Darkling the Broken Slave

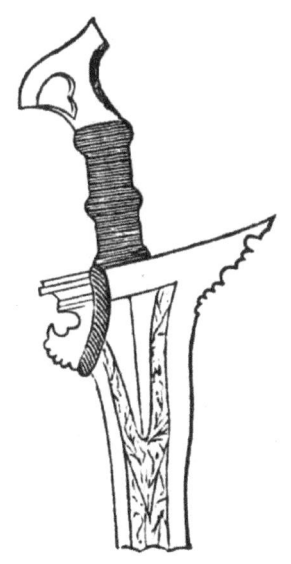

Morena Stamm

Also by Morena Stamm…

Ashta the Lion Tamer
Svetlana the Last Princess
Darkling the Broken Slave

Coming soon…

Trice the Wolf Hunter
Iris the Blood Sister
Agora the White Warrior

Carien the Shattered Heir

This is a work of fiction. Names, characters, places and incidents are products of the author's imagination or are used factiously and are not to be construed as real. Any resemblance to actual events, locales, organizations, or persons, living or dead, is entirely coincidental.

No part of this book may be used or reproduced in any manner whatsoever without written permission except in the case of brief quotations embodied in critical articles and reviews.

FIRST EDITION.

Copyright © 2021 Morena Stamm
All rights reserved.
ISBN: 978-1-7775449-2-8
Imprint: Independently published

To Bethany, an amazing, strong, kind English woman that puts up with my big brother. It takes a lot of courage to move a half a world away from everything you know and start a new life. I love having you as a sister.

PROLOGUE

⌘

Fifteen Years Earlier

SVETLANA STOOD BESIDE her mother, rubbing at the uncomfortable neckline on her court dress. Today was the first time she was at court. Her father had requested, no commanded, her mother to bring Svetlana.

Looking at her mother's pinched face, seated in the throne beside her father, Svetlana didn't understand why she had to be there. But if it made things easier for her mother, than she gladly would.

"Stand still, Mina," her mother warned her on a whisper, not daring to glance at the little girl. Instead, she kept her gaze forward and focused on the dangerous scene below.

Anichka carefully took in the room, noting that all the old families, and some of the newer families of the nobility stood present. Most concerning was the small group of families gathered together in the back. Lord Pavel stood tall amongst them, glaringly defiantly up at Anichka and her husband. The queen tightened her hands, feeling the comforting stab of pain from her fingernails into the soft flesh of her palms.

Lord Pavel was a familiar face to her own childhood. He had spent many a night in front of the fire with her own father, drinking and talking about their younger years. Often the conversation would shift to their late wives, which both men had lost at a similar time.

Anichka felt sorry for the older man and had a great love for him and his twins. She had spent her girlhood playing in the rocks with Erast and Maxim. While her father had hope she marry Erast one day, that had all changed the day her Alerik had rode into the courtyard.

Anichka looked up at her husband, her heart warm. That strong jawline. The little curl in his hair that he could never tame. Most saw a stone wall, but she felt a warmth, a passion that bubbled beneath that cold exterior. He made her feel safe, cared for. Something she had only ever felt from her father. How could she not love this man?

A tug at her hand had Anichka turning and looking into dark eyes, a mirror of her own. "Not now, Mina," she replied automatically, sensing the questions that bubbled up from her young daughter's inquisitive mind. The girl frowned but turned to face the court once more.

As if by que, Lord Pavel stepped forward. The rest of his men, and the other families behind him turned to face him.

Alerik watched them with cool eyes and waited. He would not be baited into addressing the other man. Instead, Alerik reached over the throne and slipped his hand over his wife's.

Lord Pavel's gaze narrowed on their hands with a frown. He took another step forward and made sure to capture the attention of everyone in the room. Nobles. Courtiers. Servants. The King.

"The crown has asked for fealty from all the families. And an oath of men." He paused and glanced at the other heads of family. Varlam. Dmitry. Oleg.

Turning to the King, "Have we not given enough? Has our bread, our meager wood, our best men not been enough?" He stretched his arms out as if to include the assembly. "I am not alone in feeling the effects of the last few years short summers and shorter growing season." He turned, his feet wide apart as he defiantly questioned the king, "What is it our crown needs that requires so much of the great families?"

The silence was deafening as the two men stared at each other, neither baking down.

Svetlana shifted to her other foot, rubbing her eyes. She was tired of standing but knew she was not allowed to sit until her mother said so.

Both men turned to look at the young girl. Slowly, the king lifted his hand from his wife's hand and motioned to the girl.

Svetlana hesitated, looking at her mother for guidance.

The woman said nothing, watching Lord Pavel with concern.

Irritated, King Alerik called her sharply, "Svetlana. Come here."

She moved closer. When she was within reach, her father reached out and lifted her onto his knees. She sat stock still, shocked at being held by her father like this. Her father was not an affectionate man. Except to her mother. Sometimes.

Lord Pavel frowned but pushed past the display the king put on with his young family. "The crown asked for fealty." His big voice boomed in the stone room. "Family Trofim knows no King."

The statement drew more than a few gasps.

Lord Pavel continued, stepping closer to the thrones. The berserkers stepped forward to stop him, but King Alerik waved them off. Lord Pavel continued until he stood not five paces before the couple. He pulled his sword out and knelt to the ground, staring pointedly at the young queen. Finally, he continued, his voice resonating through the hall and into the little girls' ears. "Family Zima knows no king. As our fathers and forefathers have done, I and mine pledge our swords to the true blood heir of the first Queen of our land. From this day until my last day." He held the sword out to the queen, his eyes lowered in respect.

Beside Anichka, King Alerik fumed at the blatant move around him. All the years spent bringing the families together, the years leading the berserkers, all of it meant nothing to his people. In the end it all came down to blood.

Svetlana squirmed in her father's tight grip, confused by the many emotions that floated in the air. Her head hurt as she squinted her eyes to look at the older man. His beard was long, and the red was speckled white with age. His sea green eyes were gentle as they watched her.

The silence sat heavy in the room as no one knew what to say or do.

Eventually, Anichka shifted in her seat and addressed the room. Her quiet voice, while soft held that thread of steel that had the court room leaning in to listen.

"Thank you, Lord Pavel. Your pledge to my family and our kingdom means so much in these hard times. It is with families like yours coming together that will bring Bbrski through this drought. And with my Alerik leading our Kingdom, Bbrski will be reborn into a new land. One that is more than just snow and hard people. We will one day thrive." With that, the queen turned to King Alerik, her black gaze warm with love and adoration.

Lord Pavel said nothing. He was all too aware the young king held no love for their queen. He stayed in the city for the sake of a promise to an old friend. One day the king would miss step. And on that day, the old families would come together to stand behind their queen and fight against the king's machinations.

He watched the young princess with interest. While Lord Pavel had watched the young Anichka grow into the beautiful but flighty woman she was today, time would tell if her daughter would be the same. For now, he watched her squirm, uncomfortable in her father's arms, constantly looking to her mother for comfort.

Would she be strong enough to lead a harsh people, Lord Pavel wondered? Or would she bend in the wind like her mother, the queen.

Lord Pavel stood and bowed to the young family before returning to his men. Time would tell the story of where Bbrski would go in the next years. And time would tell if the young heir would follow her family legacy.

King Alerik released his grip on the girl as he watched a few men nod in approval of Lord Pavel move. It seemed Alerik still had some work to do in his court. Some people to convince to his way. Or to be rid of.

Svetlana hopped off her father's lap and moved safely out of his reach to the other side of her mother's throne. She tried to hide in her mother's skirt, rubbing her aching head. Her mother gently patted her head and the pain disappeared instantly.

"Come Mina, it is time for your afternoon meal," her mother whispered as she rose. She gave a deep curtsy to the king before leaving the court room, her daughter in tow. Eyes followed the pair with interest. The King. Lord Pavel. Courtiers. Lady Arja. The King's berserkers. All of them wondered, and worried, what the young princess would grow up into.

CHAPTER ONE

⌘

Honour and Loyalty

DESPITE THE SUN beating down on Ashta's bare skin, she shivered. The mist and cool wind off the ocean kept her naked body cool even as it blistered from too much sun.

Across the ship she watched Augostus, her father's man, and the captain of the Bbrskian boat. The man who had ripped out the rest of the arrowhead from her leg and burned the wound closed. And burned the cut on her arm closed.

Also, the only man who came near her. Her father's warning must have reached the other men manning the ship. They watched her from distance, careful never to stare to long.

Sighing, Ashta blinked up into the sky. It had been days already, sitting out here in the open. Her wrists were rubbed raw from where she was tied to the main mast of the ship. Her shoulders ached from being pulled back. The scabs on her arm and leg itched to the point of bringing tears of frustration to Ashta's eyes.

With some effort, she wiggled and pushed against the mast until she was standing, despite her tied up ankles.

No one commented, not even Augostus who briefly looked over at her before continuing whatever it was, he did.

The standing hurt, but it made her muscles ache less. And time pass.

Sitting.

Standing.

Sitting.

Ashta leaned her head back against the mast and slit her eyes. To the others it would look as if she was sleeping, while she was actually watching them. Learning them. Twenty-four men she had counted on the ship so far. A mix of ages. There was a few younger boys. And one older man.

He was the only one who did not look at her with fear. Or disgust.

Ashta glanced across the deck and found him talking with a couple of men as they fixed some rope for the sails. The older man kept glancing over at her. His beard was peppered and tapered down his chest. His hair was in two simple braids that landed in the middle of his back.

If her memories from her governess were correct, then she would guess the man was from one of the inland clans. The ones that lived more of a nomad life similar to the zMun people or the Tripsian Alpen people.

While it was unusual to see such a man in her father's army, Ashta wasn't surprised by it. Early on in his rule her father had required that every clan and family must send able bodied men to serve in her father's army for a time. But someone so old would have served long before her father was a leader.

"Time to eat princess," a guttural voice said from beside her.

She shivered but kept her eyes closed. Augostus had kept his lust inline so far. But only the gods could know for how much longer the man would respect her father's command.

A slap across her face had her blinking as stars blinked in her sight. The pain lingered as she glared up at the red headed berserker. He smirked at her, simply grabbing a spoonful of gruel and shoving into her mouth.

She ate it, humiliated at having to be fed, more so because she had to watch him.

Once the bowl was finished, he grabbed the water skin and held it up to her lips for her to take some sips from. She coughed after a few moments and he pulled it back to wait her out.

Sensing her moment to speak before he left her alone for the rest of the evening and night, Ashta continued the long-standing argument. "I would be of more use to you if you released me from the mast. I can help with the sails, or wash deck, or-"

As usual, Augostus cut her off by putting the water back to her lips forcing her to drink or choke. She drank the water as best she could.

This time when she began coughing, he closed the skin and walked away without another word.

Ashta growled in frustration.

Yes, she knew her father had given strict instructions to have her tied up and naked. But what was she going to do now? They were days out on the water, far from any island or land mass. While she wanted to escape and return to Tripsia, even she knew it would take a little more preparation than stealing a dinghy and some food and rowing back.

The old man and his few men watched her for a long time as she recovered from her coughing fit. She finally collapsed back to the ground, her head falling forward as bits of her loosened black hair fell forward.

She waited as the evening sun slowly set and she was left shivering, her teeth chattering, out in the elements of the night.

The next day, as the sun sat in the middle of the sky beating down on her, Ashta noticed a change in the men. It wasn't anything obvious, just a few tense shoulders in some and furtive glances between a small group of men that pulled out a repaired sail for the mast. There was also a quiet between the men. No one spoke too loudly. There was no joking. No laughter.

Ashta tried to swallow past her swollen tongue. While Augostus did feed her and give her water, he was always careful to give her just barely enough.

With a sigh, Ashta shifted and tried to stand up. Her legs, weak from days of being tied up, shook before collapsing on her. Tears of frustration came to her eyes as she glared up at the sky. She hated feeling this weak. She hated even more showing this weakness in front of others.

A shout had Ashta turning her head. On the other side of the ship, a group of men including the old man, were smacking their swords against shields or against the ship handrail.

Augostus, hearing the racket, turned away from his first man and moved quickly down the quarter deck to where most of the men had gathered loosely around the main mast. And the girl. He refused to look at her, her naked body not nearly as large of a temptation as her spirit. One he relished to slowly crush on the journey back to the Issha.

Asvig stared Augostus down as he stood slightly in front of some men.

Augostus didn't like it. The old man had strong ties to the men. And to the old families. And to Lord Gleb. Augostus could not rid himself of the man without retribution waiting for him when they landed in Bbrski.

Rubbing his chin, he decided to head the old man off, shouting out, "What is the meaning of this?"

As Augostus looked at each of the men standing around, the men glanced away or shuffled their feet. Only Asvig glared back at him.

"Asvig?" Augostus called, quirking his brow.

Ashta watched quietly, her eyes partially closed. The old man was of a similar build to Augostus. Tall, wide shouldered, scars across his arms and legs. Both were formidable in their own right. Across from each other, Ashta couldn't tell who was more dangerous. There was no fear in the berserker's eyes, but the old man had age and decades of war and fighting behind him.

"It's not right to keep the princess tied to the mast like some common criminal," He turned and looked at those men closer to him who seemed to nod and agree. "She should be clothed, at the very least in simple cloths, and tied outside of the beating sun, as befits a woman of her rank."

Augostus barked a laugh, pulling his sword out and pointing towards Ashta. "That," he growled, "Is no ordinary woman. She killed our men. Beheaded our men. She is too dangerous to allow any freedoms to. Even clothes. Do you think me stupid enough to allow her free to choke me as I sleep? No."

His last word rang out with an air of finality which Asvig did not like. He widened his stance and lifted his sword up in a ready position, perfectly balanced.

Augostus' eyes widened before he growled and also readied himself for a fight.

Ashta watched in fascination as the men stood across from each other in silence. Neither moved, not even their eyes, waiting, muscles tensed and ready.

In an explosion of movement, swords clanged together as they quickly parried. Asvig ripped the other man's sword out of his hand. Then twisted his arm around Augostus neck, his sword biting the soft skin and leaving a small trail of blood on the white skin.

The sudden stillness had the crew holding their breath as they watched.

Asvig shoved Augostus away.

With the slightest nod, Augostus rubbed his neck. He glared at the men surrounding Asvig, then spat on the ground. "Fine, Asvig, you want the princess to walk around, then you can be her keeper. Only you." With that he turned and sauntered away. His own men watched him skeptically as Asvig's group separated and went back to their stations.

Asvig shouldered his sword once more and carefully walked up to Ashta's prone body. She watched him curiously, her face devoid of any clear expression or feeling.

The old man leaned down, his beard scratching her collarbone as he carefully untied the rope around her wrists, then her middle, and finally her ankles.

Ashta began rubbing at her wrists and ankles immediately, watching the man from under her eyelashes. He carefully wrapped the rope up and shouldered it. Then, slowly, he kneeled down before her, his head down in respect for her.

"My princess," he breathed out, waiting.

Ashta froze, unsure of what to do. The last weeks had finally brought her some closure on this part of her life. On her heritage.

Being confronted by her former life once more was dizzying. Had she not already made this choice before? Why was she being confronted again and again?

Instead of giving him the reply he wanted, she asked him a question. "Why did you fight against him when he is your captain?"

The old man looked up, his pale gaze swimming with age and violence. Slowly, he rose. He held his hand out to help her up.

Ashta waited, staring at him.

"Because," he finally said, "I did not join this crew for him."

His hard stare into her eyes had Ashta looking away and down at his scarred hand. She grabbed it and allowed him to pull her up.

Not another word was said as he led Ashta underneath into the hull where the crew slept. He came up to one of the hanging beds and pulled out a simple tunic and pants. Ashta took them gratefully and quickly donned only the top. The tunic hung like a bag on her, coming down past her knees. Asvig cut off a piece of rope which she quickly fashioned into a belt for herself.

She turned away from the old man and took the time to braid her hair into its familiar snail conch shape. Its tightness was the reminder that she needed that Ashta was no longer free to make decisions for herself and her own life. Every decision had to be made in the best interest of her charge. And the kingdom whom she served now. Tripsia.

"Here," Asvig's gruff voice had her turning around.

Shocked, she took the handle of the offered dagger. She looked up at him questioningly. Did he really not fear her, she wondered.

He responded simply, "Your birthright won't protect you here amongst these men."

She nodded and quickly hid the short dagger in her hair. He made no comment.

"Come," he called, turning back towards the area under the quarterdeck. On one side was the captain's quarters, on the other was the kitchen. Asvig grabbed a bowl and filled it up with porridge for her. Ashta took the bowl gratefully and quickly ate. Asvig continued, grabbing bread and a tankard of something that wasn't water.

As they stood to the side, Ashta eating, Asvig spoke. "My men and I will protect you as best we can until we reach the mainland. But there are men, boys really, aboard this ship who will do you harm. Bbrski is not the same land as it once was. Honour and loyalty are not what they used to be. It is safest for now to keep you tied up at the mast. But it won't be as bad as before. I promise."

Ashta watched him skeptically but said nothing. She did not relish the idea of being tied to the mast again. But she understood the small bit of peace between the old man and the captain was a thin piece of ice.

Once she had finished her tankard, she followed Asvig back to the mast. This time, as she was tied up, he only tied her arms together and back to the mast, leaving her legs free. She appreciated the small kindness. With the tunic covering her skin, and her belly fully, Ashta watched the men continue to work through the afternoon around her. But now she had hope of survival. And escape.

Soon, she promised herself. Soon.

CHAPTER TWO

⌘

Ivan Lucifer

THE AFTERNOON DRAGGED on for Ashta with the anticipation of being released to eat. Her wrists were still sore as the rope tugged on them, but the relief of having her ankles released outweighed the pain.

She rolled and stretched her legs as best she could, being mindful of not having any pants or underthings on. The tunic protected her from the hot sun despite its scratchy texture on her skin.

Just as the sun was setting and the men began disappearing into the bowels of the boat, the old man came over to her.

"I'll be bringing you your food up here," he said quietly, looking around at some of the men who lingered on deck. Specifically, the captain, Augostus.

The other man had kept his distance from Ashta, the hate in his gaze thinly veiled. The old man leaned over her, as if checking the rope, and carefully untied and gave Ashta the ends.

"I'll be right back," he warned, glancing meaningfully over at the captain.

Ashta swallowed before giving a slight nod.

Asvig quickly disappeared, leaving Ashta alone on the deck.

For the first time since being tied to the mast by Augostus, Ashta did not feel safe. Maybe it was the few men of Augostus who lingered on the deck, watching her. Maybe it was the tall man at the helm of the ship who purposely kept his back to her. But something had changed since the afternoon.

She was glad Asvig had untied her. She still did not understand why. But she had a dagger and the element of surprise in case anything did happen.

Soon enough, Asvig returned with a bowl of porridge and a full water skin. He made a big show of untying Ashta from the mast before helping her over to a barrel to sit and eat her meal on. He sat across from her, carefully sharpening the edge of his double-sided axe.

He let her eat in peace, which Ashta appreciated. But she also craved conversation. It had been days since she had had an actual conversation with another person.

"Your mother was a kind soul," he commented. His quiet words shattered the silence.

Ashta set her almost empty bowl down and stared at the old man with new eyes. Asvig knew her mother?

He paused to gesture at her bowl.

Reluctantly, Ashta picked her spoon up and continued.

As she ate, Asvig spoke. "I was a young man when I came to the Broskla estate. My uncle, the chieftain and head of the

Hrokr family, was of the old ways. Your mother had just turned twelve, and in tradition with the Llitha, Lucifer, your grandfather, had held a gathering of all the heads of the families in the summer." He paused in his sharpening to stare off into the distant horizon, his eyes clouded with memories.

Ashta set the bowl down and quickly downed the offered water.

Before Asvig continued, a shout let out from the quarter deck and Asvig straightened.

After having spent a week on the boat, Ashta knew it was the shift call. The night crew, maybe six men, would take the duties over until the morning sun.

Asvig gathered the bowl and carefully tied Ashta back to the mast. Before he left, Ashta called to him, "Will you tell me more?"

He looked to the quarter deck, and the approaching figure of Augostus, before nodding to Ashta in answer. "Tomorrow," he promised before disappearing beneath the deck.

As Augostus passed Ashta, he spat at the ground in front of her before following Asvig.

Ashta slept fitfully. Her mind tense with anticipation and a bit of fear. By the time Asvig came with breakfast in the morning, Ashta was too tired to hold the rope any longer.

She ate quietly.

Asvig watched the dark circles under the young woman's eyes. While she looked better, and her ankles were healing, he worried about what other damage had befallen the woman.

Asvig left the princess in her silence, and quickly joined his shipmates.

Despite the promise to continue the story, a week passed before Asvig continued. Ashta slept in the sun during the day and fidgeted through the night. On the sixth day, her body finally exhausted beyond the point of reason, she slept dreamlessly through the night. Asvig noticed the change in her, the wakefulness in her eyes that had been missing before. That evening, as she ate her porridge, he began again as if no time had passed.

"Despite your grandfather never being king, all were aware of his claim and right to the throne. Or more accurately, his young daughter's claim. Anichka was a very sweet and peaceful child. Well loved. Many worried about her good nature, so unlike our harsh people. Her cousin, Ivan, was much more Bbrskian in temperament and looks."

"Cousin?" Ashta echoed, shocked.

Asvig nodded, not seeing her pale face and shaking hands. He continued through the silence.

"Yes. Ivan was well known. Almost as well-known as your grandfather. And not for good reason." Asvig paused, glancing down at his axe, his eyes fixed on his reflection. "I should leave you for the night," he mumbled.

Ashta reached out without a thought, stopping his arm. "No," she whispered, "please continue."

He stared at her hand for a long moment before settling more firmly on the barrel again.

"I-I didn't know I had any living relatives. My father had said they were all dead," Ashta said haltingly, the words spilling out from her soul.

Asvig snorted. "King Alerik wishes they were all dead. Would have been easier."

Ashta rubbed her chest as she waited. Her eyes tracked the men still on the deck, following one man coiling the rope for the sails.

"Ivan Augosst isn't a true Broskla. His mother was your grandmother's sister. She became with child quite young and died during birth. Your grandfather took the child in and raised him beside his own young daughter."

"What was he like?" Ashta asked, her heart beating in her throat. The only thought in her mind that she wasn't alone in this world. She didn't count her father as family.

Asvig leaned in and stared Ashta in the eyes for a long time, searching. After a beat of silence, he continued quietly, his words barely louder than the crash of the waves against the ship. "Where Anichka was kind, Ivan was mean. At the gathering of the families, there was a contest for the men to show their prowess. Racing. Fighting. Archery. Ivan, being just eleven at the time, had gone into the stables before my race. I caught the little rat putting burs underneath the saddles." Asvig spat on the wood floor, the rage still fresh in his eyes.

Ashta shook her head, her emotions a mess. Why would a child put grown men at risk like that? The same action had almost cost Princess Carien her life in Naankdoen when she had ridden a torash. But then, it had been an assassin who had taken action. Not a child.

"I dragged that little shit out of the tent and in front of Lucifer and the other heads of the family, including my chieftain. Ivan began to cry, his eyes clear as tears ran down his cheeks. The young Anichka came over and begged your grandfather for his forgiveness, that her cousin didn't mean any harm. That it was a simple joke gone wrong." Asvig snorted.

The call went out as the night shift appeared on deck. Asvig shook himself as he stood up and stretched. He quickly tied up Ashta, his action automatic. Ashta grunted as the rope tightened around her wrist. She said nothing, her mind still on the news of having family.

As the moon shone high in the night sky, Ashta stared unseeingly up at the sky. It was something she had always dreamed of. Wished for. To have a family. To have siblings, cousins. Aunts. Uncles.

Her heart warmed at the idea that there was still a piece of her family, of her mother and grandfather, alive.

Tomorrow, she promised herself, she would ask Asvig about Ivan. Before she could let her hopes soar, she had to be certain he was even alive. What if her mother never spoke of other family because Ivan had died tragically?

"...just do it already. Not sure why we are waiting so long."

Cocking her head, Ashta tried to catch more of the conversation.

"The captain wanted to be sure no one from the mainland would suspect anything."

Another voice grunted in agreement.

Ashta blinked several times in hope for her eyes to adjust to the darkness. She was thankful for the bright light of the full moon. Just as her eyes cleared, she heard several ominous creaks from behind and around her.

Keeping her head leaned back against the pole in feigned sleep, she peaked out from beneath her slitted eyelids to take in the slowly gathering crowd in front of her. Most of the faces were obscured, but one stood out in sharp relief to her.

Augostus.

Beside him stood another tall berserker. This one she did not recognize. The scar running down the length of his face and his missing eye would have made him easily recognizable.

He must be part of the night crew, she thought as she noted that the crowd was slightly divided into two groups. One behind Augostus and one behind scar face.

The two men stood off facing each other, each holding a wide and steady stance. Each glaring at the other man.

Ashta shivered. Thanking Asvig for the knife. She slowly twisted her hand around while leaning further down the pole. Slowly, carefully, her fingers against the too big shirt and the small wrap that kept the knife flat against her arm. Ashta held her breath, praying fervently the men continued their standoff.

"No," Augostus said, his deep voice reverberating through the wood and in the night air. His answer left no room for argument.

Scarface face seemed to disagree, his one eye squinting in rage against Augostus. He glanced at the few men behind him before stepping forward and challenging Augostus in his space.

Ashta slowly tugged at the bandage, pulling the knife closer to her fingers. She held her breath as her fingers slid against the cool steel of the blade.

"It will be weeks before we return to the raids. Weeks of no woman. And you want to just kill this one without allowing the men to use her body first?" Scarface gestured towards Ashta with his hand.

She froze, her hand wrapped around the blade, her heart pounding in her throat. Ashta could feel the hot stares like unwanted hands stroking down her skin. She suppressed a shiver, careful to breath slowly out of her mouth. Please let them think me asleep, she prayed to the gods.

Augostus response was lost in a gust of wind, as a night storm began rocking the ship. The men were to focused on each other to see the flag whipping high above them. Or the ominous creaks of the ship below. Whatever storm was coming, it was swooping in hard and fast.

Behind the cover of ropes singing and waves crashing, Ashta carefully sawed at the rope tying her hands together behind the mast. She kept her breathing in check, only now cursing Asvig for his knot tying skills.

In front of her, the crowd swayed as men braced their legs wide, trying to catch the argument between Scarface and Augostus. At first, Ashta thought a few of the men on the fringes of the crowd kept glancing out at the coming storm. But as she cut through the last thread of the rope holding her, she caught the flicker of something moving in the corner of her eye.

Carefully, she held the rope as she feigned sleep. Several dark shadows began to form around the crowd. The air was filled with tension.

Scarface, his face red with outrage, pulled his knife and swung at Augostus.

The moment Augostus blocked the blade with a swipe of his own sword in hand, chaos erupted.

Men jumped out of the shadows, blades flashing white and red, attacked the crowd. In moments, Ashta stood still in the middle of a hurricane of blood, screams, and cries of death. Bodies littered the ship floor.

Blinking, moments having passed, silence reigned on the ship once more. Only the wind howled in her ears as the men around her straightened, blood dripping down from their swords and knives.

Standing above Scarface was Asvig, his sword buried deep in Scarface's back. Asvig scowled has he forcibly kicked Scarface off of his sword. He looked around himself, noting the other men were in similar shape, covered in blood but uninjured for the most part.

He walked towards the girl, but before he got close to her, the rope that had been around her dropped to the ground and she stood before him. The knife he had given her sat loosely in her hands.

Asvig shivered before straightening. Aware that the rest of the men, *his* men, were watching, Asvig kneeled before their princess and offered his sword up.

Ashta took in a shaky breath, watching as the men around her sank to their knees until she was the only one that stood. She was left shivering.

"Stand," she called harshly, her shock making her abrupt.

Asvig took his time, leaning heavily on his sword as his knee ached from past injuries.

"My prin-"

Ashta cut him off, glaring at him. "You will address me as Ashta or Lioness. Anything else will leave a knife in your throat," she threatened.

The men also quickly rose.

Asvig wanted to protest, but staring into a familiar hard stare not unlike her father's, he held his thoughts in. Instead, he turned to the men that were left, just over a third of the original crew.

"Throw the bodies overboard! Get a man at the wheel! Someone pullout the sails!"

The men jumped to action, leaving just Ashta and Asvig standing at the mast. He turned to her, then nodded slowly.

"With me," he commanded, turning away and towards the wheel. He did not bother looking back because he knew the princess would. She was smart. But she was also used to taking orders.

Dangerous for a woman that was meant to rule an arrogant people.

CHAPTER THREE

⌘

Familiar Black Sand

ASHTA STAYED SILENT as she followed Asvig around the next morning. The sailors that were left were kept busy manning the ship. And Asvig was busy trying to coordinate the small crew of men left.

It wasn't until the sun began to set in the west that Ashta finally had a moment alone with Asvig.

"Where are you taking the ship?" she asked, the question haunting her since Asvig, and his men had thrown the bodies over the edge of the ship and adjusted their course slightly west of the city Issha.

Asvig glanced down into her black eyes, glittering like hard obsidian. Impossible to know the thoughts behind them. With a sigh, he looked past her and into the distant horizon. Soon, maybe a few days' time, they would reach the coast. Bbrski's northern most estate, the peninsula sticking far out into the Blood Sea.

"Gallodel," he said in a low voice.

Ashta wrinkled her brow, confused at the mention of her mother's childhood home. Before she could ask further, Asvig continued.

"The capital is not safe for you, Lioness," he spat the last word out but continued despite wanting to address her by her true name. "Your cousin, Ruslan, has taken over as the head of the Broskla family. He will take care of you. I had sent message ahead and am ensured of your continued safety at your grandfather's estate."

A shout from the bow of the ship had Asvig turning and walking away from Ashta.

She didn't mind. She needed a moment to process the news.

Her mother's cousin was alive? *Ashta* had a cousin? And he guaranteed her safe passage?

She was curious to meet this family, excited even. But there was a small part in her heart, the part that her father and stepmother had seeded and watered through her childhood that wondered. She wished to believe this family would love her like her mother, especially since they were from her mother's side.

But a small part in her wondered at this cousin's motives. Why? Why would someone who had never met her, guarantee her safety? What did he gain from it?

And most importantly, why would a Bbrskian, born and bred, give up any inch of power by allowing his cousin, the true head of the family, and the heir of Bbrski, to return to the Gallodel estate?

Shaking her head slowly, Ashta also stared out towards the horizon.

She would get her answers soon enough. They had already been at sea for two weeks fighting the choppy fall waters. They were maybe three days out from the Broskla family estate.

"Lioness!" Asvig called.

She turned towards him, already walking, her hand loosely gripping her short knife.

"Help Ancel man the sails!" he said, point towards the older man with a peppered beard who was fighting with the ropes of at sail. The other man stared at Ashta for a moment when she grabbed the rope.

His pale eyes stared through her for a long moment before he nodded, looking down at the rope again. This time he offered the rope beside his own hands.

Ashta sidle up to him and together they pulled the sail in and tightened it to the foremast

These men, the ones who had sided with Asvig and decided to fight for her, seemed to respect her. Or at the very least not hate her. She hoped the tense truce between the remaining crew and Asvig would hold for the few days of sailing left.

"Land ho!" the barrelman called down to the ship crew.

Ashta, who had been in the midst of rolling rope, dropped what she was doing and ran to the starboard side of the ship. Several other men, including Ancel the older sailor she had helped the first day, lined up along the side of the ship.

"Best be finishing with that rope right away, little lion. We'll be on land by the afternoon light."

Ashta nodded, returning to her partially finished coil of rope.

Ancel sat across from her, fixing a hole in the spare sail.

The last few days had been busy. The boredom of the week before had quickly been replaced with work. The men for the most part kept themselves separate from Ashta, but she was expected to help.

Needed.

There was not near enough men to man the ship.

Thankfully, the weather had held clear the last couple days. Rare for the autumn.

The morning passed in a hurry as Asvig yelled out orders. Some men went below decks, returning in full furs, strapped with swords and axes. They had even taken the time to paint their faces in the tradition of the berserkers.

Ashta glanced at them surreptitiously.

While she had seen berserkers before, as a child, it had been from a distance. And last time, in the Tripsian desert, she had fought against them not beside. It was strange to see these wild soldiers as real men, who smiled and joked. Who ribbed each other as tension laced their shoulders.

Despite their destination being within their homeland, none of these men were from the Gallodel and surrounding lands. And clan wars had been happening for centuries.

Even Ancel watched the horizon with worry as he knotted the sail in place. The older man had shared very little with Ashta. But by the braids in his hair, she knew that even he was not from the area. Old mistrust and hate were not easily forgotten. Especially not by pale eyed man who was missing three fingers.

"Lioness, with me!" Asvig called out from the helm.

Ashta hesitated for a moment, glancing at Ancel.

He rubbed his good hand on the stumps of the remains of his fingers before looking at her.

"Go," he growled before tossing his hair back and stalking over to the door to the galley.

Ashta ran up to the quarter deck until she stood at Asvig's elbow.

His gaze never left the horizon.

The peninsula was clear in view now. Ashta could make out the black beach. The black cliffs that jutted above. The dark trees that blotted out the rest of the land.

She shivered.

It had been eight years since the last time she had stared out at the Bbrskian coast. It was as formidable and desolate now as it had been then.

"Lower the anchor!" Asvig called out as he moved towards the small dinghy.

Ashta followed behind him, noting the five men in furs and war paint standing at the ready.

With the anchor lowered, the men carefully hoisted the dinghy over the edge.

Asvig turned to Ashta, bowing low as he gestured towards the empty dinghy.

When Ashta made no move to get on the dinghy, Asvig quietly stated, "Ladies first, Lioness."

Slowly, she stepped towards the boat before carefully climbing in. She shivered. She could feel the eyes of Asvig, the soldiers, and the rest of crew watching as she clambered in, her bare legs flashing skin for all to see.

Once she was settled in the centre bench, the rest of the berserkers climbed in. Two in front. Two behind. One beside.

On her other side, and last to climb in, was Asvig. He wore his furs and battle axe making him even larger than his already formidable size.

Ancel came up beside Asvig, a thick bundle in his arms. He stared at Ashta as he held the bundle to Asvig. "For the girl," he growled in his low voice.

Asvig nodded slowly as he held the bundle for a moment before handing to Ashta.

Without another word, Ancel and another man began lowering the boat.

Ashta slowly opened the bundle. The ropes undid to reveal a beautiful white wolf fur. Its insides were well oiled and tanned. A shirt and pants lay neatly folded inside. And gleaming up at her with deadly intent, lay a short double-edged sword.

For a long moment Ashta could only stare at the bundle and its contents.

"His sons died in the Southern Clan battles," Asvig said in a low voice.

The boat rocked gently as it slid into the water. Asvig and the other soldier to Ashta's side lifted their oars and began paddling for shore.

Ashta clutched the bundle close, her eyes stuck on the shrinking ship and the old man on its bow, his braids swinging in the late day wind.

The meaning of the gift Ancel had given her was not lost on Ashta. A berserker's fur and swords were earned. The creature was hunted by the young man as a coming-of-age ceremony. He would pick a weapon and go out into the wilderness by himself. Some boys could take weeks before returning to the clan with their kill. Some never returned. The boys returned as made men, their swords and furs cared for as if they were children.

For Ancel to give this bundle, a bundle he had loved and cared for, meant everything to Ashta.

To soon, the boat scraped against the sand bars of the beach. The two soldiers in the back jumped out and pulled the boat the rest of the way onto the sand. The wood groaned as it scraped across stones.

Finally, they stopped.

The men got out and formed a line, waiting for Ashta and Asvig.

"It would be better for you to return to your family in furs, Lioness, than just that shirt," Asvig said roughly, turning his back to her.

She swallowed the lump in her throat down before carefully placing the bundle in the boat. Ashta stripped her shirt off and pulled the new shirt and pants on. Unlike the shirt Asvig had given her, this shirt was only slightly too big.

The reminder of how young Ancel's son must have died tugged at Ashta's heart.

With a deep breath, she threw the fur over her back, tying it around her neck so the wolf's top jaw jutted out from her forehead. She tied the front legs to her arms. Then, with the rest of the rope, she made a quick belt around her shirt and tucked the sword into it. She pulled on the fur lined short boots that were just slightly too large for her thin feet.

At the last second, she grabbed the short dagger and tucked it into her left boot.

"I'm ready," she said softly. She was dressed, she thought, but she was in no way ready to walk the path up to one of the few good memories of her childhood.

In silence, the men started the steep trek up the cliffside, single file. Ashta followed behind Asvig. Despite the years, her feet easily picked the path along the stone littered path.

The scent of pine and spruce with the tangy ocean breeze filled her nose and tickled her memories. Playing with her grandfather. Riding alongside her mother.

The walk passed in a blur, until suddenly Ashta found herself standing inside the stable. The air was cool and musty. She wrinkled her nose, shaking herself free of the fog of memories and getting to see for the first time what her mind was protecting her from.

Horses.

She turned full circle, her eyes frantically searching every corner, but there was nothing to see. Just cobwebs and dust in a place that once had been alive with whinnies and swishing tails. With the sweet scent of horses.

"Halt!"

Ashta blinked, then turned to look around Asvig's broad shoulders and up at another equally tall soldier.

But this man bore the familiar insignia of her family crest. A black horses head with cool blue eyes.

Another soldier came up beside the first. Both men stood warily, hands gripping their swords.

The sailors also gripped their swords and axes, anxiously glancing towards Asvig.

Asvig took a step forward his hands up in the universal sign of peace. "We come bearing the true heir of Bbrski, the first born of the Broskla family, Svetlana Anichka of the Broskla Family line. First born daughter of King Alerik and Queen Anichka. Crown princess of Bbrski." Asvig gestured behind him towards Ashta.

She took step forward and carefully pushed back the wolf's head, freeing her long black hair. The soldiers watched her suspiciously at first, but once they gazed into her eyes, each man fell to a knee.

"Your highness," the closer one breathed, keeping his eyes down as his shoulders shook in fear.

"Stand, soldier," Ashta demanded, glaring at Asvig. He wielded her true name to freely for her liking.

The men quickly stood but kept their heads down in respect.

"The princess," Asvig continued, carefully avoiding her gaze, "Seeks the protection and the right of her family's men."

The first soldier quickly pulled his sword out and held it towards her. "I live to serve you, your highness, from this day to our last day. I-"

Ashta cut him off, his quick show of fealty making her uneasy. "Take me to my cousin."

The man stuttered for a moment, the white showing all the way around his iris, before he slowly nodded. "As you wish, your highness."

Ashta kept her tongue. While she, and the sailors were aware of her situation, it might be safer now for her to pretend a bit longer to be a princess.

The soldiers turned and began walking through the stables. Ashta followed right behind, hearing Asvig step up behind her.

In moments, they had crossed the courtyard and entered the main hall. The first soldier, his curly black hair making look boyish, stopped in front of the large oak door. An extravagance that Ashta remembered from her child. She laid her hand on the old wood and stood silent for a long moment.

This door had stood watch over the great room for hundreds of years. It once protected the old Kings of Bbrski from invaders. And now it stood between Ashta and the family she didn't know was alive.

Ashta glanced behind her but wasn't surprised to see that Asvig and the other berserkers had disappeared. She stood alone now.

Taking a breath, she looked up at the engraved faces in the old door. The woman reminded her of her mother. The man of her grandfather.

Taking strength from their memory, she pushed open the door.

CHAPTER FOUR

⌘

Skirts and Daggers

THE FIRST THING Ashta's gaze caught on was the unmistakable throne in the center of the room. The chair was wrought from gold, with smooth arms and distinct edges that stood in sharp relief against the soft woods of the great room.

The throne stuck out in a noticeable way. And one that was at complete odds from Ashta's memory of the space. Where was the old dais with twin thrones?

Taking a few steps into the room, Ashta quickly took in the soldiers stationed on every meter of the wall. At least thirty men alone.

Her gaze again stopped on the golden monstrosity. But this time she realized there was someone sitting in it.

Ashta stopped dead as she stared into black eyes not unlike her own.

The man blinked down at her, frowning.

The two stared in silence, neither moving.

The man sat in the throne, his posture relaxed. He wore a robe made from white bear furs. His black eyes stood out in his pale face, his head crowned with bright red, almost orange, riot of curls.

The woman stood with her legs wide apart, arms loose but tension in the air surrounding her. Her skin was pale in spots, and dark from sun blisters across her nose and hands. Despite the Berserker dress, she looked otherworldly. Not quite Bbrskian. Yet not wholly from the Midlands.

As the silence lengthened, a shiver ran across Ashta's spine. While the dark gaze reminded her of another woman who once stared at her with love, this stranger's gaze held nothing.

No tenderness.

No worry.

No curiosity.

No tension.

No hate.

Just.

Nothing.

Not unlike the cold gaze of king Alerik, Ashta's father.

And then, in a blink, his face transformed as he leaned forward, and a slow grin spread from cheek to cheek. It looked almost maniacal.

Ashta stayed silent.

The stranger barked a short laugh, clapping his hands together before rising with a quick motion. Flinching, Ashta watched him warily. She had not sensed the quick tension in his muscles. Her gaze tracked his exposed arms and legs which showed a life of training. He may not be a weathered berserker, but he was still a deadly force to be watchful of.

"Cousin!" the man called out, his deep voice reverberated the walls.

Ashta blinked twice, again surprised by the man. His voice was so at odds with his face, just as his agility did not match his aura.

The man walked down the dais with outstretched.

Ashta made no move towards him, or to even open her arms. The man, her cousin, her family, ignored the hostile waves of tension she was giving off and engulfed her in a large hug.

Ashta was instantly nauseous from the thick cloying perfume that her cousin wore. Or bathed in, she thought darkly while standing rigid in his arms. The soldiers around the room watched the pair with keen interest but no one made a move to grab their swords.

Even so, Ashta's fingers itched to grip the short dagger in her boot.

Thankfully, the man let go of her and swept into a low bow, landing softly on one knee. "Ruslan, son of Ivan and Creta, grandson of Lucifer Augosst. I pledge this day and every day to the one true heir," he boomed. And then, on whisper that Ashta was sure she was not meant to hear. "And blood."

Before she could move or say anything, Ruslan stood up again with a flourish. His grin was too wide, making Ashta think of the similarities to the wolf's skin she wore.

"Come, come, dear cousin, you must be dreadfully tired from your journey," He pulled her hand into his arm and turned them out of the hall.

Ashta was forced to walk quickly to keep up with his long gait. She was surprised to realize that Ruslan stood a good head taller than her. And she was not short by Bbrskian women standards.

"I'm just dying to hear about all of your adventures at sea and in the barbarian lands." He gushed, all the while his eyes roamed the side hall they were quickly passing through. He did not seem to need her voice, as he continued the conversation without pause. "I've always wondered what the famed White Lionesses looked like. And their skills as guardsmen is unparalleled to all the known kingdoms. You must have killed hundreds of men!"

Almost dizzy from the speed of his thoughts, Ashta could only blink as she blindly followed him through a doorway and into another hallway that looked the exact same as the last.

A young girl in a dirt-stained dress ran into the hall from the courtyard, her bright laughter stopping mid giggle when she caught sight of Ruslan.

"You there!" Ruslan yelled, his countenance shifting instantly from joyous to anger. His mouth turned down and his brows came together in displeasure at seeing the girl.

Her face whitened but she did not move.

"Go find your keeper, have them prepare a bath in the Black Queens rooms," he growled. Just as the girl turned away, he called after her, "And have them gather clothing for her highness. It must be fit for a princess!"

Just as quick as the anger had blanketed over Ruslan, it lifted and he smiled down at Ashta, patting her hand. "It wouldn't do for the heir of Bbrski to parade about in clothes befit of a commoner." Then he eyed the wolf fur. He kept the comment to himself, but Ashta could sense the rest of his thought. Or of a berserker.

Bbrskian women did not fight. Ever. It was one of the reason's Ashta's mother never rode horses. Only when they had visited grandfather's estate, did Ashta's mother act as anything other than the wife and queen of Alerik the Ruthless, the king of Bbrski.

Despite the years of training to become a fearsome white lioness, Ashta felt her shoulders curling in as she tried to make herself smaller. Daintier. Unseen. Womanly.

Stopping in front of a great wooden door, Ruslan released her hand and swept inside the room that had once been Ashta's mother's. It still had the blue silk coverings her mother so favored on the bed and couches.

Before Ruslan could walk any further in, Ashta grabbed his elbow. He looked down at her hand in shock but Ashta did not let it stop her. Her unease at this man, despite being her cousin, had her pushing forward.

"Thank you, cousin," She whispered the last word, glancing out the window that showed the stables and courtyard. Then she looked back at into Ruslan's black gaze. "I can take care of the rest." She finished with a gentle nod to the door.

Ruslan swallowed slowly before straightening himself. This time his smile was sharper, less friendly and more like that of a wolf baring its teeth. "Yes of course," he acquiesced.

Just before he walked through the door to leave Ashta in her privacy, he turned and added. "You must join me for dinner." Before Ashta could say no, he blustered on. "It won't be a public thing. Just you and I in my private rooms. We can talk and get to know each other. It is strange and exciting to finally meet you, cousin. I have heard so much."

The last statement hung in the air with the slight note of a threat, long after Ruslan himself and disappeared down the hall.

Ashta mulled over it, not moving from her spot.

Soon enough, she heard noise from the attached bathing rooms. It was one of the few luxuries of her mother's private rooms. Otherwise, the rooms in the castle were all the same. Even the King's private rooms did not have an attached bath.

Ashta pushed into the room and watched in silence as the maids hurried to fill the tub. One of the girls was no older than when Ashta had joined the cubs training. She tripped, barely catching herself. Unfortunately, the bucket of hot water she had been carried tipped and splashed across the tiled floor.

The girl dropped to her knees, cowering on the floor in front of Ashta. The other maids all froze and watched the girl. No one dared to look at Ashta. Or up into her eyes.

Unnerved, Ashta stepped forward and picked up the bucket.

The girl flinched, making Ashta hesitate, the bucket still in her hand. She quickly glanced at the other women, then poured the remaining water in the large tub before handing the empty bucket to the girl.

At first, the girl refused to take it.

Sighing, Ashta nudged the bucket until the girls fingers slowly curled around the handle.

As soon as the girl held the bucket, Ashta stepped away and dropped her furs and rough clothing to the ground. Without another glance at the girl, Ashta stepped into the hot water. A sigh slipped from her lips as the heat wove its way into her bones.

Despite being born in this cold land, her limbs had become use to the perpetual Tripsian heat. And hopefully, Ashta prayed, she would feel that heat on her skin again.

Closing her eyes, Ashta slowly unwound the complicated knot in her hair.

A gasp.

Ashta tensed slightly, then said roughly, "Leave."

Finally, she heard the tell-tale clicks on the tiled floor as the girl, and the other women, disappeared down the servant halls.

Taking a deep breath, Ashta submerged herself. She stayed in the tub until the water was cool against her skin and a dark colour. Her skin felt raw from the rough brush she had used.

A swoosh of skirts alerted Ashta that she wasn't alone once more. Looking up, she was unsurprised that it was the young girl who had come with another fresh bucket of water.

"F-for you, m-miss," she stuttered, keeping her eyes on the tile.

Ashta stood, the cold air chilling her instantly. With a deep steadying breath, she stepped out of the tub and took the bucket. She slowly poured the hot water on her skin, hissing in pleasure.

The girl kept stealing glances as Ashta finished her bath. Another woman entered from the hall; this one held a pile of familiar clothes on her arms.

A lump formed in Ashta's throat as she took the towel from the girl, shooing her away.

"Here, your highness," the woman with the pile of clothing said as she held out a bright yellow silk skirt.

Frowning, Ashta reached below the garish yellow dress, her fingers curling around the pale blue shift edged with lace. In her mind she could hear the sweet tinkle of her mother's laughter. How in the morning light she had twirled in her mother's arms, clutching the soft shift in her grubby fingers.

Without another word shared between the women, the maid helped Ashta into the summer shift, then the under skirt. With each layer of cloth, Ashta felt the noose of her past wrapping tighter around her neck. Until finally, the maid had pulled the laces tight. Ashta's lungs complained but she kept quiet. The corsets were new. It seemed even Bbrskian style had changed since her childhood.

With a nod, the maid and girl curtsied to Ashta before scurrying down the hall.

Ashta carefully folded the furs, before gently sliding the short sword down her back. At least the tight corset, hidden under the empire waistline, would keep it snug and in place and out of sight.

Rather than having her hair down with the elaborate braids of the Bbrskian court, Ashta pulled it into the tight conch of the white lionesses. She had just tucked the short dagger into the bun when a knock rang at the door.

Hesitating, Ashta took the furs and carefully placed them under the pillow of the bed.

"Enter," she called, brushing the silk skirts down with unease. The weight of the dress was stifling, but she kept her head high and stared the soldier that entered the room in the eye.

The man looked at her in surprise, before bowing low. "You are to come with me, your highness."

The hair at the back of her neck rose at the casual use of the title. It felt wrong. But familiar.

Holding back her need to correct the soldier, she swept past him and out of the room.

He hurried to keep up with her as she led the way through the maze of halls. It may have been years since she had last been exploring the maze of halls, but her mind never forgot the way.

Ashta stopped in front of the large wooden doors that had once led into her grandfather's rooms. Seeing the familiar red sheen to the wood eased her tension. Not everything had changed.

Ashta glanced up at the soldier, her eyebrow arched. The man blushed, his breathing fast as he hurried to open the door for her.

"The princess Svetlana, master," he called before scurrying out of the room.

Ashta frowned briefly, watching him before turning towards the once cozy room. Now it was only cold. It's once warm coverings and carpets were stripped bare to the stone. Silver and gold shone coldly from the window coverings and a thick white bear skin covered most of the floor. It's head stared up at her, teeth bared.

Ashta shivered before gently stepping over the bear and towards the small table set for two.

Her cousin stood. His calculating gaze quickly shifted to humor as he opened his arms and pulled her into another uncomfortable hug. Ashta stood rigid, even after he had released her.

Ruslan chuckled, before gesturing towards the well-stocked table.

"Come, come, cousin, you must be famished from your travels."

Ignoring the barb, Ashta walked past him and pulled her chair out for herself.

Ruslan watched her with a furrowed brow before his face went slack again. He quickly shifted his weight and sat back down in his seat.

The meal passed slowly, silent except for the clink of forks and knives against plates. Ashta kept her head tilted down, allowing her to surreptitiously take her cousin in. His motions were controlled. Nothing was done by accident. Right down to the two shakes of salt onto the steak bite before carefully slicing a thin ribbon off.

Aside from his mannerisms, Ashta also took the man himself in. She tried to catalogue his features, place them against the memories of her mother and grandfather. Aside from his black eyes, similar to her mothers and her own, Ruslan looked nothing like the Broskla family. His pale skin was mottled with freckles. His hair bright and unruly. His build was toned but much smaller than her grandfather's once wide shoulders and tall person.

If he had not introduced himself as her cousin, Ashta would not have believed they were family.

It wasn't until she had crossed her cutlery on the plate, that Ashta realized that Ruslan had been studying her every movement as well.

Finally, giving into the tension, Ashta looked Ruslan straight in the eyes.

He rubbed his chin thoughtfully, looking at her hair pointedly. She ignored it. Everyone else may think her the princess returned, but Ashta knew her place. And the sooner she returned, the better.

"I had hoped we could talk. I am curious about the Midloean kingdoms," then he leaned over the table, arms outstretched, taking up as much space as he could. "Is it true that they teach all the Tripsian slaves how to pleasure a man?" he whispered.

Despite the innocent curiosity in his eyes, the hair on her arms prickled. What was his game, Ashta wondered?

Ignoring his question, she picked up her cup and finished the last bit of water. Her wine sat untouched.

Deliberately, she placed the cup back on the table and gathered her skirts before carefully standing.

A flicker crossed his face but was quickly replaced with sincerity. Ashta didn't fully believe in it. The entire evening had felt similar to that brief time in her life with Lady Arja.

She could feel something dark pushing off the man in waves. Not so different than what she felt around her father.

With a quick nod, she finally replied in a soft voice. "It has been a long day of travel."

Without another word, she twirled and walked out of the door. Her skirts were silent despite the layers of cloth.

Ruslan watched the door close behind her. He rubbed his chin again. For the first time, worry began to tinge his thoughts. She was nothing like the reports had said she would be like.

CHAPTER FIVE

⌘

Blade In The Darkness

THE PALE SUN SLOWLY rose in the east, barely lighting the blue silk room. Fog hung heavy on the castle grounds and the forest surrounding it, blanketing the world in silence.

Ashta breathed in the cold air, before bending over and releasing it in a steady warm breath. Fog rose around her in the stone room. Despite there being a huge fireplace set against the wall near the bed, Ashta had not bothered to light it.

One of the first lessons upon arrival to Tripsia as a young girl, was that the sooner she quit fighting the temperature the sooner her body became used to it. That was how Ashta found herself dressed in the simple shift of the berserker boy, carefully stretching.

Once she was warm, she attacked imaginary foes, feeling the weight of the sword in her hand, as well as the grit and slip of the stones under her feet.

Hours later, once she had dressed herself, several maids entered the room. Two carried a small table. Another a basket full of hot food. And the girl, not from the night before but from the hallway, came carrying a soft chair. Her bright red hair frizzed around her face, unwilling to stay tamed in the braid that held the longer bits together.

Ashta stood rigid in the middle of the room, wearing another one of her mother's shifts. The purple pattern glinted in the sun, hiding its secrets. Like the front stays and closure. It had been a dress from her mothers younger years, when she had been a wild and independent soul.

Now, the dress hid more than a wild spirit. The hard nob from the pommel gently pressed in between Ashta's shoulders.

None of the women said anything, seeing the lady already dressed and waiting for them. Once the table had been set, the women scurried out. The redheaded girl lingered, her big blue eyes watching Ashta with an equal mix of fear and wonder.

Ignoring the child, Ashta took a seat and quickly ate the sumptuous fare. Hearty rabbit stew. Heavy bread that barely soaked in the grease from the meat. Hot mead. It was unlike anything Ashta had ever eaten in Tripsia or Naankdoen. But it filled more than just her belly.

A knock at the door had Ashta pushing the last of the meal away, while hiding a small bun in the pocket underneath the top skirt. Ruslan walked in without waiting, his eyes quickly scanning the room.

"Ah, I am to late. You have already eaten," he joked, four women including the dark-haired girl from the bath followed behind him. Each carried several bolts of cloth in her arms.

Ashta ignored the comment, slowly standing and pushing away from the table. Her excitement a few days ago on the ship about having family had cooled considerably. Her worries from the planted seeds having now grown to great trees. Ruslan reminded her more and more of her father every day.

"Over there, and careful with that fabric. It's priceless!" He growled at the women. The girl almost fell in her haste to put the bolts down in the corner he had pointed to.

Despite her curiosity, Ashta stayed silent. It was clear the women were here to sew something. But for what?

Instead, Ashta took note of the heavy fabrics lined with gold pattern on her cousin's coat. How was it that a lesser noble could afford such fabric? Her own family line had not been poor, but they had never had the amount of wealth that oozed off of Ruslan.

Ruslan turned and a smarmy grin crossed his face. He stepped closer as if to hug Ashta.

This time, she carefully side stepped her cousin and instead walked into the middle of the room.

Ruslan frowned only for a moment before shrugging and stealing the chair from her breakfast to sit in.

"I have sent messengers to the outlying villages to gather the local nobles to a dinner this evening. Seeing as you are the heir to the throne, it wouldn't do for you to show up in rags from years past," he sneered, glaring down at Ashta's dark day dress.

She frowned but said nothing. Clothing was irrelevant to her. The new clothes did give an opportunity, she mulled as she watched two of the women busy themselves with opening up various bolts. The dark haired girl had disappeared out the door before returning with a slight stool.

"We are ready for you, your highness," one of the women said. Her dark hair was streaked with silver, its rich colour a twin to the young girls. Her mother likely.

Ashta looked to the stool the woman was gesturing to and then back at her cousin. While the nursery had removed all notions of embarrassment of nakedness out of her, she did not wish to remove her clothes and hidden weapons in front of her cousin. Or the women.

Ruslan rubbed at his chin but made no move to leave. He settled deeper into the seat, leaning back and spreading his legs to better watch Ashta.

She shivered at his lingering gaze. Glancing back at the older woman, Ashta nodded towards the private bathing chambers. "I will be a moment," she warned the woman. She gave Ruslan no time to protest, disappearing behind the door before firmly shutting it.

Taking a deep breath, she quickly removed her half sword and wrapped it in the purple outer skirt. Ashta hesitated on the final shift. While nudity did not bother her, there were some secrets her cousin did not need to know. Her scars being one.

With a final pat on her hair to ensure the dagger was still securely hidden, Ashta returned to the main room.

Ruslan flicked her an annoyed glance before focusing on his hands. For some reason, her cousin held a short dagger in one hand and was slowly cleaning the dirt under his fingernails.

The fear in the room was palpable. The white around the women's eyes flashed as they kept to the far side of the room. The woman with the streaks in her hair pushed the younger woman, her daughter, behind her.

Ashta purposely stepped between her cousin and the women before continuing to the stool. She easily alighted the stool before facing her cousin in nothing but her shift. She kept her face neutral as the women quickly began taking measurements.

"She will need a whole new wardrobe. Shifts. Underskirts. Top skits. Coats. Corsets. Capes. All in the newest styles of the great city Issha."

The dark haired woman replied in a quivering voice, "Yes, master."

Again. That word. The strange ribbons of fear and tension were impossible to ignore when Ruslan was in the room.

Ashta had no desire to stay in Bbrski longer than she needed to get a ship and get to Carien. But with each passing day another feeling grew.

Guilt.

Yes, Ashta knew she had a duty to Tripsia. And by taking the trial, she had sworn her life and death to the King and Carien. It was something that could not be undone. Only the King's word could change that fate.

But standing on Bbrskian soil, she was faced with her birthright, a duty she had not chosen but blood had dictated for her. And it was her blood that had been promised to lead this kingdom. Watching the jerky movements of the women who were so cowed by fear reminded her that the only other person in this room with more power than Ruslan was her. Ashta.

Or more accurately, she thought wryly, Svetlana.

Lost in her thoughts, Ashta reacted to the sting in her arm without thought, the gasp out of her mouth.

Ruslan stood suddenly, the chair falling behind him in his anger. He stalked towards Ashta and the redhead who still held the bloody needle.

"F-forg-give me," she pleaded, tears running down her splotchy face.

Ashta watched in horror as Ruslan pulled back his arm and punched the girl in the jaw. Her body collapsed instantly as she curled up on the floor. The other women stepped back, hovering in the corner of the room with fear. Except for the woman with streaks, she watched with equal measures of fear, worry, and hate.

The girl curled herself into a ball without success, Ruslan hurling kicks into her side and stomach.

It was her cry of pain that broke through to Ashta.

From one moment to the next, Ruslan found his arms pinned behind his back and a sharp dagger at his throat. He continued to glare down at the useless girl, ignoring the slow slide of a drop of warm blood down his neck from the slight cut in his throat.

"I would remind you, cousin," Ashta spat from her hold behind him, "That these servants, are *my* servants. This estate, is *my* estate." And then she leaned close, making sure the next words could only be heard by Ashta and Ruslan, she whispered, "And if you ever lay a hand *on anyone* in front of me again, *I* will remove that hand for you."

Releasing him, Ashta pushed her cousin aside and bent over to help the girl stand. Her jaw was already coloring, blood trickling down her lip. In a gentle voice, Ashta coaxed the girl to take her hand.

Only the girl could see the malice that clouded Ruslan's face as he glared at Ashta.

Ashta ignored his presence, keeping the girl's hands in her own. She glanced at the other women and with louder voice than necessary, she asked, "Can one of you women take this girl to the infirmary? She appears to need some Ruutka for her injuries."

Ashta was not surprised when the woman with the streaked hair stepped forward. Without looking Ashta in the eye, she replied quietly, "I will take her, my princess."

Ashta quirked her eyebrow at the changed title.

Glancing at her cousin, she breathed out a small sigh of relief when she noticed he had not caught the brave woman's words. Brave but stupid. Ashta was no one's princess. Not anymore.

Even if she wanted to be, she thought morosely watching the pair disappear into the hallway, Tripsia would never let her go.

The other women came forward and picked up the fabric with shaky hands. The shorter one said in a threadbare voice, "We will have the first dress finished for tonight's dinner, master."

Ruslan did not look at Ashta or the women. Instead, he stared out the window, shaking his bruised hand.

The rest of the morning passed by quietly without any more incidents. By the time they broke for lunch, the women had everything they needed for the dress. And Ruslan seemed to have had enough of spending time with Ashta in silence.

Not that Ashta minded Ruslan finally leaving her room. His presence wasn't as pressing as the zMun people. But there was something about her cousin that just didn't sit well with Ashta.

Ashta took a bun from the lunch tray that had been brought up to the room. Making sure no one was at the doors, she changed back into the purple dress and carefully replaced her sword between her shoulder blades.

Taking a bite out of her bun, Ashta stepped into the servant halls. She could hear the occasional scuffle in the distance but no one was close to her rooms. Thanking the deep shadows around her, Ashta lifted her skirts and picked her way through the tight halls and down several stairs. At one point, she could hear water dripping and feel her toes tingle with the wet cold of water.

Finally, she came to the small wooden door that she had discovered as a child. The door stuck from disuse, but with a hard shove from her shoulder it creaked open. And light poured into the dark hall.

Smiling, Ashta stepped out into the greenery. The door was completely surrounded by vines from the outside, being a whole head in the ground. Adjusting her skirts into both hands, Ashta carefully picked her way up the crumbling stone steps and walked into the secret garden of her childhood.

Despite the oncoming winter, the garden was a riot of colour. Gladiolas the size of fists, like bright suns in between the thick lavender wisteria. The occasional budding Hellbore Lily sparkled along the ground.

Stepping up into the sunlight, Ashta dropped her skirts and just breathed. The smell of grass, sunshine, and that hint of something sweet, like a fairy tale, hung in the air and transported her to happier times.

"Take care not to go too far, mina," her mother had warned even as she eyed the horses in the pasture.

Svetlana didn't mind, already calculating the time it would take to get back into the side doors that led to the servant halls. "I'll be fine, mama, I never get lost."

This had the queen turning away from the horses and giving her young daughter her full attention. Anichka knelt to the ground and took both of Svetlana's hands in her own. With a gentle smile, she caressed her daughters cheek, while carefully picking the right words that would frighten the girl.

"This is not Novyy Zamok castle. Or even the great city Issha, my dear mina. There are places in this castle that even I daren't walk to close to. There are things that cannot be explained that walk in these lands."

Svetlana frowned, her bottom lip pouting out. "But I don't feel anything bad when I go walking, mama."

Anichka's eyes sharpened at her daughters words. She covered Svetlana's mouth while looking around to be sure none of the Kings guards had heard.

Svetlana's eyes bulged with surprise, and trepidation. Her mother never acted like this.

Once the queen was sure no one had heard her young daughters words, she breathed out a sigh of relief before speaking to Svetlana.

"Mina," she whispered, looking deep into black eyes so similar to her own, "Promise me you will never speak of the 'feelings' aloud. No matter who asks, you will keep them inside, okay?"

Svetlana hesitated, but seeing the love and slight fear shining in her mother's warm gaze, she nodded.

Crack.

Ashta blinked several times, regaining her senses. The memory had washed over her, making her completely unaware of her surroundings. Or of the fact that she had walked through the small courtyard and around the old horse pasture to the back of the stables.

Pushing down the sensations at the back of her neck, Ashta carefully pulled her hand away from the stall that her fingers had lovingly caressed. Instead, she slowly walked further into the stables, where the light from the side entrance could not reach.

It saddened her seeing empty stall after empty stall. The stable had been a source of pride and happiness for both her grandfather and mother. And now it was slowly rotting, a forgotten relic.

Her steps were unhurried as she carefully picked her way through the darkness.

Ashta's steps faltered when she came to the second last stall. She turned and hesitantly pushed the door aside. Mold and dust scratched at her nose. Ignoring it, Ashta took a deep breath and walked into the back of the stall. Her hands reached out in memory to the smooth stone, the one her mother would rub every time she came to grab her mount, River.

A slight rustle was the only warning Ashta had.

She dropped to the ground just as the rough cloth from the man's arm rubbed across the top of her head.

The stall was in complete darkness. Ashta could not make out her hands, but she could feel where the man was.

And he her.

He scrambled, his dagger whipping close to her face as he blindly reached out, searching for her.

Ashta kicked his legs out from under him, jumping onto his chest before he had to time to move towards the stall door. The two scrambled, kicking and scrabbling in the darkness. There was the tell-tale clatter of metal on stone.

With more confidence, Ashta wrapped her arm around his neck and held him until his hands dropped limply to his sides.

After another minute of listening to the silence, Ashta was sure no one else had followed the man and her.

She dragged his body out of the stall and into the main stable, grabbing his dagger, before setting him against a stabilizing pillar. The sun washed through from above, lighting up the floating dust motes around her.

The man groaned, coughing slightly.

Before he could move, Ashta pulled her half sword out and set it against the man's neck.

He looked up at her and for a moment she stared into ice blue eyes, and then he shuttered them closed.

"Who sent you?" Ashta commanded, pressing the blade in until she could see blood dripping down his neck.

Rather than answer, the man grabbed her blade with his gloved hand.

Without thought, Ashta pushed the sword through his neck, forced to watch him choke on his blood before the light gave out in his eyes.

She ripped the sword out and cleaned the blade off on the man's shirt. Taking quick note of his non-descript clothing, she bent over and quickly searched his body for something that might identify him. Instead, she found another long dagger and a set of throwing knives.

Ashta quickly hid the knives in her hair. She took the dagger in her boot and slid it into her tight arm sleeve. Ashta took the long dagger from the man and then retrieved the one he had lost on the stall ground and quickly hid them, one in each boot.

Then, she hooked her arms underneath his arm pits and dragged his body until she reached a dark spot on the ground.

With a grunt of exertion, she moved the lid to the side and was greeted by rushing water. An underground river that fed into the castle before spilling miles down the coast into the sea. Once used to much out the stables. Now, it lay beneath the estate, long forgotten.

She dropped the body into the hole, pulling the cover over it again.

With another pat down her body, making sure everything was as it should be, Ashta straightened her back and returned to the castle. This time she took a different hall back to her rooms.

She smiled grimly to herself as the afternoon sun sliced over the stone walls and into the Dark Queens rooms. It had only been a day and she had already amassed quite the collection of weapons.

Now all she needed to do was stay alive long enough to get back to Tripsia.

CHAPTER SIX

⌘

Fox Amongst Wolves

"OH!" A FEMININE GASP distracted Ashta from her slow methodical wash of her arms.

She glanced over at the woman, one of the seamstresses from earlier in the day. Her arms were laden with thick clothes.

The evening dress for the dinner that evening.

Ashta grimaced.

The woman hesitated in the doorway, her nervous glances around her had Ashta's shoulders tightening. Did anyone know about the assassin? Were they not expecting Ashta to be alive and in her rooms?

"What's your name," Ashta asked in a low voice, turning back to her arm still in the bucket of water. She stood in nothing but her shift. The cold ground was gritty and solid against her feet.

"Petra, your highness," the woman whispered. A shuffle behind Ashta had her turning back to the woman who was now bowing, the dress precariously close to falling to the ground.

"You can place the dress on the bed. I will be in shortly."

The woman hesitated for a moment, glancing at Ashta's arms before scurrying into the other room.

Once she was gone, Ashta rubbed her arms dry and then poured the red tinted water out into the drains. With a final glance over the room to make sure nothing was out of place or forgotten, Ashta swept into the main room.

Petra waited at the bed, her eyes downturned and her hands folded together, the knuckles white.

"I am ready, Petra," Ashta said.

Despite her soft voice, the woman jumped at the words and began helping Ashta into layer after layer of clothing.

First came the several layers of underskirts, for both warmth and fashion. Then the white silk undershirt, the neckline carefully folded until it came tight up to Ashta's throat. She tugged it once before taking a shallow breath and focusing on the next layer.

The over skirt came down in clean flow of silver, ruched with bright red rubies. Ashta had to slide her arms into the top before Petra could thread the ribbon and tighten the stays under her bosom.

Ashta grunted at the final tug but otherwise kept silent as Petra retrieved the bright red cape, lined with soft silver-fox furs.

Ducking, Ashta allowed the woman to drape the cape around Ashta's shoulder before gently fastening it to the bright rubies at her shoulders.

Petra stepped back and for the first time that day, a small smile lifted at the corner of her mouth. Before Ashta could comment, a knock at the door sounded.

Petra ducked and slipped away; her slippers barely heard on the stone floor.

Rubbing at her throat, Ashta grabbed her boots from under the bed covers and quickly tugged them on. Whoever was at the door would wait. Rank required it.

She replaced her newfound daggers into the new boots before carefully sliding the half sword behind her back. She stared at the last dagger; the first weapon she had received since being taken by her father. The arms on the dress were too tight to hide its handle.

With a sigh, she hid it with the rest of her warrior clothes.

A knock rang at the door again, this time a quick rap.

Ashta smoothed her hands down her skirt for a final time, glancing around the room. Then in a loud and commanding voice, the one her father had taught her at the young age of four, she called out, "You may enter."

Ruslan slammed the door open and walked in. His face was a smooth mask.

Ashta rubbed at her throat, noting the hard look in Ruslan's face. He did not appear shocked to see Ashta alive and dressed for the dinner. Instead, his eyes quickly swept down her regal form before hesitating on her hair. It was still up in its conch shape. The slightest tightening of his eyes gave away his displeasure. But he said nothing, instead holding out his elbow for her.

Ashta stared at it for a moment before sweeping past him. Ruslan said nothing, dropping his arm and quickly catching up and walking beside Ashta.

Glancing at his reddening face, Ashta couldn't help but wonder why she reverted back to her childhood etiquette. She was not a princess anymore. And had no desire to be. But in the face of her cousin, she felt this need to remind him of his place.

The walk was filled with strained silence. Ashta refused to be the first to break it. Ruslan kept his mouth shut for fear of his tightly leashed anger coming out.

Soon enough, they came to the great room with its tall wood doors. The soldiers took one look at Ashta before opening the door for her. The man to the right announced them.

"Svetlana Anichka rightful heir and first born to Alerik the Ruthless, King of Bbrski, and daughter of the Broskla family."

Ashta swept her gaze across the room. The strange throne stood alone on its dais with a single table. In front were two rows of tables facing each other and people mingled on the edges of the room.

All fell silent and turned towards the newcomer.

With a slight pause, the soldier continued, "And Ruslan Ivan of the family Broskla."

The soldier stepped back out of the room quickly, but Ashta did not the miss the glare her cousin shot the man.

Intriguing. I wonder what they usually call him, she wondered.

Turning back to the interesting dynamics at play in front of her, Ashta carefully walked down the centre of the room and stopped in front of the dais. Turning, she faced the rest of the local nobles and elites, and Ruslan who had not moved from his spot at the door.

"It would seem we are missing a table," she said in a loud voice that reverberated clearly through the room.

A nervous chuckle passed through the crowd.

Ashta stared at her cousin. "Cousin Ruslan, send for a table and two chairs to be brought to the great room."

He stared back at her, eyes cold, shoulders tense.

Ashta quirked a brow and waited.

Finally, he nodded slightly before turning and disappearing out of the room.

The rest of the room waited in silence, waiting for the true heir to react.

But Ashta gave them nothing, standing tall in the centre of the room, her head held high.

Minutes passed, and whispers began to fill the room like the gentle sound of waves crashing on the coast. Ashta ignored it. Tonight, was a test, and she was well aware that to get out of Bbrski alive, she might need to rely on one or more of the nobles here tonight.

The great doors swung open again. Several soldiers swept in with a table and two familiar looking chairs. They had once occupied her grandfather's private room, new additions curtesy of her cousin.

Ruslan followed behind the men and came to stand beside her.

Once the table was set in front of the dais and gaudy throne, Ashta gestured to the seat on her right. Again, her cousin hesitated before moving to her other side and behind the chair.

Ashta addressed the crowd once more, now that they had quieted down. "Friends, old and new, let us break bread together."

With that she took a careful seat in her grandfather's chair. The others in the room stepped up to their plates. But no one sat, glancing furtively at Ruslan.

"Cousin?" Ashta asked without looking up. She reached for her wine goblet and pretended to take a sip.

Finally, she felt him move beside her as the chair scraped across the stone floor and he took a seat.

It was like a breath had been released and the tension in the room lessened. Ashta refused to look at Ruslan. She may have been out of practice playing the royal, but she was very aware of the importance of eyes on her.

As was her cousin, it seemed.

Slowly people sat and picked at drinks. A side door opened, and servants came bearing trays and trays of foods. Young female servers came with wine and ale, carefully refilling cups around the room. The general murmur of conversation picked up once more. But it wasn't jovial. There were a few nervous laughs and Ashta noted more than a few sly glances towards her and Ruslan.

She could feel the anger slowly rising in the seat beside her. Her snubs had not gone unnoticed by her cousin, but they were necessary. Bbrskian politics was kill or be killed. She had grown up to see more than one loud mouthed courtier be put to death in the throne room back in Issha.

Her cousin would be smart to remember his place. Because it had become very apparent to Ashta that her father's physical absence in Bbrski had shifted the power amongst the nobility.

But it wouldn't take long for her father to suss it out and put to death any rumours of rebellion. He would kill his own daughter to maintain his firm grip on the kingdom.

He *had* killed one of his daughters.

A wine server came by to refill Ashta's goblet. The girl glanced at the still full cup. Without comment, she lifted it and made a careful show of refilling it before replacing the still full cup in front of Ashta. With a careful bow, she disappeared out the side door.

After that first time, the other servers were careful to come by Ashta's table to pretend to refill the goblet. Ashta was grateful for the staff's continuance of her slight lie. While she did not care if the nobility knew of her aversion to alcohol and sumptuous foods, it helped if they believed to be the same as her.

The night wore on. Food spilled off of tables. Some of the nobles huddled in groups. Raucous laughter filled the air.

And through it all, Ashta pretended to sip wine and watch the elites.

The group to her left, two women and a man dressed in rich blue colours with mink hides were from the clan Medved. Their people were primarily fisherman. They were also one of the 'newer' great families of the nobility of Bbrski. The younger woman with shining white, blonde hair spilling over her shoulders in sumptuous braids and a deep cut dress kept glancing at Ashta's table. But it was her cousin that the woman kept watching.

A side glance at Ruslan showed his face stony and his gaze fixed to the right.

Following his gaze, Ashta noted the several noble men, braids in their beards and hair, sitting quietly in front of their plates. Hrokr people. Clansmen of Ancel who had given Ashta the sword that warmed her back. The longer she watched, the more she noticed the slight movements in the men's cheeks and tightening around their eyes.

Curiosity piqued her interest. What did her cousin have with the clansmen?

A shout from the far end of the tables had everyone, including Ashta and Ruslan, turning their attention.

A group of younger courtiers had amassed and in the middle was a young man waving his arms animatedly while the rest laughed.

The rest of the room quieted, and the words from the bright faced man could be made out by all.

"...Hair of a savage! To think the princess has spent years in nothing more than a brothel, servicing the lowest of low men? Her manners match her upbringing if you ask –" The young man suddenly stopped mid-sentence, realizing that more than just his captive audience of courtiers were listening. He looked up and accidentally caught the gaze of Ashta. His face brightened even further but he stayed quiet.

An uneasy silence blanketed the room as more than one man and woman peeked towards the princess to see her reaction.

Coolly, Ashta waved to the young man and asked in a clear voice, "Don't stop on my account."

He looked up and hesitated for a moment. Ashta wasn't sure if it was his young age or his life of partial privilege, but the young man slow swaggered into the centre of the tables. His motions were exaggerated and reminded Ashta of a court jester.

The man brazenly accepted the moment of power of the complete attention of one of the most powerful people in the kingdom.

Unconsciously, Ashta rubbed at her throat before grabbing the wine goblet to hide her discomfort. Ruslan leaned forward in his seat; arms braced on the table.

"We've all heard the tales of the kingdom of Tripsia, the so called 'jewel of the Midloean kingdoms'," he walked over to the young woman with the deep cut dress. She blushed at his attention. He grabbed her cutlery and returned to the centre of the room. "But we are all aware that Tripsia is nothing more than a land of savages. They spy on our kingdom," he said, throwing a spoon up in the air, then juggling a fork and knife. A few of the women made delighted squeals at the show. But Ashta watched the clansmen, several who had reached for their swords and axes. "They *steal* our girls. And now- And now they wage war against us, even though they are clearly inferior. I mean, they have *women* fight their battles. How good can they really be?"

And then, Ashta watched in slow motion as the man quickly glanced towards her before grabbing the knife tip and throwing it right at Ashta's neck.

Chairs fell back. The clansmen on her right threw the table over. Women screamed. Ruslan sat stone still beside her.

Ashta's right hand was still wrapped around her wine goblet. She lifted her left hand and pinched the tip of the flying knife to a stop.

Everyone stood still.

An apple slowly rolled across the stone floor. Ashta tracked its movements, her face as still as ice before she flicked her gaze back at the young man. His face had lost all colour as he clutched the fork and spoon in his other hand.

Her blood boiled beneath her calm exterior. How she wished to throw the knife in the courtier's throat. But that would not gain her any followers. Nor would leaving the man unscathed.

With a slow stretch back, Ashta threw the knife back at the man. The but end connected with the shiny brooch that protected his heart.

Clang.

And then it clattered harmlessly against the stone floor.

Ashta stood up.

Those who were still left seated, including her cousin, hastily stood as well. Walking with a slow measured step, Ashta wove around the table and stopped beside the young man.

She watched as his erratic pulse jumped in his neck.

Turning slowly and catching every person present's eyes as she did, Ashta stopped until she stared back at Ruslan. "It seems, cousin, that I am still tired from my journeys. Forgive me while I return to my rooms to rest."

She turned back until she faced the young man, who stood at an even height with her. He carefully kept his gaze straight ahead towards Ruslan. She whispered only for his ears, "I may have spent the last few years amongst savages, but I am Bbrski strong. And you know how we treat our traitors."

The man shivered, his legs trembling.

With a small smile, Ashta turned back to the great doors and walked out of the room without a backward glance.

She couldn't help but feel like a fox in the middle of room full of rabid wolves.

CHAPTER SEVEN

⌘

All Men

ON A FOGGY MORNING a week after the day of her arrival, Ashta was walking the grounds in her simple shirt and pants. With her hair under a cap, and her breasts bound by some bandage she had cut from a towel, she easily passed for a young man. The servants didn't look twice at her as she strolled through the halls and snuck out to the pastures.

Once she was sure she was alone, Ashta dropped the cap and began her sun salutations. Through the stretches her mind wandered.

Ashta had fallen into an easy routine over the past week. Her days were quiet with Ruslan avoiding her company. In truth, all the courtiers avoided Ashta. It was the soldiers, the guards, and all of the female servants who acknowledged her. They gave her quiet smiles and quick curtsies. The men nodded, holding a relaxed stance when she was near.

Slowly, day by day, Ashta won over the castle staff.

In the evenings, her cousin held smaller dinners. Often times it was the man and two women who came. Ashta came to learn that they were lesser nobles from the coast near Issha. The man was Ivan, son of Ivan, and the two women were his wife, lady Nadia, and her sister, Fevronia.

Lady Fevronia was the woman with the low-cut dress. And indeed, she kept up the practice of dressing risqué around Ruslan and Ashta at dinners. In Ashta's presence he never made note or furthered the lady's advances.

But Ashta wondered.

Though what the woman was angling for Ashta wasn't sure, as Fevronia came from little money and thin blue blood. From Ashta's very short acquaintance of her cousin, she had quickly come to realize he wasn't happy with his station in life. He played at King in her grandfathers' estate.

Though he had never sat on the throne again since Ashta's arrival.

She rolled her sleeves back and pulled out the half sword and began practising her foot work, her balance, her speed. Despite the sweat now dripping down her neck and the sun slowly breaking through the fog, her mind could not stay clear.

It would be easy, she thought, to stay here. To forget about the rest of the known world. To forget about a war being waged in another kingdom.

She enjoyed the freedom of her days. Ashta could go where she wanted, and wander without a care. There was no one to protect. No one to submit to.

Yet here she was training – in the early hours.

She laughed at herself. Yes, she thought, it was easy playing a noble born woman, but it was also boring. Ashta could feel her mind wandering, needing to focus on something. And she kept falling into the role of heir when she was around Ruslan and the other nobles.

She did not want to be princess. She had no desire to go to Issha and rule in her father's place. She could barely keep a handle on the court politics in the far flung Broskla estate, how could she survive the council?

With a shudder, Ashta dropped the sword onto the grass. With a sigh, she began her cool down stretches.

No, she thought, she did not want to be princess. And there was the constant tugging at her heart. Carien and Mina. She missed them. And she had really begun to care for her charge as more than a duty. Ashta believed in Carien as a fair ruler who could bring change to Tripsia. If she survived getting *to* the throne.

And Mina, the sweet little babe who had done nothing wrong but be born. She was a piece of hope for Ashta. Motherhood was something that had been taken from her, but with Mina it was hole that was now filled.

Had they made it back to the Tripsian palace that fateful day?

With a sigh, Ashta flopped back on the ground and stared up at the blue cloudless sky.

She needed to find her purpose. Or back to it. When she had been in Tripsia, she had felt needed and useful. Like she could make a real difference.

But sitting here in a field in Bbrski, it was hard to find that purpose again. To find the energy to work her way back to the Kingdom who owned her.

Staying in Bbrski wasn't an option, she reasoned.

Was it?

Ashta shook her head and sat up. Thinking was dangerous. She slid the half sword down her back between her breast bands.

With a quick hop, she was up and making her way back to the grounds. A growl from her stomach reminded her that it was almost the noon hour and she still had not eaten. Ashta took a detour and stopped near the kitchens.

Women at tables were rolling out bread. A young girl was bringing eggs to another white haired woman with a large mixing bowl. The room was hectic and full of life, with a light cloud of flour floating in the air. It was also warm like no other room in the estate was, filled with the occasional laugh.

Keeping her head down, Ashta grabbed a few buns off the pile nearest her. The older woman, as if feeling Ashta's presence, looked up from her bowl and began waving her spoon towards Ashta. Before expletives could fall from the woman's lips, Ashta slipped out of the kitchen and almost ran down the hall. She didn't stop until she was just outside the estate wall where the servant quarters were.

Ashta leant over, breathless and began laughing, joy filling her heart. She ripped into her bun with gusto.

But her hunger turned very quickly when she realized what she was looking at.

A girl was at the well, struggling to heave a bucket of water over the edge. Her arms were black and blue from bruises. Blood soaked through her thin servants' gown in lines across the back.

No longer hungry, Ashta dropped the bun into a side pocket and walked up to the girl.

"Here," she said quietly, offering to help the girl.

The girl gasped, her one eye wide with fear. The other was swollen shut.

Petra, Ashta remembered, the seamstress's daughter.

The one that had stabbed Ashta with the needle.

Clenching her jaw, Ashta grabbed the girl's arm and flipped her hands over. She gasped when she saw the deep lashes across Petra's palm.

"Who did this?" Ashta asked looking up into the girl's pale blue eye.

Petra began shaking, her lip trembling as she recognized the black gaze of the princess.

"Tell me," Ashta demanded.

Petra said nothing, her knees giving out as she became a sobbing mess.

With a sigh, Ashta turned and left Petra on the ground

She wound her way through the halls quickly until she found the store house. The soldier placed at the door surprised Ashta. What was there to protect in the store house?

She turned and disappeared into a different hall. This one lined with boards along the floor every few feet.

Ashta stopped at one section of wood. She looked around and strained her ears for a long moment. Sure that no one would be coming, she popped open the near invisible cellar door. She jumped down into the hole. Thankfully the hall floor only went up to her chest, far shorter than the last time she had made this jump.

Ashta lowered the cellar door over her head. Crouched down, she carefully crawled forward only a few yards before reaching above her. It took some time before her fingers brushed across the knotted wood cellar door.

With a quick prayer to the gods and goddesses, she carefully pushed the door open. It gave way easily and she found herself staring blindly in the pitch-black store room.

Carefully leaving the door propped open, Ashta pulled herself up out of the hole.

Only a sliver a of light could be made out from underneath the door. It was enough for Ashta to carefully make her way towards the door. Her hands searched beside the wooden door until it found the candle and flint she knew would be there.

Holding her breath, Ashta carefully picked up her find and took several steps back into the room.

She hesitated, straining to hear anything from outside but nothing could be heard. With a slow breath, she risked lighting the candle.

Once the wick caught flame, Ashta carefully turned so her back was to the door and covered the meagre light from the candle.

When she did look up, she frowned. Rows upon rows of swords and armor lined the side wall. In the corner stood over a hundred spears. Why wasn't it in the armory, Ashta wondered?

The rest of the store house was innocent enough, with grains piled in bags and dried herbs hanging from the ceiling.

Ashta walked to the opposite side of the armor. When she had been a child, her grandfather had taken her through the storehouse and its contents. It was here on the opposite walls that several cubbies of wood had been made.

Shining the light in each, she didn't stop until one of the last bottom cubbies. The familiar seal on the bag warmed her heart. Ruutka.

Carefully, Ashta removed enough of the herb for a poultice and placed it in her pocket. She was quick to blow the candle out before replacing it beside the storeroom door and sneaking back through the cellar door.

She hurried through the halls and back to the well, unsurprised that Petra was still there. She had taken up the rope for the bucket again. She dropped it as soon as she saw Ashta approach.

Not giving the girl any other choice, Ashta grabbed her arm and led her back to the wall. "Wait here," she commanded the girl. Petra said nothing, sliding down the wall to stare at Ashta blankly.

Sighing, Ashta went to the well and quickly lifted the bucket of water out. She carried it back to Petra.

Once it was settled on the ground, Ashta reached under shirt and quickly unbound her bands.

"What-what do you want from me?" Petra asked on a shaky voice.

"Nothing," Ashta answered honestly, placing the bandages beside them.

She carefully took Petra's hands in her own and with a washed them as best she could in the water. Ashta worked in silence. She took small pieces of Ruutka from her pocket, chewing the bits before spitting them onto Petra's open wounds.

The other girl would let loose the occasional grunt but stayed silent otherwise.

Once Petra's arms and hands were bandaged, Ashta began on her face. She could feel Petra's stare but avoided her eyes as best she could. It was unnerving but the work was soothing.

"Now for your back and legs," Ashta said, stepping back to give Petra room to stand and turn.

Petra, again, hesitated.

Sighing, Ashta held her hand out. The other girl stared at Ashta's outstretched hand for a long moment. The swelling around her eye had already come down, and the freckles stood out against her pale skin once more. Even the bruising was more yellow than purple.

Finally, Petra took the princess's hand and stood. She carefully turned to the wall and lowered her dress to the ground. She kept her naked back facing the princess, her shoulders rigid and proud.

Ashta said nothing. She simply reached down and began cleaning the cuts and bruises.

Scarring on Petra's back told a story of violence despite her young age. It was hard for Ashta to see. In her mind she still remembered the kindness of her grandfather, the soft heart of her mother. How was this man, *her* cousin, from the same family?

To see the same brutality of her father, King Alerik, on a young Bbrskian servant, the same brutality Ashta had felt on her own back in Tripsia, was heart breaking.

Could it be, Ashta wondered, that it was not just Tripsia or Naankdoen that were savage, but all people?

Shaking her head, she quickly used up the last of the Ruutka on the cuts left on Petra's back.

Once she was done, Ashta dumped the dirty water on the hard earth.

Without any words spoken, Ashta walked back to the well and refilled the water for Petra. Ashta didn't know what Petra needed the water for. She didn't need to.

When she turned away from the well, the girl stood before her. Her eyes shone with quiet gratitude. "Thank you," she whispered.

Ashta passed her the bucket, and then said, "We women need to look out for each other."

Petra gave her a wane smile before quickly scurrying back to the wall and inside of the castle.

Rubbing the back of her neck, Ashta stared up at the castle. There was no point in returning the bag of Ruutka since she had used it all.

Instead, Ashta walked the servant halls and snuck back into her private rooms. The afternoon light filtered in through the small windows.

Ashta went to the large hearth. Taking the bag that had contained the Ruutka, she carefully burned it until there was nothing but ash and the pleasant minty aroma of burnt Ruutka in the air.

She wasn't sure how long she sat crouched in front of the hearth, but the light slowly shifted across the room, lighting up the door.

Knock, knock.

Shaken, Ashta rushed up and over to her wardrobe and pulled out a dressing gown. She had just tied it around her middle when the door barged open. The wood crashed against the stone wall, making her wince.

Before she could get righteously angry for the disrespect, her cousin stood in the middle of the room, glaring at her. He announced loudly, "A messenger has arrived calling for the heir to the throne to return to Issha and the palace. To where *you* belong. We will leave post haste."

The silence following his statement seemed to suck all sound out of the room. Ashta, too shocked, stood gripping the belt around her middle tightly.

After several beats, Ruslan nodded, turned around, and disappeared back to the main hall.

Before Ashta could move, a berserker in full furs and swords stepped into the room. His dead gaze skated across Ashta before landing on the door. Carefully he grabbed it and closed the door behind him.

Ashta let out a shaky breath.

She creeped towards the door and set her ear against the time worn wood. After a long beat she could make out the light tinkle of armor rubbing against each other.

Ruslan had apparently stationed a berserker in front of her door.

Frowning, she quickly creeped into the private bathing rooms. And she came to a full stop when she saw the distinct shadow under the door leading to the servant halls.

Her mind flooded with rage.

How dare he, she thought, dropping the dressing gown to the floor and returning to the main bedchambers.

CHAPTER EIGHT

⌘

Mina

RESTLESS, WITH THE MOON hanging high in the night sky, Ashta paced the floor. Sleep would not come. She kept glancing at the entrance where she knew the two berserkers waited.

But the servants exit and the main door were not the only ways to leave her mother's rooms.

Shaking her hands out, Ashta quickly stripped the nightdress off and pulled on the simple underclothes from Ancel's young son.

With another quick glance at the door, Ashta went to the bed and fluffed the pillows until a human sized lump lay underneath the blankets. Satisfied, Ashta turned towards the chest and wardrobe on the far side of the bed.

Quietly, with only the moonlight to guide her, she pulled open the wardrobe. Each creak had her wincing and looking back towards the two other doors in the room. Nothing moved.

With another fortifying breath, she reached back until she could find the tell-tale latch in the wardrobe wall.

Ashta stepped inside and carefully closed the door behind her before pushing open the hidden door. A cool breath of air poured into the wardrobe and wrapped its chilly fingers around her in a ghostly hug.

Shivering from more than just cold air, Ashta crouched and crawled into the pitch-black tunnel. The space was a lot smaller than her memories of it. *Probably because I was child then*, she thought wryly as she pulled herself across the cold stone and wriggled her legs.

She wasn't sure if it was minutes or hours later, but her chilled hands began to catch on the soft moss that was growing along the floor.

Shaking her head, Ashta pulled herself across the last few meters before her hand was stopped by the solid wall of another door. Again, this time with trembling fingers, she pulled the latch open and crawled out into the moonlit pasture. The cool grass tickled her chin as she took in deep lungfuls of fresh night air.

With a final shiver, and a dark glance at the hole she had come from, Ashta stepped away from the stable wall.

The tunnel had been a childhood discovery from an afternoon of play. Even now she was unsure how it wound its way from the queen's chambers down and around the estate, through the ground and up out of the back of the stable.

Ignoring the puzzle, Ashta walked in the shadows of the trees and hopped onto a small piece of fence, the only proof that this had once been a well-used pasture. The scars from horses rubbing and biting the wood from years gone by stood bright in the moonlight.

Ashta settled herself on the fence, pulling the peasant top tighter across her shoulders. From here, if she looked through the trees at exactly the right spot, she could just make out the inky black waters of the ocean.

And somewhere further north, she mused, was Carien, waiting for Ashta.

Rubbing her hands to get some warmth, Ashta finally realized that something wasn't right. Cocking her head, she listened for what her instincts were screaming about.

She heard nothing.

The hairs on the back of her neck and arms stood on end.

Not even the gentle whisper of grass dancing in the wind could be heard.

Dead silence.

A flicker from the corner of her eye had Ashta grabbing her dagger and turning.

But nothing was there.

Blinking several times, Ashta turned back towards the ocean. She kept her focus to the corner of her eyes, waiting for whatever had disturbed the night to come out.

And when it did, the blood in her veins chilled.

For what Ashta saw was a ghastly white being, standing at the next fence post. It was leaned over and staring out at the water with unseeing eyes. The wide shoulders and long beard tickled an image of memory from her childhood.

Sparkling black eyes and a sense of safe that she had only ever felt in her mother's arms.

"Grandfather…" Ashta whispered, turning to face the ghastly being.

The thing turned slightly and nodded towards her.

Ashta was struck dumb. How was this possible?

Before her mind could catch up, her grandfather pushed off the fence and began walking further down the fence line.

Ashta only hesitated for a moment before jumping off the rail and chasing after him. His spirt walked, its ghostly steps gliding just above the glistening grass.

She kept a few paces behind the ghostly figure, questions bubbling up from inside of her. She wasn't sure if it was the unnatural silence or the press of the dark night around her, but her throat seemed to no longer work.

The figure glided through the pasture, turning abruptly near a thicket of trees and gliding through the fence.

Ashta did not hesitate, jumping over and chasing the figure into the shadowy darkness of the forest.

Whatever the being was made of gave off a slight glow. Enough for Ashta to see that there was a distinct path, layered with evenly spaced stones, that seemed to be leading them forward.

She couldn't be sure how long they walked through the forest in silence. Ashta only noticed when they were suddenly not in complete darkness. The moon bathed its soft light over Ashta and lit up the craggy cliff face of the Bbrskian coast.

Before they reached the cliffs, the figure disappeared behind a large stone. Heart beating to fast in her throat, Ashta hurried after the figure and stopped dead when she saw the hole in the ground, and stone stairs cut from the earth spiraling down into the depths of the cliff.

The glow from the figure slowly disappeared down the steps.

Ashta only had moments to decide.

Her skin prickled with awareness. Her stomach was a knot of tension and fear.

But her mind could not stop wondering, what if it *was* her grandfather? And what was he trying to show her?

With a final shuddering breath, Ashta raced down the steps to catch up to the figure.

The darkness enveloped her, pushed down from all sides. As she continued, her steps unwavering in their belief of the next step, she was hit by the memory of another set of steps. Ones that had led from being a cub to being a white lioness. Ones that had led to her betrayal. Ones that had brought her back to the princess. And to her trust.

But these steps, while familiar in their spiral pattern, were distinctly cold and moist, an acrid odour hanging in the air.

Until finally she stumbled out of the stone stairs and out into a vast cave. It's height and breadth was similar to the training room. The walls had been hewn into a smooth even height. The ground below her was level with a strange, grooved pattern along the entire length.

At first, she didn't understand why she could see the grooves. She blinked several times, then realized that it was the water that was glowing.

At the far end of the room was a large pool of water, its depth shining from some unseen light. Ashta walked slowly to its edge, staring at it. She could only see the grooves in the water for a few paces before they disappeared.

She shivered, despite the hot muggy air.

A movement had Ashta turning to face her grandfather's ghostly figure. He stood beside her, also at the water's edge staring down into the water. Even more strange, the figure seemed to be pulling off its ghostly clothing, each disappearing into a wisp of nothingness, before he began walking into the water.

Ashta watched in horror as the water rippled around the glowing figure of her grandfather. Until finally he disappeared in a splash down into the water.

Ashta rubbed her arms, not sure if she should follow or return to her rooms. But something called to her, deep inside of her. Something she could not ignore.

She bent over and let her fingers just barely skim over the water. The moment the cool liquid touched her skin, she was zapped with a pulse of energy and something else. Something warm and kind, the memory of it hovering at the edge of her thoughts.

Ashta jerked back and stood staring at the water for a long moment. The water slowly dripped from her fingers onto the cool stone ground. Ashta turned and took several steps back to the stairway.

But something made her stop in her tracks.

Was it curiosity for the figure? Or the faint memory of that warm feeling? She wasn't sure, but Ashta turned back to the water with a renewed determination.

Quickly, she stripped her shirt and pants off letting them fall off into a pile at her feet. She carefully laid the daggers on top but left the throwing knives in her hair.

Goosebumps flushed over her skin and the slight chill in the air had Ashta shaking. Squaring her shoulders, without giving herself even a heart beat to reconsider, she walked into the water.

This time, the energy pulse was multiplied, burning like a great fire until the last memory Ashta had was the clear blue water rushing towards her face.

Giggling.

That was the first thing she heard. Somewhere there was a young girl laughing and shrieking. Ashta forced her heavy eyelids to open. It took her a long moment to comprehend what she was seeing.

In front of her was her grandfather's estate. And there, in the pasture was a young girl running, her long black hair flowing behind her. Then the girl turned facing Ashta and for a moment Ashta swore the girl saw her, but the girl's eyes did not register anything as she turned back to her pursuer. Her black gaze was familiar but strange, her face too pale, her chin to pointed.

And then, the man appeared. Tall. Black hair instead of white. The wrinkles around his eyes weren't quite deep set yet.

"Mina!" he called in that familiar deep voice that vibrated through Ashta's core. "I'm going to catch you, little findling!"

In shock, Ashta turned back to the slowly disappearing figure of her mother as a child.

The girl laughed before taunting, "You're too slow to catch me, papa!"

But how, Ashta wondered? Shaking her head, she glanced down.

Instead of seeing her feet, she saw a swirling blue mist. Her stomach flipped as she felt the sudden need to retch.

The next time she opened her eyes, Ashta found herself in an open field. The distant shape of the towers from the estate filled the skyline, behind a thick wall of trees.

This time, Ashta kept her eyes up and watched the scene unfold before her.

Tents littered the grass; some were elaborate constructions almost like buildings. Others were nothing more than a few furs strapped together. It made for a mess of grey and brown furs, littered with the bright coloured tent like a bejewelled carpet.

In front of Ashta stood her grandfather, still a tall and imposing figure. He was dressed in royal finery. Just behind him stood Ashta's young mother, now maybe twelve. Her dress flowed to the ground in a smooth sheet of silk, clear and clean like spring water. Her eyes were on the ground, flitting from flower to flower.

Ashta watched in fascination as another man came out from the tents. He was tall and broad shouldered. His rounded belly and red face gave him a jolly countenance. Following close behind him were several men. One of them was a long-limbed teen who had not quite filled in.

The party stopped in front of Lucifer. The red-faced man bowed low before saying loudly, "We bring greetings from Trofim, and are here to pay our respects to the first family and the first born daughter, Anichka Lyudmila." The men behind him also bowed low, except for the boy who peeked up at and stared at Ashta's mother.

Ashta's grandfather nodded. "Please rise, Lord Pavel. We look forward to sharing bread with you and yours during the festivities."

Lord Pavel stood and Lucifer pulled him into a quick embrace.

Ashta's eyes widened at the public show of affection. The man must mean a lot to Grandfather, she thought.

Then she watched as the teen sidled up to her mother. Something must have caught the young Anichka's attention, because she turned and looked up into the teen's face. For a moment her face cleared and then a familiar warmth filled her gaze.

Dread boiled in Ashta's belly as she waded forward, trying to get a better look at the teen.

Just as she came up behind him, the words from Lord Pavel filtered into her brain.

"...And this is the boy I found on that fateful raid of Kae ol," He then gestured to the boy. "Come here, son, and pay your respects to the true king of Bbrski."

Ashta watched as the boy turned away from her mother, and he flipped his hair out of his eyes. And Ashta stared in shock into slate gray eyes.

Father, she thought.

And then she felt herself falling backwards as the memory kept playing out but getting further and further away. As she fell down, down, down, scenes played out around her.

Men, women.

Marriages.

Births.

Deaths.

Until finally she fell hard against the familiar stone grooves of the cave. But something was different.

Ashta shook herself as she stood. Before she could look at her feet, she became aware that she was not alone.

Standing in the middle of the room was a tall, broad shouldered man. His pale eyes tugged at a memory.

Standing beside him in the protective embrace of his arm was a small girl, maybe five years old. Her hair was black and curling in complete contrast to the man standing beside her. Both stood stock still as a pounding sound began to shake the room.

Ashta floated to the wall until she could see the man and girl's face, but both were looking down. Behind them, from the stairway came two men carefully carrying a long-shrouded body.

The men walked around the girl and man, gently setting the body down in front of the large tomb. Without any words, the men turned and left out of the stair way.

"Stay here, mina," the man commanded on a gentle whisper as he stepped forward. The girl did not move.

With great care, he pulled the shroud away, uncovering a pale faced woman. Her dark blonde hair was pulled into a tight conch shaped braid.

Without her intentionally moving, Ashta found herself standing beside the man and down into the familiar heart shaped face. Ashta knew that if the woman had been alive, violet eyes clear like the sea would be staring back at her.

The man carefully lifted her body into his arms and gently placed her inside the stone enclosure. Tear drops stained the woman's white funeral dress.

With a shudder, the man stepped back and with a grunt he pulled the stone cover over his dead wife.

He turned away from the woman and gathered her young daughter into his arms. The girl went to him without a word, tears staining her rosy cheeks.

Neither said a word as the they walked out of the cave and disappeared into the stone stairway. The cave shook with each step, an ominous hiss rising from where Ashta's feet should be.

Her legs gave way and she flipped over and caught herself on the top of the woman's tomb.

Another shake and a burst of energy had Ashta opening her eyes and staring into the stone face of the woman that was laid to rest in this tomb.

Remina the Lion.

Water pressed on Ashta, seeping into her nose as she coughed and sucked some in.

With fear and pain, Ashta shoved off of the tomb and swam up until she broke the surface of the eerily glowing water. She swam until her feet caught the grooved stone floor and she could walk out of the water.

With shaking fingers, she shoved her still wet legs into her pants. She dropped the dagger several times before shoving it harshly into boots. With her head still in her simple shirt, she stumbled towards the stone steps.

Her heart raced as fast as her thoughts. How was it possible? And what did it all mean?

CHAPTER NINE

⌘

The Golden Road

THE MORNING SUN HAD barely broken over horizon. Ashta could not lay in her bed for a moment longer. Her mind was a mess, having caught no sleep after her mad dash back to her room.

And today she was to return to the castle of her childhood.

Novyy Zamok.

She shuddered, memories of the night before mixing with memories from her childhood, shifting and swirling into an unending nightmare.

Shaking herself, Ashta jumped out of the bed and quickly bandaged her chest. She pulled on the simple shirt and pants. There was only one chest in the room and Ashta worried that the only things she could bring with were the dresses her cousin had made for her. She pulled out the white wolf fur and carefully placed it in the bottom of the chest before piling on the rest of the gowns that had been made for her.

The final dress she left out, it was a deep wine red. Its fabric was patterned with silver leaves and it was the most forgiving to wrinkles. Important, Ashta thought, when one was trying to hide clothes and weapons on their person.

She smiled to herself as she quickly braided her hair. The motion was soothing. Ashta carefully hid the throwing knives into the conch shaped braid. Then she pushed the half sword down her back in between her bandages. She tied the leather boots tight before hiding a dagger in each.

Once the skirt, over skirt and bodice were on and tightened, Ashta hid the dagger up one arm and the final throwing knife up the other.

A commotion at the bath door had her looking up in time to see several female servants, followed by a berserker, coming into her private chamber. Everyone stopped in their tracks and stared at the princess who was already dressed and ready for the ride to Issha.

Ashta's eyes caught on Petra. She gave her a small nod, and the young woman quickly came forward. Ashta handed the other women her long coat without another word.

"Thank you... for everything, your highness," Petra whispered as she fastened the coat to one shoulder.

Ashta said nothing. She was happy to see that the bruising on Petra's face was all but gone.

The main doors to the rooms opened and the other berserker stood at attention. His dead eyes surveyed the room before he stood aside.

Ruslan walked in, wearing a regal coat that was adorned with the royal family crest. Ashta stared at the familiar white bear for a long time. Her cousin was playing a dangerous game, she thought.

"The horses are ready. If we leave now, we can be at the palace by nightfall." Several male servants began streaming into Ashta's room. Four men carried her single trunk out while the rest began pulling sheets off the bed and curtains down from the ceiling.

Ruslan watched his cousin as she surveyed the men's work in the room. Her black gaze flicked to every motion and detail before stopping on him. He held back a shiver before breaking their gaze.

Without a word, the black-haired heir swept out of the room, her head held high, her profile every bit as regal as her heritage. Ruslan hurried to catch up to her, barely keeping in step with his cousin.

They quickly passed by the men and her trunk. The princess swept outside and continued down the stairs and into the main courtyard.

Horses stamped around them. Berserkers in full furs paced, agitated to get moving in the early light. And in the midst of the commotion, standing in complete contrast, was an iron wrought carriage.

The wood panelled walls were beautifully painted in scenes of summer. The cover had been painstakingly sanded and smoothed before having thin gold leaf pressed along its entire surface.

Ashta froze mid step, taking in the massive carriage that seated an entire family. Six beautiful white horses were hooked up to it. The lead horse threw his mane, his feet pawing the hard ground.

Turning slightly, Ashta watched Ruslan approach one of the berserkers that held two horses. One was a gelding, the other a large chestnut stallion. His mane was braided back. He sniffed and pranced, trying to move further away from Ruslan.

The men with her trunk passed Ashta and began carefully attaching it to the monstrous carriage. The seamstress, her dark hair streaked with silver, and her daughter Petra came running out with baskets of food.

No one looked at the black haired woman who stood stock still in the middle of all the movement.

Ruslan, with help from a male servant, got onto the stallion. The horse automatically began walking towards the princess.

"I will ride a horse as well," Ashta said in a clear voice, the words ringing loud as a bell in the yard.

Slowly, the commotion around her slowed. The berserkers quieted. Gazes turned towards her. But Ashta kept her gaze on Ruslan.

He said nothing, adjusting his seat in the saddle.

When no one made a move, Ashta turned to the closest berserker. The one that had stood in front of her private room doors. His gaze was even colder now that she stood only a few paces from him.

Ignoring the prickle of unease down her back, Ashta jutted her chin out and looked him square in the eye. "Am I not the heir of Bbrski, the first born of the Broskla family?"

She was careful not to say her name. Ashta could not bring herself to utter those words. To take ownership of that identity once more.

After a long pause, Ruslan yelled out from behind her, "You heard our heir, get the princess a horse."

When still no one moved, he yelled, "Now!"

The berserker slowly nodded, just barely moving his gaze down before disappearing into the crowd.

Ashta waited as the movement around her resumed. Ruslan left her alone, riding up alongside a soldier in the family coat of arms. He looked of the same age as Ruslan, his mouth stuck in a severe frown as if he never smiled.

"Here," a raspy voice said.

Ashta turned to see the large black stallion in front of her. He kicked his head back, stamping his feet. For a moment, Ashta's heart ached. He looked just like Starson.

No one from the crowd moved to help her. The horse had an old side saddle on, the dust streaked from where it had sat in the stables since her mother last rode it.

"Of course," Ruslan agreed mindlessly to Vlas, but his eyes were on his cousin. He watched with interest as she placed a hand on the nervous mount's shoulder. The creature stilled before wrapping its head around to nip at her shoulder.

The yard fell into a second silence as the stallion carefully kneeled before the princess. She perched onto the side saddle, and with a soft pat on the stallion's neck he stood, shaking his neck, his black hair flying.

"Haven't seen that since the late queen came out here," a low growl caught Ruslan's attention. He turned and watched Savva, one of the only berserkers who had served the Broskla family since he was a young man. His long white braids stood in sharp contrast to the red scar that slashed down from his hairline to his chin.

Savva turned and glared at Ruslan before kicking his horse to walk beside the princess. His companion, a new fighter from the deep south, followed.

Ashta turned to the berserker and asked, "What's his name?"

"Stormbreaker, your highness," he replied grudgingly before turning and mounting his own horse in one jump.

With a small smile, she pushed Stormbreaker out from the crowd. Once she was beside her cousin and the lone Broskla soldier, she adjusted her cape to fall around both sides of her mount.

"Well, what are we waiting for?" she asked, staring out to the east. Trees met her view, but she knew that not far ahead stood the great city of Issha.

Vlas stared at her, grinding his teeth.

Ashta quirked her brow, waiting for him to say something.

He shook his head, before turning towards the rest of the party. With a quick hand signal, the rest of the berserkers mounted their steeds. In minutes they were on the great silver road.

They broke through the treeline of the Grey Forest by noontime. Ashta had spent most of the morning riding beside Savva. He had introduced himself before taking up his post beside her.

In front of her rode Ruslan with Vlas, and two younger berserkers with bear skins took the lead.

While they were a small party, maybe twenty men and herself, the carriage kept them bound to the golden road. Its clatter was loud and impossible to miss behind her.

For the most part, the berserkers kept their distance from the dark haired woman. Some for fear of witchcraft, and the rest with respect to her riding skills. The Bbrski weren't known for their way with animals. In fact, it was rumored across the known kingdoms that they Bbrski feared animals of all kind.

It was only out of necessity, like today Ashta thought, that they would ride on the back of a horse. For the most part, the people walked. Everywhere.

Kind of like the zMun, Ashta mused, staring out at the dry hills that surrounded them, golden like the sandy dunes of the desert.

Slowly, small huts began to dot the countryside.

"Another hour's ride before we reach Landamot, your highness," Savva said.

Ashta glanced over at the large man before nodding.

As the party drew closer to the village, Ashta began to notice small details. Many of the huts lay forlorn. The occasional hut had smoke rising from the cooking fire. The people that dotted the fields were thin. And many were old women and children.

Where were the men, Ashta wondered?

"The past ten years have been hard on our people," Savva said, just loud enough for Ashta and none of the other men to hear.

Ashta carefully steered Stormbreaker closer to Savva.

After a moment Savva continued, "At first the rains came later. And then they stopped altogether. Many had to push further south to find feed for their herds. And those poor farmers who lived off the soil they had to leave the farm and fight for coin." Savva watched as the princess slowly nodded, her wide eyes taking in the bare fields.

"The King has been waging war for years. Far longer than any King or Queen before him. And the kingdom is starting to crack under the constant weight of feeding an army."

They approached the small cluster of houses. A small crowd of dirty children followed the party, their eyes too big and sunken in for their small faces.

Ashta swallowed hard, turning away from their hungry stares.

The children kept their distance, wary of so many berserkers. Even so, they eagerly ran beside, trying to catch a glimpse of the tall woman riding astride a horse. It was unusual. Especially since her dress was of a noble woman and not another berserker.

The White Bear Inn stood tall amongst the huts, with the only new thatched roof in the village. Its sign hung freshly painted, in stark contrast to the grey and dirty houses that surrounded the Inn on all sides.

The carriage stopped in front of the stable by the Inn. The berserkers quickly dismounted. The children scattered, disappearing into alleys.

Ashta slid off of Stormbreaker. Before she could take a step, Savva took the reins and disappeared into the stables, leaving Ashta standing there with Ruslan and Vlas.

"After you, your highness," Ruslan said with a sneer.

Ashta turned towards him but his face was blank as he waited for her to lead the way.

She pursed her lips before taking her skirts in hand and stepping into the low entrance.

The White Bear Inn was large with half the tables filled with locals. The serving wenches rushed between tables, tankards spilling with beer. Ashta took the nearest empty table. Her cousin sat beside. Despite the other two empty seats at their table, Vlas took a seat at another table.

A serving wench came by, her bosom almost spilling out of her top. Ruslan didn't even hide his staring at her chest.

"I'll have a tankard of ale and a hearty meal," Ashta said while glaring at her cousin.

He gave the young girl a lewd smile beckoning her closer.

Ashta turned away, tuning out his low voice and the girl's nervous giggles. Instead, she watched as the berserkers from their party slowly trickled into the room. They made a large ring around Ashta and her cousin, but none sat with them.

The meal passed in relative quiet, her cousin eating without any comment. Even the mood in the Inn was quiet, slightly uneasy as the locals stole glances at the unusual party.

Vlas came and stood by Ruslan's shoulder. When her cousin was finished, he shoved away from the table and turned to leave. The rest of the berserkers stood as well, some already walked out of the building.

Ashta grabbed the arm of their serving girl.

The girle looked up into the black-eyed woman with fear, her heart beating too fast. Tikka wet her lips before asking hesitantly, "How can I serve you, milady?"

Ruslan turned back to Svetlana and the serving girl. He glared at the chit. "That is, your highness, to you, wench, not milady," Ruslan corrected her in a harsh tone.

The girl paled and shrank back, finally noting the regal cut of the woman's gown.

Before the girl could say anything, Ashta asked politely, "I would like to see the Inn Keeper."

The girl nodded before scurrying off to the back.

Ashta turned and glared at her cousin. "You didn't need to correct her."

He waved her answer off, "Of course I had to. These are your people. And the sooner they know that the heir is back, the better."

Before she could wonder who it would be better for, the Innkeeper, a middle aged woman with a babe in her arms stood before them. The woman dropped into a low curtsy, before murmuring, "It's an honour to serve you, your highness."

"What is your name?" Ashta asked, ignoring Ruslan's tapping foot.

"Iness, your-"

Iness was cut off by a piercing cry from her babe.

A berserker stalked over to Iness pulling his dagger out. "Shut your babe or-"

"Stop!" Ashta commanded.

Everyone stood still. The room was blanketed in silence, save for the screaming babe. Ashta leaned over and pulled the babe from Iness' arms.

The babes face was red already from crying. The noise comforted Ashta even if her Mina had not cried often. With a happy sigh, she caressed the babe's cheek.

It stopped mid cry and stared straight into Ashta's eye.

Sleep.

For a moment the babe fought to keep its eyes open. Ashta rocked it gently, and then it was still. She held the child for a few moments longer, even though she was sure it would no longer wake.

Carefully, she transferred the child into its mother's arms. "You have a beautiful child, Iness. I only wished to thank you for the meal," Ashta said. She gave the child a parting smile before turning away.

Ruslan watched as his cousin swept out of the room. The men followed her outside. He exchanged a glance with Vlas before following behind as well.

By the time he was outside, Svetlana was already seated on her mount, looking every bit the lost princess of Bbrski. He frowned as he took in the crowd of villagers – children, women, grandfathers. All of them had the same expression on their face.

Hope.

Ruslan stomped over to his mount, Vlas trailing him with a thoughtful expression.

CHAPTER TEN

⌘

The Heir Returned

As THE SUN DRAGGED its way across the sky, the party rode closer and closer to the great city of Issha. Ashta watched as the scattered huts began to come closer. As they rode out of the last village, she finally caught her first glimpse of her childhood home.

Issha had been built along the river Loh which spilled out into the ocean. Unlike Naankdoen city, or as their people knew it as Kiang don, Issha had seven walls. The walls were short, maybe three men high, built with stone to survive the harsh winter frosts. Each wall had a great portcullis, named after each of the great families and manned by their men.

As the party neared the first wall, Ashta noticed the crumbling towers. She grimaced but kept quiet, patiently waiting as Vlas spoke with the gateman.

The soldiers kept furtively glancing over to the lone noble woman who rode astride. Her skin was dark, her hair was simply braided and completely up. No jewels adorned her neck or head. Yet there was something unmistakably regal about her.

Ruslan's face began to redden as the gatekeepers stalled, not making any move to open the first portcullis. Ashta smirked, not surprised. The Smirnov family were known for their prickly and distrustful nature. Which made them the perfect first gatekeepers to the city. Very few entered the city without a Smirnov sending a messenger to the king's advisor. Every person was tallied and accounted for except when a royal advisor grew tired of the Smirnov.

Having had enough, Ruslan rode his mount up to the man with the Smirnov crest, a porcupine, stamped in gold on his crest.

"This is unacceptable. Do you know who this is?" He asked, gesturing towards the dark haired woman. She ignored his motion, staring at something on the wall in the distance. "This is Svetlana Anichka, daughter of King Alerik and of the family Broskla, heir to Bbrski. You dishonour the crown princess with your tarrying."

The gateman snorted. "Do you know how many young women we get in a day claiming they are 'the crown princess'? We can't let just anyone have an audience with the Blacks Council."

Ruslan's face flushed to a purple, his jaw rigid. "*I* am Ruslan Ivan, the current head of the Broskla family. And *I* demand an audience with the Blacks Council or so-"

"Cousin," Ashta interrupted in a soft voice. She forced Stormbreaker to walk up to the Smirnov gatekeeper.

The man looked her up and down, frowning but said nothing. Ruslan glared at Ashta but wisely kept his mouth shut.

"The light dawns on the red lion and lights a fire on the ice," Ashta recited from memory, words passed down from mother to daughter, to granddaughter.

As the last words fell from her lips, a strange power surged in her body. Her face flushed as her skin crawled with blue illuminated shapes and lines.

Just as fast as they appeared, the light blinked out of existence.

The man, and the entire company of Smirnov gatekeepers dropped to their knees. "Princess," they called out.

Ashta ignored her cousin's curious gaze. The words had been passed down in her family for centuries, a key to the city and the kingdom, and she had never needed to use them before. "I request an audience with the Blacks Council."

The man immediately straightened, "As you wish, your highness." He turned and directed the nearest man who disappeared into the tower.

The Smirnov gatekeeper made a quick hand motion and the portcullis groaned as it opened its teeth to the small party of berserkers and the princess.

Ashta road past the soldiers, taking the lead of the party. Ruslan kicked his horse and quickly came up beside her.

Her gaze flicked over the ramshackle stands that made up the first market. Once a bustling area of gay colors and singing merchants, it now stood grey and desolate. A boy ran in front of Stormbreaker, his right hand missing as he slipped into the streets.

Ashta shuddered.

Ruslan fumed beside her, his anger palpable in the air.

They came up to the second gate quickly, the Bogomolov, which they passed through quickly. The gatekeeper had been forewarned from the messenger, his men ready, the large wooden doors open to the inner city.

The next three gates passed quickly, the streets in were quiet as the evening dinnertime pulled the city residents indoors to hearty meals around warm hearths. Even in the soft winds of fall, Bbrskian stayed wary. The winds could shift in a moment and bring snow and winter on its back.

As they passed through the Artisans market, Ashta was shocked to see even here it was dirty and many of the houses and stands stood unkempt and missing boards. It seemed the city of Issha had suffered greatly in the time that Ashta had been sold to Tripsia. A small ache started in her chest, but she pushed it down, keeping her eyes focused. Above them stood the many spired towers of the castle, and the king's seat of Bbrski.

As they passed the last gate that opened up to the main castle and outer courtyards of Novyy Zamok, Ashta could see hundreds of people lined up on either side of the path. Many were in servant clothes, with courtiers and lesser nobles standing at the front of the line.

The people gawked in disbelief as the long lost princess rode into the palace courtyard. She rode her horse with a steady hand, her body an extension of the animal so like the late queen. But her dead gaze, as it swept over and took in each person had servants shivering in recognition. The princess may look like the late queen, but she was just as much inside as the current king. How much, would be seen.

As the party neared the end of the line of people, they stopped before the steps that led inside the main castle entry. Several men walked out to stand on the slight dais at the top of the steps.

Ashta took in the six men. Each was dressed slightly different. One man looked as old as the head healer. And another, whose bright red hair shone orange in the last of the evening light, looked no more than sixteen.

She stopped Stormbreaker only two paces from the bottom of the stairs. Ruslan jumped off his horse and hurried over to the princess.

Before he could help, Ashta nudged Stormbreaker to carefully kneel for her. A gasp came from the crowd of onlookers but when Ashta swept her gaze over the two lines, everyone had their eyes firmly to the ground, bowed low in respect to her.

Frowning, Ashta slid of Stormbreaker. With a slight shake to straighten her skirt, she turned and walked past Ruslan's outstretched hand. She ignored his tense jaw.

Ruslan waited a beat, feeling the weight of the Blacks council on his back, before following behind Svetlana.

Lord Kestral watched the princess walk past the Broskla boy. He rubbed his chin in interest before dropping his hand. He had doubted the messenger from the outer gate when he had come to say the heir was here. They had been expecting her weeks ago, but no one from the council spoke up when the King's ship never arrived in Issha.

And now the lost heir to Bbrski was here, in the great city.

In that moment, the princess looked up into Kestral's eyes, and his heart froze. Her eyes, black like Anichka's were the same familiar cold as King Alerik's. Kestral quickly pushed his shaking hands behind his back where the princess could not see. No doubt, he thought, she would see everything, just like her father.

When Ashta reached the top of the stairs, she paused. The gathered men lined up of their own accord. Their coat of arms clearly visible on their chests, carefully sewn in silver and gold and all manners of colour.

Before she could speak, the man furthest away stepped forward, hands behind his back. He gave her a quick bow before speaking, "Welcome home, your highness."

A shiver broke out across her back and down her arms.

Home.

Bbrski, and Novyy Zamok, had not been a home for over eight years. Longer, if she were honest with herself, Ashta thought.

The man straightened and Ashta stared into his familiar emerald green gaze. Lord Kestral had been younger the last time Ashta had seen him in court. Fresh from the battlefield, only a man of forty summers. He had served beside her father for years, but even as a child Ashta had sensed the tension between the two.

She watched with interest as Kestral did not acknowledge Ruslan, but kept his gaze on her.

"You must be tired from your travels. A guard will take you to your rooms so you may rest and wash off your travels before the great celebration of your homecoming tonight," He said as he gestured to a soldier wearing the castle colours.

"I thank you, Kestral," She said.

Kestral, her cousin, and all of the council men's gaze's widened.

Ashta ignored them and followed the soldier inside the castle.

The experience was surreal, the halls familiar but completely different. Maybe it was because I am taller now, Ashta mused as they passed painting after painting of the royal family.

Or maybe it has simply changed, she thought grimly as they passed a blank spot where the family painting of her mother, father and herself as a babe was distinctly missing. No other paintings came after.

The soldier turned before taking a stone staircase up to the family wing. She had spent most of her childhood while her mother was alive there. Ashta was not surprised when the man stopped in front of her childhood bedroom. The one that her half-sister had taken after Ashta's mother had passed.

The soldier pushed open the door before stepping back and bowing to her.

She took a deep breath and walked through the doorway. As she passed, the hair at the back of her neck stood on end, similar to when she had passed the sword in the Cub's training hall.

Blinking several times, Ashta stared at the room. The tall windows were the only familiar thing in the room. The drapes were thick red brocade, and the bed was covered with a red velvet curtain. Gold edged the wood and the vanity. And in the middle of the room stood a large golden tub. The servants must have carried it here, she thought before her eyes caught on three women curtsied low beside the tub.

All three were dressed in similar shades of grey. Two had white blonde hair and the third had black hair similar in colour to Ashta, but curled and unruly, flowing down to the small of her back.

"Your highness," the third girl breathed out.

The door to the bedchamber clicked behind Ashta. No one moved.

She stared at the women for a moment longer. "Rise," she commanded on a quiet note.

The three girls stood up quickly, the blonde women keeping their gaze lowered while the third looked at Ashta's chin.

"I am lady Yana, and behind me is lady Agripp and lady Miroslav. We are honoured to serve as your ladies-in-waiting," the black haired woman said before dropping into another quick curtsy. The other two women, now that Ashta could see their faces, had a similar nose and eye shape. Sisters.

"I do not require your assistance," Ashta growled, stalking past them towards the bed. She quickly removed the heavy fur lined cape and dropped it onto the gold silk coverlet. She wrinkled her nose, hating the heavy colours and fabrics. It felt as if the room was smothering her in its heavy colors and fabrics, like the weight of her title smothered her in this castle.

When she heard no movement behind her, Ashta turned and glared at the women.

"Let me make myself clear," She said as she stalked up to Yana. "You are dismissed from the position, as I do not require a lady-in-waiting – *any* ladies-in-waiting. Now leave this room."

Her heart pinched as Aggrip and Miroslav trembled but did not make any move to leave.

Yana straightened her back and for the first time looked the princess directly in the eye. Her face was flushed. It was dangerous to stay but she could not fail at this to.

She took a step forward. The princess's eye's widened for a moment but otherwise her face stayed as impassive and cold as before.

"*Your highness,*" Yana bit out. "We *must* serve you. Or in the eyes of the nobility and Blacks Council we will be seen as disgraced. There will be no life for us. *Please,*" she begged quietly, glancing back at Aggrip and Miroslav with warmth in her eyes.

Ashta did not want this. Another layer of cloth to stifle her freedom and movements. Another reminder of the heavy weight of her birthright.

But watching the three women, and having been trained to protect for years, Ashta knew she could not dismiss them. No matter how much easier it would be.

"Very well," she said, and the three ladies' shoulders relaxed. The sisters glanced at each other with small smiles. "If you could have the servants draw a bath for me."

Aggrip and Miroslav curtsied before disappearing back into the hall. Yana stayed and watched Ashta expectantly. When Ashta made no move, Yana walked to the bed and picked up the cape. She carefully shook it out before going to the dressing room to hang it.

As soon as she left, Ashta turned to the curtain beside the bed and whispered. "Who sent you?"

Nothing moved.

Then in a flurry of motion, the man flung back the curtain and ran. His arm was outstretched, dagger glinting in the last light of the day.

Ashta hit his arm away.

The man's eye's widened before he twirled and tried again. Ashta pulled her own dagger out of her sleeve and stabbed him in the ribs.

He slackened, his eyes resigned and shocked.

Before Ashta could pull the dagger out, or ask him again, he stabbed himself in the throat.

Shocked, Ashta stepped back and watched the man gulp for air as blood began pouring from his neck.

"I can tak-" Yana began before gasping.

The princess twirled to the other women, black eyes flashing, bloody dagger in hand.

The man gasped once more before falling face first into the fur carpet. Yana's eyes bulged as she took in the dead assassin. She put a hand to the wall to steady herself.

"Did you send him?" Ashta asked in a deathly quiet whisper.

Eyes still on the dead man, Yana replied in a shaky voice, "Where did- How did he – Who- Who…" Her eyes rolled back, and she collapsed to the ground, her head narrowly missing the corner of the entrance to the dressing room.

Frowning, Ashta wiped the dagger off on the assassin's clanless clothes. After replacing her dagger in her sleeve, she checked over the body. But there was nothing, just a variety of simple weapons with no special marks.

She rolled up the body in the floor fur, wrapping him tightly.

"I – I have some rope in the dressing room, your highness."

Ashta turned to see a still pale Yana standing, her eyes carefully focused on Ashta.

A knock at the door had both women turning.

"I'll deal with the body," Yana said, straightening her shoulders before walking jerkily to the wrapped body.

With a slow nod, Ashta went to the door. "Lady Yana," Ashta said turning away from the door for a moment. "Tell no one of this."

The other woman stared at the black haired princess for a long beat. In that moment, she realized how strong the princess was. And how she was as hardened as any Bbrskian berserker.

Finally, Yana nodded.

"Good," Ashta said before slipping out the door to occupy Mirosalv and Aggrip as they waited for the servants to bring water.

CHAPTER ELEVEN

⌘

The Blacks Council

A KNOCK AT THE DOOR had Yana passing the cape to Miroslav as she hurried to the bedchamber entrance. Ashta watched her go as Aggrip continued straightening Ashta's skirt.

The ladies had decided that the princess would wear the only dress that had been absent of colour. Completely white. As pure as the princess.

Not an hour ago she had been dripping in blood, she thought grimly. Yana shared a glance with Ashta, both staying quiet around Aggrip and Miroslav.

Ashta said nothing to the sisters even though the white skirt reminded her of the ball in Naankdoen. Not a year ago she had stood in a dress to be presented in front of nobles. And now she was back in Bbrski, wearing a dress.

Yana returned to the dressing room with a box.

Before Ashta could ask, Yana turned to Aggrip. "Hold this."

The other woman said nothing, straightening up and taking the box.

Yana carefully opened it.

Inside lay a familiar circlet with a large black diamond in the centre.

Ashta swallowed when she saw it. The Queen's Jewel. Her mother had worn it when she was alive. But the lady Arja never wore it.

Slowly, Yana picked up the circlet and then turned to the princess.

Ashta carefully curtsied, bowing her head.

The moment the circlet touched the skin on her forehead, Ashta gasped. Her vision brightened, everything edged in white for a moment. And then it settled.

Blinking, Ashta straightened, touching the circlet with her hand subconsciously.

"You look just like the late queen, your highness," Yana breathed out before dropping into a deep curtsy. Aggrip and Miroslav followed suit.

Ashta turned away from them. Her eyes pricked.

In that moment she felt a warmth, like a hand pressing on her arm. The scent of lilies passed under her nose briefly, then cleared.

Ashta turned back but known of the ladies had noticed something amiss. Yana looked to her expectantly.

For a moment, Ashta swore her mother had been in the dressing chamber with her.

Taking a deep breath, Ashta gave Yana a nod.

She walked out into the hall where Vlas waited for her. "Right this way, your highness," he said, leading the way down the hall and back towards the dining hall. Yana followed a step behind and a step beside the princess. Aggrip and Miroslav followed behind them. Only the swishing sounds of their skirts could be heard in the otherwise deserted halls.

They stopped in front of the doors to the dining hall for a moment. Vlas spoke with one of the two guards in front of the door. A quick nod, and one of the guards opened the door. Vlas stepped inside and then to the side. "Presenting her highness Svetlana Anichka, first daughter of the Broskla family and heir to the throne of Bbrski."

Ashta waited a moment to see if he would continue, to introduce her ladies-in-waiting, but Vlas stayed silent, standing at the ready beside her.

Were ladies-in-waiting always ignored, or did she notice it now because of her own invisible position as a lioness, Ashta wondered. With a frustrated sigh, Ashta turned to the dining hall and its occupants.

The dining hall held only the Blacks Council and their families for the celebration of the princess's arrival. A small gathering of fifty people. All stood up at her arrival.

Ashta quickly walked around the tables to the head table. She was surprised to see her cousin seated with the council families.

There was only one plate set on the head table. One chair.

Ashta froze halfway to the table.

Like hell she would sit through the meal, alone, like a bird on display, she thought. She turned and caught Lord Kestral's gaze.

"I will need another chair and plate set at the head table," she said, her voice carrying in the still room. She gestured to Yana to continue walking to the head table with her.

A slight murmur passed through the hall, but nothing intelligible. Aggrip and Miroslav found their seats at the end of the tables, furthest from the head table.

Yana walked with her chin high, but her eyes lowered. For the first time in her life, she felt the full weight of the Bbrski nobilities' stares. Her heart was pounding in her throat and she could feel a slight sweat on her upper lip and forehead.

The princess walked around the head table and stopped at the chair, not taking a seat.

Uncomfortable, Yana stood to her left, waiting. The council men fidgeted, restless.

Yana breathed out a sigh of relief when she saw two servant boys comeinto the room with a chair. Once they had set a spot beside the princess, they disappeared.

And Ashta finally stepped forward and took her seat.

The tension released in the room as everyone else also took their seats, relaxing and turning to their neighbours.

Yana dropped her mouth open slightly, keeping her lips still as she whispered, "Why did you require my presence, your highness?" Her heart still beat too fast, a reminder that she was not in her country estate anymore. That there were rules to follow and dangerous people all around, listening.

And the most dangerous person in the hall sat right beside her.

Ashta reached for her goblet of wine, but rather than sip, she replied, "Tell me, Yana, how long have you been at court?"

"Since my coming out," she said slowly, her mind finally catching onto why the princess had seated her beside the princess.

"And that was how long ago?"

Servants came out and set single dishes in front of each of the nobility. Bbrski meals could go for hours simply from the amount of dishes. The first was a small fried fish with fresh greens. Ashta wondered where the greens came from as it was deep into the fall.

Yana waited until the servant had set the dish down at the head table and disappeared. The princess grabbed the fish and ate it in one bite. Several council men, including Ruslan her cousin, stared at the princess with wide eyes. Some with disgust. Others with simple shock.

Yana took up her cutlery and carefully sliced a sliver off the fish before taking a gentle bite. "It will be almost four years this winter solstice."

Ashta nodded, chewing thoughtfully. She sipped from the water goblet before pushing her plate back. The servants came rushing out and removed all of the plates from in front of the nobles. Lord Smirnov had his cutlery still in the air with his single bite of fish when his plate was whisked away.

After a few moments, the servants, rushed now, came out with the next course. Soup.

"If I must have a lady-in-waiting, it would be a great service of you to inform me what you know of each person here in celebration tonight."

Ashta turned and waited for her reply, not touching the soup. No one else moved. Many of the men stared at the princess. Lord Ivan watched the soup with longing, his stomach growling.

"Of the council men?" asked Yana, glancing out over the large crowd of people.

"Everyone," Ashta corrected.

Only when Yana nodded, did Ashta turn to her soup. To the horror and dismay of those that watched, she picked up the bowl and drank it in one tilt.

The servants, red faced and twitching, ran back into the hall and gathered the plates. No one besides the princess had been able to eat their soup.

Yana frowned, her own bowl already whisked away. The princess dressed – besides her strange hair style – and spoke like a Bbrskian highborn. And yet she had the etiquette of a barbarian.

The servants took a bit longer before they came back out with dishes for the second course. Salad. And a soft white bread roll.

The moment Ashta's dish was set in front of her, she picked up her fork. But she hesitated.

Most of the people that sat closest to the princess watched her avidly now, hands gripped fiercely around their cutlery.

Ashta ignored them. "Go on."

When Yana did not start right away, Ashta flicked a glance over the other tables in the hall before focusing back on Yana.

"I'd suggest you leave no details out. *Really* take your time on it."

Yana's eyes widened.

The princess was doing it on purpose.

With a small smile, she began detailing all she knew of the people present. And as she did, Ashta took small bites, chewing slowly. Many of the onlookers finished their meal quickly, for fear the princess would change her mind.

Lord Kestral, the head of the council, of the family Zima was already familiar to Ashta. The older man had a sprinkling of white at his temples, his sea green eyes unmistakable to the usually grey gaze's of the Bbrskian. Seated beside him were his two daughters, and both their husbands. The men were formidable soldiers, Ashta could see their large biceps even from the head table.

Beside Lord Kestral was Lord Yuri, who had just come into his seat on the council, a young man untried by war and still gangly with youth. His father, Lord Varlam, had died peacefully in his sleep the last winter. His widowed wife and four young daughters eyed the single men in the room hungrily.

Across from Lord Yuri sat the familiar long braids and fur pelts of the Rviun Tribe. Ashta had been surprised that a tribe had been given a seat on the council. Lord Gleb, only slightly younger than Lord Kestral was known for being a levelheaded man. Uncommon amongst the ice clans. Four of his men, likely brothers and cousins, sat with him.

Lord Dmitry of the family Bogomolov and Lord Oleg of the family Smirnov, openly glared at each other. Lord Oleg's silver beard was trimmed to a sharp point, matching his sharp hawk like visage. Fitting that his family crest was the porcupine, Ashta thought to herself. He was accompanied by an equally waspish woman.

And Lord Oleg, with his plump wife and equally soft son were well known for swaying with popular opinion rather than standing hard to the laws. A personal thorn of Lord Dmitry.

Finally, furthest from Ashta sat a familiar face, Lord Ivan of clan Medved, the newest family to join the council with the death of the Trofim family line. Known for his greed, Lord Ivan was a feared man in the room. What he wanted, he got. And the same for his young wife and equally beautiful sister-in-law. Ashta frowned at the beautiful woman who kept her gaze on Ruslan.

By the time the last dish came out, Yana had detailed almost everyone present.

Almost.

Ashta had stayed quiet when the other woman skipped any comments on her cousin, but now she was curious. Especially given the dynamic personalities that made up the Blacks Council. It was a wonder that they were able to rule in her father's place while he was overseas.

With a lull in the conversation, Ashta gazed over the hall thoughtfully. As usual, no one seemed to pay any mind to the staff. A server came by and made a show of refilling Ashta's cup.

There was much going on in Issha. From the way the servants moved in between the tables, refilling goblets, clearing dishes, Ashta could see that fear was not as rampant in the castle. It was likely, she mused, that when her father was present in the city that servants were more fearful. She remembered the tension from the nobility as a child and doubted her father's tactics with dealing with the nobility had changed so much over the years. But around the Blacks council the servants were calm, not quite relaxed. The only tension she noted, besides Lord Dmitry and Lord Oleg, was around her cousin and Lord Kestral.

Taking a quick sip from her water, Ashta asked quietly, "And Ruslan? What is the word in the court about him?"

Yana stalled, her cutlery shaking in her hands. With deliberate slowness, she set them down and pushed her plate away despite there still being dessert on it. Her stomach had tightened into knots at the mention of Ruslan.

She wet her lips, gazing at the familiar shock of red hair and pale face.

Ashta watched the play of emotions across Yana's face. A shiver raced across her skin. She rubbed her hand to calm it as she waited.

"He…" Yana began before dragging her gaze from Ruslan. She took a quick drink of her wine and watched her wine in contemplation instead. "He has quite a following in the city. And the younger families have gathered behind him…"

Ashta wasn't sure what to make of that. But there was more. "And?" she gently prodded.

Yana flashed her a quick glance before staring at the wine again. "He has made some," she pursed her lips, "*interesting* points on our laws. And pushed for changes."

Ashta tried to hide her shock behind her own wine goblet, staring at Ruslan with fresh eyes. Indeed, it did seem that many of the members of the younger, less powerful, families watched him with respect, if not admiration.

And Lord Kestral also watched her cousin. But his was a look of not dislike, but disapproval. And a hint of fear, Ashta thought.

Yana did not continue. She did not need to. Ashta had learned much during the short meal. About the kingdom. The council. And her cousin.

Without warning, the princess stood up.

While some of the tension from the beginning of the meal had eased by through the dinner, it took only moments for everyone to also be on their feet.

She did not say anything. Instead, she nodded to Yana. Then the princess walked around the head table, down the middle of the room and out of the dining hall. Only when the door closed behind her did people relax.

"Like her father…" Lord Dmitry said without any inflection.

Lord Kestral stared at the door for a long time, even as others sat and continued to eat and talk despite the princess having left. Lord Kestral rubbed at his chin before turning to Lord Yuri. "Be careful of that one. Her eyes are as dead as the King's."

Yuri nodded, his eyes still wide in shock from the entire evening.

CHAPTER TWELVE

⌘

Changing Winds

THE NEXT MORNING, BEFORE the sun broke the horizon, Ashta had dressed in the simple mens clothes. She felt a connection to them, and how much freedom they gave her from her title and her role as a woman.

Smiling to herself, she carefully placed a cap over her hair. Now she looked the part of a gangly street urchin.

Pleased, she stood by the door, listening to her guards. Novyy Zamok, unlike her grandfather's estate, did not have servant halls connecting the private rooms. Though it was not without its own secrets.

Ashta stuffed the cap back into her pocket and wrapped her dressing gown around herself. With a quick breath she opened the door.

The guards snapped to attention, bowing to her.

"Your highness."

She smiled stiffly at them, her lips tight across her teeth. In a low voice, she said, "Forget you saw me leave this room." And then she leaned in even closer, catching both men's eyes. "And if I hear *anything*, you will be the first to have your tongues cut out."

The men said nothing but the fear and respect in their eyes satisfied Ashta. She didn't want to be like her father, but there was a reason he was still the King and not dead at sea.

Fear moved kingdoms.

With a careful swish of her gown, she walked down the hall and around the corner. The moment she was out of sight, she whipped the gown off and stuffed it into her shirt. With the cap back in place over her hair, she looked like a lazy boy with a fat belly and no muscles rather than the fearsome warrior she was.

Good, she thought.

With her disguise in place, she skulked through the halls until she found the large kitchen that served the entire castle. The room buzzed with people. Girls washing dishes. Servants making plates of breakfast. A man in the corner carving a pig up.

Quietly, Ashta snuck into the stores and grabbed a dinner roll from the night before. She stuffed one in her mouth and two in her pocket.

Movement outside the storeroom had Ashta running to the back by the bags of rice and wheat to hide in the deep shadows. Ducking down, she waited for the occupants to leave.

She could make out two voices. A man and a woman's.

The man was the first to speak, his voice carrying to the other side of the small room, though he did not move closer to the back. Ashta breathed out a sigh of relief. It would be awkward to be caught dressed as a boy in the kitchens. Her own people would have her hand cut off before asking any questions.

"And her hair? She looks like some balloon headed man. Did you see last night?"

The girl giggled. "Yes. When I served her wine, I saw the dark tan on her hands. You would never see colour on a Bbrskian noble woman's hand."

"Shhh!" A third person came into the storeroom.

Ashta peeked from behind her spot, seeing the dowdy skirts and grey hair of the newcomer.

"It would do you both well to remember that woman is our princess," and then in a much quieter voice, the older woman continued, "The same blood that runs in his majesty runs through her veins."

"I'm not scared," The boy piped up, his voice shaky.

Movement near the back by the grain had Ashta pushing deeper into the shadows. The old woman had moved on silent feet.

Ashta held her breath, her ears straining to pick up the conversation that was not meant for her to hear.

"You should be. Her father had a man put in an oak barrel, studded with nails, dragged to the port-"

"That's just a faery story!" The boy interrupted.

A beat of silence fell on the storeroom. Ashta could make out the older woman placing things in the other two's arms.

"It's no faery story. I was a younger girl then, just a serving wench. They had us all line up outside the castle to watch. And the princess watched the whole thing, her black eyes as dead as her fathers. A girl like that is dangerous, and one who survive..."

Ashta lost the rest of the conversation as the three occupants left the storeroom. Only her loud breaths kept her company in the deafening silence.

After a beat, she snuck to the front then out and through the kitchen and back to the halls.

Her heart raced as fast as her thoughts. She almost ran straight into the guard in front of her.

"Watch it!" a familiar voice shouted.

Ducking, she ran around and down the nearest hall, hoping Vlas hadn't recognized her.

She stopped in an alcove to catch her breath. And then she realized that Vlas had been headed toward the royal wing.

Likely, to her room.

Heart racing even faster, Ashta ran down the halls, through a courtyard, and skid to a halt around the corner of her room. She hurriedly pulled out her dressing gown from her shirt.

Yelling drifted down the hallway.

"-I demand to speak to the princess right now!"

Shuddering, Ashta pulled the hat off and stuffed it into her pants.

Low murmurs from the guards could be heard, and then a scuffle. Clash of metal on metal.

With a deep breath, Ashta walked around the corner and demanded. "What is the meaning of this?"

The men froze. Vlas had his blade at one of the guard's throat, the other man stood hunched with his sword outstretched and dripping blood from his mouth.

"Princess," Vlas said in a quiet voice. With a quick glance at the other guard, he dropped the man he held. Vlas stepped past the men and towards Ashta.

His quick eyes took in the princess's flushed face, and her haphazard dressing gown before dropping to the floor. "I'm here to escort you to a private meeting with Lord Kestral this morning," and then he added in a quieter voice, "your highness."

Ashta breezed past Vlas and the guards, pushing into her private rooms. Yana stood in front of the fireplace. The woman jumped to her feet and dropped to a quick curtsy.

Glancing back at Vlas, Ashta replied, "I will need a few minutes to dress. You may wait for me outside."

He hesitated for a long moment in the doorway.

Then Yana stood and walked to the door. After a quick stare down, Vlas sighed before walking stiffly out into the hallway. Yana shut the door behind him with a distinct click.

"You as well, Yana."

The other woman only hesitated for a moment before nodding briefly. She slipped out the door.

Finally, Ashta was alone in her room.

Ashta sighed out a breath of relief. That had been too close for her comfort.

Not wasting any time, she stripped her clothes, hiding the men's clothes behind her bed. She went to her dressing room and blindly grabbed the first dress. It was only when she was straightening the skirt in front of the mirror that Ashta noticed the canary yellow set off with black piping underneath her breasts and along the skirt.

Wrinkling her nose, she turned away from her reflection and went to the hall. There was no time to change again. And, she thought hopefully, no one would notice the thickness of her forearms where the dagger handles sat nestled close to her wrists.

Yana gave the princess another curtsy before falling in step behind her. Vlas kept a space between himself and the noble woman Yana, sneering at her wide eyes and fair complexion.

Neither spoke a word as the princess led the way, without needing any direction, straight to the traditional seat and meeting place of the Blacks council. A place during her childhood which had stood empty and unused.

The guards standing at attention on either side of the entry gave a deep bow to the princess before opening the doors to her.

Inside stood all seven council members. She was careful to keep the surprise of her face. Her cousin's soldier had said a meeting with Lord Kestral not the entire council.

Ashta glanced to her cousin, who leaned against a wall rather than sat around the long table.

The rest of the men stood behind their seats and watched as Ashta swept across the room and took her seat at the head of the table. Yana stood at her shoulder. The councilmen took their seat.

Vlas joined Ruslan who remained against the wall.

Ashta said nothing, turning to Lord Kestral. With a quick nod from her, he stood and began.

Ashta sat back and listened to Kestral as he spoke of the current situation in Bbrski, as much as she watched the other council members.

The next morning, in her street clothes, Ashta snuck out of the room. The guards nodded.

Without any words exchanged, Ashta snuck through the castle halls until she came to the servants exit. While the main gates into the inner courtyard and palace proper were used by the nobility and all visitors to Issha, there was a second gate in the wall. A wide set of oak doors that allowed for horses and wagons to come through but nothing larger.

Ashta joined the fray of servants and city workers that were entering and leaving the palace grounds before the breakfast.

She followed the crowd down through the back streets of the city until she was walking through the markets of the third wall.

Ashta could not hold back the grin that stretched across her face.

The markets had been one of her favorite memories of Issha. How often had she and her mother snuck through the castle in the early hours of the dawn, dressed as maids? It was those mornings that she had her first taste of being something else. The weight of her family legacy was gone in the lively streets as vendors tried to catch her attention and street urchins tried to coax her into games.

The market was still busy, with the crowds brushing shoulder against shoulder, four men wide. But the colour seemed to have been washed out of the streets. Ragged and sun bleached cloths covered stalls. Thin faced women with sunken in eyes tried to push their wears into passersby hands. Even the children running around were different. Dirtier.

Ashta followed the flow of the people until she was almost at the end of the market. A flicker of blue had Ashta turning towards a small stall, no wider than a person. The woman seated behind worked diligently on her knitting, needles flying. At her side stood a young girl, her eyes old with the ways of the world.

Those eyes watched the dark eyed stranger approach their small stall.

"I'll give a gold coin for a bloom and that apple, mina," The stranger said, pointing to the large apple sitting beside the young girl's arm. The apple had been a hard earned prize this morning, something sweet for her mother and sisters to share.

Jutting her chin out, she bartered fiercely, "Two gold coins."

She waited for the dark-eyed stranger to counter, but he simply smiled.

Ashta dropped three coins in front of the apple. Then she quickly took the prize and the voluminous blue bloom of the hellebore lilies that had drawn her attention to the stall in the first place.

The young girl said nothing, pocketing the money and sharing a long look with her mother that Ashta did not see.

With a sigh, Ashta quickly left the stall, the memory of quick fingers and short knives a hard lesson learned as a child. She kept moving, the crowd slowly thinning as she approached the fourth wall. A small gate pierced through the centre of the wall. Beyond it lay a small, enclosed garden. And beneath the soil lay the final resting places of the greater and lesser families of the city.

A man jostled her, almost distracting her from the slide of small fingers into her pocket.

She whipped her hand out and caught the little mugger's thin wrist.

The boy stared up at her with wild wide eyes, like a starved dog.

Before he could bite, Ashta yanked the boy closer to her, and further away from the stream of people coming from the market.

"Don't," she warned as he tried to wriggle free.

The cold threat in the man's voice slid down his back and had the boy's muscles freezing up.

"You should take more care to who you pick pocket," she whispered glancing meaningfully over at the berserker who had been following her since the palace. The berserker's eyes widened before he turned and disappeared into the crowd.

The boy also watched the berserker with wide eyes.

Ashta pulled the apple the boy had reached for out of her pocket, and carefully placed it into his own pocket. With a final look into his eyes, she straightened and released him.

For a moment the boy stood there in shock.

Frowning, Ashta waved him off. "You best run along now, before he comes back."

He needed no more warning, turning and diving into the crowded streets. The red apple flashed in his hand, a bite already missing from it.

Smiling to herself, Ashta turned back to the gate and pushed inside the small piece of heaven.

She had been visiting the garden that fateful morning she had been taken and sold to Ennris. Now she was returning as a grown woman, a trained lioness. And a disgrace of a princess.

Sighing, she weaved through the gravestones and tombs. As she passed the statue of her grandfather, the feathered wings on his back almost fluttered. Her fingers trailed across his grave marker, but she didn't let herself stop. Her prize lay deeper in the cemetery.

She did not stop until she reached the large weeping willow tree that her mother had favoured. The only space in the garden that Ashta had been allowed to bury her mother.

The coward's death, the people had called it. Only Ashta knew the truth, that it had been a broken heart that had killed her mother.

She pushed the long trailing branches of the willow aside, before coming to an abrupt spot.

There, in the spot that she had planted her mother's favourite flower so many years ago stood a sturdy plant, now as tall as Ashta, and as wide filled with blooming white hellebore lilies.

Her legs pulled her closer as she stared in awe at the flowers. The blooms purchased from the market fell from her fingers. And then her knees gave out as she fell before the plant.

She reached a finger out and gently rubbed the edge of the leaf. The smell of citrus and moonflowers filled the air, and with it the memory of black eyes filled with love and warmth.

Mother.

Sighing, Ashta closed her eyes.

Someone had come and cared for the plant. Watered and fed it. Had taken the time to trim it.

Hot tears trailed down her cheeks.

Ashta had expected the people to forget her mother as quickly as they had forgotten their princess.

But now, facing the many blooms of the single plant, she knew that to be wrong.

Bbrski needed a strong leader more than ever right now. The meeting of the council members, and all she had learned from their reports of the kingdom, haunted her.

Famine. Drought. Rebellion from the southern ice clans.

Since setting foot on Bbrski, Ashta had been reminded again and again of not only her birthright, but her born duty to her home. Her people.

Yet even now, surrounded by the scent of her family and reminded of the power of her title, caramel eyes tugged at her heart. Soft and filled with warmth and concern. Love like no other Ashta had felt before, not since her own mother and grandfather had passed.

Carien had lived through so much already as the young princess of Tripsia. And she had a softer touch than her fathers. She was trying to bring change to her kingdom, to her people. And she needed and trusted Ashta to protect her, to get Carien on the throne.

And to keep the princess on the throne.

A wind ruffled the swaying branches of the tree, singing a soft rustling lullaby.

Ashta swayed with it, her heart torn.

She opened her eyes and was faced with the lavender tinted cut blooms from the market. Their colour soft and ethereal, reminding her of another lavender gaze that had brought her warmth and that same feeling of home.

Shaking her head, Ashta stood up. She needed to make a choice. There was no way for her to help bring lasting change to both kingdoms; Bbrski and Tripsia.

And if she died where she was now, as she was now, nothing would change.

Yes, change was coming, she thought, whether she wanted it or not. And she knew she should feel blessed to have a choice in that change.

But it was not an easy choice to make.

CHAPTER THIRTEEN

⌘

The Old Ways

THE FOLLOWING DAY, ASHTA and Yana are seated in one of the courtyards, with the fall sun weakly warming their faces. A table was set between them with a variety of Bbrskian foods. Ashta waited for Yana to try a piece of each food before sampling it for herself.

"There is talk amongst the nobility that the Mabron feast will be larger than normal this year," Yana said, her gaze flitting across the dismal gardens.

Even in the Bbrskian summer, the plants had no chance to grow as luscious as the gardens in the Tripsian palace courtyard. Just another reminder that she was not where she was needed, Ashta thought.

She made a noncommittal noise, chewing slowly on the candied meat pieces.

Yana took it as a reason to continue. "Issha is abuzz with having the heir to the throne living in the city again. To have things happening again."

The princess lifted a black eyebrow, her gaze still blank.

Yana quickly explained herself, "Not that the counsel has done nothing these past years. They have done much. But it takes more time. And especially during such turbulent times, every month counts…" she trailed off, looking to the princess hesitantly. The dark eyed beauty was a mystery, as much an unknown as a foreign King. But surely, she would be better than her father, Yana worried.

They sat in silence as birds flew over top towards the distant ocean.

Suddenly, without warning, Ashta stood, sweeping her skirts aside and walked to the edge of the courtyard, where the wall stood at waist height. Below her, steepled, stood the sprawling city of Issha.

Yana hurried to follow, her gaze constantly flitting to dark spots. She did not understand why the princess refused the castle soldiers, or the berserkers, to follow and protect her.

"Tell me, Yana," Ashta whispered, her mouth barely moving. "What do you see."

Focusing on the woman beside her, Yana stepped beside her and leaned over the wall. The city lay below, the seven walls dividing up the people. Far below was the port and the harbour where trade ships and war ships docked.

"I see the city below us, your highness?" She asked, in a quiet voice, not sure what the secrecy was for.

The princess did not move. She replied, "Is that all?"

Frowning, Yana looked back over the wall. Beyond the final wall stood fields of black earth, the farms bare from the harvest and the drought. "I see the black dirt of the farms. And the many ships in the harbour."

"Hmm."

The two women stood in silence, both in their own thoughts.

Finally, Ashta said, quietly for she saw the movements in the shadows of the courtyard. "I see thatch that hasn't been fixed in years. I see crumbling pieces of wall," Yana's eyes sharpened as she saw the slow deterioration happening below them. "I see dark alleys of crime, and berserkers roaming in the daylight covered in blood. I see the fresh wood of the warships, outnumbering any other in the dock. I see the white salt on top of the black dirt, where nothing green will grow for the next generation, if not longer."

Yana stared out at the view with fresh eyes, not understanding how on first glance she had not seen the same as the princess. She had lived in Bbrski her whole life. And in this city for the last year, and yet the princess in a moment saw more.

"You are a true princess of Bbrski, your highness," Yana breathed out, turning to the other woman and bowing deeply.

"Stand!" the princess hissed.

Yana looked up, bewildered but did as she was told. It was then that she realized the princess did not only see the city, but saw the men stationed around the courtyard as well. She shivered. This was no ordinary noble woman standing in front of her.

Ashta gripped the other woman's elbow and pulled her close. She walked with measured steps back towards their table, and behind it to the entrance into the palace.

As they moved, she whispered, barely audible. "Many see what they want to see, but it is an outsider who sees everything."

Yana said nothing, but her lips pressed together.

Once they were safely back in Ashta's room, Ashta dismissed her lady-in-waiting. The other woman left without further comment. Thankfully, Ashta thought.

With the door closed, she carefully walked around the space, her hand gripping the hidden handle in her sleeve. She had not been sure if those that had watched the last week from the shadows were friendly. Or deadly.

Or if they knew about the others who watched her from the shadows.

But she wasn't going to test her luck.

She had just cleared her dressing room when there was a knock to her door. She swept back into the main room and took a careful seat at the settee in front of the fireplace.

"Enter," she called, her gaze firmly on the flickering flames.

She watched from the corner of her eye as the doors swung out and one of the soldiers guarding her room stepped inside. "Ruslan, your highness."

Ruslan stepped in, and Ashta watched with satisfaction as he realized that she was not standing at attention for him. He quickly shook himself off and glared at the soldier.

The door closed with a loud *snick*.

Without moving her eyes, she watched as he took a deep breath, something crossing his face. And then he was bearing a fake smile as he stepped towards the fire and took the armchair to her left.

She sat in silence. Waiting.

The flames flicked and danced, their warmth glinting off of the gold buttons of her cousin's coat, and the many rings on his fingers. She wondered how it was her cousin could afford such opulence during such hard times in the kingdom.

Ruslan began to fidget, small movements. A twitch of the finger, a slight roll of the shoulder.

The princess kept her back ramrod straight, her pose leisurely with how far back she sat in the settee. But Ruslan did not misjudge her, as her body was tensed and ready to fight. He would not misjudge her again. His cousin was a dangerous ally, and a lethal enemy.

"You must be wondering why I request an audience, cousin," he asked, his voice offhand.

Ashta heard the slight shake in the last word. She said nothing but inside she was smiling.

When she gave no indication to answer, Ruslan continued on his own. "As you may have deduced, I have been representing the Broskla family on the council for the last years."

She lifted her hand and flicked a non-existent piece of lint from her skirt before letting it drop into her lap. He did not see how the fingers slipped beneath her other sleeve.

Ruslan hated how easily she manipulated him. But he also respected it. Only his uncle, the king had ever done so before. One disastrous meeting, and he had been careful to never meet the King in person again. Lest he end up in the sea with a knife between the eyes, the kings mark on its hilt.

As his brother had.

"There are many in this city who are terrified of your father. Of what he has done to those who stand in his way. As I'm sure you remember from your own childhood in the castle."

Now she looked up and stared him in the eyes, her black gaze glittering and dangerous.

"The council is weak. With your father gone, we have a chance to rebuild. To spread the wealth from Issha, from our ports and trades with the Midloean kingdoms, to our outer and inner lands. There is so much that can finally be done that has been ignored the last decades of his rule."

"Like what?" she asked, interrupting his rant.

He stood and paced in front of the fire. Ashta watched him with curiosity. And a bit of admiration. No one was perfect. She knew that better than most.

"Like, like – the southern wall!" he spun around and faced her, his face bright red and angry.

But at this, Ashta was confused. "What of it? The wall has stood for thousands of years between the ice clans and the deep south." But her tone was questioning.

"Have you been to the wall recently?" he asked harshly.

The princess shook her head once, her chin barely moving. Her eyes never left his.

"I have." He fell back into the ottoman, the energy leaving him in a gust.

Ashta wasn't sure if he was this passionate or this good of an actor.

"There are parts of the wall that have completely crumpled to the ground. It would take nothing for an army to crawl through. Or a sShaxah."

Ashta shuddered, the memory of long ago lessons bringing up the image of a great beast as tall as the wall, long tusks and sharp claws on its forelegs.

"Surely, the King has been informed," she said in a low voice. But even as the words left her mouth Ashta knew the answer. Her father wouldn't care. He had been bent on being the greatest king to every be. And as far as the Bbrskian living on the coast knew, sShaxah were nothing more than myths.

Her cousin laughed mirthlessly and shook his head. "I had been sent to the wall by the King himself. And do you know what his response to my letter detailing the necessary supplies and human labour to fix the problem was?" He stared into the fire, before whispering. "That it would not be necessary. I was there simply to remind our men and women who manned the wall that if they failed, that it would be better for them to die than to seek refuge in the northern lands or in Issha itself."

The two sat in silence, each lost in their own memories of a King that was not easily forgotten.

Finally, Ashta shifted on the settee until she was facing Ruslan. "Have you brought it to the councils attention?"

He leaned forward, his hands clasped, and his elbows braced on his knees as he stared deep into his cousins, the princess's, eyes. "I am one voice of seven. And not all agree with me. Many would rather sit and hide in this city, waiting for the terror from the south or the evil sailing in the north to come here." He turned away and mumbled something, his eyes on the fire.

Ashta's gaze sharpened. "What was that?"

He sighed then looked her in the eye again. "It would be a lot easier if it was only one person who could make decisions. Our King has many faults, but many opportunities to move fast. As fast as an heir would."

"An heir could do nothing," Ashta spat out. As years before her father, the Blacks counsel ruled until a King or a Queen took the throne.

His eyes glittered, and small smirk graced his lips. Ashta wanted to cut it off of him. For a moment, she had almost felt bad for her cousin. "You know as much as I cousin about the new Kings. But what of the Old?"

"You mean my family line," she asked quietly, realizing where this was going.

Now it was the princess who glared into the fire.

Ruslan watched her. Not sure if he pushed too far. If she was aware of her power here in Bbrski. Not even her father could stop her, if she chose it.

"It's not as simple as that," Ashta whispered, her ribs itching with the reminder that her body was bound to another Kingdom.

Ruslan stood, brushing his hands on his legs. He knew there was no more to be said. But the look on her face, that she was thinking about his words, was what he had expected. It was more than he had before. And while the princess was a wild card, he would have a better chance with her than with the King.

"I will leave you now. Until the morrow, your highness."

Ashta said nothing, waiting until the click of the door closed behind her cousin before relaxing against the back cushion of her settee.

Oh, she was aware of her power as the heir, and as a daughter of the Broskla family. The old ruling family of Northern Bbrski. The first kings and queens.

She stared at the fire for a long time. Maybe minutes, maybe hours. And then an idea flitted through her thoughts. A way out. And maybe, just maybe, a way for everyone to win. Carien. Her cousin. And the Bbrskian people.

Ashta was not surprised when the next day a messenger came with an invitation to the next council seating. She *was* surprised to see her cousin in the council room. But he stood against the wall, and the seat for her family sat open.

Ashta walked past it and instead took the seat at the end of the table.

Her father's seat.

Lord Kestral gave her a brief nod before standing and addressing the rest of the councilmen. "I would like to start-"

Ashta stood, "Actually I would like to start, Lord Kestral."

He whipped his head around and stared at her, his eyes hard. But Ashta didn't back down. He may be older than her and wiser in years, *but she was the heir*.

After a long moment, he broke their stare and took a seat.

Ashta then focused on the rest of the council men.

Lord Kestral, a fair man who was battle hardened. Lord Yuri, young and untried. Lord Gleb, his familiar clan braids making him look as formidable as he was. The waspish Lord Dmitry and the easily swayed Lord Oleg. Lord Ivan, who's greed pushed him, and was only kept in check by Kestral and Gleb.

Finally, her gaze stopped on her cousin. Ruslan. He watched her, that familiar heart shaped face like her mother's. With her heart beating fast in her throat, Ashta made a decision. She wasn't sure it was the right one, but right now, it was the best one.

Taking another quick look around the table, Ashta took a deep breath and straightened her shoulders.

"With the council as my witness, I, Svetlana Anichka, head of the Broskla family and heir of the new and old royal families of Bbrski, renounce my birthright."

Gasps filled the room, but Ashta turned her gaze to Lord Kestral. The older man glared at her but could do nothing.

Aware that the next words would change the fate of the people in this room forever, in a slow and clear voice, she said, "And, as is my right by the old ways, I give my cousin, Ruslan Ivan, grandson of Lucifer Augosst, the place as head of the Broskla family. And as the *next true heir* to the Broskla family."

The room was dead silent with six pairs of eyes glaring up at the former princess.

CHAPTER FOURTEEN

⌘

Son of Alerik

ASHTA TURNED TO LORD Kestral, ignoring the rest of the room. "As your duty to the Blacks counsel, and to Bbrski, Lord Kestral, you will write up the necessary paperwork to be signed and witnessed in the throne room with Bbrski watching."

His right eye twitched but he made no other move.

But Ashta had said her piece, and she knew that everyone in the room had heard her words.

Finally, since the words had left her mouth, she looked up at her cousin. His eyes were wide and his face bloodless. She gave him a small nod. At the motion, he gave her the barest smile with a nod.

Good.

Her cousin had not expected that move. Nor had anyone in the room.

That was fine with her. Ashta needed to focus on what was truly important. On her *true* duty. And that was to the Princess Carien of Tripsia, and her adopted daughter, Mina.

"Councilmen," she said, with a quick look around the room. The councilmen stared back at her with mixtures of fear, disgust, respect and admiration. And soon she would never look upon these men again. With a quick nod, she pushed back form the table.

The other men around the table scrambled to their feet, but she didn't care. She swept out of the room and didn't stop until she closed the doors to her private chambers behind her.

For a moment she rested her forehead against the hard wood door, just breathing. *What have I done?* She wondered.

It was one thing to tell Carien, tell zHavier, and even herself that she was no longer a princess to Bbrski. But telling and making it so was very different. Now that she had started the process to removing herself from her family tree, her heart ached terribly with the betrayal to her mother, to her grandfather, and to every heir that had ever been before her.

Who was she to take power over her own name, and to take her name out of history?

She shuddered, the ache in her chest growing, until it was a dark cloud swallowing her whole. She stumbled to her bed, and crawled under the silk sheets, dress and all. For all she knew, tonight might be the last time. Because after the papers were signed, Svetlana Anichka of the Broskla family would truly be dead in the eyes of history.

And all that would be left was Ashta the Lion tamer. A nobody. A slave to Tripsia.

No daughter.
No mother.
No one.

The sobs wracked through her body, but she kept a stranglehold on her throat, not allowing a single sound to pass her lips. Not a single tear passed her eyes. Instead, she lay there, shaking, as the sun sunk over the Blood sea, and night fell over the cold wasteland of Bbrski. What once had been her homeland, and now was nothing.

The next morning, Ashta broke her breakfast in her rooms. Staring sightlessly at the fire. She forced her hands to push the food in her mouth even though she tasted nothing. She didn't know the next time she would eat.

The doors to her chamber slammed open.

Ashta jumped, her eyes clearing for the first time as she turned to the door.

A seething Yana stormed towards her, the guards quickly closing the doors behind her. Her face was flushed, her eyes flashing with each step. Ashta frowned, her hands fluttering down to her skirts, useless.

Yana didn't stop until she stood toe to toe with the princess. And then, she shocked herself, when she poked the princess in the shoulder, whisper yelling, "How could you!?"

The princess blinked several times, that black gaze cold and distant. It enraged Yana even more. After everything the princess had said the day before. And now this.

"How could you-you- leave our fate to-to-to that *man!*" Tears filled her eyes, her throat closing up as the horror of the gossip she had heard this morning finally filtered through.

And even as Ashta stood there, still and dispassionate, deep inside of her another piece of her heart broke off. No, she wasn't sure about what she had committed to yesterday. But with the oath out there, there was nothing left to do but fulfill it.

And she would.

Just as she had done with every oath she had taken in her short life. She was not much, but an oath breaker would never be it.

Ashta watched Yana cry for a minute before walking away from the lady and taking a seat again at her chair. She lifted the bread to her mouth, staring at the fire with unseeing eyes.

Yana felt embarrassed, following the princess and falling onto the settee. How could the princess eat when it felt like Bbrski first chance at life without a cruel King at its helm had just been ripped away?

When her sobs finally quieted to the occasional hiccup, the princess turned to her. "At least Ruslan cares about Bbrski. Unlike my father."

Yana glared at her but couldn't disagree. Taking a steadying breath, she leaned forward, keeping her gaze on the princess's. "But not much more. You've seen the way he flashes his family's wealth. And how he treats his servants-"

"Stop," Ashta motioned, glancing meaningfully at the door. Yana's cheeks turned bright red, but she did not turn away from Ashta. "Whether you, the counsel, or the people of Bbrski like it or not, He *will* be king one day. It would do you well to remember that."

"It should have been you," Yana whispered.

Ashta shrugged, turning back to the fire. In a distant voice, she replied, "The crown was never meant for me." And then she added quietly, as if it was an afterthought, "Any crown."

Yana deflated, falling back into the cushions, staring bleakly at the fire as well. To have hope ride into the city astride a horse, strong and capable, and have it torn away so quickly was too much for her.

But there was nothing she could do.

The words had been said. And so, it would be.

"Yana," Ashta called, her voice still filled with that distant quality.

Yana looked to her, sitting up slightly.

"You are dismissed. I will no longer be needing your services by this evening."

It was too much for her. Yana stood on shaking legs. Her anger still fueling her, she said in a quiet tone for just the princess and herself. "I hope you remember what you have done for the rest of your life." And then she turned, her skirts swishing as she almost ran back to the door.

With another final click of the door, Ashta was alone. As she always seemed to be, she thought wryly. Now all there was to do was wait.

Just as the sun passed over the city and began its descent into the ocean, the four berserkers walked through the halls. Servants and courtiers watched them with fear.

The men did not stop until they reached the princess's quarters.

The guards stepped aside.

Daniil took the lead and pulled the doors open with a satisfying crash. He stomped into the room, and then stopped. Filat slammed into him, swearing.

Daniil glared at him, then nodded his head to the still figure of the princess in the middle of the room. She was dressed in another one of her royal dresses, the gold glittering in the sunlight as if she was a living goddess.

"Your highness," Daniil growled, but he refused to bow. If the rumors were true, then this woman did not deserve his respect. To spit on her blood the way Ruslan said she would do this afternoon. It was disgusting.

The girl turned, her black gaze pulling the berserkers in like her mother had done so many years before. Finally, each man dropped to his knees.

Even Daniil fell to his knees, at a loss for words at seeing the late queen Anichka in the flesh before him.

Ashta said no words as she walked past them. The berserkers trailed her quietly, their party somber as a funeral procession. Servants, courtiers, nobles, all crowded into the halls to catch a glimpse of the final steps of their princess.

The doors to the throne room creaked open. And then Ashta stood before the seven councilmen.

In front of the throne stood a small table. Lord Kestral stood to the left, his mouth in a grim line, his eyes hard as he glared at Ashta. His opposite in every way, Ruslan stood to the right, his clothing was rich as if he had been born to the place of prince. His eyes, so similar to her own were bright with excitement and something else.

Ashta swallowed hard but continued her slow procession. Past the courtiers. Past the councilmen. She took the steps up to the throne and stopped in front of the table.

From this close, she could see that there was a hard edge to her cousin's gaze that made the hairs on the back of her neck stand up. Was she doing the right thing, she wondered not for the first time?

She fell to her knees before the two men, her head bowed.

Silence blanketed the room. Ashta listened to the quick beat of her heart in her ears.

Kestral glared down at the slip of a girl before him. In one swoop she had cut away everything he had been working toward his whole life. When she had first come back to the palace, he had hoped the girl took after her mother. But now, standing in the throne room with Ruslan gloating beside him, Kestral knew that she was no different than her cold father.

Cornered, he could do nothing but his duty and continue his work in the dark shadows of the kingdom.

Taking a deep breath, he addressed the room and the upper crust of Bbrski. "We are gathered here today to witness the first born of the Broskla family, Svetlana Anichka of the Broskla Family line. First born daughter of King Alerik and Queen Anichka. Crown princess of Bbrski renounce her birthright."

He watched as several people shifted, as people shared meaningful looks. The room was tense with uncertainty. Kestral hoped his allies stayed strong through this blow from the royal family.

"And as per the old laws, from the time of our first king and queen, Lucifer and Illya. King Lucifer named the young daughter of his wife as his true heir, so does Svetlana Anichka name her cousin Ruslan Ivan as the head of the Broskla family."

He turned to look at the young man to his left, puffed up like rooster that had just walked into a henhouse. Kestral's hand itched to pull out his old scabbard and fight the man in the old ways of their people. But not yet.

With a deep breath, he said in his loud booming voice, "And, she declares Ruslan Ivan as the next *true heir* to the Broskla family".

The silence, which had been tense before, now seemed to consume the throne room's occupants.

The councilmen at the foot of the stairs watched, mute, as the princess stood and signed the traditional papers. And when the Royal lineage book came out, Yana watched with a sickening horror, as the princess took her feather quill and crossed her name out and wrote in her cousin's name instead.

And then the girl, princess no more, stepped back and fell to her knees once more. Lord Kestral's voice rang with the finality of deaths bell. "From this day forth, Svetlana Anichka, daughter of Alerik and Anichka, shall be no more, and this woman before me shall be a Bbrskian woman of no name."

He stepped forward and took the small circlet off the crown of her head, and then he stepped behind Ruslan. And begrudgingly, he announced, "From this day forward, Ruslan Ivan son of Ivan and Creta, shall be no more and instead this man will be Ruslan Alerik, of Anichka and Alerik, true heir to Bbrski."

He stepped back and bowed, breathing out, "My prince."

The room seemed to hold its breath, before slowly, one-by-one, each person bowed or curtsied, and the words "My Prince," rang through the room.

Ruslan stepped forward, and everyone quieted. "Rise, my people," his baritone voice shook, and he watched with glee as everyone, including his cousin stood.

"Dear cousin, I will never forget this day. You may return to the former princess's rooms to collect what you need, and I will give you my men to take you wherever it is you wish to go."

Ashta dipped her head, then rose, turning and leaving the room as fast as her shaky legs would let her. She did not dare look anyone in the face. She could feel her people's horror, disgust, and fear. But it was done. Svetlana was dead.

And now, she truly was Ashta the Lion Tamer.

She was only thankful that her cousin gave her the small mercy of returning to her rooms, rather than sentencing her to death right there in the throne room. Something her father would have done without hesitation.

The halls were empty, the guards no longer stood before her former rooms. But it did not matter to her. She simply needed to rid herself of this dress and then she could disappear into the bowels of the city before her cousin could change his mind.

Ashta pulled the doors open and hesitated for only a moment.

Before her stood five men, dark clothes, and short swords at the ready.

Recovering quickly, she stepped inside and pulled the doors closed behind her. Before the men could move, she had pulled her two short knives from her arm sleeves.

The group of men hesitate, eyeing the wicked curved blades. Ashta shuffled to the side, drawing them away from the door and towards the fireplace.

The men fanned out, four of them closing in on her as the fifth man hung back near the doors.

As the first man lunged, Ashta side stepped him, stumbling slightly in her skirts, her knife landing with a thud in his shoulder rather than his heart.

He grunted, stumbling back out of her reach, as the next man stepped in, his axe swinging.

Ashta fell to the ground, her leg coming out and tripping the axe-swinger. He fell towards the ground his wrist out to catch him. But Ashta was already pulling around, her body thrown over his back and her sword slicing deeply across his neck.

She shoved off his body just as a sword from the third man swung down, slicing deep into the second man's shoulder. Ashta rolled to her feet.

The fifth man was edging closer to the door, but she pulled a throwing dagger out and her aim was true, landing in his throat. The man stumbled back, clutching his throat before falling on the carpeted floor.

The fourth man eyed her as he moved to her left, the third one – sword bloody, to her right. From the corner of her eye, she watched the man with the knife in his shoulder fall back against the settee.

Taking a deep breath, she reached down the back of her dress. The third man, pushed forward, his sword coming down in a heavy swing for her shoulder.

The clang of her own short sword parrying his blow, surprised both men. After a short, block and parry, she stepped past the third man. He grunted, not expecting his partner to stab him in the shoulder.

Ashta continued around the back of him and came out the other side, left hand gripping the fourth mans sword handle as her blade sliced cleanly through his throat.

She flipped around, the new sword blocking the third man. She wrenched out her own sword, and then with double blades, assaulted and attacked the man until he stumbled back into the fireplace.

His attention diverted for a moment behind him, she struck out like a snake and shoved the sword to the hilt into his heart. He fell back into the fireplace, his mouth falling open as he groaned. Then stuck in cream as the fire caught his hair.

But Ashta ignored him, instead, focusing on the final man, sweating and breathing hard on the settee.

He pulled the knife out of his shoulder, but before he could take his life, Ashta swung her sword and sliced off his hand.

He screamed. Then sat silent as blood trickled down his throat from where she had the sword point jammed against his Adam's apple.

Before she could question him, he stepped into her blade, taking his own life. But his eyes flashed open to hers and in that moment Ashta had her answer.

It was Vlas.

Grim faced, she shoved the sword through his throat, skewering him to the settee.

Dead men couldn't talk.

CHAPTER FIFTEEN

⌘

Secret Filled Walls

ASHTA STARED WITH unseeing eyes at the carnage around her. How could this be? Her cousin had let her go. Why would he try to quietly kill her in her rooms and not have her put to death publicly?

Shaking her head, she pulled her knife out of the dismembered hand sitting beside Vlas. A quick glance down had her grimacing. Blood. Lots of blood.

She took the blade to her skirt and cut through the layers. The sharp edge separated the silk easily, cutting through the over skirt and petticoats in one. Once the weight of the long fabric fell to the ground, the rest flounced around her hips. It was no leather skirt, but it did provide some modesty. And a lot more movement.

Still reacting without thought, Ashta quickly walked to the doors. A quick glance down the halls showed that it was still eerily quiet. Good.

She quickly picked through the darkening halls, the sun setting in the west. When voices could be heard in front of her, she would slip into an alcove or just inside a doorway. Most of the rooms in her mother's wing of the castle were empty anyways.

Slowly but surely, she made it to the traditional rooms of her grandfather. The rooms that were for the head of the Broskla family and had not been used since before her grandfather had been born.

She smiled grimly, seeing the two guards posted before the door. The men didn't even have the chance to open their mouths, her flying daggers reaching their marks without fail. She pulled the first man down to the ground and caught the second man, laying his body on top of the first.

Then she pulled the doors open. Her cousin sat at a table set for himself, food almost dripping over the edges, enough to feed the council. Behind him were two guards. But in between the table and Ashta were two berserkers, still in their furs.

She pulled the doors closed behind her, grinning wide at her cousin's bloodless face as he looked at her.

The berserkers were quick to react. The first pulled his half sword out, but Ashta had pulled her long knife from her boot and lodged it in his chest.

As he fell, she ripped the sword from his grip, whirling around and parrying with the second man. He was tall, lumbering, and with a slight hitch in his left leg.

Ashta could see from the corner of her eyes one of the guards pulling her cousin further back into the room towards the bed, while the other came towards her, his own sword at the ready.

Not wanting to test her luck, her muscles straining from the tussle with the assassins in her room, Ashta ducked and sliced at the berserker's right leg.

He fell to his knee but didn't lose his grip on his sword.

Ashta swiped at his blade, and it fell from his grip. She watched the cold acceptance of death in his eyes and grimaced. This was not an assassin. This was a man who had been in the wrong room, protecting the wrong man.

She shoved her sword with both hands through his chest. He gripped the blade as it slid in, blood dripping from his mouth.

"The goddess welcomes," he choked out.

For a moment, Ashta was frozen, caught in this ancient right. Of an honourable death. Of a soldier who fought the fight he did not believe in.

And it was this moment that the guard swung at her back. She caught the movement and tried to bend out of the way, but the blade caught on her skin, slicing from shoulder to the opposite hip.

With her heart racing, Ashta fell to the ground and rolled to the side, narrowly missing the guards second swing. By the third swing she was on her feet, parrying, gritting her teeth as the blow shook her to her teeth.

The pain in her back pulsed, but all she could see was her cousin's face, smirking from the bed.

Biting down on her lip, she pushed past through the pain. Parrying, advancing, pushing the guard back until he was the one on the defensive. His foot slid in the blood from the berserker. His eyes slid away from Ashta for a moment.

It was enough.

She swiped his sword aside and hacked at his neck, the sharp Bbrskian blade easily slicing through skin and muscles and bone.

The head rolled across the floor as the body fell to its knees in front of Ashta. Her stomach rolled, the nausea of all the blood slowly seeping into her mind. But she wasn't done yet.

She advanced on the last guard, and her cousin. The man only took two steps before he fell to the ground, her final dagger lodged deep in his neck.

Ashta continued walking towards the bed.

Ruslan scrambled backwards, trying to move as far away from her as possible. He fell of the edge of the bed, arms and legs sprawled.

Ashta did not hesitate, hopping onto the bed and following him as he crawled to the wall.

"Stop," she commanded, her short sword coming down and pressing into his shoulder. He flipped around and looked up at her, his eyes filled with fear and hate. In that moment, he looked more like Ashta's father despite the blood that flowed between them being from her mother's side.

She pulled the sword back and stood before him, panting. The pain along her back pulsed, growing slowly as her heart slowed too normal.

"I should have killed you that first day we met, with your self-righteous ass sitting in my grandfather's room and that gaudy throne you built for yourself," Ashta spat out, glaring at the shaking mess of a man beneath her. The only thing still was his glare on her face. His hands, his legs, his whole body shook with the fear and knowledge of his impending death.

Mad at herself more than her cousin, she dropped down and spat into his face, "I gave up my birthright for you! I thought I saw something in you, something more human than what lives inside my father." Looking down, she glared at the blood that had begun to dry on her hands, like a tattoo on her soul. "More than what lives inside of me."

Shaking her head, she stood and held her arm up. There was nothing left to do but end this before it became worse.

Ruslan held his hands out, as if they would stop the blade. Just as her arms tensed, readying to swing the blade, he yelled, "I had no choice! I had to kill you!"

Ashta hesitated. "What do you mean?" She growled.

His hands lowered slightly so she could see his eyes on her. In a slow voice, he spoke, each word hitting her with its truth. "It was on your father's orders. He had sent a messenger ahead of your ship."

She blinked down at her cousin, seeing past him to the human beneath. A young man who had grown up surrounded by evil. Pushed and poked until he built up his armor, his reputation.

It all made sense, why her father sent her, alive, back to Bbrski. He had not meant to keep her in the line. Her father knew as much about the slave laws, and magic, of Tripsia as she did. He knew she would find a way to leave, without her birth right.

She dropped to her knees, coming close to Ruslan's face, so close she could she the creases of age start to show around his eyes. "If you try to follow me, or kill me again, I will personally come back here, cut your stomach open, pull your entrails out and hang you from them," She threatened.

What little blood that had returned to his face, disappeared.

She stood up, her legs shaking. Ashta dropped the sword and took a step back from him.

Ruslan scrambled for the sword, but Ashta lashed out with her foot, catching him in the temple. It wouldn't kill him. But it would give her time to get out of this mess and disappear into the bowels of the city below.

Her hands shaking, her back burning, she stumbled to the last guard she killed. She pulled the knife out and wiped the blade on her bloody skirt before shoving it into her hair. She continued to the door, bending down to grab Ancel's son's half sword.

Glancing at the door, Ashta knew she could not return that way. She needed the shirt and pants that she had hidden under her bed. Dressed the way she was, blood splattered all over, dripping down her back, any street urchin would look twice.

Gritting her teeth, she turned back to the dressing room. Her grandfather's rooms in the palace had one thing in common with his own estate. Hidden tunnels.

She pulled the dresser aside, her back screaming at her, sweat pouring down her face. Once moved, she stabbed at the pale wall. The knife cut through the mud and fabric of the fake wall.

With a deep breath, she centered her pain inside of herself, focusing on the goals. Get bandaged. Get changed. Get out. The rest, she would figure out later. If she was still alive.

She stretched the sword in front of her and carefully stepped into the cool, dark passage. Time stretched on with each quick step. She kept her right hand on the wall. As the passage went, it slowly became damp, with the sound of dripping water breaking the silence. She was getting deeper.

If she remembered right, this passage led straight past the wall and outside of the castle. But there were a few off shoots. And one would lead her to the hall of paintings, from there she would only need to sneak a short way to her rooms.

Shaking her head, Ashta reminded herself that they were not her rooms any longer. That she had no right to anything in this palace anymore.

The cut on her back pulsed, the edges itching already.

Finally, she came to the spot, another doorway sized length of fabric with plaster on it. She stood before the spot for a long minute. Only when she was satisfied she could hear nothing, did she crouch down and cut a hole near the bottom. She held the groan of pain in as she felt the cut stretch and rip wider.

Gritting her teeth, she crawled through the small hole and waited inside the darkened hall. No one had come through with the evening torches yet. Good.

She carefully skulked in the shadows, limping slightly as the pain in her back could no longer be ignored.

Once she got to her former rooms, she carefully slid the door open and peaked inside. She almost retched, hit with the smoke from the half-burned body in the fireplace.

Taking a deep breath, she slid inside and closed the door.

She hesitated for a moment on whether she should drag something in front of it. There was no time and hopefully she would be out of the palace in minutes.

She hobbled to the bed, pointedly ignoring the bodies that littered the main room. Ashta pulled out the plain clothes and bandage for her breasts and dropped them on the bed. Next, she dropped what weapons she had left. A knife in her right boot. The half sword in her hands.

Grimacing at the pitiful amount of weapons on the bed, she glanced over at the bodies. With her knife, she cut the remains of the dress off her body, frowning at the blood soaked back. Maybe she would need to find a cloak before disappearing into the city.

The door banged open and Ashta jumped, naked except for her boots, arms trembling in pain but still outstretched and ready.

Yana gasped, her eyes quickly taking in the scene.

Then she turned and promptly closed the door. She then dragged the only free chair over and propped it against the door. With that done she turned back to the former princess, who had dropped the knife and turned away.

"You should leave," Ashta said in a low voice, pulling the pants over her slim hips, the fastenings just barely able to hold them up.

Yana walked towards the woman, "I came to warn you," she whispered, taking in the bodies on the floor and the legs sticking out of the fireplace. She shuddered. Yana had known the former princess was strong, but she had not imagined her able to withstand a small army.

"You're too late," Ashta growled, frustrated with her back as it twinged every time she reached around with the bandages.

A soft hand on her shoulder had Ashta tensing. She turned to look down into Yana's pale face. Yet the other woman's hands did not shake as she took the bandage out of Ashta's hands. "Here," she whispered, "let me."

Ashta said nothing, she closed her eyes and stood still, focusing on her breath and trying to block out all of the aches and pains.

Yana stared at each of the cuts and red marks that were already bruising on the other woman's bare top. She carefully wrapped around the princess's back, grimacing at the long gash, the blood dried black in spots.

This woman, Yana though, was strong beyond imagination. Bbrski had been robbed the future of a true queen ruling with a firm and just hand.

When Yana had just tucked the end in, Ashta stepped forward and out of the other woman's reach. "Thank you," she grunted, pulling the loose shirt over herself.

As she strapped the arm guards on, she spoke. "I am leaving. And I will never return." She looked up to gauge Yana's reaction, but the other woman was already going over the bodies, pulling out knives and half swords as she went.

Frowning, Ashta shoved the hat over her hair and walked over to Yana. "You should find somewhere else to be. Your connection, however short with me, is dangerous to your life," Ashta said as she grabbed the throwing knives from the other woman's hands and shoved them under the edges of her cap. They would be easy to reach from there.

Yana stared down at the bloody knives and sword in her arms. "It's too late for me as well, your highness."

Ashta froze.

Yana looked up and Ashta was caught in the warmth and the fierce loyalty in her gaze. "I am no one now," Ashta whispered.

"Then what should I call you?" She asked.

Ashta quickly slid knives under each arm band and one in her boot. The other already had one. She grabbed the half sword, thankful for the holder strap. She would rather the sword hidden from all, but it would serve to hide the already bleeding wound on her back.

As she adjusted the sword on her back, she looked Yana in the eye. "The Tripsians call me Ashta the Lion Tamer."

Yana cocked her head, noting the strange tone to the former princess's voice. "That's not the only name you have, is it?" she asked quietly.

Brushing off her hands, Ashta looked to the door then back to the dressing room. "No," she answered honestly, her mind already on to escaping the palace. "Those who knew me best call me Darkling."

Yana reached out and pulled on Ashta's elbow to get her attention. "Wait," she said.

Ashta hesitated.

"I can get you out of here."

Ashta grimaced, "I need out of Bbrski, not just out of this palace."

Yana nodded, "I know some people. They can help."

Ashta watched the other woman's face closely, suspicious.

A knock at the door had them both turning.

"Alright," Ashta whispered. "But we leave the palace my way. Now."

Yana didn't even have time to nod before Darkling pulled her towards the dressing room. Darkling pulled her knife out again and cut at the corner wall, behind the large standing mirror. Yana gasped, stumbling behind the former princess into the depths of the palace.

The walls held as many secrets as the woman in front of her, she thought, hearing the splinter of wood of the doors being broken into the main rooms.

CHAPTER SIXTEEN

⌘

Stowaway

Ashta led the way as quick as she could, her hand outstretched in the pitch black, Yana gripping her other arm with the sword. It wouldn't take the palace guards long to find the hole she had left behind in the dressing room. But they only needed minutes.

Her hand suddenly fell away and Ashta turned into the new passage. Her mother had told her, when Ashta was a little girl, that all the passages would lead to the seventh wall if she kept her hand on the left wall.

And so, Ashta did.

The only sounds that followed them was their heavy breaths and the crunch of stones in the hall.

Long minutes passed. Ashta could not hear any pursuers.

Suddenly the stone floor softened. Packed dirt. They were near the end.

Ashta slowed.

Yana felt as if the guards were almost breathing down her neck. She whispered harshly, "Why are we slowing?" She kept looking back over her shoulder, even though she could see nothing in the pitch black.

"We are at the exit. We must be sure it is clear before using it."

Slowly, the tunnel began to lighten until Ashta could make out the shape of her hand before her. Her outstretched hand connected with a wooden door. Like the one that had been in the Blacks Queen rooms at her grandfathers estate. She felt around until she found the lock.

"Stay close," Ashta whispered.

The clang of metal began echoing from behind them. Some of the guards must have found the path the two women had taken.

Gritting her teeth, Ashta pulled the ancient lock until it creaked open.

"Hurry!" Yana whispered, crowding Ashta against the door.

Ashta took a breath and shoved the ancient door until it was just wide enough for them to slip through.

She slid against it, grunting as the stone wall scraped against her cut. Her hand swiped the brambles aside, leaving enough space for Yana to step out beside her. Then Ashta closed the door and shoved the sword into the dirt ground. It wouldn't hold the guards back forever, but it would slow them.

That's all that they needed anyways.

Yana stayed quiet beside Ashta, her arms shaking, her skin pale, but her eyes were bright. "Now what?" she whispered.

Ashta held a finger to her mouth.

Yana's eyes widened, and she squeezed her lips closed. It was too late.

Ashta crept around her to the edge of the bush. One of the few bushes growing in the older passage that the servants used to navigate from the palace to the wall and the outer city. The small section was dark, with the wall ahead of Ashta, the height of two men.

Ashta listened hard. The quiet laugh of a maid coming towards them rang across the stones.

Then a second woman's voice spoke.

Then the loud squeal of a boy.

Perfect.

Ashta pulled Yana out from the bush. She waited until the group passed ahead of them before pulling Yana onto the path and began walking towards the second gate. The one that lead back to the city.

Suddenly, the shadowy darkness of the tunnel brightened under the pale full moon.

Ashta looked up at it for a moment. She had wasted too much time in the palace. She never should have gone back to confront her cousin. It had been rash. And now she was paying for it.

Her shoulder itched from the corner of the long cut down her back, another reminder of her thoughtlessness. She was a lioness. She should have been able to let go of emotion and do what needed to be done.

Shaking her head, she focused on the woman beside her. Yana was still dressed in the clothes of a noble woman. At least under the cloak of night they wouldn't be as noticeable. But Ashta would need to do something about the other woman's presence. Soon. Or risk both their lives.

"Now. Where to, your ladyship?" Ashta whispered.

The maids ahead of them turned off the path and down a thin laneway, leaving only the two women out in the open.

"To the Inn. But I'll need to change first."

Before Ashta could complain, Yana grabbed her hand and pulled her down the laneway and inside a noble house. The kitchen was filled with bodies as everyone ran about cleaning and finishing the evening meal. No one noticed a well-dressed lady and a peasant boy in their midst.

Yana darted through the crowd, leaving Ashta on her own near the exit. Antsy, Ashta backed closer to the wall. Her fingers bit into her palms as she ignored the creeping itch down her back. It would heal soon enough, she reminded herself.

Yana appeared again; a simple dark cloak wrapped around her shoulders. She held out the second cloak to Ashta.

The two disappeared back into the streets. This time as two hooded figures. Maybe lovers disappearing for a tryst. Maybe a couple of maids looking for trouble in the night.

Yana grabbed Ashta's hand, then led her through the lanes. With each wall that they passed, it became harder for Ashta to breathe.

By the sixth gate, Ashta tugged on Yana's hand.

The woman turned around, shocked to see Darkling leaned over her legs. Panting.

"Darkling?" she whispered, her eyes skating over the rough houses in the Bogomolov district. A lone fiddle could be heard playing. The occasional rush of bawdy laughter filled the night air with a shock of warmth from the inns that lined the streets. But these were streets best traveled in light. To many of the Bbrskian berserkers and fighters roamed the Bogomolov district, waiting for their next fight.

"I-I just need a mo-moment," Ashta said, trying to suck the air through her nose. The itching in her back was now burning like an unholy fire. Ashta straightened.

Yana's eyes filled with relief as she half turned. They were almost at the inn.

Ashta took one step, then stumbled.

Yana caught her arm, shocked at how heavy the other woman was.

"Poi…" Ashta mumbled.

"Your back," Yana finished. She should have realized. The green ooze from the top of the cut. Likely one of the blades had been poisoned.

Yana pushed underneath Ashta's shoulder, wrapping an arm around the other woman's middle.

With effort, she lifted the other woman slightly. Together they continued through the night. Yana prayed fervently to the goddess. *Please deliver us to Ishmeer without any incidents.*

She listened to Darkling's laboured breaths, each one rattling through her lungs before she paused for so long that Yana worried it was her last. And then another rattling breath.

By the time they had stumbled through the street and down the lane, Yana wasn't sure that the other woman would survive the rest of the night. Worried, she stopped and settled Darkling against the wall. The other woman was so far gone that she did not notice they had stopped.

Saying another quick prayer to the goddess, Yana ran the last few metres in the dark until she stumbled into the back of the Black Goat Inn.

A young man, golden hair with warm eyes and a soft face looked up from the kitchen sink. "My heart, what are you doing here?" he asked, dropping the pot into the water in surprise. He did not notice it splash in his face, so focused was he on Yana's pale face and shaking hands.

"I-I-" she panted, pointing her arms wildly back out the door.

He turned to his mother who had just entered the kitchen through the swinging doors. His mother took one look at the woman before turning to him. "Go. I will get your brother to finish in here."

He nodded, following Yana out into the night.

Yana broke out in a sprint again, ignoring Ishmeer's shout. What if she was too late, she worried?

As they came back to the alley, she breathed out a sigh of relief at the dark shape against the wall. Yana stopped in front of Darkling, trying to catch her breath.

"Careful-" Ishmeer tried to warn Yana but she waved him off.

"Help me carry her."

He hesitated, looking down at the sweat soaked face of the street urchin. He turned back to Yana and her eyes pleaded. He sighed, knowing that he could never say no to his love.

Ashta groaned, her whole body aching. It was not unlike when she had woken in the Tripsian desert.

"She's awake!" a small voice said.

Ashta tensed.

Where was she?

The creak of a chair and stomp of feet moving away had Ashta relaxing slightly. She stretched her body, taking stock of her tight muscles.

The last thing she remembered was running through the streets with Yana...

Her eyes popped open as she sat up. Instantly she groaned, her back tensing with fiery pain. The damn cut hurt worse than the arrow in her chest, she thought.

She looked around herself, at the simple wood walls and door. The plain weave of the sheet on the bed. An inn's room.

Her head swam as she was pulled back into another room, eight years before. When she had been a grief stricken girl, trusting her mother's guard.

Moments later, Yana appeared in the doorway, her eyes weary as she looked over Ashta's seated form.

"Careful. The wound needs time to heal," she said, coming to the bedside with a cup filled with water.

Ashta forced her hands to be steady as she took the cup. She drank from it thirstily, not caring that water dribbled down her cheeks and onto the bed.

Yana sat in the only chair in the tiny room.

Ashta lowered the glass and looked at the other woman, noting her plain dress and the simple braid in her hair. And the happiness that burned bright in her dark eyes.

"How long?" Ashta asked, her voice raspy from disuse.

Yana looked confused for a moment before realizing what Darkling was asking. She looked down at her hands as she admitted her failure. "Three days."

Ashta gasped. So long?

Yana fidgeted with her hands, the skin already starting to roughen from the hard work of the kitchens. With a sigh, she looked to the door before continuing in a quiet voice, "There have been palace guards patrolling the city streets. And especially around the docks."

Ashta was still stuck on the fact that three days had passed. No wonder her muscles ached so.

Ishmeer appeared at the door with a bowl full of food and hearty bread.

Before Ashta could ask, he smiled and said, "I heard voices and thought you might be hungry now that you are awake." He held the bowl out to Ashta, but she only stared at it. Yana had said they were going somewhere safe. But Ashta had no idea where *they* were right now.

"Thank you, Ishmeer, I'll make sure she eats some," Yana said with a small smile, her cheeks reddening.

He handed her the bowl, his hand lingering on her wrist before he left the room.

Making sure Darkling watched her, Yana took a large bite from the food and broke off a chunk of bread to chew. Then she passed the bowl to the other woman.

Wearily, Ashta took a bite. It was then that she realized how hungry she was. It took barely a minute for her to devour the contents of the bowl and the loaf of bread. When she was done, Yana held out the cup of water to her. Ashta looked to the jug that had been beside the bed.

Without a word, Yana took a sip before passing it to the other woman.

With her stomach full, Ashta's mind began to wander to other problems. "The guards…" she started to say, her eyes glancing wearily to the open doorway.

Yana stood and closed the door before returning to the bedside. "The palace guards have been roaming the upper city streets. No one knows what or who they are looking for. But it is apparent that they are looking for something." She hesitated a moment before continuing, "It's not the palace guards I'm worried about. There have been some of the paid men, the berserkers, who have taken to scouring the alleys and docks at night."

"They know I'm missing. And they think I'm on or will get on a boat to leave the city," Ashta guessed.

Yana nodded.

Rubbing the back of her neck, Ashta carefully rolled her shoulders. Her back twinged but felt tight. No pain. She reached back with her hand and was surprised not to find anything but raised skin.

Before she could ask, Yana answered, "When we got you to the Inn, the poison had spread. Ishmeer," She blushed, "had been a soldier for the King on the southern wall. When he lost his hand, he came back to the inn. He was the one who knew it had been Lohte. He still had his medicine bag from the Rviun tribe that he had been fighting alongside with. I'm not sure how it works, but he said you would only be tender for a week."

Ashta's fingers still felt the ridge of hard skin as she processed the other woman's words. For so long she had thought the Ruutka from the Alpen people was the best healing medicine to known man.

She smiled. "It seems our people have more secrets than they care to admit to," Ashta whispered. She pushed off the bed and stood.

Yana also stood, her hands fluttering as if to stop Ashta. "You should rest," she murmured, glancing back at the door again and again.

"I'm fine," Ashta replied, stretching to the ceiling before bending over to her toes. Everything felt as it should.

Remarkable, she thought. It was too bad she was leaving for Tripsia immediately, or she would have liked to learn more about the Rviun medicine. Once she was standing again, she turned to Yana. "I'll need a clean set of men's cloths. And then I will be gone."

"Are you sure-"

"Now," Darkling growled, her black eyes flashing. Yana swallowed her fear and scurried out of the room as fast as her shaking legs could take her. She had almost forgotten that the woman behind her was not only a former princess, but a formidable warrior.

With Yana out of the room, Ashta felt along her hair and was happy to note that the throwing knives were still there. A quick check of her boots confirmed the long knives were as well. All that she missed were the ones on her arms and the sword that was buried in the wall of the palace.

It was enough. It would have to be.

Ashta snuck out the door, glancing down the hall. A small window let a tiny amount of moonlight into the dark hall on the right side. On the left were the stairs.

Quickly, Ashta darted to the window and slipped outside, thankful for the dark of night. While she felt bad slipping away from Yana, it was safer for Yana if Ashta simply disappeared.

Her back was tight as she carefully shimmied down the rough stone wall of the Inn. She dropped the last few feet and took off at a run, ignoring her screaming lungs and every other ache in her jostled body.

Several times she had to duck into a dark shadow as loud voices broke the night ahead of her. Far more than had been on the night she first left the palace.

By the time she reached the docks, the horizon was beginning to lighten. To her luck, a reddish ship, its black sails distinct was anchored along the port. Headed for the Bbrskian fleet, the Black Death, to bring supplies and men for the war.

Ashta snuck around to the edge of the dock, a ships length down from the trader's ship.

She carefully climbed over the edge and underneath the wooden slats of the dock.

From underneath she easily bypassed the soldiers above her, crawling under the gangplank and waiting for a moment of silence before sneaking up onto the deck.

She quickly hopped into a crate filled with chickens.

The animals stayed quiet, quickly finding perches on Ashta's arms. She smiled, keeping a giggle inside. If a berserker opened the crate, he would be in for the shock of his life, she thought.

Soon enough the crate was jostled around before being moved below deck. Once everything was settled, and the voices disappeared above deck, Ashta carefully got out of the crate. She winced at every creak and groan of the wood.

By the time the men came down with the next load of cargo, she had hidden herself in the back of the ship, a simple shirt and pants laid out on the flour bags underneath her.

Grinning, she settled in for the long sail to Shadow Island. Then to Tripsia. To Carien.

And more importantly, to Mina.

CHAPTER SEVENTEEN

⌘

Revenge Over Duty

AFTER A WEEK OF sailing on the open ocean, Ashta could feel her mind spinning. The only time she moved was to steal food during the night shift, and to dump her piss pot by the chickens.

That second one had brought her enormous happiness. Twice she had heard the soldiers being told off by the captain for not pissing over the ship deck. Though after the second time, Ashta had to adjust her hiding spot as some of the men decided to look for the culprit.

But now, with the hot chinook sun beating on the deck, making the berth hot and humid, she could do nothing but lay on the flour bag, in complete darkness. With nothing but her thoughts to occupy her time. For even sleep evaded her. She was rested enough, her muscles itched to move, her feet begged to run, to jump, to do *anything*.

Sighing, Ashta shifted slightly on the bag. The slight creak from her weight change had her tensing for a moment. But nothing moved in the main berth.

Breathing in slowly, her mind settled on other things. Like her father.

The more time that passed, the surer Ashta was that it had been her father who had tried to get rid of her in the palace. Who was responsible for her sale to Tripsia? Who had tried to kill her, multiple times in Tripsia, and in Bbrski?

Her cousin was able, but what did he stand to win with killing off Svetlana?

Her birthright, Ashta thought bitterly.

But then, even if he had killed Svetlana, before Ashta had given her rights away, her cousin would have gained nothing. The bloodline, and the power with it, ran through the women. Not the men. And with Ashta's death, the bloodline would simply have died.

And someone had been trying to kill her since she was forced on that boat, naked and helpless, bound for Issha.

No, it wasn't her cousin.

But her father didn't care about Ashta's bloodline. Not since her mother had died and no male heir had been conceived from his family line. Ashta's existence was a reminder to her father that he would never have complete control of the kingship of Bbrski. That one day, somehow, someone that was not of his choosing could usurp his power and position. Simply by being married to or born from Ashta.

The more and more she thought about it, the more Ashta became certain that it had been her father who had tried to kill her.

But what she couldn't understand was why he had not done it earlier. Why send her on a boat back to her birthplace? Why not have her killed on the island when she was first captured? Or even before, when she was nothing but a nameless slave in the Tripsian Nursery.

One question that haunted her mind, and made her both angry and sad, was far simpler than the rest.

Why had he let her live?

It would have been easy enough to have made a baby girl disappear. It made no sense to Ashta, why her father had done or not done the things that made up her past.

At the edge of her memories was something, a niggle that had a taste of answer to it. But no matter how hard she tried to remember or think about it, the memory was just a shadow. She could feel its presence but not see its source.

Days later, her musings were broken up by a shout.

"Land ho!"

Tensing, Ashta carefully rolled over, making sure her hair was still tucked in under her cap, and that her knives were secure.

It was finally time.

She could almost hear Mina's sweet baby laugh. Never had she felt so close in the last months to her charge and babe.

Amidst the bustle of the ship, Ashta strained to listen to conversations. Any bit of information. At one point she heard one of the sailors complaining, loudly, to his friend.

"...won't even bother unloading, what with the coast needing supplies now. We'll be docked for a day, at most, before heading north."

Another voice, much quieter, replied. Ashta strained to make out his words. "...be worse...a night on land...heard some women in the…" And the rest was lost as both men climbed back up to the deck.

Ashta smiled. She was in luck. She wouldn't even need to find another ship heading back to Tripsia. It seemed this one was destined for the coastline. And from there it would be a matter of a day or two travel to the ruined city of Trian and the palace below.

All she needed to do was wait aboard for another night, hoping that the men did not need to go through or load up more supplies in the boat. And then she would be set.

That evening only one man could be heard climbing down below to the sailor's quarters. It seemed that the rest had taken the liberty of a night on land.

With his gentle snores keeping her busy mind awake, Ashta waited. Sleep would come, eventually, she hoped. For now, her mind kept going back to her father. And the gnawing need to know.

And tonight, her father was on the same island as her.

She could get her answers tonight, if she wanted to, Ashta mused. She could even kill her father. While it wouldn't end the war, it would cause mass confusion. And she was sure that her dear cousin, Ruslan, would be more than happy for her father to die. Then he could claim the throne for himself.

Her hand curled around the knife hidden under her other wrist cuff.

She pulled it out and rubbed her finger up and down the sharp edge, her eyes watching the movement, mesmerized.

It would be so simple.

Easy even.

She had come close to killing her father before.

This time, she was prepared. She felt cautiously optimistic that her cousin, even the council, could lead her people.

She hissed as the blade just barely sliced into her pointer finger. She shoved it into her mouth, the metallic taste of blood exploding on her tongue.

For a moment, she imagined it was her father's blood.

A shiver of pleasure rippled down her spine at the idea.

Suddenly, she sat up, her ears listening for the gentle snores of the lone sailor. This time, she did not hesitate, sliding over the barley bags and landing on silent feet on the floor. She moved quickly to the stairs and did not hesitate above deck.

"Changed your mind, did yah?" a voice called from above deck.

Ashta grunted, not breaking her stride to the gangplank.

Once she was behind the first row of tents, she turned off the path and hid in the darkness of the night and the deep shadows of the Bbrskian tents surrounding her.

The smell, somehow in the past month, had become so strong that it was unbearable. Her eyes watered. She covered her nose and lips with her arm and barely breathed through the crack in her mouth.

The fall had not been kind to the tent city. Her mind raced with the implications. Her father was a well-known general. Surely, he would be planning to move his men before an outbreak of cholera blazed through the army.

As she wandered deeper into the tents, lights flickered across walls from makeshift fires. The occasional bout of raucous laughter broke up the unbearable quiet.

The hairs on the back of Ashta's neck stood on end. Where were the screaming women? The blood-soaked men wandering between tents. That former layer of manic ecstasy and death that blanketed over the makeshift city.

Something had changed since last she had been here, and Ashta could not pinpoint what. Her instincts screamed at her to turn around and return to the boat. To stick to the original plan and return to Carien and her babe.

But her anger was too strong to let go. She was too far into the tents, her legs beginning to burn from the incline that led up to her father's tent. She could see the black flags waving and snapping in the wind above the city.

Damn it, she was too close.

Too close to answers.

Too close to revenge.

And at the back of her mind wriggled the smallest doubt that she would ever get the opportunity to be so close to her father again. Once she was back in Tripsia, she would return to her sworn duty to the princess. There would be no time for personal revenge. To leave the princess's side.

Unlike now, when she was not protecting anyone, and no one knew where she was. For all of the known world might write down in history, it may have been a simple soldier, a stranger, that killed the Bbrskian King. Not his own daughter. Not a White Lioness. And definitely not the heir to the Bbrskian throne.

A man stumbled into the darkness ahead of her, leaning over his knees to puke.

Ashta hesitated. Her fingers itched, the cold steel of the handle of her blade a heavy reminder. But this soldier had done her no wrong.

She nibbled at her lips.

The man wiped his mouth, then stumbled past into the next tent.

Ashta let out the breath she didn't realize she was holding.

With the adrenaline of almost being seen pumping through her veins, she swiftly traversed between the rest of the tents until she came to the slight raised hill where her father's tent sat in front of her. There was a slight distance of clear rock and tufts of grass between where she stood and the back of the King's black tent.

The moon was a dark shadow, lost behind a cloud in the sky. The shadows of the night clung to her.

This was it.

She took a deep breath, her nerves settling with cold determination. Ashta crouched down and waited for the guard at the corner of the tent to turn away.

When he did, she sunk low and quickly ran to the back of the tent. She stayed low, the flickering fire light from inside playing across the tent canvas.

She listened hard, stilling her breath.

Ashta could just make out the quiet steps of her father's guards as they began their slow patrol to the back of the tent. From inside, she heard the clatter of cutlery against dishes. One set. No other voices.

He was alone.

Before the steps from the guard could reach the corner of the tent closest to her, Ashta carefully slit into the canvas with her sharpest knife. She slipped inside swiftly, not hesitating.

The king of Bbrski sat at a table for one, his back to her. His broad shoulders were hunched over, his silver hair thin, his widows' peaks reaching far back on his head. His once neatly trimmed white beard was scruffy and unkempt.

Ashta moved quickly to him, knife ready. It would be so easy, to slide the blade across his neck and slip out of the tent without anyone's notice.

But her hand hesitated. The blade wavering slightly in the air, inches from her fathers turned back.

"What are you waiting for," her father asked in a deep voice.

Ashta's eyes widened, but she did not move.

Alerik carefully set his knife and fork aside. Then, in a slow and deliberate motion, he pushed back from the table and stood before his daughter.

Silence reigned as the two took the measure of each other.

Father saw a made woman, determined, confident, but still weak with misplaced family loyalty.

Daughter saw an old man, deep wrinkles, dark bags under his eyes, but a cunning and cold intelligence in his eyes.

A shout came from the back of the tent.

Still neither moved.

A guard rushed in from the front of the tent while the second guard rammed through the slit, stopping dead when he saw the young lad before his king.

Alerik held up his hand. The guards stopped, swords at the ready but no other motion.

Cold fear gathered at the back of her neck, making Ashta shiver. She glanced at the two hardened soldiers. Neither was familiar to her.

She looked back at her father, who was now smirking.

"Ask," he demanded, his eyes never leaving her face.

Ashta wet her lips, her throat suddenly clogged. She coughed slightly, then finally the words slipped from her mouth. "Why did you send me home only to send assassins after me?"

He cocked his head, his thoughts closed to her. She shivered from more than just cold. It had always been like that with her father.

"Do you really believe that *I* sent those assassins, daughter?" he whispered.

She winced. Her heart ached. The tiniest voice inside of her suddenly doubted herself.

She shook her head and glared at him instead. "Who then?" she asked sarcastically.

The guard slowly inched further back, sliding into the princess's blind spot. The King gave the slightest nod, then stepped the other way to distract his daughter.

"What would I gain with you dead?" he asked, her black eyes tracking his movement. "My entire kingship relies on my marriage to your mother, and your birth. I am no leader of a family, I have nothing outside of my blood that flows through your veins."

Her brow wrinkled as she heard his words, her doubts growing.

"But Tripsia," he whispered, taking another step. Her eyes never left him. "They would gain everything with you dead."

She slowly shook her head.

It was that moment, that the soldier jumped forward, quickly pulling her arms behind her back. She didn't even have a moment to think. Her knife clattered to the ground, bouncing off an uneven stone underneath the canvas carpet.

"Take her to the others," Alerik commanded, his voice cold once more. He turned away from his daughter as if she wasn't standing in the tent anymore.

Ashta's heart ached even as she tried to squirm against the soldier's immovable hold.

What had she done, she bemoaned, the hairs on her neck standing on edge as her stomach roiled.

CHAPTER EIGHTEEN

⌘

A Girl Named Era

ASHTA STUMBLED FORWARD, out into the pitch black. This time the walk down to the rest of the tent city was loud. It was as if a fog had lifted from her ears and she heard every screech, every moan, every clang of metal on metal. The soldier who held her from behind, stopped her in front of the second soldier who held a length of rope.

Working with quick and efficient pulls, the second man had Ashta's arms tied behind her back and enough of a lead that she could walk forwards. If she walked.

The first soldier grunted, taking the rope and pulling out his sword. He pushed the tip between her shoulders. "Walk," he growled.

Ashta stumbled down the path. Her only directions were the slap of the flat side of the sword on her left or right shoulder.

Her cheeks were warm with humiliation, her gaze scoured the ground so that she would not drop and accidentally find herself impaled to the stone ground.

Quick peeks about her confirmed that they were on the other side of the hill, further away from the dock and the ship that would have taken her to Tripsia in the morning.

She cursed herself the whole walk, her eyes pricking with heat. *Why had she let her revenge cloud her mind?*

If she had stuck to her original plan, she would have been in Tripsia in a few days' time, taking up her duty as a white lioness to the princess. Instead, she acted as a free person – as a princess – able to control her future.

And this was the cost.

Thankfully, the night kept the berserkers and soldiers in their tents, giving only the occasional man a glimpse of the former princess.

"Stop here," the soldier commanded.

Ashta halted, her eyes moving up to take in a row of large unassuming canvas tents, one connected to the other. There were maybe six of them. Three of which had a soldier stationed at the front flap. The first, third, and sixth.

They had stopped in front of the second one.

Another soldier came up from behind Ashta and pulled up the flap. The first soldier jabbed the sword into her back, making her gasp as she stumbled forward. She fell to her knees in the centre of the canvas tent, dirt and rocks pressing into her skin.

The inside of the tent was pitch dark. Then three men, one holding a torch, followed her inside. She looked up at them, sweat dripping from her brow and down her back from the walk.

"Hold her," the first soldier commanded the newcomer who had held the tent flap open.

The second soldier gripped her biceps hard. The first soldier, with a deft flick of his wrist, cut the ropes, her shirt, and pants off. His face was shrouded in shadow as he put the sword in its shaft and stepped towards her.

A deep sense of despair filled her, weighing her thoughts, and limbs down. Ashta watched as if from a distance as the soldier stripped the clothes off of her. He was careful to remove the knives from her wrist guards. His touch was cold and abrupt, removing her boots with practiced ease. She shivered at the thought.

"To the post," he grunted at the soldier who still held her. His hot breath stuck to the back of her neck. He jerked her none to gently backwards, allowing her to see the only other thing occupying the large tent.

A large wooden pole.

She could not make anything else out with the flickering light of the torch.

Hands on her naked back had her shivering but standing with a stick straight back. The man easily pulled her arms around the pole, tying a new knot if rope around her quickly.

She ignored the chuckle from the soldier holding her. A smack on her naked butt cheek had her yelping in surprise more than pain.

Before she could say anything, the first soldier pulled his sword out and slammed it into the soldier behind her. Ashta could make out the gurgle of blood in the soldier's throat.

The tent went eerily silent.

The first soldier looked into her eyes briefly, his were cold, dead. Then he glanced back over her shoulder at the remaining soldier.

"Get rid of the body before you take up your post."

He walked past Ashta, leaving her to stare at the blank back wall of the tent. Her ears strained as she caught his whispered words to the third man. "And if she has any new marks on her body, or breathes a word about anyone besides myself touching her, it will be your body beside Adrian's."

There were shuffling noises behind her.

Then darkness.

Suddenly alone, Ashta collapsed onto the ground wrapping her legs around the wooden pole, her head leaning on it for rest. She closed her eyes as shivers wracked through her body.

What had she done, she asked herself again?

A week, maybe longer, passed when Ashta finally discovered the soldier's names. The shifting light on the canvas tent was her indication that time had shifted. The men came at the strangest times, releasing her briefly to eat and drink and stretch her legs, to use the latrine.

She was thankful for the movement, but also wary. How long did they plan to keep her here, she wondered?

This morning, as the light just washed over the tent and Ashta could barely make out her fingers, a rustling caught her attention. She shifted slightly so she could stare with slanted eyes, at the newcomers.

The first soldier, his short cropped hair white with age, held a bowl. Ashta's stomach growled at the sight, even though she knew it would be more of the tasteless gruel she had been forced to eat this last week.

The men were in the midst of a heated conversation. Her ears sharpened at the mention of Tripsia.

"... ships bound for Tripsia have been diverted to Trimont and to Malten," the older one whispered.

The younger one, still carrying a torch, burst out. "Malten! I thought we were at war with Tripsia and Naankdoen, not half of the known kingdoms!"

The first soldier glared at the young man. "Keep your thoughts to yourself Beltus, or the king will cut your tongue out." And then he added in a low mutter, "if you're lucky."

Beltus, his eyes wide with shock and cheeks red, glared at the older man's back. But no other words were said as the first soldier undid Ashta's ropes.

A few days later, Ashta heard shuffling behind the canvas wall beside the tent opening. The wall glowed from a torch on the other side. Ashta strained her ears, trying to catch anything.

So far, time had passed uneventfully. The thick canvas walls muffled almost all noise from the outside world.

"…deserves it, for being what she is," said a familiar rough voice. The older soldier.

"Always did have strong morals, Wulf," a new voice joked, chuckling loudly. Ashta couldn't identify the male voice, maybe a new soldier to be posted in front of the tent beside her, she wondered?

Wulf, the older man, muttered something but Ashta couldn't pick up a word. The other man laughed loud again before everything fell quiet once more. Soon after, the glow of the torch disappeared and Ashta was left in the pitch black once more.

A blood curdling scream woke Ashta. She jerked against the ropes, cursing them as they pressed hard into the raw skin around her wrist.

Shaking her head, she shuddered as another scream broke the night. This time, she noticed that it was coming from the tent beside her. Ashta squinted but could make out nothing, not even the slightest movement, in the pitch black.

With a sigh she leaned her head against the pole, her shoulders tense.

It was only when she heard the loud, distinctly feminine, sobs, that Ashta took a deep breath. She was sure that there were soldiers around the tents, listening to any words the prisoners said. But her heart ached at the fear emanating from the wall beside her.

"You are not alone," Ashta called out, tensing at the loud ring of her voice in her head. How long had it been since last she spoke aloud? At all?

The sobs hesitated. A sniffle. And then in a high pitched voice, the woman asked in the native tongue *Kiang*, "Are the soldiers with you?"

Frowning, Ashta responded honestly, switching effortlessly to the Naankdoena tongue. "No. I am tied up to this pole, naked as the day I was born."

The woman snorted. Then another sniffle.

The silence was long but Ashta could feel the fear diminishing.

"What's your name?" the woman asked softly.

Ashta hesitated. If the woman was from Naankdoen, she had likely head of Ashta the Lion Tamer, the Tripsian princess's white lioness. And Ashta wasn't sure if she could trust the stranger. She would not put it past her father to send someone here to try and get Ashta's trust.

After a long pause, Ashta finally said in a strong voice, "It's Darkling. And yours?" she asked right away, not giving any room for the woman to question Ashta's answer.

The woman replied quickly, in the same even voice. "Era."

Another pause.

With another sigh, Ashta said quietly, "Get some sleep, Era."

The next morning, long after Wulf and Beltus had left, Era spoke up. "Are you a spy as well?"

Ashta hesitated.

If she escaped, she was sure to give Carien any and all information about the island, as well as the state of Bbrski. But spying was not who she was. At least not by nature.

But her curiosity was piqued now, that the woman would ask that first.

"Of a sort," Ashta answered honestly.

A flicker at the back of the tent caught her attention.

A scuffle. The thud of flesh on flesh.

Silence again.

Ashta sat tense, her shoulders aching, as she took shallow breaths. But nothing changed.

When her eyelids began to sink from exhaustion, Era spoke up again.

"I had never planned to leave Naankdoen. Life was peaceful. Until a year ago."

Ashta grunted, flashes of flaming arrows and the thud of stones against the thick city wall crossed her mind. It felt as if the whole episode had been a day ago.

Maybe it was from being a prisoner once more. Time moved differently. Her memories became brighter. She seemed to keep ending up as a prisoner, she thought, laughing to herself quietly.

Then Ashta asked aloud, "Has prince zHavier returned to the city?"

Era was quiet for a beat. If Ashta hadn't been listening for it, she would have missed that slight shock. "Only just. But without any allies. My king hadn't trusted prince zHavier's plan, and sent us out to-"

"Talking, are we?" the deep voice of King Alerik cut Era off.

Ashta sat up, her skin buzzing as her fingers tensed. What was he-

The unmistakable thud of flesh on flesh.

A groan.

And then-

"Fuck you," spat Era.

The king laughed, and then said something to the spy just quiet enough that Ashta couldn't make out any words. Damn that canvas, she cursed to herself, her whole body strained as she tried to catch anything.

Instead, she listened to the muffled beat of fists against flesh. Of groans. Wheezing. Spitting. And never a word in Bbrskian.

It continued until the sun set.

Finally, silence settled over the tent.

Her father said the first clear words since the afternoon. "Until next time."

And then the light from the torches disappeared, leaving Ashta in the pitch black, listening to the harsh breathing in the tent beside her. Eventually, Ashta fell into a dreamless sleep.

The next day, again after Wulf and Beltus had left, Era spoke. "Have you ever been to Kae ol?"

"No," Ashta said. Green eyes haunted her at the mention of the jungle kingdom. "My-" she hesitated. Ceerie had been more than a friend. And yet not. "...friend," she continued in a quieter voice, "was from there."

Era did not notice or seem to mind the awkward pause. Her voice was warm as she fondly recalled her memories. "I had been spying in the west for years. My great-grandmother was from the People of the Blue Lagoon. When she was alive, she would tell me stories of her girlhood. Of horses made of water, and birds made of leaves. Trees that walked like men," and then in a dreamy voice, she added. "Of elves."

"And you believed her?" Ashta asked, her mind turning to the two books Ceerie had gifted her. She had only been able to read a few stories. But even then, even after all she had seen, she was skeptical of such tall tales. Of wolves that were men. Of a city that could read minds. Of people born of tree's blood.

Sure, there was truth in stories. In legends. But she knew how details could be changed. Made bigger. More dramatic. Memorable.

Era laughed, which quickly shifted to a heavy cough.

Ashta grimaced.

"No," she finally replied. "But there is something magical about the forest. Timeless."

Ashta smiled. "Like the desert," she said. Purple eyes flashed in her mind's eye while she stared numbly at the unending canvas around her.

They both fell into a silence. Ashta wasn't sure if the other woman slept. It would be better for her, Ashta thought, her own body feeling the aches of previous fights from months and years past. Her chest pulsed with a special ache, one she wasn't entirely certain was her own.

CHAPTER NINETEEN

⌘

The Twins

ILLA STUCK HER TONGUE out as she focused on the almost still water of the ocean. Nearby, a sea eagle slowly circled above, hunting for fish. The smooth rock on her hand was gripped firmly, but with lightness, just like zHaveek had showed her.

With a slow breath in and then a slow breath out, she whipped her hand out, releasing the smooth rock. She giggled with delight as she watched it skip twice before falling into the water.

"Good job, my star," zHaveek praised, a fleeting smile stretching across his weathered face.

Her twin brother, zHaviel, stood beside the tribesman, scowling at his older-by-a-few-moments sibling.

"Let me try!" he demanded pushing past Illa until she lost her footing.

"Careful," zHaveek called as he gently picked up the princess and set her on her feet. She was quiet but he could feel her thoughts brewing with hurt and embarrassment.

He crouched down until the little girl looked up into his face. Her violet eyes were not unlike her powerful fathers. Which worried zHaveek. He had watched her father struggle with his power for years. He would try to help the young majik woman find the path.

He held his hand out, another smooth rock waiting in his palm.

Next time, raise your elbow slightly. Then the rock will skip all the way out into goddess's belly.

Slowly the anger around her mind dissipated and she smiled up at him, her eyes clear with joy. While she and her brother were still too young to send clear thoughts to others, they were already powerful enough to affect others with their emotions.

"Thank you, zHaveek," she whispered.

They both turned in time to watch her brother throw a rock and it fell straight into the water. Not even a hesitant skip over the edge.

Upset, zHaviel kicked against the sandy beach, his anger blanketing over zHaveek. With a deep breath, he cleared the emotion from his mind. He was unsurprised that the sister stood beside him and watched her brother, unaffected by his power.

Both were more powerful than either of their abled parents.

zHaveek worried how the prince and princess would come into their power as they aged.

The daughter was curious and sweet, wild as the wind of the desert. But her brother, the tribesman worried, was like the immovable stone walls of Kiang don. And each day it seemed he was a little more like his grandfather, and the city dwellers ancestors.

"This is stupid," zHaviel complained. "I want to go back to the castle and practice sword fighting instead."

zHaveek stood and gently patted the young boy's shoulder, "To be a great sword fighter, or any fighter, you must practice. You must move with precision and agility. You must have patience." He reached down into the sand and pulled out another smooth rock. Making sure the boy saw, zHaveek carefully threw the rock. It skipped into the horizon, no one hearing it fall to its eventual resting spot in the water. "It took your father many years before he could make a rock skip even once."

The boy stood beside him, quiet. The anger was still there, but quieter. With something else mixed into it.

Illa took that moment to step forward on the beach, and with the accuracy of a warrior twice her age, she threw the rock. Like zHaveek's, the rock skipped into the horizon.

Filled with joy, the princess jumped with glee. Her joy crashed through zHaveek and filtered up into the city, where he could feel his people and the city dwellers dance and smile without understanding.

zHaveek would be sure to let the king know later why his daughter had been overfilled with joy this afternoon.

So lost in the happy feeling was zHaveek, that he reacted to late when the boy jumped forward and pushed his sister into the water.

Anger crashed over joy, hitting zHaveek in the chest, strong enough to bring him to his knees. He watched in shock as the sea eagle dove down, its caw screeching, clenching around zHaveek's heart.

In horror he watched as the birds outstretched claws sank into the boys shoulder and pulled him back onto his butt.

Illa!

At the feel of her father's powerful voice, the girl lost her anger, and her grip on the sea eagle's mind.

By the time zHaveek had both children standing and cleaned off and dried, the King was hopping down the rocks lining the cliffs edge beside their small strip of beach.

Despite the years living behind the city walls, King zHella's skin was bronzed from days under the sun. Much to his wife's dismay, the king wore just the loose pants of his own people throughout the day as he worked with the zMun and Don people.

It had been years since the famine had struck their people, but zHella still worried about the farms of the Don drying up.

zHaveek nodded his head in respect to the king, and his tribe leader, as the other man stormed past and dropped to his knees in front of his two children.

What have I told you two? zHella asked, looking into twin gazes. Both daughter and son looked shocked at their father's sudden appearance.

Blood dripped down zHaviel's bare arm, while sea water clung to Illa's hair.

King zHella gripped their small hands in his own. Despite their age, only six, both had far surpassed the powers of any zMun child. And while the outburst would have meant very little in the desert, it was disastrous for the city.

Even now, he could feel the ripples of shock and fear from his wife's people flowing through him. It would not do if their people were terrified of the heirs to their throne. zHella was all too aware of what fear made people do.

Listen closely, my stars, he said. Both children kept their gaze and their minds open to their father. Satisfied, zHella continued. *You both have been blessed with great power. It is very dangerous for either of you to forget this. You must be aware of your power and use it with that awareness or you risk mine, your mother, the city, and your own, lives.*

Illa whimpered, sadness weaved its gentle touch through her thoughts.

Her brother on the other hand stuck his lip out, his brows coming together in anger. "But it was Illa's fault, father," he whined.

zHella shook his head. *It does not matter who is at fault, or who started it, it is up to both of you on HOW it ends. And I will tolerate no violence between you two.*

"But..." zHaviel whined.

zHella scowled. *None, zHaviel.*

zHella did not have to remind his daughter for she was a gentle soul.

"Now," he said aloud, for the benefit of zHaveek, "It is time for you two to return to the castle for dinner."

At the mention of food, zHaviel perked up and ran back towards the cliff face with the tiny goat trail up to the city walls.

Illa was more hesitant, taking her father's hand as they followed her brother. She rubbed her chest, looking back at the rippling water of the ocean behind her. As always, it called her, but she cuddled into her father's side, taking comfort from his warmth.

Once inside their private chambers, zHaveek bowed and left the royal family in peace.

Queen Iara stood in the centre of the room, dressed in a regal gown that shimmered like the ocean on a sunny morn. Illa stared at her mother wearily as her father let her hand go.

zHella smiled, grabbing his wife around the waist and pulling her into a kiss.

The queen laughed, half-heartedly pushing away from his strong embrace, her cheeks reddening.

Illa snuck around the couple and tried to disappear into her own chamber. Before she stepped through the doorway, her mother's voice stopped her.

"I expect everyone remembers that we are hosting the royal entourage of Lupuain for dinner tonight and will be dressed accordingly."

zHella groaned, nuzzling his wife's neck. "Must I wear the silk suit?" he asked, sucking on a sensitive spot that had Iara leaning back.

But his distraction didn't work.

"Yes. And you look handsome in it," she said on a sigh.

The two exchanged a look that Illa was very familiar with. Her parents would be very busy, and likely late to the dinner.

She stepped just inside her room and waited a minute. Once she was sure her parents had disappeared into their own rooms, Illa snuck back into the foyer and slipped out of the doors.

With quick feet and a gentle nudge on any stray eyes to forget they saw her; she was able to get out of the castle and down to the beach. The water lapped at the sand; its whispers made her smile. She sat on a small bit of sand and leaned back until she could see the darkening sky. Soon enough it would be nightfall.

There was nothing Illa hated more than the state dinners. Normally her mother allowed her to dress and run and be a boy, as was normal to her father and his people. But state dinners meant tight dresses and being quiet and sitting still.

She *hated* being still.

Sometimes, Illa wished her mother wasn't a princess. And that they could have all lived with her father and his people, roaming the desert. When zHaveek talked about the times before the zMun had come to the city, Illa listened carefully.

It all sounded so free. To move and be a part of the sand and the wind. The only worries were taken care by the great mother.

So long did Illa lay in the sand, dreaming of a people she had only ever heard of, that she dozed off.

Illa woke with a start. The first thing she noticed was the moon high in the sky. It was very late in the night.

The second was that she was unbearably cold, the night air cooling her bare arms and chest and legs.

The third, and the reason for why she had awoken suddenly, was the splash of water from the ocean.

She stared out into the night and could only see a dark shadow in the water. Was it a torash, she wondered excitedly? She had heard many tales from the cook about the flesh eating creatures that hunted on the coast at all hours of the night.

Illa sat still, pulling her emotions tight to her like zHaveek had taught, and waited.

It was only when she was staring up into a pair of steel grey eyes that she realized her mistake. But by then it was too late for the little girl. The strange woman grabbed her from the beach and covered her mouth.

Scared, Illa kept an even tighter grip on her emotions. She closed her eyes and bit her lip, hoping to wake up from the horrible dream. Soon her mother would come into her room and gently shake her awake. Her father would kiss her forehead. And zHaviel would be whining that he was hungry.

So lost in her thoughts was she, that Illa hardly felt the jostle of her body as it was lifted. She did not hear the crashing water and creaking wood over the quick rhythmic beat of her heart.

It was only when the hot sun beat down on her face that she was forced to open her eyes. And realize that it had not been a dream.

She looked around herself and saw dozens of little girls, like her, dirty and hungry. Instinctively, Illa reached out for her mother's comforting thoughts and was met with silence.

Horrified, she carefully sat up and looked over the ship walls and saw water all around them.

One tear slowly streaked down her face and dripped onto the soaked barge floor. As the unending day continued, her emotions drew closer and closer to her heart until all she felt was numb.

CHAPTER TWENTY

⌘

Sons and Daughters

ASHTA WOKE WITH A start. For a moment she was disorientated by the pitch black. Was she still dreaming?

But movement at the back of the tent, a grunt, and silence again, reminded Ashta that she was still, in fact, in the canvas tent. Still a captive to her father. Taking deep breaths, Ashta tried to calm her racing heart and the fear that still gripped her from the dream.

As her breath slowed, she became aware of another noise. It was just slight enough that she might not have noticed it. The slight creak of wood. The slap of skin on skin.

She turned her head, her ears sharpening.

A low grunt. And this time, she knew that it came from the tent beside her. Era.

Shuddering, Ashta turned her head away from the tent and where the noise was coming from. She tried her hardest to tune out everything, but with only darkness surrounding her, she couldn't help but hear everything. Not even sleep would come and relieve her of the nightmare happening beside her.

Hours later, Ashta glared with dry eyes at the tent flap entrance to her prison. She wasn't sure when the noise had stopped in the tent beside her, only to be replaced by soft crying. Her heart ached, her mind whirred, knowing all to well of what was happening not only in the tent beside her, but on the island as a whole. It seemed that the depravity the spring had not lessened at all. It had just become quieter.

And for once, Ashta was thankful for her blood. It protected her from the worst of man's depravity.

It hadn't saved Ceerie, her mind reminded her.

Grimacing, she argued with herself. *My blood protects me on this island, from* Bbrskian *soldiers.* Glumly, she knew that it would not protect her against Tripsian soldiers. Or Bbrskian people who did not know who she was. Or from any other man, she slowly realized.

A weight settled on her chest as she struggled to breathe through the realization. And the sudden fear she hadn't known that she needed to have before.

Of course, she understood that sex, and rape, was a normal occurrence for other people. A dark necessity of life. She had just never understood, soul deep, that it was only a thin barrier, an invisible name, that stood between her body and another man's. Or woman's.

Before her mind could spiral into darker corners, the tent flap shook, before it was pulled aside.

At first Ashta was thankful for the distraction, her stomach grumbling from the limited food they had been giving her once a day. But instead of the grim faced Wulf walking towards her, she stared up into a familiar steel gaze.

Her father.

King Alerik walked into the tent and stopped just before his daughter. Despite weeks of limited food and movement, he was surprised to find her looking so healthy. Viral even.

He would have to crush that.

Alerik turned to Wulf. He had entrusted the general with the prisoners of war. So far, the man's tactics had worked well in retrieving information. And retrieving spies.

"Untie her," he demanded.

The other man hesitated a moment before going to the dark hair woman. He quickly loosened the rope, shoving it into a pocket. He stood behind the woman, looking to his king for direction. But the other man had only eyes for the woman.

Ashta rubbed her wrists automatically, purposely not looking her father in the eyes. She knew how much he hated it. How much he needed attention. It was the only way to command others.

"What do you know about the access points into the underground palace? Into the ruined city of Trian?" he asked, crouching down until he was eye level with Ashta.

She ignored him. Ashta dropped her hands to her lap and waited.

"What are the supplies of the city?" he continued.

Silence.

After a beat, he asked in a deceptively soft voice, "How many men does the city have to protect it?"

Ashta said nothing. She focused on keeping her muscles loose, her fingers loose, her feet soft. It may have been weeks since she had properly stretched, but with surprise, she could still attack her father.

The tent flap moved aside, spilling the early morning light into the tent and briefly blinding Ashta. When she blinked her sight clear, she was surprised to find four men, including Beltus spread around her.

Wulf gave a terse nod to the other men. He had seen the dark haired woman fight the first time they had captured her. He was not underestimating her abilities. Even if her body was weaker now. Her mind was still sharp.

"Fine," her father said as he stood up. He motioned to Beltus and another soldier.

The men stepped forward, each grabbing an arm, lifting Ashta up to her feet, then stretching her immobile. She strained against their hold but could only feel her own muscles twisting.

Alerik smiled darkly at his daughter. Despite looking so similar to his late wife, Svetlana had the same strength as he did. "You will talk. One way, or another, you will tell me what I want to know, dear *Mina*," he spat.

The soldiers all looked spooked at hearing their king say the term of endearment. Wulf's gaze went from the dark-haired woman to his king and back again. The King had not told anyone who the woman was. Just that she was a Tripsian White Lioness. But Wulf had wondered about it after his King had sent the woman on a boat back to Bbrski.

Then again, his King had done many a thing that Wulf did not understand or agree with. He had been there when the King had his second wife put to death. Had watched the King walk behind the barrel. Had seen the pleasure cross the other man's face as blood splattered across his face.

"Wulf!" the king commanded tersely, his glare filled with impatience.

Taking a quick breath, Wulf pushed down the memories of his own sweet daughter and stepped around the dark-haired woman. He pulled out his short blade, holding the handle out to the king.

Roman grabbed the handle, enjoying the familiar weight in his hands.

Ashta fell slack in the soldier's arms, her muscles releasing at the shock of her father holding a knife. Her entire childhood, she had known that there was something dark about him. Something that hung over him. But she had not seen *him* physically hurt someone.

Oh, she had seen him easily wave a hand and let *soldiers* do the deed. But he himself had always seemed separate from it.

Not anymore.

Ashta swallowed hard, her gaze caught on the glint of the knife blade. Her father held the knife with ease.

Alerik stepped in front of her, his gaze flitting from one spot of skin to the next. His mind was alive, energy pumping through his veins. He had not felt this good in years, he mused.

Finally, his gaze stopped on his daughter's familiar black gaze. The same as his late wife's. He wanted to cut them out of her head. But she would need them for what he planned to do with her.

"It's uncanny how similar your looks are to your mothers," he whispered, gently tracing the knife blade from her temple to her mouth.

Ashta held her breath, unable to look away from the strange look on King Alerik's face. It was the most interested he had looked at her. Ever.

"The same black hair... The same skinny arms." In a move too quick for Ashta to follow he slashed down her forearm. The cut was shallow. Its angle made sure it would not bleed her out.

But it would hurt.

And it did.

Clenching her teeth, she turned her focus from her father to the flap on the tent. It gave the faintest flutter as if a wind whipped outside.

Alerik grinned. She had not made a single noise. He watched the blood pool and slowly drip to the ground. Her blood was red like his. Like her mothers. Like the infernal Lucifer.

"I was surprised to learn that you did not become a whore like all the other Tripsian slaves," he said thoughtfully.

Then he slashed down on her opposite arm. Her only movement was the jump of the muscle in her neck as she tensed.

Alerik stepped in closer, enough that only Svetlana and he could hear his next words. He whispered, "But then, half your blood is mine."

Ashta turned and glared at him. She was slightly mollified to find that she looked him straight in the eye. He had always loomed in her memories, and now he was just a man. Not even taller than her.

Alerik brought the blade up and wiped the flat edge off on her collar bone. Slowly.

Smiling, he took a step back.

"Ah, and there it is. The famous Broskla stare. The one that brought kings to their knees. And made birds dance in the sky," he said with derision, snorting.

The soldiers on either side of the girl shuffled their feet but kept their grip steady. Their gazes, on the other hand stayed near the bare floor. It was Wulf, who stood slightly behind and to the side of Alerik, who watched his king. And the girl. And began to connect the thoughts in his head. He kept silent.

"There are legends about the Broskla. How the bloodline could never have more than one child. Or sons," Alerik muttered. Slowly he pressed the blade just underneath her collarbone, until it just slipped under the skin. Bright red blood beaded on the blade.

With deliberation, he slowly dragged it down along her collarbone until he reached her sternum.

Ashta shuddered, the pain a bright spot that would not be ignored. With shallow breaths, she kept her eyes open and her focus on her father's face. Treat it like the tattoo, she told herself, it is nothing more than the sting of the needle. Slow. Precise. Unavoidable.

Alerik lifted the blade and cleaned it on her other collarbone. Then pressed the blade into her left side and slowly dragged it down.

As if unaware of his words, he continued speaking in a monotone voice. "I didn't believe in the legends. Nothing more than stories meant to scare off a weaker person. If they had been true Lucifer Augosst would not have been born." He came to the end and wiped the blade on her neck. He inspected the red ribbons on her chest, the slow drip of the blood down her body.

His eyes moved slowly, lazily, before coming to her face.

Ashta's eyes widened as he pressed the blade just under her temple. She could see the deep wrinkles around his eyes as he focused on her skin. She could make out a small scar above his left eyebrow. And the shift of blue and green flecks in his eyes, that looked like steel grey from a distance. This is what she focused on, rather than the burning line down her cheek.

"All I needed from your mother was a son," he whispered, his lips barely moving.

Ashta's eyes did not move, but she could see Wulf take a step to the side, the soldier's gaze focused on her father's lips.

Alerik breathed in, his heart racing but his mind relaxed. He stopped at the apple of her cheek, keeping the blade there for a long moment. He watched the blood pool on its silvery edge, mesmerized.

He released a shuddery breath, his hand shaking the slightest bit as he quickly wiped the blade on her neck and began on her opposite temple. "A son would have ensured my hold on the kingdom. A son I could raise and mold into the king I needed him to be."

His eyes flashed, his face only a hands breath away from Ashta's. For a moment she was caught in his cold glare. "Instead, that bitch gave me a useless *girl*," he spat.

In a movement she could not see, he pulled her close and slid the blade easily between her ribs.

Ashta gasped at the burst of pain.

As fast as it had come, it dulled. Unlike the arrowhead which had lodged into her chest and irritated her for three days, the blade easily slipped out, leaving only a trail of blood behind.

Panting, Ashta strained against the soldier's arms, needing to move. To get away. To do something.

Alerik stepped back and watched her, his face blank. The blade hung loosely in his grip, slowly dripping blood to the sandy ground.

Angry, unable to hold her thoughts at bay, Ashta lashed out at the king with her words. "Maybe if you hadn't been busy fucking every other woman in the castle, you might have had another babe with the queen."

The air in the tent froze.

The cloud of confusion lifted over the soldier's eyes as they understood the gravity of the situation. And the importance of the woman they were holding.

Wulf's throat ached, finally realizing that the woman in front of them was their future. And as was the way of King Alerik, he ruined it for the Bbrski and her people.

Alerik's fingers twitched, clenching the handle briefly. Instead, he took a deep breath in and smirked. "Oh, how blind you are, daughter of mine," his voice was rough, his eyes never leaving Ashta's. "You were not the only babe of mine your mother bore."

Glancing at the soldiers faces, he frowned. He had no intention of giving these men any more than they already knew. Even then, likely he would have to rid himself of the soldiers.

His gaze flicked to Wulf.

Everyone except his general.

He took a step forward again and whispered into Ashta's ear. "You were the only *living* child born to me."

Ashta shook her head slowly. His words cut deeper than any knife.

It wasn't possible. It couldn't be. He had to be lying.

And yet, flashes of a swaddled babe. Of her mom being in her bed for months. Of hugging her mother and feeling her swollen belly underneath the layers of her court dress...

Could it be?

Alerik stepped back. "Tie her back up," he demanded of the two soldiers.

Then he stepped closer to Wulf. "And don't feed her. Water only. Until she breaks."

At his words Ashta glared at the man, the *monster*, that was her father. She didn't fight as the soldiers tied her arms around the pole once more. But before her father could step outside of the tent, she yelled out. "You will never break me. I am stronger than she was. Then you are!"

He hesitated at the tent flap, his back rigid. He turned slightly; his profile lit by the morning sun.

Then, in a deep voice that had shivers running down her back, he said, "We will see."

CHAPTER TWENTY-ONE

⌘

Death in the Dark

EVERY MOVEMENT BROUGHT new aches with it. Ashta sighed, trying to stretch her back without disturbing the stab wound between her ribs. But it was of no use.

With no food, her stomach cramped, a constant ache reminding her of the hopelessness of her situation. Had it only been this morning that her father had come to the tent? The whole event felt to her as if it had been days ago and not merely hours.

Sighing, she leaned her forehead against the pole and focused on her breathing. Anything to distract her mind from the pains of her body.

A shuffle in the tent beside her had Ashta's ears perking. Era.

Ashta had forgotten that she was not alone. That there were others close by who had heard her situation. Who may have heard her father?

But her thoughts could not focus on the gravity of that knowledge. Instead, she focused again on her breathing, wishing for time to pass.

The next morning, as the sun just began to lighten the canvas walls, Era called out in *Kiang*. "You will survive this."

Ashta snorted. What did Era know? There was no one who would come to save Ashta. None of her fellow white lionesses were allowed that freedom, the princess Carien thought Ashta was dead, and her own people would gain nothing from a woman who gave up her birthright.

"I know I will," Era continued, ignoring Ashta's silence. Her voice became softer as she mused over her own situation. "Even now, tied to this pole, on an island surrounded by enemies, I know that I will survive. I *have* to."

Licking her dry lips, Ashta managed to croak out, "Why?"

Era was quiet for a long time.

The silence was welcome.

Ashta's own mind raced as she tried to answer that question for herself. Why did Ashta need to survive? Was there anyone who really needed her?

The princess had a host of other women to choose from to be her guard. Kkaar had Lucy, and Lucy had Kkaar. Even little Mina had the protection of a princess. There was no one who truly *needed* Ashta.

"Because-because I can't let them win," Era finally replied.

Ashta snorted, turning her head so she could stare blindly at the canvas wall that stood between Era and her. "What does it matter if they win, you would be dead and nothing in the living world would be your worry anymore."

"You are wrong, princess-"

Ashta snarled, "Don't call me that."

Era asked, tentatively, "But that is your title? You are King Alerik's first born, are you not?"

Ashta glared at the canvas. "I may have that monster's blood in my veins, but I am no one." And then, in a quieter voice, she admitted, "I gave up my birthright. Signed it to my cousin. Svetlana is dead."

Stunned silence.

Ashta strained to hear Era's response but none came. Ashta's focus waned and she found herself falling asleep.

Maybe moments, maybe hours later, Era finally replied. "Svetlana can never truly die. Her name still lives in record."

Ashta blinked awake, the tent was brighter now. She could make out a thin white line of sunlight that peeked through a hole in the flap door.

Shaking her head, she focused on the words that woke her. Her voice was shaky, uncertain. "For now. Soon that name will be struck out of the records and she will be as if she had never been born."

Ashta swallowed, her mouth dry. Surely Wulf would be coming by soon with water?

Era snorted. "Do you really believe it is so easy to disappear from history? From existence?"

Ashta's brows furrowed. *Wasn't it?* She thought.

The other woman laughed quietly. Then she added, thoughtfully, "There are very few of the royal bloodlines that have simply...disappeared. And even then, there existence, that they *did* live at one point is well remembered if not recorded.

And Svetlana, even if she disappears, even if she dies, will be known by someone, some forgotten written record, some legend, that she *had* in fact been born. And she had lived for a time. Her *whole* story may not be known, but then, whose is?"

"My mother's was," Ashta said softly. The stark black ink in the history books stating her mother's birth, her mother's marriage, her mother's death.

"The late queen Anichka." Era said it as a statement, though she was not sure of the truth of the other woman's heritage.

Ashta neither confirmed nor denied her mother's name. Instead, she continued on the path her thoughts had begun to stray on. "What parts of her life were not recorded in the written accounts, were well remembered by the other's that lived around us. Except…" and she remembered her father's words. Of her *brothers*. "Maybe not all of her story was remembered."

And then, as if she had forgotten, Ashta added "You're right. The whole story is never known."

Then another thought struck Ashta. She voiced it, not separating thought from spoken words. Her tired eyes swam with shadows and lights, yet the canvas had not shifted colour. "Then why do we record anything?"

Era was silent, mulling over the question as well.

In the meantime, the canvas flap shifted. Like a mirage, Ashta watched as the shaky image of Wulf materialized before her, water skin at hand. She opened her mouth without thought, leaning back and greedily gulping down the cool liquid. Her stomach ached, tight and hard, wishing for more than just water.

And then the water stopped. By the time Ashta blinked her eyes open, Wulf was gone. She licked her lips, her mouth dry once more.

Had it even happened?

"To remind us."

Blinking several times, Ashta turned and stared at the canvas wall once more. Likely Wulf would not come back again today with water. She would have to wait until the next morning for more.

Sighing, she leaned against the pole once more, her muscles as relaxed as they could be.

"To remind us of what?" Ashta finally asked, only half listening to Era.

"Of whom we are. Where we come from." And then in a hard voice, Era added, "Why we keep fighting."

Ashta asked in a detached voice, "And who will remember you, Era of Naankdoen? When you die, who will write your name down to be remembered. To know that you lived once?"

Ashta had expected Era to reply right away. But Era was silent too long for it to be comfortable.

Worried, Ashta shifted her body.

Eventually, Era replied. "No one." Her voice was hollow, filled with immeasurable pain. The old kind of hurt that had festered and worked itself into the very core of one's body.

Ashta's heart ached because it was the same for her. Who was left in this world that would remember Svetlana? Who would care enough to repeat that name over and over and make sure the true story lived?

"I had a sister once," Era said, jogging Ashta from her dark thoughts.

She closed her eyes and focused on Era's clear voice.

"Innes." Ashta could hear the smile in Era's voice. "We were close in age, she was only a year older than me. Innes was fearless. We would play zMun and Don in the streets, and she would fight the other kids, fearlessly protecting me from the evil king. I thought nothing could stop her," she chuckled darkly.

"What happened?" Ashta asked. Era had said she *had* a sister.

"She was taken by Tripsian slavers."

Frowning, Ashta blinked open her eyes and glared out at the canvas flap door. Her whole life, where she was sitting right now, could be blamed on Tripsian slavers. On Ennris.

Era continued, her voice aching with shame and anger. "My father had decided to take us out of the city to go fishing. My sister and I had been excited, helping my mother pack a small meal for the noon-day. The morning had been filled with laughter and smiles. My sister had convinced my mother and I to play hide and seek. I thought…I thought I'd be smart," she said, her voice breaking, but she continued, "I quickly climbed up from the beach edge, and snuck into the forest. My sister had never said how far we were allowed to go to hide," she reasoned as much to herself as to Ashta.

She stayed silent for so long that Ashta spoke up, prompting her. "And then?"

Era laughed darkly again, "Night fell and still my sister had not found me. I was tired and hungry, so I decided to go back to the beach. But my sister and mother were nowhere to be found. Instead, a spear pinned my father to the sand, the blood having dried already. They told me there was nothing I could have done…But surely if I had been there, I could have called someone. I could have stopped them."

"But your sister and mother still live. You are not alone," Ashta said tiredly. Her father wanted her dead. Her cousin was glad to be rid of her. And her own bloodline would die with her, Tripsia would make sure of that.

If she even returned. The slight swirling in her vision had her questioning if she would come out of this alive. She had survived her father last time. But she wasn't sure he would let her go so easily again.

"I joined the guild as soon as I came of age. One of my first missions was to Tripsia. I found out my mother had died on the boat…"

"And your sister?" But Ashta had a feeling she already knew. She had seen the teeming floors of children in the Nursery herself. Only a few *chose* the test. Even fewer survived.

"I had thought her strong," Era spat bitterly.

Cocking her head, Ashta said rather than asked. "She didn't take the test."

"I wish she had," Era replied, hurt bubbling forth. "It would have been easier than finding her in that house. The glazed look in her eyes. The worst was she didn't even recognise me."

This time the silence was heavy.

Ashta had never seen one of the other slaves before.

"The women in the pleasure houses. The luckier woman would be purchased to live in the estates, forced to serve only their lords and no other man."

Ashta shivered a little, thankful for what control she had over her body. Over her life.

"Did you help her escape?" Ashta asked, even though she knew it would be impossible for a slave to escape. *All* slaves were marked with their ownership. Her own tattoo itched, as it often did. She was never able to completely forget its presence on her ribs.

Era snorted. "We both know that is impossible. My people especially."

Ashta frowned, sensing more to those words. "What do you mean your people?" she asked, her words almost echoing in their starkness.

Era hesitated. Ashta could hear the other woman shift, the scrape of rope against the wood.

Ashta prodded again, her mind picking out memories, details from her own short stay in the guarded kingdom. "Why do Naankdoena people never travel?"

Era stayed quiet for a long minute before releasing a shaky breath. "I-It's hard to talk about."

Ashta waited, her eyes closed. Her heartbeat slow, distracting her with its calm rhythm. It was soothing. Familiar. She felt herself losing awareness of her limbs as she was lulled into a trance.

Era's words filtered through, painting pictures in her head. Blue and violet eyes. A young girl. The desert. Blue marks twirling and twining on a wrist. "Our people have a special hate for the slaves of Tripsia. Never has a Naankdoena girl been willingly sold to Tripsia. They are always stolen. For centuries Tripsia has stolen our girls. But that never stopped our people from traveling. It is hard for us to be out in the known kingdoms, to be surrounded by people and feel so alone. To be reminded with each meeting that we are not quite the same as others. It's hard to want to live with that feeling year after year. That's why not many of our people join the guild. The guild…" She hesitated for a long moment as if the next words were being ripped out from an especially deep part of her soul. "The guild came from the time of zHella and Iara. Before that our people never left our walls. But Tripsia had gone too far. They had stolen someone far to precious. And the King refused to let her simply go. The shackles of Tripsian slaves runs deep, pulls on old majik that hasn't died. Yet."

The hairs on the back of Ashta's neck stood on end. She knew the legends of the White lionesses well. But majik? Real majik? And by the way Era spoke, she knew more about this so called majik. Her heartbeat picked up as a slight sweat broke out across her skin. She licked her lips, barely able to wet them, before asking, "What do you know ab-"

But she was cut off of by a high-pitched scream.

Ashta stilled, her ears almost vibrating as she listened hard.

A squelching sound.

Then again.

And then a thud.

Finally, the distinct sound of someone choking.

Then silence.

Ashta stilled her breath, scared to make any noise. What happened, she wondered?

Movement at the front of her tent had her looking up.

A berserker, one she had never seen before, stepped inside. His eyes were glazed over, blood splattered across his face and dripping from his right hand.

Shivering, Ashta watched in silence as the man took a step, then another step towards her. Before he reached her the tent flap moved again.

"What are you doing in here?" Wulf's low growl filled the small space. Ashta was never so glad to hear it.

The other man grunted but his crazed eyes never strayed from Ashta's.

Wulf grabbed the man by the shoulder and hauled him back outside. A thud followed by cursing echoed in Ashta's ears.

But she saw nothing. Her vision swam as a far off ringing swirled around her.

She was dead.

Era was dead.

Dead.

Everything went black.

CHAPTER TWENTY-TWO

⌘

The Witch

THE GIRL HAD GONE mute. Wulf checked the tent several times to be sure she was even there. He had a strong fear that the girl would somehow sneak out.

Her silence unnerved him.

And her lack of movement.

She was like a statue. Her unseeing eyes stared through him every day. The other soldiers kept their distance, even Beltus refused to come near inside tent.

The king asked for an update each day. Wulf's stomach turned remembering the day he told the king that the Naankdoen spy was dead, and that his daughter had gone silent. The smile that lit the other man's face was nothing short of evil.

It was inhuman.

And so, the days passed. Wulf watched as the roundness from the girl's shoulders sharpened to points. Her face hollowed out, deep bags grew underneath her eyes. What little colour her skin had was now pale and sallow. Her hair was matted in its strange braid. After a week and half, he noted small flies crawling out of her hair mat.

But she drank each morning.

Despite the silence, she had not completely given up on life.

Sometimes, when he entered the small tent, he felt something strange. Like the soft brush of feathers across his forehead.

In the last couple of days, the feeling washed over him more often. He swiped at his forehead but found nothing.

Beltus' eyes had changed in the last couple days. The whites could always be seen. And the other man's gaze skittered across people, the dark bags under his eyes giving away his lack of sleep.

Wulf came this morning with the daily water for the girl. But this time Beltus was writhing in front of the tent, pulling at his hair, deep scratches bleeding from his face.

Wulf dropped to his knees and grabbed the other man's hands. Beltus' eyes had rolled back, only the white being seen.

"Beltus!" Wulf commanded tersely, his grip firm despite the ripple of fear washing down his back.

The other man's mouth opened, but an unearthly moan came out. Wulf shook the man slightly, but nothing helped.

He called out to Orvin who was guarding the only other living prisoner. The other man refused to approach, staying in front of his post.

Unable to allow Beltus to hurt himself further, he punched him hard enough to knock him out. Then Wulf walked quickly to Orvin.

The soldier watched his approach suspiciously but kept his gaze turned away from Beltus.

"How long has Beltus been like that?" Wulf demanded, glancing back to confirm Beltus was still prone on the ground.

Orvin stayed silent.

Wulf turned back and glared at the other man. "Answer me!"

The soldier swallowed hard. "I-I don't know, sir, I came with the first light, same as Beltus. He wasn't himself even then." Then the soldier glanced at Wulf before whispering, "I think he's been possessed by the witch."

Wulf jerked up, shocked by the words. "Witch?" he said without thinking.

The soldier nodded before jerking his head to the tent. "Strange things been happening around the island since the witch has been here."

Wulf could not say anything. She was the Kings daughter, but she wasn't a witch. He shook his head. "Send for Makar and Gerasin. They will be on guard duty for the prisoner until Beltus comes back to himself."

When the soldier did not move, Wulf yelled with irritation. "Now!"

The other man jumped before hurrying out of sight into the tent city. Leaving Wulf alone in front of the tents. The hair at the back of his neck stood on end. With a deep breath he walked to *her* tent and shuddered at the now familiar brush on his forehead.

Orvin ran, glad to be free of his duty for a short time. All morning he had felt the strange pressure on his head. The first night he had thought it from too much to drink. But with each step away from the tents, the foreboding sense of doom lessened.

The pressure on his head did not.

Shaking his head, he continued through the tents, until he reached the one he was sharing with the other prisoner guards. Gerasin was not sitting out front by the fire. Makar and Hristof were both drinking from large tankards.

Makar squinted as he looked up at Orvin. His lips pursed as he struggled to not slur his words. "Aren't you supposed to be on today?" He glanced behind him but didn't seem to see what he was looking for. "Or is it Nikifor's turn?"

Orvin shook his head. "Lieutenant Wulf is looking for you and Gerasin."

The other man frowned. "Why?"

Swallowing hard, Orvin replied as he glanced back over his shoulder. "Beltus has…fallen ill," he whispered the last words.

But both men heard, both shifting in their seats in front of the fire. Makar spat on the ground as the other man muttered, "Damn witch."

Orvin didn't disagree. Strange things had been happening on the island since the prisoner had appeared. Some of the men said that the woman was a kelpie or skin shifter. Orvin didn't know if he believed the rumors but nothing could make him go nearer to that canvas tent than he absolutely needed to.

"Have you seen Gerasin?" he asked the men.

Makar shrugged. Hristof took a long gulp.

Rubbing the back of his neck, Orvin left the men behind and pushed the tent flaps aside. No one else was inside.

Damn it, where was Gerasin, he worried.

"Shut up, bitch," Gerasin growled at the cowering girl. But the girl continued to cry as she shook in the corner of the bed.

It wouldn't do. Gerasin had paid a pretty penny, and his best sword – and killed a few men – to get his hands on a woman.

And he was damned well going to enjoy her. Even if his head ached.

He ripped up some linen and advanced on the shaking body.

Her eyes flickered up for a moment, landing on his. She jumped back. But not quick enough.

Grinning, Gerasin wrapped his spare hand around her bicep and threw her back to the tent ground. Before she could get up, he slapped her hard enough across the face that his hand stung. It was satisfying.

Almost as satisfying as her silence.

He quickly wrapped and tied the linen around her mouth, then pushed up the rags of her skirt.

Finally, he thought, his heart beating fast. It had been months since last he had been on land and enjoyed a soft body.

Yevgraf bit is fist to keep from crying. The shifting sounds of cloth and the grunt of Vladislav were unmistakable behind him. Thankfully the barrels hid him from view.

"That's right, boy, keep your mouth shut," breathed out the berserker. "We'll make a fucking man of you."

Yevgraf shut his eyes and wished he could close his ears. Boris and he had become quick friends on the sail from Bbrski to Aishma. Neither had been prepared for the depravity of the army.

Or the berserkers.

Yevgraf had managed to evade the berserkers after the first night he had been caught. But Vladislav had been hunting him and Boris through the camp. Yevgraf hadn't dared to sleep in the last week for fear of Vladislav.

His other hand cramped around the handle of the short knife he held. It would do him no good against the monsters. He had stabbed the last berserker when he had been cornered by the ships, but the berserker had only laughed, the crazed look in his eyes bringing real fear to Yevgraf.

All he wanted was to go back to Bbrski. Starving on the land, watching his sisters and mother starve, was far better than this hell hole.

But there was only two ways off this island. The ships. Or death.

Boris screamed. Yevgraf flinched.

The pain in his head spiked as he tried to curl even tighter into himself.

Sozon could barely keep the disgust off his face as the younger men around the fire joked about the women, and the *boys*, they had used.

He was thankful for his long beard hiding his face, because he was sure that a knife would have been slipped in his chest otherwise.

Instead, he kept his mouth shut by taking another hardy drink. Soon enough this fool's errand of a war would be over, and he could return to his clan. He had little hope that his wife would still be alive. She had been ailing before the king's armies had come through and taken every able body. Likely his sons and grandsons were somewhere on this godforsaken island.

Or dead.

Wrinkling his nose, he took another hardy gulp before rising on steady legs. The other men quieted, looking up at him curiously.

Sozon rubbed his forehead as a wave of dizziness washed over him. "About time that fucking witch dies," he cursed.

Several of the other men crossed their hearts and muttered similar curses. No one paid him any heed as he left the fire and wove through the tents. As the afternoon wore on, the slow cacophony of screeches and screams rose from the tent city.

Sozon shuddered.

The young berserkers were nothing like the honour bound men of old. Sure, he had felt the call of bloodlust in his younger years. But these men, no, these monsters, were something else. They had no respect for the other men. The way some of them watched the younger boys made Sozon's stomach flip.

No, it wasn't like it used to be.

He was just thankful for his armor and his quick sword hand, or he was sure the monsters would come after him in the dark of the night.

A young boy, blood streaming from his lip, ran past Sozon. He paused for a moment, not surprised to see a berserker stalking through the tents after the boy.

Shuddering, he moved quicker through the tents until he reached Timur's tent. A night of drinking and telling stories of home sounded much better to him than thinking about the hopelessness of this island, this war. Of his people.

May the gods burn every last one of these monsters to dust. Because Sozon knew that restless berserkers without a war to fight, were far more dangerous to Bbrski than they were on this island. At least here they could only destroy each other, and not their villages and clans.

"Sozon!" Timor called out from the fire. Several other older faces looked up and greeted Sozon. He smiled grimly as he took a seat by Timor, rubbing his head.

The night air was warm, the wind like sharp daggers on the torash's oily fur. It sniffed the wind, scenting blood close by.

With a shake of its wet mane, it galloped across the sea, the scent of blood getting stronger.

But the scent of humans also grew stronger. The closer it galloped to the island on the horizon, the louder the noise of the humans became.

At the last moment, the torash nickered and dove under the water, turning towards the south instead. Where it was quieter, easier hunting.

Kirill glared at the back of the king's head. He had been left waiting here for the better part of an hour. The king ate his meal slowly.

Kirill knew it was just a power play. He himself used many such subtle shows of power on the other men and especially on the berserkers.

It was necessary. Otherwise, there would be total chaos in camp.

But that did not mean he liked having those same power plays used against him.

He shifted on his feet and took a quiet breath. Kirill didn't want to give the king the impression that he was uncomfortable.

Instead, Kirill went over the numbers in his head again. The reports from the fleet from the eastern and western kingdoms were promising. The walled city would eventually run out of supplies. It had been well over a year since the people last could leave Naankdoen City, Kiang don. At maximum, Kirill believed it would be another year. He hoped for it to be this fall before the harsh winds of winter came. In the next few weeks, the winds would blow, making sailing the final stretch through the Blood sea more difficult.

The constant pain above his eyes was worrying. Kirill squinted, not trusting himself to close his eyes in the presence of the king. But it was difficult. When the war was over, he hoped the aches and pains that tore at his body and mind would loosen their hold.

One could hope.

King Alerik finally set his cutlery in the plate. From the front entrance, a servant came running, quickly clearing the plate from the table. A second man came and cleared the food off the table.

Kirill waited. Soon.

Breathing through his nose, he tried to focus on something else. Like his son.

The thought brought a small smile to his face. Kirill was proud of his son. He was a damn good fighter and was showing a real interest in strategy. Kirill thought the move to put him at the front of the western Black Feet taking Kae ol and Malten had worked well in his son's favour.

"Come forward," King Alerik called as he leaned back in his chair. The servants appeared again and finished clearing the last food off the table. The king made no indication that he was going to move from the table.

Kirill walked to the king's right side, forced to stand since the king sat in the only chair in the tent.

"Your majesty," he started, keeping his gaze on the kings folded hands on the tabletop.

"How is your son, Luka?" King Alerik asked.

Kirill stuttered, losing his breath for a moment. He dared to look into the king's eyes and saw the glint in his gaze.

"G-Good, your majesty," he finally got out.

"Really," the king said smoothly, "Only good? Surely a father hears more from his son than the tallied numbers of our dead and our enemies' dead?" His tone was laced with poison. Not for the first time, Kirill wished he could kill the king. Protect his son. Protect the people he loved.

But he was trapped, especially since the king had a large number of loyal berserkers who were barely more than animals. But lethal. And following his son.

He swallowed hard.

King Alerik smiled inwardly. He already knew Kirill's son had reported a number of soldiers who were loyal to him and his father. And not the king.

But Alerik wouldn't kill the man yet. He had proven himself useful, easily taking the land and holdings from the Malten people. With far less casualties than his men at Tripsia, or even Naankdoen. Both kingdoms had one central city, one central stronghold. And it was proving difficult to break them.

A brush like sensation had Alerik leaning back in his chair.

Hmmm. He thought with satisfaction. *It seems you possess the same abilities as your mother.*

CHAPTER TWENTY-THREE

⌘

Wedge in the Crack

ASHTA SHOOK HER head, her neck aching from stiffness. She blinked several times, seeing the canvas tent around her for the first time in weeks. The flap had a thick layer of grime on its edge from Wulf's hands gripping it open. A short path to where she sat dug into the packed ground.

How long had she been here, she wondered?

Ashta blinked again.

A flash of a memory, a berserker sprayed in blood, stepping forward and attacking her. She shuddered, shaking her head as if to dislodge it.

And like that, the memory was gone, the constant ache from her stomach was gone. All that was left was an awareness that she was here, nothing more and nothing less.

Noise outside of the tent caught her attention. She shifted her head slightly to watch the tent flap.

King Alerik waited impatiently for Wulf to open the tent. His own personal guards hesitated around him, refusing to step ahead inside the tent.

But Alerik wasn't worried.

"Your majesty," Wulf nodded.

Alerik gave an annoyed glance at Wulf, before stepping inside.

Kirill hesitated a heartbeat, taking a deep breath before following his king inside.

Wulf waited, arching a brow at the other guards. Each man shifted nervously on his feet before following inside. Wulf took a quick sweep of the area, not surprised at the lack of men around the surrounding area around the tents. The few guards that were stationed around him kept their backs to the tent.

With a sigh, he brought up the rear of the small party, letting the flap settle behind him.

The first thing he noticed was that the girl had moved. Just slightly. Her head wasn't the same angle. It bothered Wulf that he noticed such a small detail.

The second, was that the guards had settled themselves into the furthest corners of the tent. Only Kirill stood slightly behind and to the side of the king. Wulf stood to the king's other side, briefly glancing at Kirill. The other man's face was impassive, almost bored.

The king took a step forward before settling on the ground in front of the dark haired girl. He took the time to sit with his legs crossed. Wulf kept his surprise to himself, forcing his gaze to the back of the tent instead.

Alerik stared at the girl. Much had changed in the passing weeks. Svetlana resembled a skeleton more than a living body.

He could count every rib. He could see the pop of the tendons underneath her skin.

The most satisfying change was the blank look in her eyes.

He smirked.

Then he pulled out a small loaf of white bread that he had pocketed from his breakfast meal. He carefully pulled the crust apart, its skin breaking and releasing the succulent scent of its yeasty goodness.

With deliberate slowness, he pulled a small piece of the soft, still-warm innards out, and placed it in his mouth.

By the third bite, Svetlana's eyes cleared.

When he had almost finished half of the bread, she blinked several times.

Good. It was time.

He opened his mind, ignoring the strange pressure on his mind.

Alerik looked over his daughter with a critical eye again. A lesser man would have gone crazy by now. Or died.

But not his daughter. She was strong. She came from strong blood.

More than that, there was that innate *thing*, something Alerik knew could not be taught, that was inside of her. It had always been there, even when she had been just a mewling babe.

Alerik was annoyed at her strength, it made everything more difficult. Everything took longer. He had thought to break her when she had been a young child, but she never gave up that goodness inside of her. That piece so like her mother.

But he was also proud of her. He had broken stronger men, berserkers, in a matter of days. And this slip of girl had survived weeks of his direct attention. Longer, if he counted her childhood.

Her mind was finally opening itself up but was far from broken. He would find the crack now that he was inside, and he would enjoy the ensuing deadness that would filter from his daughter's eyes.

Like her mother's.

Alerik took another bite of the bread, slowly chewing it. He enjoyed the flavour, the rough texture, and the warmth on his tongue.

Ashta's eyes tracked his small movements but otherwise she was still. Quiet. Waiting.

Wulf and Kirill watched the pair as well. Kirill did not understand why the king was being so deliberate, but Wulf had seen a simple cup of water drive a man crazy. If they were close to the edge. As far as his trained eye could see, the girls mind was still clear. Her muscles did not shake. She did not swallow convulsively as she watched the king.

She was just still. Very still

Like a snow snake before it struck a snowshoe hare through the thin layer of snow lying above it.

The girl blinked occasionally, but nothing else in her face changed. And though her eyes tracked his movements as he slowly finished the bread in front of her, nothing else moved.

When Alerik got to the final piece of bread he hesitated, holding it out just under Svetlana's nose. Her face twitched, she blinked twice rapidly, before frowning at him.

Alerik had not believed the food would break her. She had already survived weeks without it. He wasn't sure how much of the strength came from her training as a lioness or her childhood. He had only heard rumours about the white lionesses.

Oh well, he thought, shoving the last piece in his mouth, chewing it with satisfaction as she watched his jaw with a small frown marring her face.

There was bound to be a crack. There always was. Alerik just had to find it.

He held his right hand up without looking away from the black eyes so similar to his late wife's. Deep black holes that sucked people in, but never him. He felt the pull, but he had always been able to hold himself separate.

An idea flickered across his mind, but he quieted it before she could hear. Alerik let the cool feel of the vessel being placed in his hand flood his mind.

Ashta blinked once before her vision blurred slightly.

Alerik glanced at the girl before taking a long drink of water.

But her eyes did not stray to the droplets he felt making their way down his chin.

He finished the water in another long pull before holding it back out, not caring who grabbed it.

Wulf took the flask and holstered it once more. It had been for the girl, her daily ration. But it seemed the king wanted to starve her of even that. He glanced briefly around the room, noting everyone's tense positions. Only the girl and the king seemed relaxed, their muscles soft. Wulf fought the urge to rub at his forehead. Barely.

"Since you don't seem to be hungry or thirsty, maybe I shall entertain you with some stories. Stories of the past. Like your mother…"

Svetlana stared deep into his eyes, giving him a slow blink.

But Alerik was not deterred. He brought the memories he was looking for, forward in his mind, slowly reliving each moment.

His young wife, naïve and happy and free, rode beside him to the castle. She looked up at him, those black eyes filled with adoration and love. And all he felt was cold. Which would not do to keep his young wife close. So instead, he let go just a little bit of that warmth, that affection he could not feel but knew others did.

Her eyes brightened at the feelings and she smiled up at him, grabbing his arm. The bright heat of her skin was like a bucket of ice and he closed his mind again. Anichka's eyes clouded with confusion and she quickly let go of him.

"*Are you well, mina?*" she asked in that soft voice of hers. She always sounded like she was a word away from breaking. It disgusted him.

But he needed her to gain the kingship.

He pushed past his discomfort and patted her hand briefly. "*We must be proper for the kingdom. It does not do well to show to much affection.*" And then he took his hand back to his own mount.

She looked up at him, the confusion slowly shifting to understanding. She nodded to herself, her expressive face giving away all of her thoughts. "*Of course,*" she said with a laugh. "*As long as you love me in private,*" She added with a wink before pulling back from him.

His revulsion for women, for people, was strong, but he hid it well. Had hid it his whole life. It was necessary, in order to move up and gain the power he craved.

Alerik blinked several times and was surprised to see no change on Svetlana's face. He was sure she had seen it all. Instead, he went to the next memory.

"*The queen is dead.*" His man whispered in his ear. Lady Arja stood across from him, with the other nobility. It was supposed to be a quiet bruncheon.

Alerik blinked.

The other woman's blatant stare was beginning to annoy him. While she, and her father's gold and abundant crop of men, had served Alerik well, it seemed the woman was forgetting her place.

Sighing, he turned to the soldier. "Take me to her bed,"

The soldier was pale as he shook his head.

Alerik turned completely to the soldier. He had been sure his wife would simply die from wasting away. She was pathetic. Weak. With the occasional glimpse of Broskla fire.

"She jumped, your majesty," the boy stuttered.

Alerik was shocked.

He gazed down at her mangled body, the strange angles of her legs and neck. The blood that had pooled around her. Even in death she was beautiful. Ethereal.

He felt annoyed by that truth.

"*You killed her,*" a quiet voice spoke from the bushes.

Alerik looked up and was again surprised, as the morning seemed to be filled with them, to see his daughter sitting in the tree branch staring at him. Her face was clear, her eyes hard. Not even her nose was red.

For the first time, he wondered about her. "*Your mother jumped. I did not push her.*"

The girl stared at him, her eyes so similar to Anichka's and so different. The longer she stared the more he wondered. But unlike her mother, there was no pressure when he was around his daughter. Just silence. Deafening silence.

"Where are your words now, daughter?" he asked harshly.

But she did not flinch.

Anger began to bubble up. Everything had begun to fall into place. He had the support of Smirnov, Bogomolov, Trofim, Medved. And the rest he had coerced. He had the kingship. All he needed was a son.

And now his damned wife was dead.

He would have to marry quick. Maybe Lady Arja would give him the son he needed?

Sneering, he knew it wasn't enough. The lady did not come from the right family. He glared up at his only living daughter from his fragile – now dead – wife. To be so close to everything he had been trying to achieve his whole life, and have someone who was stupid, as weak, as his wife throw it all away.

"Get rid of the body," he growled at the soldiers who had followed him. He turned away from both mother and daughter. Neither would serve him any use now.

Blinking, Alerik looked up into Svetlana's face again.

Still no change.

Annoyed, he was about to go into the next memory when movement at the tent entrance distracted him.

"What is it?" he growled, not looking away from the girl.

The soldier, panting, quickly spoke the message. "No change from Tripsia. We are still at a stalemate. The outer rooms have been blocked off with boulders making it impossible to get inside the cave castle. And the ancient walls from Trian are still holding."

When the panting soldier did not leave right away, King Alerik demanded, "What else?"

This time, the soldier hesitated, glancing out uneasily at the other soldiers in the tent. He noticed the girl for the first time and quickly averted his eyes. In a quieter voice, he continued.

"There are rumors that the Tripsian princess serves on the frontlines, with the healers. And…" he hesitated even longer, his discomfort at the next words palpable. "And that she has a baby on her hip."

Alerik watched with interest as his daughter's eyes suddenly sharpened, focusing on the soldier behind Alerik. "The bitch has a babe. I thought she was to be married in three years' time?"

A low growl released from the girl's throats, making every man in the tent, except the king, jump.

The king smiled.

"You know about the babe?" he asked in dark whisper.

Ashta feels her lips curl as she glares up at her father.

He smirked. His mind spun and Ashta found herself caught in a strange vision of Carien and Mina on the wall. Of Mina being caught by a stray arrow from a berserker. Blood. Screaming. And Carien dropping the dead weight over the wall, her eyes dead.

Svetlana jumped at the king, her face millimetres from his, her mouth foaming as she growled like a wild animal. Alerik grinned. "You may leave now," he called in a distant voice.

The soldier didn't hesitate, quickly leaving the tent.

But Alerik was just getting started now that he had found her crack. He carefully wedged himself further into it, playing out fantasies and memories until it all became a vision of death and cold princesses.

He stayed late into the evening, until she was a whimpering mess, unable to cry because she was too dehydrated.

Finally, as Wulf had to send for a torch as the sun sank below the horizon, Alerik got up.

As he walked past his second, and Wulf, he whispered. "Prepare the ship. Tomorrow she sails."

Wulf shuddered.

Ashta sighed, her mind finally releasing her to a deep sleep.

CHAPTER TWENTY-FOUR

⌘

Moss and Steel

THE FIRST THING ASHTA noticed was the cold stone under her hands, rather than the hard packed earth.

She pushed off the ground to sit up in the darkness. Before she moved again, she looked down at her hands in amazement. The ropes were gone. So were the deep welts from the rope, replaced by soft scars and faint lines of blue.

Frowning, she rubbed at her wrists as something tickled the back of her brain.

"Darkling?" a familiar lyrical voice called out.

Ashta gasped, scrambling up from the floor.

It couldn't be! Ashta had watched her die!

And yet, as she scrambled to the door, she could hear Ceerie's' clear voice calling out again, "Darkling?" followed by a slight whimper.

Ashta pushed against the large wooden door, shocked that it easily gave way. She didn't think about it, her feet taking her straight to the chamber beside her own.

The door was slightly ajar.

Again, she pushed against it without any resistance.

Her eyes took a moment to adjust to the darkness of the chamber. It was exactly like the one she had, except for the small pallet in the corner and the body huddled into the corner.

Ashta fell to her knees and pulled Ceerie into her arms. "It's okay," Ashta murmured, her heart aching, "I'm here. I'm here…"

Ceerie's lithe body had grown thin, her bones poking into Ashta's flesh. Her gossamer white hair hung in limp clumps around her face, shorn to her shoulders. Ashta could feel each of her friend's vertebrae as she rubbed her back protectively.

Slowly, Ceerie's shaking subsided and her whimpering calmed. Ashta could feel her friend relax. And it was then that she noticed Ceerie's arms curled around her wide stomach.

Ashta blinked several times. She had never seen Ceerie pregnant. *Had she?*

Before she could ask it aloud, Ceerie grabbed Ashta's hand and laid it over the taught skin. It was warm. Hard. Unnerving.

And then it moved underneath Ashta's palm.

Ashta gasped, trying to pull away but Ceerie had a vice grip on her wrist.

"Promise me," Ceerie whispered, her moss green eyes shining with an unearthly glow.

Ashta tried to look away but couldn't. Her tongue was stuck. No words would come out.

"Promise me!" Ceerie demanded, her face shifting into a cruel glare. Her teeth were bared, a growl leaving her throat, reminding Ashta of the wolf fur with red ruby eyes.

"Promise me…"

Ashta heard her friend's voice as everything faded around her. She reached out, uselessly, trying to grasp the warm flesh of her friend.

But nothing could bring her back.

"Ceerie!" she called into the oppressive darkness.

But there was no echo. The darkness swallowed her voice as it pressed down on her throat. Hot tears pricked her eyes but could not fall.

"Ceerie!" she screamed again.

And then Ashta found herself standing in the desert. Sand dunes stood around her, tall as mountains, almost touching the sun. A single palm tree could be seen in the distance.

Rubbing her arms at the strange cold, Ashta began walking.

She tripped over a rock, her hands coming out in front of her to catch herself. She gasped when she saw her hands.

Blood.

But whose? And from where?

She looked down at herself and realized she was naked. Her body was covered in blood and soot and something else. Something that burned hot on her skin and the more she felt it, the dizzier she became.

Shaking her head, she stumbled to her feet and continued to the tree.

"Ceerie!" she called, but her voice broke, hoarse from use.

The sand dragged at her feet. Each step she struggled to pull her foot up. Crying, with fear, with heart ache, Ashta closed her eyes and dropped to her knees.

"I'm sorry," she whispered, the sob wracking her body.

Something soft brushed against her arm.

Ashta looked up and her gaze was caught by familiar golden eyes.

The lion. From the test.

As the thought crossed her mind, the roar of the crowd broke through her focus.

In shock Ashta looked up and realized that she was back in the pit. But this time, she recognized the on lookers. There at the top, sat King Roman. His eyes cold. The barest of smiles crossed his face. Beside him, sat Carien. Her caramel eyes glittered like amber jewels.

Not understanding, Ashta stood, reaching her hand out to the princess.

But the other woman's gaze was as cold as her kingly father's.

She will never trust you again.

Ashta looked around, her eyes wide with fear. "Who said that?" she whispered, her gaze searching for someone, anyone who was close enough to hear her words. But all she saw was the lion. Who also did not look like the tall, proud animal she had met in the pits that day?

This lion was gaunt, his ribs protruding. His thick mane was matted, and his eyes sunken in.

Let her go, came the rough voice, edged with a growl.

Ashta shook her head. No, she thought, this wasn't possible. She could not hear his thoughts.

Look inside you, child.

But she only shook her head, stumbling backwards and falling hard on her tailbone. The whites of her eyes flashed, no sounds came to her throat.

The lion sniffed, taking a slow leisurely step towards her. Ashta shivered at his rough tongue on her toes.

This wasn't real, she told herself, this cannot be real.

The lion snorted, his gaze flicking up to hers before turning back to the stands. *If you will not look inside, then look around you.*

Despite her fear, she did listen to the lion, following his gaze. Her eyes landed on the familiar group of lionesses.

There stood Kkaar and Lucy. In the back, standing on someone's shoulders, was Trice. Her hands were around her mouth, as if she was trying to call to Ashta. But Ashta could hear no noise.

The ground began to shake.

The roar of the crowd died down to absolute silence. So quiet that Ashta could hear the clang of swords. The thud of a thousand footsteps.

The hairs on the back of her neck stood on end, but she could not stop herself from turning to the other side of the pit.

And there, clothed in furs, war paint streaked across chests and faces, stood the Bbrskian army. Berserkers with swords out. Their wide smiles filled with glee and malice. And standing above them all was her father.

King Alerik.

But unlike his army, he had no sword. He wore a simple peasant's shirt and pants. His steel gaze blazed even from this distance. For the first time, Ashta could feel his emotions. His hate, his fear. And deep down, so far that she thought it was no more than a drop, was guilt.

She blinked up at the nightmare before her. The Bbrskian army to her left. The Tripsian court, all of the white lionesses, all of the people she loved, stood to her right.

The lion nipped her toe, bringing her attention back to his skeletal face. *Now do you see?*

Before she could ask, the lion crouched, a deep growl rumbling through his chest. And then he pounced on her.

Without thought, without time, she closed her eyes and rolled aside.

And fell into cold water.

Spluttering, she waved her arms and legs, not able to find up from down. She opened her eyes and closed them against the brilliant light.

A pair of warm hands gripped her arms. With a strong tug, she was pulled out of the water. Ashta fell against the lush green embankment, coughing water.

"Than-Thank you," she growled, looking to her right.

A flash of familiar green eyes peered down at her. But these were set off by the darkest hair Ashta had ever seen. It was as if the woman's – or mans? – hair sucked the very light out of the forest.

Before Ashta could say anything more, the – *thing?* - scuttled into the foliage and disappeared, leaving Ashta alone.

She rubbed her eyes hard. Her temple ached, as well as her heart. She could not seem to understand what was going on. Where was her father? The army?

And had she really heard the thoughts of a lion?

Shaking her head and realizing she could not feel the familiar weight of her hair, Ashta reached up to her scalp. Her fingers rubbed against soft stubble, feeling along her scar-ladened scalp.

Frowning. Ashta reached down and realized that her whole body was covered in a mass of scars.

"What the…?" she asked aloud, her breath rattling through her still sore lungs. Completely naked, her skin was a mess of mottled red and blue and white. Some of the scars were old, their edges deep. Others, her hand ran over and felt only smooth skin, but had coloured the skin to the point of being unrecognizable.

Fear drove Ashta to her feet, as she looked away from her strange appearance and focused on the thick leafy forest surrounding her. Some of the trees looked familiar, like the palm fronds of the oasis. And others, whose leaves were dark hearts the size of her head, had Ashta backing away in fear.

Her foot crunched over rock, her heel sinking past the grass. She turned and took in the small blue pond. The water was crystal clear and yet she could see no bottom.

Svetlana, a voice like a thousand screaming men, the roar of lions, the screech of eagles, the crash of the ocean, called out.

Ashta jammed her hands over her ears. But it was no use as the voice echoed through her soul.

"That's not my name!" she cried out. "I am no longer the heir!"

The water began to shimmer, a fog appearing in the center. Rising up from the centre was a woman, her skin dark as the raw earth, her hair the soft yellow of the desert grass. Her face was too bright for Ashta to look upon. Ashta squeezed her eyes closed as tears streamed down her cheeks.

That may be, the voice whispered. The words rattled through Ashta, shaking her to her soul. *But you are my daughter.*

Molten hot hands cupped Ashta's cheek. And then a hot streak brushed across her forehead.

For a moment her heart was filled with warmth. With the protective embrace of her own mother. The smell of lilies wrapping itself around her soul.

You have travelled long but it is not quite time, yet.

Before Ashta could ask, the heat wrapped around her. She felt as if she was boiling alive. She screamed out for help, but no sound left her throat. Her eyes burst open but only darkness met her.

As the heat increased, and Ashta thought surely she would die, it disappeared.

Blinking hard, she realized that she was in the tower again, but it was darker. The shadows wrapped around the walls and the crevasses, reaching out to her.

Scared, Ashta slammed through the door and into the room beside. But it was empty. She checked the next room. And the next. But all were empty.

Panicked she took the spiral staircase down.

No, she thought, I can't be too late.

But dread filled her stomach as the steps wound deeper and deeper into the darkness.

"No!" Ashta screamed, as the last light from the tower was swallowed by shadow.

A moment passed. A flash of light.

Ashta stumbled from cold stone to hot sand, her eyes stinging from the too bright sun.

Before her stood Ceerie, a white shift floating about her quaint limbs.

"Ceerie!" Ashta called, walking out into the sand.

But the other woman did not turn around. A pride of lions paced before her. The gaunt male stood at the centre, his piercing gaze on Ashta.

He licked his lips.

In horror, Ashta watched as Ceerie's figure bent down. Ashta tried to run to her, to save her from her death. Ashta's hands were outstretched but never came closer to the other woman and the lions.

And then Ceerie stood, turning away from the lions.

Ashta stilled.

Green eyes like the forest shifted to a familiar steel grey. Ashta could only stare as the woman that had been Ceerie looked with King Alerik's cold eyes at Ashta.

"You promised," the strange woman growled, her voice like Ceerie's. But her mouth was too wide. Her chin to sharp.

The NotCeerie ran at Ashta, a sword brandished in her hand. Ashta ducked, feeling the cold wind of the blade pass her cheek.

It was then that Ashta noticed the small bundle in front of the lion. Her eyes widened as Mina whimpered. The soft cry grabbed the attention of a dozen hungry gazes.

"No," Ashta whispered, as she ducked the next swipe and pushed past NotCeerie's gaunt body.

The lion glanced down at the pale babe before looking at Ashta.

Ashta cried out, the hot slice of metal cut through her legs cutting her down. She fell helplessly, her hands just catching her.

"No…" she whimpered, as a shadow fell over her.

The lion leaned down, sniffing the soft skin of the newborn.

Mina's whimper grew.

Ashta watched as the lion opened its great mouth, its teeth sharp as they came down over Mina's small head.

NO! Ashta screamed, her soul splitting into a thousand pieces, her gaze going red.

"No," Ashta moaned as she sat up from the hard ground. Her eyes felt crusty. She tried to clear them, but her hands pulled uselessly against rope.

A dream, she thought. Shaking, she sobbed in the early morning light. Her heart pulsed with pain. The feeling grew and grew until Ashta worried that she would be swallowed by it

Please let it be a dream, she prayed, as her tired mind dragged her back down into sleep.

CHAPTER TWENTY-FIVE

⌘

Dead Eyes

KING ALERIK RETURNED in the early morning. The arrangements had been made. The ship was ready. The only thing left was the cargo.

Wulf and Kirill walked behind him, the other guards were left outside of the tent this time. Wulf rubbed his head; the ache having gotten stronger overnight. He noted the dark circles underneath Kirill's eyes. And the soldiers. His instincts screamed at him. But he pushed it down. To not follow the king would be to sign his death. And he couldn't do that to his daughter. His life was the only thing keeping her in relatively good care.

Alerik stepped inside and watched Svetlana's curled form with satisfaction. The mind was a tricky thing. Which was why he toed her shoulder. When she jerked her shoulder away from him, he growled, "Get up."

She twitched, rolling onto back her eyes opening slowly. Her black gaze was dull and lifeless. Alerik smiled. "I said, get up!" he commanded.

And with great effort, with three men watching her, Svetlana rose. Her legs were shaking from weeks of minimal use. She stood before him, her back straight, her eyes cast slightly down. The perfect soldier.

Alerik rubbed his mouth to hide his smile. To use Tripsia's own hand to strike its head off was beautiful. Poetic even. He could not have planned it better himself.

And he hadn't.

Ever realistic, he had various other plans in motion. Starving the city. Storming the city. Laying siege to every estate along the coast until all were under his thumb.

This one had been a lark.

But it gave him great joy. The same joy he had felt for the first time in his young life as he watched the life leaving his brothers eyes.

Alerik turned to Wulf. "Take her to get cleaned up. Clothe her and arm her."

It was Kirill who stepped forward, shocked. "Your majesty, you can't-"

Alerik turned his back on the girl, cutting Kirill off. "I am king. And I have given you an order," He said with a meaningful look at Wulf.

The other man nodded slowly.

Alerik turned to his second, already calculating how to be rid of the man. His use as a great strategist was invaluable. But Alerik didn't need people with opinions around him. And not ones who questioned his command. "You would do well to remember your place, Kirill," he whispered.

The other man gulped, otherwise his face stone still.

He turned back to Svetlana, reaching out and pulling her chin up until she was forced to look into his eyes. Beneath the dead gaze was a kernel of rage. The same rage that would wash over his berserkers in battle, making them uncontrollable killing machines.

"We have intercepted a Naankdoen spy," he said the words low so only his daughter and himself could here.

She watched him. Or stared through him, more accurately.

The king continued; she kept her gaze on his. "Princess Carien has not left her quarters in days." And then leaning in to whisper directly in her ear. "Rumor is King Roman had ordered the babe killed. Quietly."

Rage and hate washed over Alerik.

Wulf and Kirill gasped.

Stumbling back a step, Alerik quickly rubbed his head and gained control again. He watched the woman with wary eyes suddenly.

He nodded to Wulf, who stepped forward, and with the slightest tremble in Wulf's hands, the man cut the girls bindings.

Her hands dropped to her sides, tight fists. Her eyes never left Alerik's. Waiting.

Alerik placed his hand on her shoulder, surprised at the heat of her skin. Looking deep into her eyes, in a low tone, he said, "You are to silence the King and his heir." Her eyes sparked for a moment. Alerik leaned closer, whispering, "The heir is no better than her father. A heartless ruler with an iron grip, playing with the people's emotions to get the support they need in this war." The spark fizzled out and Alerik continued. "Kill the King. Kill the Heir. Make them pay."

The storm of rage that surrounded him was absolute. Flashes of things he had not seen went through his mind – a throne room, a whip, sand walls, golden eyes. And then everything quieted as suddenly as it had come over everyone.

She nodded slowly.

With nothing else to say, Alerik nodded to Wulf. "Have her fitted and fed."

He turned without a backward glance. He didn't need to look. His control over the girl was absolute. And he knew with complete certainty that she would follow through with the order. With the King and his heir dead, Alerik knew the people would finally give in.

Kirill quickly followed the king out, leaving Wulf alone with the girl.

Her eyes were blank, unfocused. Wulf shivered. He wasn't sure what had come over him, but he knew that the sooner the woman was off the island the better.

"Follow me," he growled, turning to outside. He glanced back once, surprised that she was only a step behind him, her gait strong and sure despite not having eaten in weeks.

The few soldiers still on guard duty stepped back, eyes averted as Wulf and the girl passed. Indeed, even as they walked through the crowded tent city towards the supplies tent near the pier, the soldiers gave the girl a wide berth.

A silence he had never heard seemed to have fallen over the island. No one dared to speak, or laugh, or breathe.

By the time Wulf and the girl made it to the supply tent, they were alone once more. "Stand there," he pointed to the entrance, disappearing inside.

He came out briefly with a fresh flask of water and some dried meats and fruit. He held them out.

At first the girl didn't move.

"You need to eat, or you'll pass out before you get in the palace," he growled.

She stared through him for a long moment. Right as he was about to drop it onto the hard background, she reached out and took them.

He waited until she placed a piece of meat into her mouth, chewing it mechanically before taking a sip of water. With a nod more for himself than for her, he returned inside.

He quickly pulled out a set of trousers and shirt for the young boys. It would fit her well enough, a little short was better than too much cloth that could trip a man. Next were the leather cuffs, vest, and boots. He glanced back at the girl and switched out the boots for a smaller pair as well.

He unloaded the haul on the ground, noting her hands were empty again, the flask thrown carelessly on the ground.

"Dress."

And this time she did not hesitate. He watched her for a moment, uneasy with her fluid motions. Was this the same woman that had been left to starve bound to a pole the last weeks?

Another thought crossed his mind. *Who was she really?*

At the thought she looked up, mid tying of her cuffs. It was the first time an awareness was in her eyes as she looked at him. Really looked at him.

Wulf quickly turned back to the tent, his legs shaking as he went to the weapons. Out of her sight, he quickly crossed himself and sent a quick prayer up to the great gods.

He grabbed a short sword out of a barrel. He turned around and jerked to a stop.

Surprise froze him.

The girl stood right in front of him. Her steps had been so quiet that his years of battle instincts had not heard it.

She took the sword from him, her other hand outstretched for the scabbard. He quickly passed it to her before taking a step back and crossing his arms – more to hide his shaking fingers than anything.

Without looking up at Wulf, she asked in a dull tone, "And what else?"

At first, Wulf did not understand what she was asking. She glanced behind him at the wall. His eyes widened with understanding. With grunt he shook his head. "That's all you'll be needing."

She looked at him again. The dull look was familiar to Wulf. He had stared across from that look for decades. Which was why he kept his stance firm.

When she didn't look away, he leaned forward. "You only need one blade to kill a king."

For a moment her eyes flashed before returning to their dull glaze. Wulf wondered if he had even seen it.

The girl nodded once, slowly. The sword rested comfortable at her hip at odds with her baggy clothing. She looked like a youth and yet had the aura of a berserker.

She would survive the men just fine, he thought darkly.

"Follow me," he called as he left the tent and went out to the pier. Only one ship was loaded, men leaning on the rails, ready to be off to sea.

As Wulf and the girl walked past, the men watched the pair wearily.

Wulf didn't stop until he stood beside Captain Prohor. The other man looked at him before glancing at the girl.

He quickly returned his gaze to Wulf. "General." He gave a quick nod in respect to Wulf.

"Captain," Wulf replied with a nod.

"The girl comes with, King's orders. Keep your men away from her," he warned needlessly, the other soldiers avoiding looking at the girl as they moved as far from the bow as they could.

Prohor nodded his agreement.

Wulf glanced out into the horizon to the north. Somewhere out there, his people were waging a war. Swords clanged and hearts bled.

Without another word, Wulf turned and left the ship. He watched several soldiers cross themselves as they threw weary glances at the wraith that stood beside the captain.

"Anchors up!" Captain Prohor called.

The men jumped into action. Within the hour they were at sea, Aishma a distant spec behind them.

The girl had not moved an inch from the bow. Her arms hung loose as she stared unseeingly at the island.

"You'd best be getting down underneath for some sleep and a meal. We'll be joining the rest of the fleet at Trian in two days' time."

The girl looked up at him, her black gaze piercing yet familiar. He shivered but kept his back straight. He'd captained many a ship, moving berserkers from one raid to the next. He was familiar with their mindless bodies.

Without a word, she turned on her heel and disappeared below decks.

Prohor resisted the urge to cross himself, instead focusing on the waters ahead, and the dark clouds from the east. It looked like they would be sailing straight into a storm.

Several of the sailors stepped out of the way of the wraith as she walked with sure steps to the kitchens below. She filled her bowl and ate without thought. Her movements deliberate. Nothing more. Nothing lingering.

Yevgraf watched her with fascination. He had volunteered to go on the ship destined for Tripsia. It was either this ship or stay longer on Aishma.

Shivering, he shook his head to release the memories of night terrors and focused on the woman instead.

He had heard whispers through the camp of the witch. But she looked like his mother had before Yevgraf had been stolen from his family to join the war.

Skinny but arms that were strong with years of hard work. Pale skin that was splotched from sunburns over the years. The only thing that gave Yevgraf pause was the strange blue markings on her hand and the wrapped braid that resembled a conch shell.

"Oye, boy, best get down under and get some sleep. You're on deck in the morning," Prohor, said with a slap on Yevgraf's back.

Yevgraf nodded, quickly cleaning his bowl, and disappearing to the hull where the sleeping hammocks were. The smell was strong, the heat almost unbearable. The hairs at the back of Yevgraf's neck rose as his heart picked up speed.

He couldn't stop from checking around him. Had Vladislav made it on the ship? Were these men any better?

Instead of taking one of the empty hammocks, the boy crawled behind the bag of supplies. He pulled his short knife out, his back against the ship wall. Slowly the rock of the water pulled him into sleep.

Gasping, Yevgraf sat up, sweat trickling down his back. With wild eyes he looked around him as his trembling hands brought the knife in front of him.

But no berserker stood over him.

After a couple of seconds, he calmed down enough to hear what had woke him.

Thud.

Then a groan.

Too scared to try and sleep, Yevgraf crawled out of his space to peek out of the supplies.

At first everything looked as it should. His eyes used to the darkness below could make out several lumps in hammocks.

But then he noticed an arm hanging awkwardly from a hammock. The steady drip of something hitting the galley floor. The tangy smell of blood hit his nose at once.

Before Yevgraf could back into his hiding spot, he caught movement near the other end of the galley. Another inaudible thud.

Shaking, Yevgraf pressed his back into the ship holding his knife in front of him, silent tears streaking down his cheeks.

He had hoped getting off the island, being free of the berserkers, would save him. He had ignored the rumblings from some of the older soldiers, the crossed marks across chests, the pounding in his head. Anything had seemed better than staying on shadow island.

Suddenly, something stood across from his spot. A flash of the moon on a blade lit up black eyes and pale skin. Yevgraf closed his eyes, hoping it would be over soon. At least the pain would finally be done.

But nothing happened.

After a long minute, he finally opened his eyes.

The woman was gone again.

After a long night and most of the morning of drifting in and out of a light sleep, Yevgraf finally dared to move. His stomach growled and his bladder hurt. He carefully crawled out of his spot. The floor of the galley was slick in spots, sticky in others. He ignored it, instead focusing on getting above deck.

With his knife leading him, trembling from his nerves, he stepped out into the late day sun. *Shouldn't someone have come for me?* He wondered.

Gulls cried above. The ship swayed softly in the waves. As Yevgraf looked up he couldn't help but notice the almost clear sky.

Hadn't the soldiers talked about a storm coming in today?

He walked to the starboard side and saw with amazement the short slip of beach. And the cliffs behind.

"What th-"

A rough hand covered his mouth. And then darkness.

The next time Yevgraf awoke, he realized he was no longer rocking. He squirmed to sit up, the scratch of sand against his hands odd.

And then he realized his knife was gone.

Scrambling to his knees, he patted his shirt down before sifting through the sand around him.

"Here," a quiet voice said.

Blinking several times, Yevgraf looked up into black eyes.

With an impatient wave of the knife blade, the woman continued holding the handle out to him.

Yevgraf grabbed it before turning the knife back at her.

She looked down at, her eyebrow rising but no other words.

"Wh-where am I?" he choked out, his throat dry from days of no water.

The woman turned without answering, walking up the beach towards the cliff face.

Yevgraf looked around himself for the first time. Sharp rocks stood out in the beach with low shrubs rising up until to the bottom of the sheer cliff face behind him. In front lay the calm blue waters of the ocean, the only break in the cloudless sky coming from smoke.

Squinting, Yevgraf could just make out the masts of the sails sticking out. *The ship...*

But if it was out there, burning, how had he gotten on land? And where were the soldiers?

Fear, true fear like that which followed him in the night, crawled up his back. His eyes widened as he tried to make out where the woman was. He started to run in her direction, stumbling as he went.

"Wait!" he cried out, hot tears streaking down his cheeks.

The woman whipped around, her half sword outstretched and stopping him mid step. He glanced down at the sharp edge, flecks of black and red still visible on the smooth surface.

"Please," he begged, falling to his knees. "Please just kill me."

Yevgraf was ready to die. He had wanted to for months now. With the ship burning and the soldiers gone, he knew there was no way for him to survive. Not in a kingdom he knew nothing about.

And he couldn't return to his own people because they would mark him as a deserter.

He waited. And waited.

When he finally looked up, the woman was crouched in front of him, also frowning.

"You can't come with me." Her voice left no room to argue.

"I can't go back!" his voice shook with fear as stories of what happened to deserters flashed through his head. He shook his head as tears continued to run down his face. "I can't." His voice broke.

The woman turned away, facing the ocean for a long minute. With a sigh and a drop of her shoulders she looked back at the boy.

"Go up the beach, away from the sun. You will come to a shack. An old man will be there. He will take you in." She stood up and continued up the beach, towards the sun.

Yevgraf watched her back until she disappeared.

Then he got up, the tears finally having stopped, leaving behind streaks of dirt on his cheeks. With a sniff, he turned in the opposite direction of the woman and began the stumbling trek up the beach.

CHAPTER TWENTY-SIX

⌘

King and Heir

AS SOON AS THE BOY was gone, Ashta focused on the beach. In her head, her father's words kept repeating themselves. *King Roman had ordered the babe killed.*

Slowly, over the night as Ashta took one soldier after another's life, the words had shifted. *King Roman killed Mina.*

Green eyes looking up at her, accusation and hurt warring with each other. *You promised.*

Shaking her head, Ashta focused on the mission. Kill King Roman. Kill Carien. Leave no witnesses.

The last her father had not said, but Ashta didn't care. She knew well enough that he had wanted Ashta to lead the soldiers inside the palace. But a part of her, the only part that still held any warmth, remembered that Kkaar was still in the palace. She was the only person left that Ashta cared about. And she had been guileless in the King's machinations.

Caramel eyes battled with green eyes.

Carien.

Shaking her head again, Ashta focused on the cliff face ahead of her and the shadow that marked the entrance into the palace.

She easily slid past the crevasse, not bothering to trail her right hand along the cave wall. Confidence, and something else, told her which steps to take.

She easily walked up the pitch black tunnel, bending over once and picking up the dagger that had been there a year ago. In one sweeping motion, she stood and tucked the blade in her hair.

The sound of crashing waves quickly dissipated to a hollow ringing, leaving behind the chatter of drips from the moist cave walls.

Either a moment or hours passed when Ashta reached the end of the hall. Her legs burned from so much walking. Her eyes were weighed down, having not slept in days. But the fire within pushed on. She needed to kill the king. She needed to keep her promise to Ceerie.

And a hint of fear reminded her that she did not trust what she would see in her next dream.

Shaking her head, she stepped out into the main on silent feet. Ashta glanced to the right. Not far down the hall were Luci and Kkaar, guarding the gates to the lion pits. She could feel them, their thoughts were fuzzy, as if both women were standing inside a fog.

The sensation was unlike any of the soldiers on the boat, or from shadow island. The men's thoughts had been clear, ringing, constant. Their emotions bright spots that were impossible to ignore.

Even her father's thoughts had been crystal clear. She grimaced at the memory of seeing her dead mother's body splattered on the ground.

Stealing a quick breath, Ashta turned the other way.

A stabbing sensation, like a prick of a needle, on her conscious shook her. But it was too light to burst through the fog of her own thoughts, and the one thought that kept circling her mind.

You promised.

Ashta snuck down the hall, her steps quick and deliberate. Unlike last time, there were no soldiers walking the halls. There were no lionesses in the training complex. There was no one down in the depths of the castle except for Kkaar and Luci.

Ashta's skin chilled at the reasons why, but her mind pushed on. She hopped up the fourth hallway and climbed the winding stairs without hesitation.

At the top, she collapsed at the entrance of the deadly hall, her lungs begging for breath. She gave it to them, her nose filtering in the new smells of fresh turned earth, ripe bodies that had not bathed in months, and the familiar tang of fresh blood.

Once her breathing slowed, and the stitch in her side dissipated, Ashta stood up. Her legs wavered before locking. There was no time to wait. It needed to be done now. Her body was starting to slow from the weeks of starvation at her father's hand.

She crept along the side of the hall before sneaking up the steps. All her senses brightened as she realized that the main door was slightly ajar rather than locked from the outside as it should have been.

Pushing down the shivers at the back of her neck, Ashta pulled the door just wide enough to slip through before closing it soundlessly behind her.

Now that she stood in the main palace complex, voices began to filter through the halls. The palace was otherwise quiet, a brief respite from the constant bombardment during the daylight hours. Even the formidable Bbrskian fleet, the Black Death, needed to rest and gather supplies.

Blinking, Ashta easily slipped into that strange place in her mind that had unlocked during her time on the island. The sun would be rising in a few hours. How she knew she could not stay long.

She waded even deeper into the fog and felt the soft haze of the thousands of thoughts around her. Sleeping.

A few bright spots were in the haze. Soldiers. Lionesses. Guards.

Ashta clenched the handle of her half sword, the only link to her time on the island. She carefully slid it away, leaving her hands free.

Torches lit the way as Ashta snuck towards the closest bright spot. In one of the gaps between the torches, just a few paces of shadow, Ashta flattened herself against the wall.

Her body vibrated as she listened to each careless footstep. Not a lioness.

By the time the man was close enough to notice her within the shadow, Ashta wrapped her arms around his neck, choking him, as she kicked his knees out.

Despite her shaking limbs, she was able to slowly pull him to the ground. He wriggled for long minutes before finally his hands fell away from her arms and his mind fizzled. She loosened her hold.

Listening with both her ears and her mind, she waited. No one was coming. A couple of bright spots were near a corner, but no one moved toward this hall.

With a quick breath, she stood, quickly taking off the man's clothing, switching it for her own. She strapped the leather breastplate and back plate together, then the leather shin guards and arm guards. She switched her scabbard and half sword for a pair of knives from the man. Surprisingly, he wore a bronze helmet over his head, protecting his nose and neck.

Just as Ashta settled the still warm helmet over her head, the man began to move. His chest rose with a quick breath.

Before he could sit up Ashta was crouched over him, her knife at his throat. Blood trickled from a thin line at his Adam's apple. Dark eyes glared up at her.

"Don't scream or you'll be dead before the first word gets past your lips," she hissed.

The man looked into her black eyes, fear slowly slipping inside his mind, its cold tendrils taking over reason. He swallowed nervously, the knife pushing deeper into his skin.

When he gave the slightest nod, Ashta pulled the knife back far enough to no longer have the blade kissing his skin.

"Where is the King?" she demanded in a low voice.

The man stayed quiet as he looked up at her. The fear grew larger, but at the back of his mind was a thought.

I can't tell him. I'm not a traitor.

She quirked an eyebrow. Clearly the man had misidentified her.

With a subtle movement, she pressed a second blade into his chest. Her first blade slid up his throat, lying flat to his chin. She tipped his head up, stretching his neck.

"I said. Where. Is. The King," she emphasized, each word by digging the knife in a little deeper.

The man closed his eyes, quivering now, but still he made no move to talk.

Frustrated, rage poured through Ashta. In a move that felt both foreign and natural, she tipped her forehead against his.

The moment her skin touched his, she was hit by every thought he had, everything he had seen, every word he had heard. Tears pricked at her eyes as blood slowly trickled down her nose. With unseeing eyes, she quickly shoved through the memories, sifting until she found what she was looking for.

Bryant smiled at him, slapping his back. "To be on king's duty. Who would have imagined, Farrio?"

I smiled back at my good friend despite the jealousy that wormed its way through my guts. It should have been me on guard duty. Not Bryant.

A cry of warning from down the hall broke through the memories. Without thought, Ashta shoved the second blade deep into Farrio's chest. The man's eyes widened.

Before any words could pass his lips, she slashed his throat, then jumped back on her heels.

The clatter of armor as several soldiers ran towards her was deafening in the stone walls. Ashta grimaced, a flicker of regret passing through her before she shut it down. Cold purpose seeped into her limbs, pushing thought behind. All that was left was instinct. And a ringing voice.

You promised.

Turning, Ashta threw the first knife even as she reached down for her half sword.

The first soldier fell to the ground, the man behind him stumbling before continuing. Ashta threw the second knife. It hit its mark, lodging deep into the throat of the third soldier.

Leaving only Ashta and the second soldier.

Ashta raised the half sword over her head, stilling crouching, blocking his first blow. She slid to the side and stood, stumbling as her legs screamed at her. The second soldier quickly raised his sword and swung at her.

They parried before she ducked under, her reflexes still strong as she came up with her other hand and the short knife she had found in the secret passageway to the beach.

The man's eyes widened before he stumbled back in shock. Ashta ripped the blade out, her sword quickly coming up and in a single blow punched through his chest, skewering him on his knees.

He fell, still clutching his chest, eyes wide.

Shouts rang in the hall. Ashta could feel several bright points nearing her.

Without time, she shoved the knife under her arm guard and quickly pulled the knife out of the first soldier's throat. She hid it in her other arm guard.

Then she turned around and ran down the opposite way of the hall, popping out into the courtyard that was still lush with greenery. The night air was sticky, hitting her like a wall. But she ducked down, waiting for the group to pass.

As she waited, her mind sifted through the bright points, looking for Bryant.

All of the rooms that had once lined the cliff face were devoid of life. Ashta wasn't sure, but it felt like some sort of wall separated the outer rooms to the inner rooms of the palace.

Likely the King would be somewhere in the centre, not to close to the trebuchets from the water, but also not to close to the army of Bbrskian soldiers that sat above the palace.

There. A man looking to his partner.

"I got to piss. Be right back," I throw over my shoulder, not bothering to see if Bryant agreed or not. New guy would get used to it soon enough.

Besides, we're useless here what with the King having two lionesses inside the room.

Ashta quickly homed in on the bright light, turning her head as she mapped out the halls towards the room. It had been part of the lesser nobilities' rooms. Far from the kitchens. And the infirmary.

That was fine, Ashta thought as the grass under her chin tickled her nose. Crouching low, she quickly moved through the courtyard, entering the halls from the other side.

She moved quickly, keeping out of the way of people. The alarm hadn't made it to this side of the palace yet. But it would soon.

When she came to Bryant, she snuck up beside him, slitting his throat before he could turn and see her.

Knowing her time was limited before the other soldier returned from his leisurely walk to the kitchens, Ashta pulled the body aside and laid it gently on the floor, out of sight.

Then she slipped into the darkened room. The only light came from the raging fire in the fireplace.

Without thought, she threw her first blade in the direction of the foggy beacon.

The lioness twitched from where she had been resting against the wall, the handle lodged in her throat as she silently choked to death.

Unfortunately, the other woman noticed Ashta immediately, her sword out as she came at the dark-haired woman. Ashta reached her other arm guard and pulled out her last knife. She threw it, but the other woman ducked, the blade harmlessly flying over her head and lodging into the wooden four poster bed.

Ashta got her half sword up in time to block the first blow from the white lioness. But she knew that she didn't have much time. The other woman was stronger, faster, and well rested. There would be only one chance.

On the second blow, Ashta checked her shoulder against the other woman. Both lost their balance and fell to the ground, their swords clattering out of their reach.

The silence was filled with grunts as either woman tried to get a chokehold. They grappled, until Ashta found herself losing air as the woman had her in a choke hold.

Desperate, Ashta felt around until she found a blade handle inside the woman's leather pants. Ashta threw her head back as the same time as she blasted the other woman's mind with the cold memory of the lion coming at Ashta.

The woman hesitated, her arms slackening in shock for a moment.

It was enough.

With her other hand wrapped around the handle, Ashta pulled it out and threw it behind her.

The blade lodged into the other woman's throat.

Ashta grimaced as the woman choked, blood gurgling past her lips. Slowly, her arms and legs released Ashta until the woman fell back into a pool of her own blood. Her eyes were wide as she looked up at Ashta, recognizing Ashta for the lioness she was.

The woman's death brought no satisfaction to Ashta. She pushed off the ground and grabbed the bloody half sword. Taking a step, she gasped in surprise as pain sliced up her leg. She turned back in time to see the woman fall back, the blade that had been in her neck wrapped around her hand. It clattered to the ground.

In shock, and anger, Ashta whipped around, and with one hack took the woman's head off.

Ashta's left leg felt as if it was on fire.

But there was no time. Ashta could feel a bright spot coming towards the King's room. The four dead soldiers from earlier must have been discovered.

Limping, Ashta slowly made it to the bed, the curtains an dark silk, impenetrable to the flickering light of the fire. But Ashta could feel the mind on the other side.

With a swipe of her bloodied blade, part of the curtain fluttered to the ground. There, laying in the middle of the bed, lay King Roman.

Gone was his silk turban and crown. His cheeks and eyes were hollowed from the weight of the war. His long bony fingers clutched a short dagger flush to his chest. Gone were the loose silk pants and shirts, instead a simple silk robe, loosely tied at his waist covered the king, protecting his modesty.

Ashta stared at him for a long minute. Eight years ago, she had not thought she would be standing here, killing the man who was responsible for so much pain in her life. The same man who gave her a new purpose in life.

His breathing shifted, his eyes fluttered open. He turned his head and his familiar grey eyes gazed up at Ashta.

There was no shock. No fear.

Just quiet acceptance.

Ashta could not stop her mind as she saw his wife's lovely face cross his thoughts, so similar to Carien's.

Shaking her head, not wanting to feel his love, his quiet happiness, Ashta gripped the sword handle with both hands and swung.

His head rolled off the bed and hit the floor, his eyes closed in peace.

But death was not instant. Ashta felt his shock of pain. And then his final thoughts. *I will be with you soon, my heart.*

Shouts from the hall reverberated through the room.

With no time, tears she could not control streaming down her face, Ashta ran out of the room and into the adjoining servants' quarters. She dropped the sword on the ground and grabbed the thick cloak laid out onto the bed.

She pulled it over her head and ran to the door. The moment she felt the bright spots of people enter the main bedroom of the king, she eased the servant's door open and ran down the halls.

The fear of being caught dampened the pain from her leg, allowing her to run swiftly through the halls, despite the bloody trail she left behind her.

Quicker than she had expected, Ashta found herself in the infirmary. She dropped the cloak to the ground. Her hands gripped the warm metal of her helmet and readjusted it.

The room was dark with the exception of a single lamp.

The healer looked up to see who might need her in the middle of the night. Her eyes watched a limping Ashta warily. She quickly rose from the bed she had been hovering over, leaving the lamp on the ground.

She took two steps, Ashta crossed the rest, her arm swinging around the woman before a cry could leave the healers lips.

Slowly, Ashta brought the woman down to the ground, her arms loosening as the woman's still body fell the rest of the way. Ashta didn't bother to check her heartbeat because she could feel the fog of sleep clouding her mind.

With quick jerking steps, Ashta moved to the corner where she felt the familiar edge of minty Ruutka and the crisp shock of glacier water. Until this moment, Ashta had not realized that she had felt Carien in this way.

The thought had her hesitating, her blade outstretched.

And in that moment of quiet, where the world was still asleep, and dreams kept chase through the halls of the palace, Carien flipped over on her cot.

And Ashta was faced with bright, moss green eyes. Vibrant and dark like the oasis at night with a full moon hanging high above.

The blade slipped from Ashta's grip and clattered to the ground.

She winced at the sound, stumbling back from the cot.

A couple spots in the room brightened up, the fog of sleep dissipating at the noise.

Ashta turned and stumbled the rest of the way out of the room. Her breath wouldn't return, leaving her gasping as stars glittered at the edge of her view.

What have I done?

CHAPTER TWENTY-SEVEN

⌘

Last True Friend

THE WALK WAS A blurry haze. Her instincts were the only thing keeping her alive and outside of discovery of the many soldiers in the halls.

Ashta stumbled in a daze, her world off kilter.

The moment Mina's eyes had connected with hers, Ashta realized what she had done. And what she could never undo.

The fog of her father's words and his persuasion were lifted instantly, but it was to late. King Roman was dead. Tripsia would be racked in turmoil in a time when they could not afford to be. Would the council take over? Would Carien be forced to step up?

Carien.

Horror and shame washed through Ashta's body at the realization she had almost killed the princess. Her charge.

Her chosen sister.

What kind of person was she?

Ashta's hands shook as she pulled herself along into the depths of the castle, not recognizing where she was. Or caring. She let her feet lead her while her mind swirled around and around.

I killed the king.

Suddenly, her stomach flipped, and she turned, falling to her knees, puking up what little food she had eaten on the ship. Her eyes stung. The acrid taste of puke lingered.

Bodies passed around her, not noticing a dirty soldier, thin from the war rations. Ashta was invisible.

Luckily.

Shaking her head, she stumbled back to her feet, the pain from her leg coming back in full force. She limped, leaning heavily against the wall.

I killed the king.

Just outside of the fog of shock and horror sat something bigger. Something that threatened to break the woman.

But she hid deep inside her mind. Ignoring all and everything except for the physical pain. The pulse of heat in her leg kept her alive. And moving.

"Who goes there?" A voice broke through the haze.

Ashta blinked several times to clear her vision. Coming towards her was Kkaar, her familiar warm complexion and round face, her brown eyes warm with concern.

Frowning, Ashta looked around herself and realized she was in the hall that led towards the lion pits. How did I get here, she wondered as her leg finally collapsed underneath her?

She barely caught herself on the wall, sliding down the rough stone. She left a bloody trail as she landed hard on her ass.

Kkaar stumbled, doing a double-take of the soldier. Familiar black eyes flashed from beneath the helmet.

Not a soldier. A woman. Darkling.

"Luci, with me!" Kkaar called out as she skidded to a stop in front of her long missing friend. She quickly fell to her knees, ignoring the sharp jab from the rocks below.

Her hands shook as she grabbed the helmet and gently lifted it off the other woman. Darkling groaned, her eyes squeezed shut as her head fell back against the stone. Her hair was limp and matted. There were deep bruises under eyes. Her cheekbones stood out in sharp relief, from weeks of hunger.

Kkaar gave her a gentle shake. "Darkling," she whispered, while her eyes tried to find an injury.

Luci skidded to a stop beside Kkaar, frowning down at the woman passed out against the wall. Her eyes quickly tracked the bloody trail behind Darkling, then caught on the blood soaked pant leg.

She crouched down and carefully pulsated around the leg. When she pressed near the deep cut, Darkling's eyes flew open as she gasped.

Frowning, Luci said, "She'll need stitches. It's deep."

Without another word, Luci got up and ran down the hall.

Kkaar stared after her lover.

Ashta reached up and grabbed Kkaar's hand. "Kkaar," she whispered.

The other woman blinked several times before focusing on her friend's face. Her black gaze threatened to swallow Kkaar whole, the pain reflecting in them deeper than Kkaar had ever imagined from her friend.

"What happened Darkling?" Kkaar asked, the shock of seeing Darkling finally wearing off as the questions rushed to the surface. "It's been months…" she added, looking down at Darkling's battered nails.

Ashta swallowed, shaking her head in hopes of clearing the fog. But all she could see was little Mina. And the king's head rolling across the stone floor.

Her hand tightened on Kkaar's arm, threatening to leave bruises.

"Kkaar, promise me."

Kkaar frowned. She stared at the hand before looking up into Darkling's eyes. For the first time, she saw the edge of fear ringed around the other woman's normally confident self.

The hairs on the back of Kkaar's neck rose. Something wasn't right.

Something was terribly wrong for her incredibly strong friend to be almost shaking with fear.

"Anything," Kkaar whispered, her gaze shifting back and forth into Darkling's eyes.

Ashta closed her eyes, seeing the trust and feeling her friend's warmth and worry. She didn't want to ask her this. She didn't want to know how true of friend Kkaar was, when all Ashta did was hurt the people she was supposed to care for.

With a shuddering breath, Ashta made a decision. Carien wasn't safe. Especially from Ashta herself. With a trembling voice, Ashta asked, "Promise me you will sneak Carien and the babe out of the palace."

Kkaar fell back on her ass, the movement breaking the contact between Darkling's hand and Kkaar's arm.

Ashta dared to open her eyes. Her friends normally warm complexion was pale as her mouth lay open, no words coming forth. Even her mind was blank.

Squinting, Ashta wished fervently to just shut it off. She had lived her whole life without this constant awareness, why did it suddenly come on now? And why couldn't she stop it?

Instead, Ashta pushed off the wall and shakily got up on her two feet.

Kkaar quickly bounced to her own feet, her hands out to either catch Darkling or push her back down to rest. She wasn't sure which she wanted to do more.

"I don't understand," Kkaar said, her voice flat with shock.

Ashta fell back against the wall, letting her head lean back to rest. With her eyes closed, she tried to explain as best she could. "The princess is not safe in the palace. The assassins-"

Kkaar cut her off. "The princess is constantly surrounded by people. She is always with either Ennris or one of the other older white lionesses. Even the King has Kkell and Pria. No assassin will get past-"

"They have!" Darkling shouted, her eyes flashing with anger and something else.

Kkaar took a step back, shocked at her vehement response. She frowned as she tried to connect what Darkling was saying. "But it's not possible…"

Ashta stepped away from the wall, her body vibrating with anger and purpose. She needed to protect Carien. She needed Kkaar to take the princess far away from the palace and the imminent threat of Ashta's father.

"Kkaar, listen to me," she grabbed onto Kkaar's shoulders, both to steady herself and to grab the other woman's attention.

Kkaar slowly lifted her chin to look at Ashta. Once her warm gaze was on Ashta, Ashta continued, "I need you to get them out of the palace and to the Alpen people. She will be safe there. They both will be."

She waited, looking into both of her friend's eyes. Kkaar still wavered, her duty as a lioness at war with her loyalty to Darkling and Carien.

Then her gaze slid past Ashta, to over her shoulder.

Ashta already knew Luci had returned, her brightness impossible to ignore. The sting of jealousy and suspicion strong.

"It looks like we don't need to stitch that cut up," Luci's voice dripped with sarcasm.

Ashta dropped her arms from Kkaar's shoulders. Luci stepped past Ashta, her shoulder purposely shoving hard against Ashta as Luci stepped up into Kkaar's arms.

The bigger woman took her lover into her arms without thought, her eyes still on Ashta. Her thoughts shifted before loyalty finally won. Kkaar gave Ashta a slow nod.

"I'll do it."

Ashta breathed out a sigh of relief, the energy releasing from her as she stumbled back against the wall.

Frowning, Kkaar pulled out of Luci's arms. "But first we need to fix that leg."

Luci stood rigid, her glare on Ashta palpable as she asked in a deadly whisper, "Do what?"

But no one answered her. Instead, Kkaar fell to her knees again and pulled up the pant leg. "Pass me the thread and needle, love. And the Ruutka."

Luci hesitated for a long minute. Kkaar turned and glared up at her, barking her name. "Luci!"

Still frowning, she kneeled beside her lover. Together, they quickly stitched up the cut and cleaned it as best they could.

Ashta sighed as the cooling effect of Ruutka numbed her to the physical pain. Ruutka helped, but it did nothing for her emotional pain.

Done, the three women walked back to where Kkaar had the great sword leaning against the wall to the nearest gate.

"I'll stay here," Ashta said, finally breaking the silence that had fallen between the three women.

Luci frowned but didn't say anything.

Kkaar nodded, picking the great sword up with ease before holding the pommel out to Darkling.

Ashta stared at the pearl, the awareness of it washing over her body in waves. It both lulled and awakened her. Her mind quieted from its pain and focused on another emotion. One it had experienced often.

Revenge.

Ashta shook her head once, her hands in tight fists at her sides.

Kkaar frowned. "To protect the gate," she said, her chin nodding to the still closed gate behind her.

"I can't," Ashta gritted out.

Luci stepped forward, "You were the one who asked us to watch the gate. We have been down here for *months*. If you're not back here to protect the princess, then why are you here?"

"Luci," Kkaar admonished, her hand holding the sword lowering as she turned and placed a hand on Luci's shoulder.

They shared a look.

Luci took a deep breath, the tension releasing from her shoulders as she turned blank eyes on Darkling.

Kkaar watched Luci's face for a long moment before also turning to Darkling. "Something is coming," Kkaar said rather than asked.

Ashta nodded slowly.

Kkaar sighed, looking down at the sword again. "You should take the sword then. I don't know what is going on, but you need something to fight this war."

Again, she held out the sword.

Ashta was tempted to take it. To feel the strength of it wash through her body. To have the memories running through her veins as she fought better warriors then herself and killed them with ease.

Her fingers on her right hand even uncurled themselves.

But she couldn't.

King Killer.

The thought whispered across her mind and had her face crumpling in pain.

She stepped back from the pair and violently shook her head, her gaze never leaving Kkaar's. "I have no place amongst the white lionesses. Not any longer."

Kkaar dropped the sword to her side again, her other hand sliding off Luci's shoulder as she stepped towards Darkling. Something in her eyes, a familiar shame, similar to what Ceerie had once held inside, now looked out from Darkling's black gaze.

But Darkling did not want her comfort, taking another quick step back from Kkaar as she continued to shake her head.

Kkaar opened her mouth, forgiveness and acceptance on her tongue but Darkling spoke quicker.

"I cannot return, Kkaar. I have done something unforgivable." And then, shocking both Luci and Kkaar, Darkling added in a quieter voice, "Please."

Kkaar stopped moving, trying to find answers in Darkling's face. It was then she really looked at Darkling. The baggy shirt that hung off of her sharp shoulders. The tension that vibrated through her body.

In this moment, Darkling stood tall and stoic like the day she came to the cubs in training. Much had happened in the months since Carien's mysterious return through the tunnels with a crying Mina.

The woman that had left to save the Tripsian princess had been strong. Determined. Duty bound.

The woman that stood before Kkaar now was still strong, but there was another feeling that came off her in waves. A cloudy uncertainty.

Kkaar slowly nodded. Then, before anyone could speak, she crossed the space between her and Darkling. She grabbed the back of Darkling's head and pulled her close until their foreheads touched.

Too surprised, Ashta closed her eyes and simply breathed, comforted by the warmth and closeness of her friend. Enveloped in her kind thoughts.

"You are Svetlana the princess of Bbrski. You are Ashta the Lion tamer and white lioness of the Princess Carien. You are Darkling, stronger, faster, smarter than the rest of us." And then she whispered across Darkling's lips, "No matter what you have done, remember, you are my family. And I will love you. Always."

They shared a breath as both women fought back the tears of the moment.

Ashta sensed that this moment was likely the last time she would see her friend. There was no place in Tripsia for Ashta.

With a shaky breath, Ashta replied, "Always."

Kkaar let Ashta go and stared at her face. Ashta also tried to memorize Kkaar's face. The laugh lines around her mouth, the little crow's feet that had already deepened around her eyes. The twinkle in her brown eyes.

With a nod, more to herself than to the other woman, Kkaar turned away from Darkling. She ignored the questions in Luci's eyes, instead grabbing her hand and pulling her along. Luci for once stayed quiet, knowing Kkaar would speak when she was ready.

She looked over her shoulder once. Despite her jealousy of the other woman, all Luci saw was a woman tired and broken, and incredibly alone. Luci gripped Kkaar's hand tightly as she turned back and followed her down the hall and into the bowels of the palace.

Ashta took a deep shuddering breath, letting the emotions of the moment wash through her. Everything felt so final. For the first time in years, she didn't know what to do next.

Her mind wandered and she watched dispassionately as bright lights lit up in the palace. And then lights in the distance. Behind her.

She turned slowly towards the ancient gates that lead to the three different lion pits that lay in the midst of the ruined city of Trian.

With trance like slowness, she went to the wall, pulling the handle out and turning it completely.

Click.

Silence.

Then the slow creak of chains as the gate slowly raised up from the ground before disappearing into the darkness above. Ashta hesitated for a moment, staring into the darkness, then down at the corpse on the ground that leaned against the wall. The fur covering the head was beaded with moisture, looking as fresh as the day it had been skinned. The skin underneath had tightened until the face was unrecognizable.

A Bbrski berserker.

Ashta stepped towards him, leaning down and carefully prying the man's half sword out of his mummified hands. She stayed there for a moment and just stared at the body.

Months had passed.

With a quick breath, her mind already forming around anew call, she went to the next gate switch.

She was already a king killer. What was one more king to her?

CHAPTER TWENTY-EIGHT

⌘

The Lion Pits

NIKANOR LOOKED OVER at the other men around the fire. Tomorrow they would storm the Tripsian palace. The land trebuchets from Malten had finally arrived, after weeks of travel across the jungles of Kae ol and then by sea.

General Yustin had already warned the soldiers to not drink too much because at first light, the trebuchets would begin the bombardment on the west well. And when it crumbled, Nikanor and his men would be there, running into the fray.

He took another sip of the harsh whiskey before passing the flask to Samuil who sat beside him. All the faces around the fire were grim. Not a one could sleep.

General Yustin turned to the other generals in the tent. All of them leaned over the best map they could make from their scouts reports through the ruined city. All the scouts that had been sent from the cliffside never made it back to the camps.

"I want the archers covering our men. They will still be at an advantage, having the wall as their coverage. Our men will be going in blind."

"Not for long," General Arhip grumbled.

Yustin turned to him with a quirked brow.

Arhip coughed before gesturing to the side of the tent.

The two men quickly stepped outside while the rest argued on how many men should be placed where and when.

In the cold night air, Arhip leaned into Yustin, speaking almost inaudibly. "One of our scouts saw a woman from the beaches disappear into the cliff face east of the palace. We've sent a small contingent to investigate…"

Vladislav smiled grimly as the boat crashed through the stormy waves. His three brothers smiled as well. The glittering eyes of the furs on their heads matched the dead looks in the men's eyes.

Finally, the rough scratch of sand on the haul shook the boat.

Vladislav turned to Alexie who stood beside him.

The other man pulled out a short dagger with a wicked curve at the end. He took the blade and slowly sliced down the middle of one cheek. Then the other. Alexei smeared the blood in two lines across his forehead and down his neck.

Vladislav reached down to his own dagger and followed suit.

"For the dead. For the living. We are the goddesses warriors," Vladislav chanted.

The other men joined in, louder and louder until some signal had them standing up as a one. They jumped into the icy cold water and trudged up onto the rough beach.

Adrenaline shot through Vladislav's body as he looked ahead with glee. The corners of his vision darkened to red as his mind emptied of thoughts and memories, leaving behind an unquenchable lust.

Kkaar leaned over the princess's body, gently shaking her shoulder.

Carien sat up quickly, jostling Mina. The young child cried out, pulling out of her mother's arms, and sitting up on her own.

Kkaar reached down and pulled Mina into her arms, the child snuggling into her shoulder. Carien frowned as she wiped her eyes free of the last dregs of sleep. And the strangest dream.

"What is it…" she asked, her voice scratchy.

Kkaar held a hand out to the princess, which Carien took automatically, standing up.

Kkaar pulled the princess through the infirmary, all around them men and women slowly rousing from sleep to another day at war.

In the hall, Carien jerked Kkaar's arm back as she looked up into Luci's familiar cold gaze.

With confusion, she looked back up at Kkaar, her mouth opening.

Kkaar interrupted her, "We must leave, your highness."

When Carien still did not move, Kkaar hitched Mina higher up. Before she could say anything, shouts from down the hall rose up. The clanging metal and screams of confusion had Kkaar, Luci and Carien tensing up as they stood outside the infirmary.

Luci grabbed the princess's arms and pulled her with. "We go. Now!" she hissed, Kkaar already leading the way opposite of the noise.

Carien shut her mouth, following the woman even as she looked back to see what the commotion was about.

General Yustin watched as the rest of the generals filed out of the tent. Before he could turn back to the map, a commotion at the tent flap had his mouth dropping open in shock.

King Alerik, with his dark crown glinting in the candlelight stalked into the centre of the tent. The other men returned back to around the map, all glancing into each other's face.

Yustin quickly shut his mouth before falling into a quick bow. "Your majesty," he breathed out, keeping his eyes down as he waited.

Alerik glanced around the room until every man bowed down, eyes averted. With a grim smile, he spoke with certainty, "Tomorrow we will take the palace."

Yustin frowned. While they planned to take down the wall today, he knew there were to many soldiers behind the wall that were ready to fight to their dying breath. It would not be easy to capture the kingdom. Or its king.

King Alerik stepped forward to the map. Then with a quick flick of his hands he stabbed the centre where the palace was marked on the map with a short dagger. "King Roman is dead. Tripsia is ours."

A low grumble filled the tent.

Yustin rubbed his beard, looking down at the map. He had heard no such news. The palace so far had been impregnable. How could king Alerik be so sure the Tripsian king was dead? Had one of their spies gotten through?

Ashta shook her head. Her father was here. Standing somewhere above her. And she had given him the key into the palace. Shaking with anger, at herself and at her father, Ashta stalked forward to the next door switch and twisted it with a violent jerk.

She ducked under the metal trellis as it continued to rise. She stalked past multiple bodies of the rest of the berserker group that had tried to sneak into the palace months ago.

Spikes of brightness ahead had Ashta grinning with grim determination.

She stopped and turned back to the bodies, scanning them with cold eyes. She quickly pulled out several daggers from their pockets, and one that had been resting in the hollow chest cavity of a soldier splayed out in the middle of the hall. Ashta placed a dagger down each boot, ignoring the tug on the stitches of her leg. The third dagger she placed on her belt, wishing it were small enough to put in her hair.

As she returned to the final gate, she slipped a half sword out of the soldier's hilt. She grabbed a second half sword from the next body. Ashta placed it into her own hilt, the other sword still in her hand, ready.

With a quick breath, she pulled and twisted the final switch before quickly stalking into the middle of the gate.

Click.

Silence.

The creak of rusted chains shifting. The trellis slowly rising.

A shout.

Another shout.

Smiling to herself, Ashta ducked under the gate and came face to face with a tall soldier. Behind him she saw another man, except furs were pulled over his head.

Bbrski berserker.

Good.

The first man ran at her, sword outstretched.

But Ashta was ahead of him, already ducking under his arm, her sword arm coming up with deadly accuracy as the soldier impaled himself on her blade.

He gasped, his dark eyes widening in shock and recognition. His lips pursed as he tried to warn the other two men behind him.

But it was to late.

Ashta's motion continued as she released the sword, letting the man collapse to the ground on it. With her other hand she reached for the dagger.

The berserker, shock shifting quickly to anger, pushed up from the wall, a blood cry leaving his lips and reverberating in the small stone enclosed hall.

Ashta threw the dagger quickly, already reaching for her half sword. She just barely got the blade up to stop the berserker from his first blow.

She smiled with satisfaction as the light of the third soldier behind the berserker quieted. She briefly let her gaze fly past his shoulder to confirm the death. The soldier lay back against the wall, eyes wide, the hilt of her dagger glinting wickedly in the torch light.

That brief look gave the berserker an advantage, as he came in close and smashed his fist and hilt against her sword hand.

Grunting, Ashta dropped the half sword. It clattered to the stone ground, ringing with finality. The berserker's eyes lit up with victory as he reached out to grip her neck in one hand, sword hanging to the side in the other hand. Another lust blazed in his eyes as he stared down at her feminine face.

Ashta growled, pulling her knee up quickly into his groin and smashing her fist into his chin.

The berserker dropped his sword as pain briefly flashed across his face.

Ashta ducked down, whipped a dagger out from her boot. The man grabbed at her. She twisted, tripping him to the ground.

He reached out and pulled her with him.

For a brief moment, fear flashed through Ashta. And pain from her leg.

Her dagger fell just outside of her reach. The berserker saw it as well.

They briefly grappled with each other. Ashta used her smaller size to get around onto his back. She pulled out her final dagger and quickly slid its sharp blade across his throat.

He choked, his hands desperately reaching back behind him. Ashta shoved off of him and rolled away before crouching. Her leg screamed in pain. Likely she had ripped some of her stitches.

Grimacing, she panted and watched the other man. Slowly his arms stopped moving. Then he stilled. The light went out.

Dead.

Ashta spat the blood in her mouth to the ground, ignoring the acrid flavour at the back of her mouth. She could not afford to puke. There was already nothing in her stomach.

She rose quickly, stumbling as her head spun briefly.

With a deep breath, she straightened and then walked with a distinct limp down the hall. She recognized the walls. The stench of sweat and horses. And something else.

A smell that she had been close to only once. With it came something else. It seeped through the stone walls, hungry and desperate. Whispers crossed her mind, their jagged edges unlike the berserker's minds.

These were the thoughts of something else.

Ashta stumbled through the now pitch black space. Somewhere on the wall was the switch that would open the fighter trapdoor to the pit.

A growl rumbled through the darkness, setting every one of Ashta's hairs on end. Her eyes widened as she slowly turned to an area she had never been to before, far from the horse stables and the infirmary. And yet so close to the pits.

Ashta turned back, the fizzled out torch the berserkers had lit was several lengths away, the flame gone.

Shaking, she turned back and walked through the pitch black until her hands met with rough wood. She slowly felt her way down until she found a wooden slat. She pulled the board up and pulled the entire door open.

Moon light from above filtered through the same mirror system as the infirmary where she had gotten her fateful tattoo. Ashta stared around her with wide eyes.

Lions.

Big tawny eyes watched her from all angles. Over twenty males and females paced in their enclosures.

Ashta took a tentative step further into the room. Her eyes glided over their emaciated forms, the saliva dripping from their mouths as they took her in.

She stepped up to the first cage where two large males laid, their heads resting on their crossed front paws. She could feel their hunger, but beneath that, Ashta could also feel their fear. And their anger.

They wanted revenge against their keepers. The men who abused them, who barely fed them. And who had left them to starve here beneath the pits, majik keeping them barely alive.

Ashta nodded once.

A low growl left the first lion, the one closest to her. The male rose onto his feet before stalking towards her. Ashta did not move as he came right up to the metal poles, his breath stinking of rot and death. His growl shook the night. His mouth fell open as he tasted the air.

Then silence.

He sat back on his haunches and watched her.

Ashta reached to the side, noting the cages had the same opener as the gates that cut the pits off from the palace.

Even with the exhaustion of the last day weighing on her – the last weeks – the realization that the pits were likely a part of the original palace, before the rainforest had disappeared, disturbed Ashta.

Had there always been lions in the pits?

No.

Her eyes widened as she watched the male. Shaking, she reached out and turned the switch before pulling it.

Click.

As one, the rest of the lions in the other cages stood up and began pacing.

The two in front of her waited as the trellis slowly rose before disappearing into the stone ceiling.

She waited. Watching.

The male lay back down and huffed, nodding his head to the other lions.

Ashta nodded.

She turned and opened the five other cages.

When she returned to the first male lion, the rest of the pride paced behind her. Waiting. For her.

The male slowly rose to his feet.

Out. They needed to get out of here.

Ashta searched the walls, until she saw a lever, similar to the lion cages. She limped over to hit it, feeling the hot blood of her wound dripping down onto the stone floor, and twenty lions watching her back. Growling.

She turned the lever, then pulled it down to slip it over a hook.

Snick.

And the hiss of sand shifting.

Slowly, the ceiling lowered. When it was to her chest height, she quickly unhooked the lever, stopping the platform.

Silence.

And then the male lion padded past her and jumped onto the platform. Ashta winced at the movement, feeling the clang of the male's bones inside of herself.

He hesitated before jumping all the way out onto the sandy pit floor. The rest followed, until it was only Ashta standing in the dark room.

She clambered onto the platform, her arms shaking from exhaustion. Sweat dripped down her back. Her mouth was dry. And her skin crawled with the itch from weeks of dirt and hours of blood dried on her body.

She shakily climbed the rest of the way until she stood once more in the centre of the lion pit.

How many years had it been since she stood here, a young girl forced to make a choice that wasn't really a choice? The moon shone bright, lighting the white sand. She smiled as her gaze caught on the rough wooden ladder opposite of her.

The lions prowled around the pit, growling, their eyes darting everywhere. Only the large male watched Ashta with curiosity.

Ashta limped to the ladder. She gripped the edges, and then, with gritted teeth, she climbed. When she finally stumbled to the top, she was panting. Her entire body trembled. But not with exhaustion.

As she stepped past the lip of the pit, she stared with shock at the sea of tents before her. The Bbrskian army.

Creaking behind her had Ashta turning in time to catch the large male hop onto the packed dirt beside the top of the ladder.

His eyes were silver disks in the night, cold with determination and hatred.

He slowly stalked forward until he stood right beside her, his gaze on the tents. The ladder shook as the other lions followed suit.

Ashta turned, her gaze falling back on the sea of white. In her minds eye it was a cloudy fog filled with bright spots, like stars in a night sky.

The male growled, the sound shaking through the air and tingling Ashta's core. Without thought, she placed her hand on top of the male's head.

He fell silent mid growl.

And then a different rumbling began in his chest. The male leaned into Ashta's hand as the pride lined up around them, all watching the tents with hunger.

Ashta's fingers slid across into the male's mane, combing it as she watched. And rested. The purr of the male soothing her thoughts and her pain.

In the east, the horizon lightened with the oncoming morning.

CHAPTER TWENTY-NINE

⌘

Chaos

THE LIONS WIND THEIR way closer to Ashta's body, licking her arms, her fingers clean. Ashta felt their rough tongues, their strength washing through her despite their hungered state.

She bit her lip as she stared over the sea of tents. In the distance she saw movement close to the western wall of the palace. Hollowness filled her chest as she began to stumble forward into the encampment.

The lions made a semi-circle around her, keeping close. The male stayed on Ashta's left side, where her ankle throbbed. She gripped his mane to steady herself.

Slowly, they walked across the dirt packed ground, a light wind lifting the dust and sand from the desert beyond up into her face.

As they reached the outlying tents, Ashta watched curiously as the tent flaps swayed in the wind. Nothing living moved among the tents.

When she came to the first one with a foggy light inside, Ashta ducked inside the tent. The male lion settled on his haunches at the flap, waiting for her.

Ashta padded as quick as her leg allowed across the floor. She spied the sword on the ground. The berserker lay on his back snoring loudly as drool dripped down his cheek.

Ashta grabbed the sword. Without any hesitation, with both hands on the handle, she swung hard, his head rolling off, eyes still closed in sleep.

A growl rose from the lions outside the tent.

Ashta wiped the blade on the man's body before checking the corpse for daggers.

Only one. It would do.

Before she left, she turned and spied a flask. She swiped it, sniffing first before chugging down the entire contents in one. She immediately bent over, coughing, the heat of the whiskey spreading its insistent tendrils from her belly outwards.

Grimacing, Ashta crawled along the floor until she found a second flask. This one with no smell. She drank it just as quick, the water sitting like a rock in her belly.

Suddenly, the hunger that had always been there came to the foreground. Shocked at her own growl, Ashta tore through the bags until she came upon some dried meats.

She shoved a piece into her mouth, shoving the rest of the bag into her pocket.

One of the lions loosed a low yowl that set the hairs on the back of Ashta's neck standing.

She quickly rose, swaying at the rush from the whiskey. Shaking her head, she walked confidently towards the tent flap and out into the beginnings of a sandstorm.

Ashta smiled.

Perfect. Her father could control much, but not the weather.

Taking a deep breath Ashta turned towards the north, her eyes tracking the sand dunes. But nothing moved. A dark cloud slowly rose from the North east. The heat of the oncoming storm blew into Ashta's face, a welcome warmth.

For a moment Ashta thought she heard something on the wind. A voice, its low tones tugging on her heart. And her memories.

Frowning, she shook her head and turned back to the male that stood at her side. He chuffed, turning back to the tents, his gaze focused beyond the ancient city towards the walls of the palace.

Ashta turned as well.

Gripping the male lion's mane, they began walking again, towards the ancient crumbling wall of Trian, and the palace beyond.

The soldiers that were still left in the tents surrounding Ashta and the lions had been left behind. The main force was ahead of them, gathered at the west wall. Ashta was sure of it.

Today her father would try to take the palace and gain a stronghold in the Midloean kingdoms. And Ashta would be there to do everything she could to ruin her father's plans.

She stalked through the barren city streets, the burn of the whiskey now tingling across her whole body. Her head spun as the world seemed to tilt a little. A giggle fell from her lips, though she felt no joy.

The lions spread out, some disappearing into buildings. Only the male stayed closed to Ashta, her sole companion in her march to deaths door.

A thud reverberated through the air.

Frowning, Ashta jerked to a stop and looked around herself in confusion. *What was ...*

Another thud. This time followed by the unmistakable roar of screams.

Ashta's heartbeat picked up. *Was she too late?*

She let go of the male and began running through the streets. The lions kept pace, jumping from roof to roof, bounding through the streets. Their feral hunger surged through Ashta, as her fear energized the pride.

With each thud of the trebuchets, Ashta pushed herself harder. Faster.

There wasn't time.

Just as the walls of the palace came into view above the crumbling buildings, the chilling battle cry of the berserkers rent through the morning air.

"No!" She growled in frustration.

She veered right, into a dark alley. Her mind was alive with light, blinding her to the darkness surrounding her. She tripped, her knees skidding across the street, ripping her pants open.

The male lion growled in frustration as he came to her shoulder and nudged her. Ashta scrambled up and continued running, this time with a hand in the male's mane. Her steps were weary, her head spinning, as she desperately sifted through thoughts and feelings.

And then the first wave of berserkers clashed with the soldiers on the wall. Ashta no longer was sifting but swimming through the bombardment of pain and fear and lust.

Her eyes stung as blood slowly dripped from her eyes and her nose.

Light ahead warmed the stone road. Ashta and the pride turned and suddenly came upon the rear right flank of the Bbrskian army.

The sheer volume of men, and their incessant thoughts, had Ashta falling to her knees clutching her head. It was too much, she screamed to herself as blood dripped from her ears.

The male rubbed his nose on her forehead before chuffing his hot breath over her. The lights dimmed slowly, until Ashta could finally open her eyes again. Dimly she felt the rub of furs against her back as the pride converged together. The male gently licked the blood off Ashta's face before nuzzling her shoulder briefly.

Ashta gripped his mane with both hands. "Thank you," she breathed out.

His chest rumbled in reply.

Ashta's smile wavered.

A horn blew into the air.

Looking up, Ashta watched as dozens of soldiers lined up along the remaining wall, their bows nocked as they carefully let loose their flaming arrows. The ground suddenly lit with fire, separating the berserkers fighting in the rubbles of the wall from the majority of the army.

The horn blew again, and from the east, flowing through the palace gates, were dozens of riders.

Ashta blinked in shock, and then realized it wasn't just Tripsian soldiers. The riders were white lionesses.

The men closest to the horses turned and began to run to the palace gates. Ashta watched in horror as hundreds of men shifted their aggression from the wall to the women.

There were too many of them.

And there were girls riding amongst the lionesses. Cubs with barely a year of training.

Growling, Ashta stumbled to her feet. She picked up the half sword she had dropped. And then, she let loose a might war cry, louder than humanly possible. The male lion joined her, his roar reverberating through the air, followed by twenty other lions.

The back half of the army, several dozens of soldiers turned in shock behind them to see Ashta, her sword raised, followed by a pride of blood thirsty lions.

It was chaos.

A red haze creeped over Ashta's vision as she ran towards the men, and sliced into the first soldier. She was already past him, stabbing into the man behind him, the crunch of bone behind her letting her know the male lion was right behind her.

The rest of the lions spread out into groups of three or four, picking off the soldiers that were brave enough to raise their swords and fight.

Ashta left the lions behind, cutting her own path of destruction through the men.

The lionesses on horseback crashed through the first wave of soldiers. Men screamed in agony as hooves connected with bones. Ryce and Penny led the charge of women, their spears bloody as they stabbed down into the men below them.

The younger girls watched with wide eyes, gripping their spears tightly. Blood splattered across their faces, across their mount's backs. The stink of sweat had several girls puking over the sides of their mounts.

Penny screamed as a hulking man with a battle axe slammed into her horse. The animal screamed as it stumbled. Soldiers from the other side quickly cut into its legs.

Grimacing, Ryce dropped her spear and jumped off the back of her horse, her hands already pulling out her swords. She screamed as she ran at the nearest berserker.

He smiled.

From the wall, the Tripsian soldiers struggled under the onslaught of the blood thirsty berserkers. General Driet yelled out commands to the men who stood with swords ready, knees shaking, watching the battle in the wall.

Around them women screamed, and babes cried as civilians tried to run as far from the battle as they could. The crowds crushed bodies. Boys lay whimpering on the courtyard grass. Women screamed as hands slipped into skirts and knives slid between ribs.

Driet growled in frustration watching the pandemonium around him. Where was General Ttaabit?

He grabbed the nearest boy. The child's face blanched as he looked up into the general's cold face.

"I need you to get a message to the council," he barked.

Before he continued, a court soldier, out of breath and panting came up behind him. Driet spun around. His instincts screamed at him even as he shut his emotions down. "What?" he bit out, his eyes assessing the berserkers that were beginning to get through the rubble and inside the wall.

The soldier panted several times, before finally saying, "The king is dead. The princess is missing."

General Driet swore as he focused on the soldier again. He grabbed the man's shirt and lifted him up to within an inch of his face. "What did you just say?" he hissed, dread dropping like a cold lump in his stomach.

The soldier's eyes widened until the whites showed around his irises. He stuttered again, "Th-The king is dead. The princess is-is missing."

Driet swore again and dropped the soldier.

He took a quick breath, feeling the gaze of the few dozens of men who were the final wall between the Bbrskian army and the rest of the kingdom.

"What about the council," Driet finally asked, icy calmness flooding his veins.

The soldier nodded several times. "They are in the council rooms now, general Ttaabit is commanding the palace guards as we speak."

Driet nodded once. The war was not lost yet. There was still reason to fight.

Before he could turn his attention back to the wall another soldier came from the palace, his head bloodied, his left arm hanging limply from his side.

Driet frowned.

Before he could ask, the man spoke. "Berserkers in the palace. In the tunnels. Need more men to fight in the palace, head them off before they get to the infirmary."

General Driet quickly glanced back at the dozens of men, barely able to hold their swords. Knowing there was nothing else he could do, he called out to the first dozen by name. He pointed to the bloodied soldier. "Bbrskian in the palace. Follow his orders. Go now!"

The men's faces paled as they ran after the soldier towards the palace. Just over fifty men were left in the small courtyard, eyeing each other worriedly.

General Driet turned to the wall. The fire line was slowly dissipating, the oil used up. Soon, they would be over run. He turned to his men.

Ashta growled, her sword easily slicing through the berserkers unarmored chest. Her arms shook.

Another man replaced the one who fell before her. She grabbed her dagger and threw it past him as she slid across the ground and hacked the man's legs off. The soldier behind him clutched his throat as he stumbled into the man beside him before collapsing.

The growls and roars of lions surrounded Ashta on either side. Men screamed as they were ripped apart from limb to limb.

Slowly, the Bbrskian soldiers backed away from the wall of lions and into the western flank with the trebuchets. Ashta turned towards the west, her eyes catching the wave of a single flag.

Her father.

She turned back to the soldiers around her and was surprised the men backed away, swords up in defense.

Frowning, she turned further, seeing the wave of horses pushing past her and towards her father. A dozen women still rode their mounts as they hacked at the men below.

A flash of milky white stilled Ashta's heart.

No, she thought, squinting ahead at the women who were getting increasingly closer to the trebuchets. Past them, the fire line around the fallen palace wall was slowly dissipating, but no Bbrskian soldiers moved towards the walls.

The berserkers, their furs unmistakable, ran with glee towards the women on horseback.

But otherwise, the more Ashta looked around the more she saw men lowering their swords. And then a break in the line as dozens ran back into the crumbling ruins of the city.

Ashta's gaze did not falter from the woman. Her heart beating fast, she ran behind the trail of bodies left by the horses, blood rushed through her ears. Another flash of milky white, a spray of rainbow in the dissipating sun.

No.

Ashta stopped mid run as she pulled inside of herself. The male lion ran to her, circling her as he growled at any Bbrskian soldiers who dared look her way.

"Slow down!" Carien hissed as she clutched Mina inside her cloak.

But Luci ignored her words, pushing their mounts faster through the barren city streets. To their left, flashes of the sea speckled with ships could be seen. To the right, the sky darkened with an oncoming sandstorm.

They needed to be past the ancient city walls before the storm hit. There were safe huts on the old trail to the alps that would protect them.

Luci swore as she eyed the storm and then the mass of bodies fighting on the wall. She should have fought Kkaar harder. But she couldn't say no to her lover. The need to make her proud stronger than her duty to the Tripsian royalty.

Yet here she was, running from the battle, protecting the princess. By herself. She wasn't the princess's white lioness. Darkling was. Darkling should be here, Luci thought bitterly as she squeezed her mounts sides hard.

"No…" Ashta gasped as she blinked, seeing the mass of arms and blood and men around her.

Kkaar was supposed to go with Luci and Princess. She was supposed to be safe.

The male lion let loose a roar. The soldiers around Ashta fell back, in shock and fear. Ashta blinked again, her hand tightening on her sword handle as a flash of opal could be seen above the fray.

Kkaar was in the middle of the battle. And just above the mounted lionesses, Ashta could see her father's flag.

It was too late to swear at her friend. Kkaar needed Ashta. Now.

Ashta's emotions slid off her like sweat, leaving cold determination behind. Her whole body vibrated as Ashta took off at a run, stumbling over bodies, chasing after the mounted lionesses.

CHAPTER THIRTY

⌘

Darkness

C*LANG!*
 Ashta's teeth shook from the berserker's great sword connecting with her half sword. She was as surprised as he was that her sword did not break on the impact.

Before she could move, the male lion lunged past her and sunk his teeth into the berserker's neck. The man thrashed, the sword useless in close combat as it smacked the lion.

But the male had already released the berserker and returned to Ashta's side.

Those that had seen the attack watched Ashta wearily, crowding in from behind but not making a move on her. She gritted her teeth, as she stumbled past the still breathing berserker. She lifted her sword with both hands and speared him through the heart. His light went out instantly.

Ashta rose on shaky legs, her arms strained to pull out the sword from his chest. She fell back and tripped over another body.

A Bbrskian soldier lunged forward, sword swinging.

The male lion pounced on the man.

His screams were drowned out by the clang of swords and thuds of bones breaking.

Ashta blinked and tried to rise up.

Another soldier was before her, his axe coming down on her. She closed her eyes, hand outstretched, waiting for the pain.

None came.

Ashta opened her eyes to a lioness, her spine split as she held onto the soldier's head while the light went out of her eyes.

Ashta stumbled over to the lioness, pulling out her dagger. With a quick motion, she killed the animal. Its eyes closed.

The rest of the pride felt the loss, a growl reverberating loud enough to be heard above the din of the fighting.

More men slowed their motions as they realized that they were at war with more than just men.

Ashta took a deep breath, then pushed off the females back to stand. She ripped a half sword from the body beside the lioness and rushed forward again.

"With me!" cried a familiar voice ahead of Ashta.

She glanced over in time to see a flash of the silver great sword and brown hair towering above the men and women.

Ashta didn't see the sword coming at her until almost too late, pulling up her own barely in time. The blade slid down the length of her sword and sliced into her hand.

Ashta gasped at the blinding pain, her vision blurring as she fell back. Before the man could lift his hand, a lioness from behind him pounced on his back. His eyes were wide as he fell forward.

Ashta dropped to the ground and lifted the sword with her left hand, thankful for her training, and Lem. Her other arm hung limply at her side.

King Alerik glared down at the monster of a woman cutting a swath through his soldiers. He turned to the nearest man, "Take out the sword wielding woman."

The soldier's eyes widened.

Alerik growled and stepped forward.

Yustin stepped in between. The King looked him in the eye, his steel gaze threatening to swallow Yustin. He glanced away.

"When that woman is dead, the rest will give up. She's the last energy in this battle. The wall has fallen. We have more men than they do."

Yustin nodded. He turned to the soldier at his side and gave him the signal. The soldier nodded and disappeared behind them.

Shaking, Ashta frantically searched the fight for Kkaar. Seconds felt like hours as she barely hacked her way through. The two lionesses and the male lion stayed close to hear, their yowls and roars scaring most of the men. Their quick lunges killing the rest.

Ashta panted hard, the pain flaring with each breath. A slight gray haze dimmed her vision to two points. She had lost a lot of blood. She needed to do something about her hand but all she could think about was getting to Kkaar.

A riderless horse, its back legs bleeding, screeched as it galloped past Ashta. She turned back ahead and realized that none of the lionesses were on their horses.

A break in the fighting ahead, as soldiers parted on either side of Ashta, gave her a view of her friend.

Kkaar stood tall as she swung the great sword around her with ease, fighting off four soldiers. Her brown hair shone, the glint of knife hilts shining in its conch braid, in the orange haze of the sun.

The wind died down, the slight sand cloud clearing just enough for Ashta to see everything in crisp detail.

The men that littered the ground.

A lioness to the right of her, eyes wide as her legs were cut from beneath her.

An *actual* lion pouncing onto the back of a berserker, ripping the wolf skin from his neck with fervor.

And Kkaar, the sweat dripping down her neck. The blood splattered in a perfect line from shoulder to opposite ear. The flash of her eyes as she growled out commands to the women near here.

The opal on the great sword pulsed with light, as the shadow of another woman, from another millennium moved with Kkaar, strengthening her in the fight.

Ashta's left hand slowly fell to her side, the sword tip sinking slightly into the blood soaked ground.

For a moment, Kkaar turned her head, her gaze on Ashta. The slightest smile crossed her face as her eyes warmed with recognition.

Ashta's chest warmed as they shared a long moment to themselves in the midst of the battlefield. Her friend was here. She was alive. Ashta had not failed everyone she cared about. Not yet.

Ashta blinked.

Her eyes widened.

Her sword came up.

Her mouth opened to shout, to do anything.

The spear sliced through the air, cracking through Kkaar's skull as it impaled her to the ground, Kkaar's wide gaze still on Ashta.

And then her light went out.

Ashta stumbled forward, screaming, trying to get to Kkaar. The men parted around her as she neared her friend.

But it was too late.

The battle disappeared around her, as Ashta fell to her knees in front of Kkaar's body. The other woman's eyes were still wide as blood streamed out of her eyes, her mouth. The sword lay beside her, its opal pommel dim.

The male lion came up beside Ashta, gently hitting his head into her shoulder. She didn't move, wordlessly staring into Kkaar's warm brown eyes.

A hole bloomed inside her chest, aching. Pain. Anger. Fear. Shame. Guilt.

And love.

It threatened to kill her as her gaze blurred with tears and sweat.

The lion gently nipped her arm, licking above her hand.

All of it felt like it was happening to another person. Another body. Ashta could feel her soul loosen as she slid above the battlefield. All around her was death and pain and fear. Men and women fighting for themselves. For their kingdoms.

All to just survive.

The sun darkened, a red ball of fury in the sky as the wind picked up, spitting sand and rocks into the fray. In the distance, the sandstorm dragged the sky down, lightning splitting through the black.

And through it all Ashta watched. And waited.

She watched as her body's right hand reached forward and gently rested on the opal pommel.

Ashta gasped as white hot heat flooded through her fingers and up into her arms.

It's not yet time, my daughter.

Ashta blinked, her eyes clearing as she gazed into Kkaar's dead eyes, her skin unnaturally pale.

With me, a memory from the sword swirled around and through Ashta. A shadow stepped inside of her. Pulled her to her feet. Wrapped Ashta's hands around the hilt of the sword.

You promised…

Ashta shuddered.

In a matter of a few short years, she had lost everyone and everything that mattered to her. She had lost those she had loved, those she thought she had loved, and those who had loved her. She had lost her past, cut the head off of her future.

And now she stood here, in the centre of a battlefield, and all she felt was alone.

Completely.

Utterly.

Alone.

The pain intensified. Multiplied. Her pain mixed with Remina's. The opal glowed white hot, lighting up the battlefield.

Ashta leaned back, her eyes closed as she cried out, the pain threatening to tear her apart.

Like a wave, the pain rippled through the battlefield, men and women alike stumbling and falling to their knees in shock and agony as they clutched their heads.

The dozen lions that still lived joined her cry, roaring with their own fury and pain and suffering.

The berserkers dropped their weapons to the packed earth and lifted their throats to the sky. Tripsian soldiers and white lioness fighters trembled as they turned towards the light. And the woman standing beside it.

Hot tears streamed down Ashta's face and dripped to the ground around her. The ground that was soaked with Kkaar's blood.

Finally, when the pain threatened to kill her, the male lion came up beside Ashta and gently licked her bloody hand.

The sting of his rough tongue on her fingers broke through the fog. Ashta's cry was cut off as quick as it started. Pain was overshadowed by purpose.

Her father had done this. Her father had killed Kkaar.

And Ashta would kill him.

With a growl, she turned towards the slight incline where her father still stood watching over the battlefield. She could feel his steel gaze on her. His shock and his horror.

Ashta smiled. Clutching the pommel of the great sword, she used it as a crutch as she stumbled through the soldiers. Bbrski men stepped back, giving her a wide berth as they dropped to their knees in fear.

Her lions slinked through the men, only the male staying at her side. *Don't let him get away.*

Low growls answered as swishes of tails disappeared amongst the soldiers.

A whisper began on the battlefield as a few men recognized the woman that stumbled across the dirt. Her black eyes. Her strong aura. For she had spent the last months surrounded by her countrymen. And she had not gone unseen. Or unremembered. Slowly, man by man fell to his knees whispering, "Princess."

The whispers rose to a chant, until the ground reverberated with the acknowledgement. What was given to her upon birth could not be ripped from her in life. Or at death.

The Tripsian soldiers and lionesses looked around in confusion.

Ashta focused only on taking each step. One after the other.

Weapons fell to the ground. Curious refugees and palace guards doted the not-too-distant wall, watching the strangeness unfold.

All watched as the black haired woman stepped onto the slight ridge, a blood soaked lion at her side, his mane glowing white in the strange light streaming from her sword.

General Yustin and the rest of the generals behind him fell to their knees. This was no ordinary woman. This was the divine right, the gods and goddesses chosen one.

Ashta halted, leaning heavily on the sword. The male lion sat back on his haunches beside her.

The chanting stopped, as silence weighed down on the army, only broken by the occasional groan of a wounded soldier.

Then a cry rose from ahead of her. Growls and roars.

Dragged through the soldiers by three lionesses, was a familiar shock of white hair. The lionesses let go of their quarry and fell onto their sides, a dozen of them lying in a semi-circle, their fur white from the light and sprayed with red blood. Tails twitched. Paws were licked.

Wide amber eyes never left the man at the center.

CHAPTER THIRTY-ONE

⌘

The End

ASHTA STOOD BEFORE her father. The man who had brought so much suffering to her life, and to countless others. A man who *enjoyed* other people's suffering.

And now he sat before her, bleeding from shallow bite wounds along his arms and legs. His steel grey gaze never wavered on hers, his glare burning into her soul.

In the stillness of the battlefield, with sand and rocks whipping around them, Ashta stood still and reached into that place inside of herself. The sword pulsing with energy in her hands, its tip resting in the blood soaked dirt. She closed her eyes, and a moment later she could see again.

But this time through another's eyes.

King Alerik glared up at the woman. A few short days ago she had been broken. Her mind gone. Her body his to command.

When he had heard the reports of the ship missing, he had thought nothing of it. He had lost many ships in his navy. But he had known, deep inside of himself, that *she* would have made it ashore. And that *she* would have completed the mission he gave her.

And yet now she stood before him like a goddess of myth, the Black Queen herself, unlike anyone he had seen before. Her mother had only shown glimpses of this strength.

Now Svetlana stood tall, the strange pommel on the great sword she leaned on giving an eery glow in the darkness of the coming storm. Her eyes were shut, her pale face dirtied with sand and sweat and blood.

She shouldn't be still standing, he thought.

Her fingers twitched on the pommel of the sword. Her hand was steady as it gripped the handle. With an ease that should have been impossible considering the size of the blade, Svetlana lifted the sword up high.

He glared at the gleaming edge of the blade.

Alerik had always known he would die at the hands of a blade. To die on the battlefield was an honour. His name would live on forever.

His gaze shifted from the blade and back to the girl whose eyes were still closed. Blood slowly trickled from her eyes, dark tears of pain.

A small shiver set the hairs on his nape on edge.

In her face he could see his young wife. Naïve and fragile. Her eyes broken with every still birth she suffered through, clutching their bloody and blue bodies. He felt both the annoyance and relief of seeing his wife's dead body. The relief of knowing he did not need to rid himself of his queen. The annoyance that he would never have a legitimate male heir.

He saw Lady Arja and the look of glee as she had informed him that she had gotten rid of his daughter. He saw her eyes widen in shock as he had slid the blade between the ribs in her chest.

He saw two girls flitting through the courtyard, one darkness and one light, giggling.

He felt the salty spray of the ocean on his face as he watched the barrel light on fire in the Naankdoena port. Felt the numbness at hearing another child of his was dead.

The male lion at Svetlana's side growled low, his eyes gleaming silver in the strange light. King Alerik blinked several times, caught in the predators eery yet familiar gaze.

Another shiver ran through Alerik. A ripple of fear. He closed his eyes trying to be rid of it. To not think of it.

The screams of the man in the barrel. The blood. And the hate that had boiled in another silver gaze.

Ashta's eyes flew open as she swung the sword, shifting its path and the blade landing harmlessly at her father's side.

Murmurs spread through the crowd of soldiers and berserkers.

Calmness fell over Ashta as she realized that her father's head was not hers to take. His death was not hers to dole out.

She slowly turned and gazed into the men's eyes around her. Bbrskian soldiers stared back up at her. Waiting. On their knees, throats bared.

Ashta's gaze caught on General Yustin.

The man flinched at the woman's intense black stare.

She raised her bloody hand and spoke, her voice hoarse from her cries earlier. "I, Svetlana Anichka, the last princess of the

Broskla family, charge you Yustin Donat with escorting this man, this traitor, to the council of Bbrski, where his fate will be decided."

General Yustin's eyes widened slightly before he nodded.

He glanced at the King as realization set in. Seeing the two side by side, Yustin could see the future and the past. And he, like many of his countrymen was tired, hot, and hungry. He missed the ice of his homeland. The long winters inside. The whiskey strong enough to take a grown man down instead of soft Midloean wine.

He stood up and nodded to his men.

The gods and goddesses had brought the answer to his deepest desires. And Yustin was happy to shuck the shackles of fear.

He motioned to two soldiers behind him. The men hesitated as well, before stepping forward to grab Alerik.

Alerik snarled at the men, stumbling to his feet. He was not used to pain any longer. It had been years since he had been this bloody.

He turned on his daughter. "You have no right! You are no longer a princess!"

Ashta gave him a slow smile.

Alerik stepped toward her. The male lion at her side stood and let loose a low growl that shook through the men nearby.

Ashta set her bloody hand on his mane. The lion quieted once more but did not sit. His gaze never left the former king's.

"I am *your* daughter. Do you deny that?"

King Alerik shook his head.

But General Yustin answered for him. "I have not lain eyes on you in this lifetime, princess, but I, like all Bbrskian see the marks of the Broskla family in your eyes and at your side." He nodded to the lion, then continued, gesturing to all the Bbrskian soldiers and berserkers who watched avidly. He could almost make out the faint smell of hope amidst the blood and grime of battle. These men were ready to return to their lives as farmers and tradesmen. The berserkers would continue to follow the path of war without the army.

Yustin stood tall as he looked every soldier, every berserker in the eye. "Does anyone deny this woman her birthright? As a woman of the great family Broskla whose roots run deeper than the ice in our land?" He yelled out.

Silence met his questions.

The Tripsian soldiers glanced around and shifted anxiously. The berserkers watched with dead eyes, not caring either way. But the Bbrskian soldiers gave small nods, shifting with excitement and hope.

Yustin turned back to the princess and the King. "But she is not just a princess."

Ashta looked to him questioningly.

The general lifted his sword up high. "Blood chooses our kings and queens, since the Black Queen. By the blood that runs through you, Svetlana Anichka, daughter of the Broskla family, I give you my sword and declare *you* my Queen."

Long moments passed as Ashta stared at the general in shock. Her fingers were frozen as she blinked at the man.

And then, slowly, like a ripple through a still pond, swords raised up and a shout arose. "Queen Svetlana! Queen Svetlana!"

Ashta shivered. Never had she thought to hear those words. Only a few weeks ago she had given up her birthright. Her name.

And now, because of blood, she was given a power that could not be denied. Could not be ignored.

No matter how much she wanted to run from those words, from the power behind them, from the hope in the soldier's eyes around her, Ashta knew that she had to take action. She had to take the mantle of her name, her blood, not for herself but for these people who needed a saviour.

With a strength she did not feel, Ashta raised her own sword.

The shouts cut off as men lowered their swords, standing to watch their queen. Ready to fight for their queen.

Ashta spoke slowly, "As your queen, I command you to put down your swords today, to return to your ships and sail back to Issha."

When no one moved, Ashta turned a full circle, glaring out at the sea of men. The sword pommel pulsed with magic, shaking the men into action.

Swords fell to the ground as men ran on shaky legs. Bbrskian soldiers lifted the wounded as they hurried out of the ancient city and back to the tents outside Trian's walls. Berserkers replaced their weapons as they marched wearily past Tripsian soldiers, sneering at them.

The few Tripsian soldiers and Lionesses in the field carefully marched back to the hole in the west wall where refugees had piled out to watch the miracle unfold.

The sandstorm that had threatened to take the city shifted and moved westward, to the alps. The late afternoon sun bore down on the field, lighting up in crystal detail the dead bodies that littered the field.

Only one body stood partially up, a spear keeping it lodged, forever on her knees.

Ashta's eyes caught on Kkaar's body. Pain threatened to pull her under once more. She closed her eyes as she breathed through her nose. Instead, she tried to feel the matted mane of the lion between her fingers, the desert sun burning her exposed neck.

"My Queen," Yustin asked, his gaze never leaving the former king. Soldiers held him by each arm, their grip firm despite his ranting and raving.

Ashta blinked several times, the silence inside her popping suddenly as she finally heard the noise around her. The clang of swords. The grunts. The cries for help. The distant shout of hope from the palace.

And her father, screaming that he was still king.

"I am your *king*! You cannot touch me! I will have your head! I will-"

Ashta swung back to her father. She stabbed the sword deep into the packed earth. Then she stumbled forward until she was nose to nose with the man who had killed her mother.

She pulled out a dagger from her shirt.

Yustin's eyes widened with shock. The soldiers watched her wearily.

Ashta placed the blade underneath her father's head, the blade pressing just hard enough to leave a thin streak of blood.

Her eyes were fire as she spoke in a deadly whisper. "It would be easy to take your life, right here, right now, with all of your men watching. But there is only one death for a traitor."

For the first time in decades, true fear shot through Alerik's spine. The whites of his eyes popped against his steely gaze. His mouth opened and closed as realization settled into his stomach.

Ashta smiled coldly, stepping back and replacing the dagger in her shirt. Loud enough for the generals and soldiers in hearing distance to make out every word, she spoke. "Your fate lies in the hands of the council, and *Prince Ruslan Alerik, son of the Broskla family*."

She nodded to the soldiers, "Take him to the ships. Make sure he is never alone. And that he cannot take his own life before the council has decreed his fate."

The men gave her hard smiles as she felt their satisfaction. And something darker.

Ashta turned away, not wanting to see what would come of the man that was still her father. Would always be her father.

A part of her was relieved that she would not have to live with his death on her hands, another part was simply tired. Tired of fighting. Tired of killing. Tired of surviving.

She watched as men began to pile up the bodies on the field and light them on fire. The stink of burning flesh wafted around them. To her left she could make out the shift of the army disappearing in the horizon towards the beaches. The men would not stay longer than they needed in this foreign kingdom.

She sighed, the pain and hunger and weariness of the day settling on her shoulders suddenly. It was all she could do to simply stand still and keep her eyes open.

"My queen?" a voice asked, jogging her from her daydream.

She turned weary eyes on General Yustin.

"We should return now. The ships will be at the beaches until midnight before sailing back to Aishma to gather general Kirill and the rest of the army, and then to Bbrski," he spoke, his gaze on the field aflame behind Ashta.

She shook her head.

He turned and really looked at the woman. She suddenly looked impossibly young in the setting sun. Too young to have stopped a war in a single battle.

She looked up at him, her long eyelashes fluttering with a world weariness that surpassed even his own age.

He was not surprised when she said, "I will not be returning with you."

Yustin frowned. He glanced behind the fire and saw a small regiment of Tripsian soldiers gathering.

"You must. You are our Queen now."

She gave him a sad smile. "I am no queen." She turned to also gaz at the gathering soldiers, sensing their thoughts. "I am no princess either. I am simply a slave."

A shout from the palace. The gathered Tripsian soldiers moved as one around the flame, their gaze on the incline and on Ashta. Sighing, she turned back to the general. "Lead the men. Ruslan is still a prince, not a king, the council will steer him."

He nodded slowly. There was an air of acceptance around her. Yustin had seen it many times in his years battling on the southern walls, and now in the Midloean kingdoms. Of men who knew their death was imminent, and they were ready.

Yustin turned back to the small group of soldiers that had waited with him. Without another word spoken, he led the soldiers back into the ancient city and out to the beaches.

Ashta closed her eyes. The pain came back, swallowing her, as her knees buckled.

A low growl shifted behind her, then disappeared. The pride hesitated, the male watching the woman. The soldiers were almost upon them.

One raised his bow and shot at the lion's foot.

The male lion growled, turned, and ran. The dozen lions and lionesses that had survived ran with him, disappearing into the sandy city and freedom.

Ashta stared out over the fire, her gaze fixed on one person. She watched as the flames burned higher, until she could no longer see Kkaar's body, only the tip of the spear flashing in the white heat.

She did not flinch when the blade pressed on the back of her neck.

"Ashta the Lion Tamer, you will come with us," a deep male voice demanded.

From her periphery she watched as the rest of the Tripsian soldiers circled her. She slowly pushed onto her feet, stumbling as she put weight on her foot.

The men shifted nervously but did not help her.

The soldier who had the blade to her, spoke once more. "Walk."

And she did.

CHAPTER THIRTY-TWO

⌘

Sister

THE HEAT OF THE fire from the burning bodies was excruciating on Ashta's face. But she couldn't look away, her eyes entranced by the licking flames and what they meant.

"Keep walking," the solider at her back barked.

Ashta grit her teeth and continued her slow limp across the dirt field.

Around Ashta were women and children pulling bodies to the piles, picking up weapons to be brought back to the palace. Despite the stink of death, a little girl twirled in the blood soaked field and giggled.

The battle was over.

The enemy was no longer standing on the other side of the wall.

The dozen soldiers that had been sent to retrieve the white lioness kept a tight circle around her. Yet even they could not completely hide the woman.

As they passed through the hole in the wall, people who had gathered to clean up the debris stopped in their work.

Eery silence followed the woman as she slowly limped through the gravel.

Black hair, blacker eyes. Blood soaked. Dirty.

And their saviour.

A child broke from her grandmother's hold and ran to the soldiers. The men paused in their slow pace across the courtyard. The small boy, his eyes large from months of hunger, stepped up to the woman and gripped her cold, blood soaked hand.

Ashta gasped at the shock of heat from his little fingers, and the strength of his warm thoughts.

Hero.

She looked down at him and realized he had placed a plum in her broken hand. Before she could ask, the boy scampered through the soldiers and back to where his mother anxiously wrung her hands. He smiled at Ashta.

"You said that men need the food, to stay strong and fight. I gave her my food mama, now she can keep fighting for us."

Ashta winced, hearing his words distantly and inside of herself.

She did not lift her hand. But she did not dare drop the food either. These people had been starved by her father's fleet for months. She would not spit on their suffering.

But she knew that she would not need food. She would not live much longer. She *could* not.

"Walk," the soldier growled, eyeing the gathering crowd warily. The woman was a prisoner of war. But the people did not look at her with fear and hate.

Ashta stumbled forward, the blade slicing into her back and leaving another open cut.

Several of the people gathered cried out.

"Hey!"

"She saved us…"

"Watch it!"

"…'d be lying dead in our own walls if it wasn't for her…"

The soldier glanced around more nervously. The crowd had doubled in size, three times more people than his small band of men.

Ashta didn't see anything. Or hear anything. She only felt the soft skin of the purple plum.

The soldier put his sword arm down and shoved her with his free hand.

She fell forward onto her hands and knees. The plum rolled away from her.

The crowd pushed against the ring of soldiers. Screamed into their faces. The sheer amount of people surrounding her, overwhelmed Ashta as her pain was overshadowed by the thoughts and fear and hope pressing down on her.

Gritting her teeth, she stood again.

Once she was on her feet, several people from the crowd quieted. She continued walking, shoving through the soldiers and into the crowd. The men tried their best to follow behind her but were swallowed up by the crowd as dozens turned to hundreds. People spilled out of the palace, from the walls. Everyone wanting to touch the warrior. To touch a living goddess.

There were so many people that all she could see was arms reaching for her, grabbing her, blocking out the sun. She felt wrapped in a cave of human flesh.

And the first trickle of fear spilled down her spine. Her breath quickened. Her heartbeat picked up. Her eyes widened as she focused on taking one step after the other, her memories guiding her to the to the front steps of the palace.

Only when she reached the top, was she able to breathe again. Lionesses, still streaked in blood from the battle, stood shoulder to shoulder, swords out. Their feral faces kept even the young children at bay, watching them cautiously.

Penny stood at the front, her gaze never leaving Ashta's. There was a weariness in her eyes, a suspicion that had not been there before. She stood aside without a word.

Ashta slipped by.

The coolness of the palace laid on her like a blanket, shocking her sensitive skin as shivers wracked her body. Ashta hesitated, looking around the unusually quiet great hall. Not even servants moved about. The opulent entrance was dark and gloomy. At odds with the near jubilance outside its great doors.

"This way," a voice called.

Ashta looked up to see the head of the lionesses standing ahead of her. His milky white gaze scrutinized her before he turned away. She clenched her teeth, trying to quell the shaking as she shuffled behind the honorary councilman. No people moved about the halls. No words echoed.

Only the shuffle of her feet and the dripping blood trailing behind them made any noise. Even the councilman's steps were noiseless.

For once, that strange hearing that had fallen over Ashta on the shadow island was quiet. And the stillness around her only brought forth the strength of her pain.

They moved through the halls slowly, finally stopping in front of a door to a room that once was a servant quarter.

Kaos stepped inside and held the door open.

Ashta followed him without thought.

Soon this pain will be over.

Another thought followed it.

I did the right thing.

Yet she was faced with a room of stony faces that said another story.

Of the dozen councilmen that had been before Ashta disappeared in her rescue for Carien, only seven remained.

And of the generals, Hariim was still missing.

As was the King.

His place at the makeshift table was left empty.

Ashta stood opposite of it, for all the councilmen to stare at. A soldier she had not known was standing at the door came up beside her. He grabbed her hands roughly and tied them behind her back.

Pain like fire pulsed from her partially severed fingers.

The soldier hesitated, before looking at the general. General Ttaabit nodded. Only then did the soldier speak. "Some of her fingers on her right hand are severed. She needs-"

Baron Tamor burst out, his complexion as red as his face. "She is a war prisoner! She will not be coddled as one of our own. She is a traitor! We should take her head now-"

General Ttaabit glared at the man. He banged his sword hard onto the table. Baron Tamor fell silent but continued to glare at Ashta.

General Ttaabit turned to the rest of the council men before saying in calm voice, "We are gathered here to decide the fate of this woman. To let her die from blood loss, or infection, is not giving due justice. Justice to her. Or justice to our late king. Are all in agreeance?"

No one moved. Tamor continued to glare at Ashta but kept his mouth closed.

"Good," Ttaabit said more to himself than to the gathered men. "Then you will send for a healer and rags. She can be tended to here, under our watchful eye." Then he muttered quietly, "Where she is less likely to disappear again."

The soldier turned and swiftly left the room.

The click of the door behind him acting like a signal to the men. Each took their respective seats leaving five seats open between them. The head chair, where the king sat was also noticeably empty.

General Ttaabit sighed as he shoved his hands through his hair before dragging them down his face and rubbing his eyes.

Ashta had not paid attention to the other councilmen when she had walked into the council room with Carien ages ago. Kaos the bone breaker, head of the white lionesses, milky gaze watched the rest of the men. His seat honorary, the expectation of his silence weighing on him. But the others, Ashta could see the lines around their eyes, the hunched shoulders. The thin cheeks. The last months had been hard on all the Tripsians.

General Ttaabit finally spoke up, breaking the tense silence. "I have reports from several scouts that the Bbrski ships on the cliff face have left. As well as the ships carrying the army along our eastern beaches are gone under the deliverance of the full moon."

Despite this good news after months of war, no one relaxed. Baron Tamor looked even more edgy.

Ttaabit looked out at the men before letting his gaze fall on Ashta. "Even if the Bbrskian Black Death returns, it will be weeks. It should give us time to rebuild and regroup, trade with Trimant, Malten, and Naankdoen for food and supplies."

Several men nodded.

The door flew open, a healer bustling straight for Ashta. Her covered head and plain dress marking her position. She set the bucket of water on the stone floor, the stained rags teetering on the rim.

She looked at the woman's bound arms with a frown. Without hesitation, or approval, she pulled her short knife out and cut through the binds.

The councilmen and general watched. Despite the gatherings purpose to decide the woman's fate, no one it seemed wanted to begin the talks.

The healer muttered as she worked. "Be lucky to have any of them working after this... At least they were cut clean...start a rebellion, fools..."

With quick, precises movements, Ashta's fingers were cleaned and stitched together before being bandaged. The woman eyed her ankle, which was also dark with blood.

She leaned down to touch it but Baron Tamor stopped her with a word. "That is all. She will not need the rest seen to."

The healer stood, and despite the vast difference in their status she looked the councilman in the eye. Glaring.

"You called me here, away from the dozens of soldiers and lionesses who needed tending from the battle, and from injuries these past weeks, to look at this woman. And I will tend *all* of her injuries." Despite her words, Ashta could see the shake in the other woman's hands as she spoke.

Baron Tamor stood up, the vein on his forehead popping. Ttaabit touched his arm and gave him a meaningful look. Tamor hesitated before sitting down.

General Ttaabit turned to the healer. "Continue," he gestured before sitting back in his seat. He made no motion to talk, taking the short reprieve to rest his eyes.

The other councilmen shifted in their seats, surreptitiously glancing at Ashta and the healer.

The woman took a deep breath before turning to the black haired warrior. She glanced quickly at the table before turning her gaze back to Ashta. "Can you take the pants off?"

Ashta did not respond, her uninjured hand coming forward and loosening the laces at her waist. The pants slipped to her feet. She tried to step out of them but stumbled. The healer quickly squatted before her and carefully gripped the leather boot.

The right boot came off easy, the bottoms of her sole bloody from her walk into the palace. The left boot, the healer carefully cut of her foot, grimacing as the ragged cut in the leg came into view. The skin around was already inflamed.

She reached behind her for a rag and carefully washed and stitched. Long minutes passed as she worked her way up Ashta's legs, applying Ruutka on even the smallest cuts.

Ashta grit her teeth, trying not to hiss at the cool sting of the medicine. By the time Ashta pulled her shirt off, a pleasant numbness had stolen the physical pain from her body.

And by the time the healer was done, the water in the bucket was black. The rags matching. And Ashta stood before the council, naked.

The woman busied herself, replacing the Ruutka in her pockets and folding the bandages away before picking up the bucket. "I will return with the lioness clothing for."

This time it was the general who spoke. "Thank you, but you needn't bother."

The healer stopped where she was, her back rigid as she waited for the general to continue. She looked over at the black haired woman, could feel the strength and the weariness coming off of her in waves. The woman should be treated as a war hero, the healer thought, not a common criminal.

Ttaabit watched the emotions play across the healer's face as she watched Ashta. He rubbed his bare jaw, worry over the conundrum that stood in the room seeped deep in his bones. Tripsia was still weak, she could not survive a rebellion.

Despite the unnecessity of needing to explain himself, he spoke to the healer's questions. Likely the entire city, the kingdom, waited to hear the words this woman would speak as she returned to her duties. "This woman is a prisoner of Tripsia, and under a fair trial by the council. She will not be returning to the white lionesses until the trial has come to a close."

Satisfied, the woman turned and left without another word.

With the snick of the door closing once more, Ttaabit leaned forward and looked each councilman in the eyes.

Everyone sat forward, hands on the table, eyes bright as they focused on the general and his words. He had become the spokesperson in the council, because of his experience and his control of the entire Tripsian army.

He began, "As you all know, we are gathered here today to decide on the fate of this woman, given name of Ashta the Lion Tamer. She comes before us on the grounds of treason. The accusations that have come to this council are for plotting against the kingdom, regicide, abandoning her place-"

Bang!

The door swung back closed, as swiftly as it had opened.

Ashta turned in time to see steel eyes, and a blade coming towards her.

In a quick sequence of motion, Ashta ducked, the soldier pulled Ennris's shoulders back, and the general leapt from his seat, sword outstretched as he jumped between the two women.

Ashta stared wide eyed at the other woman. She was unrecognizable, her long hair curling down her shoulders to her hips, heavy streaks of silver running through its cloudy mass. Her eyes were red, her cheeks tear-stained. And there was a wildness in her eyes, like a wounded animal.

She growled, easily twisting out of the soldiers hold. She tried to step around the general and lunge at Ashta. But he kept standing in between.

"Enough!" he shouted, his sword coming up and stopping at Ennris's throat.

The wildness in her steel-grey eyes calmed as she finally looked into the general's eyes.

In a quieter tone he continued. "This woman's fate lies in the hands of the council. *No one else,*" he warned.

Ennris glared at him, her back rigid as her fingers gripped the dagger with white knuckled strength. "I demand her death. And you will give it to me Ttaabit," she hissed.

Lord Pelop stood up. He looked to the broken lioness with curiosity before turning to Ennris. "No one has come forward to confirm that it was Ashta the Lion Tamer who killed the king. The soldiers and white lionesses who guarded him are dead. And the rest were with the other guards patrolling the rest of the palace. No one has seen *this* woman in months."

Ennris growled as she turned to face the table, she pointed at Ashta, the gleaming edge of the blade shining wickedly in the torch light. "It is damn convenient for her to suddenly show up, *on the battlefield*, after weeks of being missing. Our last report of her was that she had been taken by the Bbrski King on Kijarhro. And now she is standing here, my niece is missing, and my *brother* lies dead, in his room, headless!" She screeched, spit flying in the air. Her body shook with anger.

Ashta gasped, the sound lost in the shouts between Ennris and the council. *Niece? Her brother?*

Ashta blinked and for the first time looked at the woman who had bought her. Who had been the driving reason that Ashta took the test and joined the white lionesses.

It was in the curve of her cheek. The shape of her eyes. Just like Carien's. And her hair was the same brown streaked with silver as the king's. Her eyes the same steely grey. *How could I have not seen it?*

Ashta blinked several times, finally listening to the words the general's deep voice said. "...and after fair trail, *we*, the council, will dole out the punishment. If you have nothing else to add, you are free to leave."

Ennris turned to glare up at the general.

Ttaabit eyes softened, but his stance remained rigid. "I'm sorry-"

"I don't need your apologies," she spat out before turning and leaving without another glance at Ashta or the councilmen.

Sighing, Ttaabit relaxed as he turned to the soldier. "Lock the door. I don't want any more surprises."

The man swiftly did as the general said.

Ttaabit returned to his seat, setting the sword down into the middle of the table. "Well, councilmen. Let us begin."

CHAPTER THIRTY-THREE

⌘

The Second

AFTER HOURS OF ARGUING, the councilmen were beginning to wane in their fervor. The general began to snap at the men, rather than respond in his usual cool manner.

Ashta watched it all pass, floating in a cold cloud of numbness. The occasional sharp cold stab reminded her that the Ruutka was working its way through the many wounds.

She stood at the end of the table, swaying with hunger and fatigue, but did not stumble or fall. Her brain had become numb to the stinging dryness of her eyes.

Another hollow pain fought for control of consciousness.

Knock, knock.

The soldier opened the door to several servants carrying in dishes of food, and large vessels of water and wine. The councilmen and the general sat back as the servants laid the meal before them. It was simpler fare than Ashta was used to seeing in the palace.

A hand at her elbow had her turning. A woman stood beside her, her eyes downcast as she held out a large bowl of papna. Ashta did not hesitate to take it, quickly shoveling the gruel into her mouth. Never had she been so thankful for the plain food that was for the soldiers and the lionesses.

She scraped the bowl clean in seconds, her belly uncomfortably full for the first time in months. The woman took the bowl and passed her a flask.

Ashta drank it in one swallow.

The entire exchange passed before the general was able to rip off the first bite of bread. The servants left in a bustle, leaving the warm scent of stew and wine in the air.

Ashta held in her groan. Despite the fullness of her belly, she felt ravenous. The men ate in relative silence, the meal passing in an abrupt manner unlike Tripsian affairs.

Finally, Lord Pelop put down his fork and spoke to the group. "We will not come to an answer in one sitting, councilmen, general," he nodded to each. "As such, it would be prudent for us all to retire and return at first light."

Baron Tamor muttered, "We all know she is guilty. This debating is a waste of time."

Ttaabit glared at Baron Tamor, snapping, "It is not just about the consequence of one life but of the entire kingdom. We cannot *afford* to be hasty in this decision. Bbrski has only just left our shores."

Baron Laem lifted his hand, stopping the oncoming argument which was only a reiteration of the past hours of debate. "I agree with Lord Pelop. We should retire. Allow the evening rest to clear our minds to all arguments. Clarity comes with a good rest and a good meal."

The other three Councilmen nodded in agreement with Baron Laem.

General Ttaabit stood, reaching for his sword and replacing it in his scabbard. "Then we all shall retire. Ashta the lion Tamer will remain in this chamber."

Baron Laem and Lord True shared a look. Lord True spoke up, his soft voice filling the air. "And what of Ennris the Lion Killer."

The general's face hardened. "*I* will be staying in the chamber, in case of any other unwanted visitors." He turned to the soldier at the door. "Send for Bruno and Matthen. And a cot for myself." He glanced at Ashta, before adding, "And chains for the prisoner."

The councilmen quickly filed out of the room, leaving Ashta and the general alone in the dark room. Ttaabit looked over Ashta's body before relaxing against the wall, his grip still forms on the sword handle.

"You can relax now," he said, his eyes watching the door.

Ashta said nothing. She feared she would collapse if she dared move her feet.

Ttaabit took her silence as stubbornness. He growled, "Until the entire council agrees on what to do with you, we will damn well keep you alive. Whether you want to be or not."

The door swung open. Several soldiers entered and quickly placed the cot at the other end of the room, near the Kings seat. The rattle of chains caught Ashta's attention.

She watched as Ttaabit came to her and quickly locked her ankles together, before straightening and locking her wrists together. He let go of the thick metal cuffs.

The sudden weight of the cuffs and thick chain threw Ashta's balance off. She stumbled forward.

Ttaabit caught her. His hands tightened around her thin shoulders. *She shouldn't have been able to walk let alone fight in a battle. There's nothing but skin and bones on her.*

Ashta jerked back, hard enough to stumble backwards until she landed heavily against the wall. She slid down its length. Her head fell back.

The weariness of the day overwhelmed her, pulling her deep into a dreamless sleep.

Days passed as the councilmen deliberated. Baron Laem would not be swayed. And Ttaabit continued to bring up the Tripsian people's reaction to her. Baron Tamor was adamant in her guilt, calling for her immediate death several times.

Ashta stood at the table during the deliberations. Each evening she fell against the wall. Her belly may be full, but a hollowness had settled deep inside of her. Her thoughts were cloudy, leaving her a ghost that watched but did not speak.

By the fourth day, Baron Laem had brought several of the ancient books and scrolls from the library. His face was triumphant as he slammed down a familiar old tome into the middle of the table.

"We cannot use the death penalty on Ashta the Lion Tamer as she has not technically broken any laws."

Baron Tamor spluttered, rising to his feet.

Laem continued, speaking over Tamor. "According to the original laws that bind the lionesses, there is only two instances that an *earned* white lioness can be given the death penalty."

General Ttaabit shoved Baron Tamor into his seat. Baron Laem, flipped the book open to the specific page that Ashta remembered reading. *Had it really only been months ago that I was fighting to save Ceerie,* she thought bitterly.

Baron Laem continued in a more controlled voice. "The first being if a lioness' charge dies, then that lioness will be put to death in the same or worse manner as the charge died. The second," He looked up into each of the councilmen eyes, "and only other instance, is if a lioness has lain with a man, *any man*, even if no child is born of such union."

Baron Tamor sat back, his eyes wide. "B-But surely there in must include something about regicide or-or abandoning the kingdom," he spluttered.

Lord True sighed. "How can we say she abandoned the kingdom when she returned without our having to retrieve her?"

Baron Rine jumped in, "And there is no proof she killed the king. He was beheaded with the Kkell the Fearless's own half sword. For all we know, the assassin is one of the other dead bodies in the king's quarters."

Several men shifted in their seats.

General Ttaabit leaned in, "So according to the law our land is bound to, we *cannot* call for the death penalty." He waved his hand to cut off Timor, "And even if we found another reason to put her to death, the people will not allow it."

Baron Rine nodded. "I've heard the whispers amongst my own servants. I'm sure the rest of you have as well."

Baron Laem and Lord True nodded.

General Ttaabit spoke fiercely, his nostrils flaring, his eyes wide. "Tripsia cannot afford a rebellion. *We*, the council, cannot afford a rebellion. It is a long road ahead of us to rebuild the palace. The people are looking to us," he gestured to the men around the table, "For direction. For leadership. And for hope." And then in a whisper, "And we cannot be responsible for crushing our people's last hope."

Lord Pelop spoke up, "Then there is only one solution to this problem."

All the other men, and Ashta turned to the ruddy faced Lord Pelop. He had not spoken out in the debates. Now, he stood, pulling out a sealed letter. Ashta caught the sight of a familiar white bear flash before the letter hit the middle of the table.

Lord Pelop said with complete conviction, "We free her."

All the men stood up. Baron Timor began shouting at Lord Pelop.

"Silence!" Ttaabit yelled, slamming the hilt of his sword on the table. Everyone stilled, backs rigid, cheeks red. Ttaabit gestured to the letter on the table. He spoke one word. "Why?"

As Lord Pelop spoke, Ashta realized that he had listened carefully to all the other men's arguments. "If Ashta the Lion Tamer is free from being a slave, then she will live and continue to be a symbol of hope for the people."

"Freeing a slave is unprecedented. It has only been done once before." Baron Laem rubbed his beard worriedly.

"And what's stopping her from returning to Bbrski and giving all of our weaknesses away to the enemy?" Ttaabit asked.

Lord Pelop gestured to the letter. "I have received official correspondence from the crown *prince* of Bbrski that the traitor and former king Alerik has been set to be executed by horse and barrel." Ashta shivered. Before she could think about what the words meant, Pelop continued. "And in the same letter the crown prince distinctly states that Bbrski recognizes no other heir except himself, and that anyone else who claimed to be an heir to the ice throne would be immediately executed."

Baron Timor shifted, his eyes brightening.

Ttaabit's gaze turned pensive.

Lord Pelop smiled as he finished, "She has nowhere to return to, she is no weapon to be used against Tripsia. No-longer Ashta the Lion tamer will have nowhere to go and no one to turn to. And while *we* cannot make the call to put her death, we can pay our allies to deal with her once she is past our walls and beyond the gaze of our peoples."

Baron Timor smiled. Several of the men nodded.

"Let there be a vote," Baron Laem called. "All in favour of freeing the slave Ashta the Lion Tamer, say I."

Five voices echoed as one, the first time everyman was in agreeance. Kaos' milky gaze burned into Ashta's side.

Ashta shivered.

"So, it is decided," Lord Pelop said in a quiet voice, as everyone moved in nervous anticipation.

It was not what Ashta had expected.

At all.

The men filed out of the room, leaving Ashta alone with only a soldier. She began trembling from her fingers, to her arms, to her legs, until her entire body was shaking.

I was supposed to die.

Her breath whistled through her lungs as spots began to blur her vision.

When she came to, two soldiers were dragging her limp body up. She wriggled, trying to shake their holds despite her chains.

The men quickly released her and stepped back.

That is when she saw the third man in the room. Enzol. The head healer.

His beard was still long, the white ends dragging on the stone floor. His stooped back spoke of years that his sparkling milky gaze denied.

"And so, we meet again, Ashta the Lion Tamer," he said in his raspy voice. "Follow me."

He turned.

As his robes shifted Ashta noticed the metal bound book in his arms. A tickle of fear, and something more, whispered down her back. She could not take her eyes off of it as she shuffled behind the head healer.

When they came to a stop, Ashta blinked. They were in the infirmary. There were still people in beds. Children coughing. A woman crying.

Enzol pointed to the first cot.

"You will sleep here tonight. I will see you in the morning." And then he left, leaving Ashta with two soldiers and a roomful of eyes on her.

With nothing else to do and feeling bone-deep tired, Ashta shuffled to the cot and laid back on it.

They might still kill me, she thought before giving in to her body.

CHAPTER THIRTY-FOUR

⌘

The Burning

Ashta woke up suddenly. She gasped, almost choking at the pressure of the blade crushing her throat.

"Not a sound," a familiar voice whispered.

Ashta opened her eyes.

Steel gray eyes looked down into hers.

"I should cut you open and slowly take your insides out so you can feel the pain that I feel," she hissed, pressing the blade deeper.

The cut flared with pain. Ashta didn't dare swallow. She simply waited.

Ennris's eyes glittered with tears, her pain echoing through Ashta. The love between brother and sister was as strong of a bond as that of mother and daughter. Ashta could still feel the hollow loss of losing her own mother.

But her mother had taken her life.

And Ashta had taken the King's life.

Her heartbeat echoed in her ears, drowning out any other noise.

A single tear ran down Ennris's nose before splattering on Ashta's cheek. Ashta felt that tear in her soul. All the pain and suffering she had doled out.

It was better that she died.

She kept her eyes open, meeting death head on. She watched as Ennris pulled back her arm. The knife edge flashing from the single candle that flickered in the room.

The bloody tips of Ennris's fingers, as if she had scratched her way out of a room. Or in to one.

Ashta breathed in her last breath, tasting the stale palace air, the stink of blood and infection and uncleaned bodies strong in the room. The slightest tickle of something sharp, cold.

Ennris swung her arm down, the knife just above Ashta's middle. It would not kill her. Not right away.

Ashta did not look away from Ennris's eyes.

"*Flersium ti Voleantis.*"

The blade suddenly glowed green as it flew out of Ennris's hand. The woman whipped around, giving Ashta a clear view of what had stopped Ennris. Or who.

Enzol held his hand out, the blade still glowing as it lay flat on his palm. His eyes were an eerie glowing green as he stared at Ennris. "Her life is not yours to take Alexandra."

Ennris growled, before disappearing out of the infirmary.

Ashta blinked several times, sitting up in a daze.

Enzol came to her cot and sat beside her. He lifted one finger and traced the cut on her throat, the blood still dripping down her neck.

Enzol frowned as he finally looked up into Ashta's eyes. "I had hoped for more from Ennris the Lion Killer. I apologize, my child."

Ashta said nothing, her stare unblinking, her eyes blank.

He sighed, carefully rising up again.

"Come then. We can begin now. It is not safe for you to stay in Trian."

Ashta slid off of the cot, the chains rattling as she stood. She winced at the loud clinks. She turned to face the wall and noticed the slumped body on the ground.

Before she could ask, Enzol spoke in that soft raspy voice of his. "He will wake. His friend will not."

Ashta turned to the entrance of the infirmary where the other soldier lay against the wall, the blackness staining his front from his lifeblood spilling out of the smooth slice across his throat.

Ennris had dared to kill one of the Tripsian soldiers. She would not hesitate the next time she came near Ashta.

Shuddering, Ashta shuffled behind the head healer. The glow of the dagger dissipated, replaced by a warm orange glow coming from infront the man. Ashta kept her gaze down, focusing on not making too much noise with the chain.

Soon enough they entered a hall, the air shifting from dank to damp. The warm light completely disappeared leaving only the cold light of the moon. Ashta gazed out into the courtyard and up at the star filled sky. The moon was waning, hanging low enough that Ashta was sure she could touch it.

How had she never seen the moon before? The sky?

Cold fingers touched the back of her hand, a shock of heat and something stronger raced under her skin. Ashta turned with wide eyes to the head healer. "Best not to linger this eve," he said, his milky gaze seeing what Ashta could not.

She shivered, but continued to follow him, mutely.

Once she entered the familiar room, Enzol slipped behind her and locked the door.

The room was as bright at night as it had been during the day, the one and only other time she had been here before. The mirrors glinted, bouncing the soft blue light across the room.

"Here, let me take these off," he said before muttering words that Ashta had never heard before.

Her wrists and ankles flashed hot before an ominous click shattered the silence. The chains fell to the ground in a heap before her. Ashta quickly rubbed her wrists, frowning at the already dissipating green glow from the chain.

"Lay down. I have not finished preparing the acid for removing your tattoo."

Ashta shivered again at his words. She quickly walked to the cot in the centre of the room, scooting onto it to face the wall of jars, pots, and brushes.

Enzol muttered quietly to himself as he began pulling bottles from the shelves. Ashta watched with a mix of fascination and horror as the bowl began to glow from within, pulsing purple smoke slowly rising from its centre.

He turned to read from a thin book metal bound book. The paper was near translucent covered in an ink made spiderweb of scrawling script.

Finally, finished, he carefully closed the book, the metal edges clicking together. He grabbed the bowl and shuffled to the table beside the bed. He turned to Ashta with soft eyes. "Lay back, my child."

She did, as fear finally wound its way through the fog of her emotions. She shivered at the feeling of his cold hands as he lifted her arm over her head. Then Enzol grabbed the bowl, carefully titling it to pour down onto Ashta's chest. Ashta could see the bubbling mass of sludge, a purple cloud of smoke hovering over the mass of swirling colours in the liquid. For a moment Ashta thought she saw a face in the glassy surface. Then she blinked.

"I'm sorry," Enzol muttered, and then tilted the bowl a little more.

The first drop stung. The second burned.

And then Ashta was screaming, her chest arching, her eyes rolling back as the pain overwhelmed her and cut right past her soul to another binding from centuries ago.

Blackness settled over her.

Ashta found herself in the room again, but this time she was standing to the side of the table. Beside her was a man with a short white beard and bright blue eyes. He was gesturing with arms wide, his cheeks red as he yelled.

Before him stood a short man that was familiar to Ashta. She frowned at his brown hair and short stature.

A movement from the table had her turning to see a familiar woman. Ice blue eyes.

Remina the Lion.

Ashta whipped back to the other two men as she could suddenly hear the words flying about the room.

"-to simply speak the words is not enough to free her. There is deep magic in the tattoo. To truly free her of the binds of slavery, we must burn the majic out of her!" The white haired man yelled.

The king glanced at Remina worriedly, eyeing her curves with lust in his gaze. "The process. Can it be done another way, without melting her skin?" he questioned, finally looking back at the white haired man.

The other man frowned, and, in that moment, he looked achingly familiar. "No, your majesty. This is old majic, far before my time. The elven that gave Tripsia the *binding* also gave only one answer to it, *the burning*."

Alerik frowned. "If there is no other way than we are done here. The court room is ready for us. Come Remina," he called as he turned to leave the room, not bothering to look back.

Only Ashta saw Remina reach out to the white haired man.

"Do you understand the consequences of freeing her without removing the shackles?" White-hair whispered, his eyes never leaving Remina's.

The king was the one who answered. "I don't care. I am King. You are only the head healer, Enzol. You will do as I tell you. And I have decided that she will not be disfigured."

Ashta gasped. For the briefest moments, Enzol turned to Ashta's ghostly figure and their gazes caught.

Then blackness.

Ashta groaned when she came to. Her chest and side burned. The pain pulsed with a fire she had never felt before. Even the poisoned arrowhead had not burned like this. It was as if a part of her, something so intrinsic, was suddenly gone.

Firm hands gripped under each arm. A wind tickled her face.

Two lights beside her. *Orders. Bring her alive.*

Frowning, Ashta blinked several times, her eyes feeling gritty. It was then that she noticed that she was being carried by two soldiers.

She squirmed. The men tightened their grip.

"Let me walk," she croaked, her throat dry from screaming.

The men slowed down as they lowered her enough that she could walk, but their grips on her arms did not loosen.

The small party continued to walk.

Lights ahead. Two lines. *Freedom. Warrior. Hope.*

Ashta kept her head up, her instincts on high alert. They were nearing the palace entrance. The hall opened to the main hall that led outside.

And suddenly they were surrounded by people.

Men. Women. Children. Soldiers. Slaves. White Lionesses.

All stood motionless as Ashta and the soldiers passed by. As they neared the great wooden doors, opened up and spilling the bright afternoon sun into the dark corridor.

Ashta blinked several times, squinting through all the light. Her head pulsed in rhythm with the wound on her side where her tattoo had once been. Her good hand burned.

As they reached the top of the steps, the soldiers halted.

Ennris walked steadily toward Ashta, her gaze burning. Her hair was back in its tight conch bun, her bindings tight around her chest, the skirt loose on her suddenly thin hips. She looked harder than when Ashta had first met her. Older. In a way that time did not touch the skin, but pain did.

Ennris lifted her arm and pulled Ashta close into a one armed hug. The soldiers grip tightened enough to leave bruises.

Hate flowed through Ashta, shocking her at its strength. It burned brighter than the sun, almost blinding her.

The cold prick of a blade at the back of the neck cooled Ashta's blood. Her heartbeat picked up as she breathed shallowly.

Ennris leaned into her ear, whispering tightly, "Know that if we ever cross paths again, I *will* kill you. And I will take my time." Her words chilled Ashta as goosebumps flashed across her arms, down her back and her legs.

Ennris stepped back, her smile cold as she rejoined the white lionesses that served the court who were lined up against the entrance.

The soldiers continued, half dragging Ashta to the top of the steps. The general and the councilmen suddenly stood beside her. Ashta looked out past them, her eyes aching at the brightness. She tried closing them, but it was as if it was still daylight shining before her. Each person clearer with her eyes closed than open.

"By unanimous vote, it was decided that this woman, who courageously fought for Tripsia and saved our kingdom from being raped and killed by Bbrski, will be rewarded with the freeing of her bindings to our great land of Tripsia."

Ashta trembled as the shouts and screams rose around her. The sheer glee forced a smile through her that she did not feel.

Baron Laem raised his hands. After several heartbeats, the people quieted. He turned to Ashta and continued. "We are gathered here today to witness this woman, Ashta the Lion Tamer, being freed of her bindings to Tripsia from this day to the end of time."

More roaring from the crowd.

A single droplet of blood seeped out of Ashta's left ear.

"Let us bear witness as she begins her journey as a free woman!"

Another droplet of blood seeped from her nose. Ashta swayed.

One of the soldiers gave her a push.

Wide eyed, Ashta stumbled down the steps. She could not even hear her heart beating rapidly over the roar of the crowd. The ground trembled at the noise.

She shuffled forward, hands touching her, pulling her, pushing her forward. She bit down on her lip to keep from screaming. It was a nightmare with no end. She could not ignore the intense sensation that she was walking straight to her death, not to a new life as a free woman.

The sensation was not unlike the blurred memory of Lily's death procession.

This time, it was Ashta who led the march, blood dripping onto the packed dirt as her eyes, her ears, her body ached.

Until suddenly she stood before the open gate of the palace walls. The crowd fell silent behind her, the heat of thousands of eyes watching her burning her back. The abandoned city of Trian lay before her, blissfully dark. The sun shone hot on her face.

Without a backward glance, Ashta took a step forward.

CHAPTER THIRTY-FIVE

⌘

Into the Rain

THE FIRST STEP WAS slow. Tentative.
The second more sure.
The third was quick.
And then she broke out into a run towards the buildings.
Her back burned. She could feel the hate still burning, from more than just Ennris. One well-placed arrow was all it would take.
Suddenly, Ashta didn't want to die. Not here, not now.
She ran hard, her legs pumping fast. Her chest ached as she clutched her breasts close to her. The sun burned across her pale skin, unused to its stinging heat.
By the time she reached the first alley, Ashta was panting. She darted sideways, before turning back and continuing north. Her pace did not slow as giddy excitement and fear rushed

through her, energizing her. She did not feel as the healing wounds on the soles of her feet opened new cuts slicing them from the loose rocks on the path.

Suddenly the sun disappeared, and darkness fell over the city.

Ashta did not slow, her gaze focused ahead, needing to get as far away from the still bright light behind her. It felt like a beacon and she could not get away fast enough.

Then something cold splattered on her leg.

Ashta came to an abrupt stop. Frowning she looked up. The sky was dark, flashing as it often did with sandstorms. But this was not a desert storm.

To her amazement, another raindrop splattered onto her chest. Then on her cheek.

In all the years she had lived in Tripsia, never had she felt the cold wash of rain on her skin. She turned her face up to the sky, smiling.

The steady trickle shifted, the drops getting larger.

A laugh bubbled up from deep within her. Her soul stretched out in relief. Ashta threw her arms out and slowly twirled, the cool rain washing her naked body. Reminding her she was alive. That she could feel.

Lightning flashed, lighting up the blurry street for a second. And then in the next moment-

Boom!

The thunder shook the air, the buildings, the very ground even as another flash lit the sky.

Boom!

Ashta shoved her hands over her ears helplessly. Suddenly she felt chilled to the bone, shaking in the middle of the street. She ran to the nearest door. Slamming into it, the door opened. But there was no roof. Only more rain.

Ashta ran to the next building. The door was missing, and all the walls behind it had crumbled to sand.

She hesitated underneath the entrance, the slight reprieve of the pounding rain giving her a moment to breath. She rubbed her arms, glaring out into the dark and blurry alley. She was a league from the crumbled walls of the outskirts of Trian. She needed to get out of the city before Ennris, or someone else, could send their blades for her.

Taking a deep breath, she squared her shoulders and ran down the alley. She flitted between collapsed overhanging walls and broken down entrances. Her fingers and toes began to ache with cold numbness. Her teeth chattered hard enough to shake despite her clenched jaw.

The rain began to penetrate through the tight conch braid of her hair. Everything was cold. Finally, Ashta knew she could go no further. She just hoped she was near the outskirts.

She spied a promising dark shape, a low hanging hovel. She slipped into the darkened entrance.

A corner of the roof still stood against the test of a millennia of sand and wind. Ashta stumbled to the corner, a dry patch just larger than her curled up body underneath. The rain drove down in sheets, pooling quickly on the unforgiving cracked earth.

She slid down the wall and for a moment just sat, finally out of the rain. Shivering.

With trembling hands, she reached up and fought with the soaked hairs of her braid. For the first time in months, her long black hair spilled down her back, curling around her like a blanket of warmth.

Despite her achy limbs, she felt a live and awake. Watching the steady sheets of rain come down just in front of her, Ashta slowly worked her fingers through her hair untangling the months of hair loss. She massaged her neck and scalp as she worked until she was pleasantly warm. Her fingers and toes still ached, but the rest of her felt clammy with heat.

Ashta wrapped her arms around her legs and stared out at the rain, a smile still on her lips.

Ashta woke to the gentle beat of a heart and warmth along her side. Her fingers clenched around damp hair. Sitting up Ashta looked into the familiar golden eyes of the male lion.

"You again," she spoke aloud. She was surprised that he was still in the city.

Looking around herself, she noticed the rain had let up slightly, only a gentle patter like the rains of summer in Issha.

And that there were no other lions around them.

She frowned. "Where is the rest of the pride?"

The lion huffed, slowly stretching his back before rising onto his legs. Without a backward glance he padded through the doorway. The rain collected in tiny drops along his thick mane, not strong enough to wet the hair.

Ashta quickly clambered to her feet. Her hair tangled around her arms and back. Frantic, she clawed at it, trying to get it over her shoulder and out of the way.

"Wait!" she called as she watched the lions tail switch back and forth in the entrance before disappearing.

Her fingers quickly parted the hair into three parts, braiding it in a child's pattern. By the time she reached the end, the thick length came down past her belly button. She pulled the end into a knot, not wanting it to unravel.

Ashta threw the thick rope of hair over her shoulder and ran into the rain. The shock of cold woke her mind and senses, allowing her to feel the lion, who was almost at the end of the block of ruins.

Ashta ran through the rain and puddles, clutching her chest again. The air was warm. Humid. There was a lightness to the sky, despite the unending clouds above.

The lion chuffed as she came alongside him. Ashta slowed to a walk, her shoulders tingling, her eyes weary as she searched the dark corners and rooms they passed.

A day had passed since she was freed.

Too much time.

The water in the street began to flow steadily, a stream weaving its way northwards. The water was dark and muddy from sand. Despite her thirst, Ashta hesitated. It was only the first day since she had eaten and drank. She had survived longer without either.

Her fingers in her right hand found their way unerringly into the lion's mane. She could feel the gentle rumble of his purr, its tingles soothing her mind and hunger.

The stream rose until Ashta and the lion were forced to edge along the buildings. The centre of the street was knee deep and moving swiftly. And the rain continued.

Finally, the crumbling walls of Trian rose before her, the water pooling along its length, steadily gaining height.

Worried, Ashta looked to the east. More water. She turned to the west. A league down the wall, the water was running to the northern entrance before flowing out into the desert.

Before she could move, the lion chuffed. Images of her on his back flashed through her mind.

He walked into the water, the level rising up to his chest quickly. Ashta quickly followed before diving into the murky depths. She swam to the lion and gripped his mane, letting her legs float behind him. She could feel his shoulders and hips moving beneath her.

With the currents aiding them, they quickly slipped through the entrance. On the other side, floating in a lake of dirty water, were canvas tents and furs.

Ashta released the lion and swam as quick as she could towards the nearest tent. Luck smiled down on Ashta as her hands wrapped around a berserker's cape.

She dragged it with her back out of the tent. Her feet struggled through the sludge, as she collected a still full flask and leather bags with dry food inside.

By the time she reached the relative dry earth, the walls of Trian were a blurry distant speck in the distance.

The lion stepped out of the water beside her. He stopped and shook himself, the water colliding with rain. His mane puffed up again, relatively dry.

Smiling, Ashta pulled the cloak around her shoulders. She greedily drank from the flask, only leaving it half full. Turning, she began walking along the packed wagon path that eventually trailed eastward to Naankdoen.

Two years ago, she had left for Naankdoen, a white lioness to the Princess of Bbrski.

And now, she walked the path, alone, a free woman.

She yelled out in triumph, her heart beating fast.

The lion joined her, his roar shaking through her body.

Ashta smiled.

Then together, with the rain still steadily pattering down on them, Ashta and the lion began walking north into the desert.

As the day wore on, the reality of her life began to settle over her. And the immediate danger of being hunted down waned.

She was a free woman. But Lord Pelop was right. She had nowhere to go. She had no home to return to. She had no allies.

Suddenly, the years of running and loneliness ahead of her bore down on Ashta. She trembled with grief and despair.

What was freedom with no one to share it with?
Ashta stumbled.
The lion pressed closer. His warmth did nothing to fill the void that had suddenly opened inside of her.
Sightlessly, Ashta continued through the sand.

With no stars to guide her and sand all around her deep into the horizon, Ashta worried she was walking in circles. It had been days since she and the lion had last walked on the packed earth of the trading path.

At night she would set the flask out to refill it with rainwater. She then gathered the cape over herself and the lion. She would unravel her hair for an extra layer, wishing she had found more than just a single cape in the lake outside Trian. She huddled underneath the relative dryness of her cape, the lion warming her with his body heat.

And in the morning, she would wake up, alone, the rain still falling steadily. She would carefully chew a small amount of the dried meats and fruits in the leather bag. And then she would walk all day until the lion appeared from the mist again.

After a week, she ran out of dried food.

Days passed after that, an unending gray sky that only changed to darker or lighter gray. Sometimes the rain came down in sheets like the first day. Sometimes it barely rained, a gentle mist that sparkled across the desert making it impossible to look up.

The weather matched the fog surrounding Ashta's inner thoughts and feelings.

Sometimes all she could think about during the hours alone trekking through the sand was the look of shock, of love and acceptance as Kkaar stared back at Ashta right as the spear pierced her to the ground.

Other days she could remember herself walking through the cliffs with her grandfather, happy and carefree.

One morning Ashta woke and the heat of the lion was still at her side. She frowned but did not say anything. Her steps were weak as she stumbled through the sand, falling more than once to her hands.

Her chest and side where Enzol had poured the acid over burned hot. Her skin was clammy all day despite the relative chill in the air.

It was also a day where the rain poured down in sheets.

The male lion nudged her. She grabbed onto his mane and pulled herself up, swaying. She did not bother pulling her hood back over her head, letting the rain cool her skin.

In a haze, she held on to the lion's mane, following his lead.

Through the blur of the rain, a dark patch blocked out the sky ahead.

Ashta frowned but continued.

As they neared the dark patch, the rain came down even harder. Each drop sharp as a blade against her skin. The cuts bled; the blood washed away with the next drop.

The lion suddenly began to run towards the dark patch, his tail twitching. Ashta stumbled, fear gripping her for the first time in days. She couldn't lose him! He was all she had left in this hazy world.

And then the rain stopped.

Or rather, Ashta stumbled underneath the shelter of a massive black stone. The space was big enough for her and the lion. And high enough the water ran away from it and down the sand dune.

Ashta fell before the lion, curling into his middle and clutching his mane. Her breath came in fast as her body shook with tremors. The lion leaned into her and licked her shoulder, his purr for once doing nothing to sooth her.

His ears twitched. He turned his amber eyes outwards and squinted into the rain. A low grumble shook through him, low enough not to wake Ashta from feverish sleep.

Through the rain, a shadow emerged.

A tall man with purple eyes that glowed despite the dark sky. He nodded to the lion.

The lion chuffed, gently nudging Ashta off his body so he could stand. He walked out into the rain, looking back once.

The man carefully gathered Ashta into his arms, his gaze gentle as he placed a soft kiss on her forehead.

The lion grumbled to himself before turning and disappearing into the gray.

CHAPTER THIRTY-SIX

⌘

All of Time

SOMEONE WAS CRYING. Ashta could not say if her eyes were open or if she was awake. She could not feel her limbs. But somehow, she sensed someone was crying.

And then the room sharpened, the familiar stone walls. A woman sat, alone, on her settee. A great tapestry lay across her lap. She pulled the thread through, meticulously embroidering the small face of a child.

Iara.

"My star," zHella called out quietly as he stood just inside the room. "Did you hear me?"

A deep sadness weighed his shoulders down.

The queen continued to cry, her tears staining the tapestry, but the needle never wavered.

Sighing, zHella walked into the room. He knelt down before his love, pulling her from the settee and into his lap. She came willingly, clutching his shirt to her.

Grief washed through him from their connection. He berated himself for not protecting her better. For not protecting his *family* better. He slowly pet her hair, trying to sooth the ache from losing one of their babies.

"She is alive," he whispered between soft kisses on her cheeks and over her eyes. "We know where she is. Is that not a blessing?"

Iara began laughing historically, her face a twisted grimace as she cried out, "Blessing? We can never hold our *daughter*, our little star, in our arms again. You know as well as I the laws of Tripsia."

Alerik said nothing. Just continued to hold her as her tears slowly waned.

"Why can't we steal her back?" a voice asked from the door.

Iara and zHella turned as one to their son. Prince zHaviel had become silent since the disappearance of his sister. Not even they could hear his once open thoughts.

The King was the one who replied, on a weary sigh. "Tripsia was built on the blood of elves. The people are bound to the land as the land is bound to the people, forever and for always."

The boy watched his father silently. His gaze suspicious.

Iara carefully untangled herself from her husband and walked to her son, pulling him into her arms. He watched his mother with his unbalanced gaze. She looked deep into his eyes before whispering, showing with her mind as she spoke. "Your sister is now as bound to the land of Tripsia as your fathers' people are to the desert. Never has a slave left Tripsia."

Carien hummed under her breath, her arms full off soiled cloth used to swaddle the little one. Mina babbled behind her from the sling she was tied in.

The stream was close to the village. A short walk around a large cliff face.

"You should have sent the old hag to wash the babe's clothes. She offered," Luci grumbled, her gaze weary as it constantly searched the trees and rocks around them. It had been weeks of silence. They should have heard something by now. Kkaar should have come for them.

"That *hag-*"

But Luci had already come around and pushed Carien against the cliff face. Wide-eyed Carien looked past Luci's shoulder to where the lioness was staring.

Below them, a single Tripsian soldier, his bronze helmet shining against the grey rock face, picked his way along towards the village. Neither woman spoke, their muscles rigid.

"Come, come, my stars," the majik woman called out.

zHar gripped the woman in his arms close to his chest as he ducked inside the Yer.

The woman let the flap settle, closing them off from the continuous rain and cold.

Inside, a hot fire burned, a stew bubbling. zHar caught sight of a bowl of some poultice, already finished, sitting to the side.

Bring her here, there is not much time left.

zHar's heart ached. Had he been too late? As soon as he had felt her call, he had left for the ancient city.

He carefully set her down on the furs. She looked so small. Thin. Her cloak fell open, baring the black mess on her chest and side to the fire.

zHima gasped as she stumbled and quickly knelt at her side. "The idiot..." she muttered as she carefully picked at the edge of the crust. A piece came off, bright green puss oozing out from beneath.

The smell of rot and death filled the tent. zHar gagged, quickly turning away and covering his nose.

"It's far worse than I feared. Send for jHora and Amkan and zHeezek."

zHar nodded but did not move, his eyes on her pale face. On those black eyelashes that fanned out along her cheeks. He gently grazed a finger along her cheek bone. *Please, my star. I've only just found you again.*

Carien walked through the court. Nobles and courtiers, slaves and servants lined the walls. All watched her silently.

She pushed back her shoulders.

Ahead of her stood the council, Baron Laem in front of the throne her father had once sat on. Her chest ached at the loss.

Taking a breath, she shoved the emotion down, practising her stone face. *Don't let them see, or they will tear you apart.*

She did not look away from Laem, her steps measured as her sash dragged behind her, almost the same length of the room. It's weight a symbol of the weight of Tripsia, which now sat on her small shoulders.

She stepped up to the throne, slowly turning to face the court. Briefly, she let her gaze sweep around the room.

He's not here.

She bit her tongue to ease the sting of her heart.

Baron Laem stepped up beside her, holding her father's crown.

Carien reached for it, surprised at the weight of the gaudy thing. She lifted it over her head for all to witness. Then she placed it over her silk covered head.

Baron Laem, "Queen Kehlani, first of her name!"

People stepped forward, screaming and shouting their approval. Their roar of jubilation filling Carien's heart.

I did the right thing.

The full moon hung in the sky, its white face shining down over the rolling sand hills. The alps of the east slowly shifted and moved west before crowding the sky in the north.

On the edge of the desert stood a woman. Her sky blue gaze cloudy as she stared out at the unending sea of sand.

"The clansmen are ready. We should go while the night is still young," a man growled behind her, his gaze never leaving her face.

But the woman did not see it.

Absently she nodded.

He waited a moment for her to speak. But words did not come. He turned, stalking over to the men. Anger burned through him.

Before he could yell out the command, wolves and men alike spilled from the trees surrounding them.

The men quickly ran to encircle the woman. But she pushed them aside and met the wolves head on, her twin blades glinting in the moon. A smile lit her face.

Darkling screamed as she crushed the hand clutching her left hand. Her taught belly convulsed.

One more push, and the little one should be here.

Darkling grit her teeth as she looked over her belly at the woman. The pain was unimaginable. Her back burned. Tears streamed from her eyes as she growled and pushed down once more.

Except it was not one little one.

The woman carefully laid out the babes, a boy and girl on Darkling's chest. Smiling, Darkling gathered her arms around them. Her heart was full.

Remina carefully snuck through the dark halls. Most of the servants had gone to sleep in the household. And the guards sat together playing dice. She would have to tell Justus, she thought, frowning at the men.

Finally, she eased open the door and stood before the great bed.

"You came," Justus whispered from beside the door.

Remina whipped around, her gaze hungry for him. Those black eyes that were always warm around her. That unruly hair.

He walked towards her, slowly, giving her time to change her mind.

But she wasn't going to back down.

Justus stopped before her, his chest almost brushing across hers.

Remina shivered, the heat of him intoxicating.

She shouldn't be here. Biting her lip, she instead stared down at the little patch of hair that curled over the V in his shirt. A need burned in her core, that could not be ignored any longer.

"Mina," he whispered, his hand slowly coming up and cupping her cheek.

She leaned into it, her eyes fluttering closed as she sighed.

Before she lost her nerve, she whispered, "I love you, Justus."

Justus stilled; his body suddenly tense.

Frowning, Remina pulled out of his hold and looked up at him. She gasped at the heat of his gaze, the sharpness of his clenched jaw.

Without another word, he wrapped his arms around her. Remina wrapped her legs around him, trembling as her heart beat to fast in her chest. Justus walked until his legs hit the bed then tumbled down onto the soft mattress.

No more words were spoken.

Standing before Darkling was a young woman. Her hair was white blonde. Her skin was red, peeling across her burnt nose. But what stopped Darkling's heart was the other woman's eyes.

Forest green. Lush like a jungle. Crawling and alive.

Ceerie's daughter.

Darkling was not surprised when the girl, glaring at Darkling with her back rigid, growls, "I am-"

"Mina," Darkling finished.

The girl stopped, her eyes widening in shock.

Darkling sighed, "Come inside."

The hole inside Darkling threatened to swallow her. It was worse than losing Kkaar. Than Ceerie.

Worse than losing her mother.

Her hands shook as she reached down to his still hands, rigid in death. Tears refused to come. Shock had her slowly shaking her head as she sunk to her knees, looking into his still face.

Ashta did not feel the heat of the familiar grip on her shoulders. She did not hear the others words. All she could see was his face.

Why does everyone I care about die?

CHAPTER THIRTY-SEVEN

⌘

Taken Name

S*HOULDN'T SHE HAVE woken up by now?*

Patience, child, she has had a long journey from the golden palace. It won't be long now.

Ashta could hear movement near her. The rustle of fabric as someone moved in their clothing. A quick wisp of cold air, as if someone had entered. Or left.

The waves of heat from her right.

She carefully tensed her fingers and toes. Her right hand itched, something tying the fingers tight.

A hand pulled her left hand into a warm clasp. A thumb gently rubbed the centre of her palm. The touch soothed her, as much as it warmed her.

Ashta stretched her neck and groaned as the movement ached along her entire back. How long had she been laying here, she wondered?

Two fortnights.

Ashta froze, her breath caught in her chest.

The gentle rubbing motion on her palm continued.

She breathed out as she continued to stretch her arms and legs, gently testing her range of motion. She wasn't alone. And she wasn't sure if the person holding her was an ally or an enemy.

Friend. Or at least I hope to be.

Frowning, Ashta was sure she had not spoken her thought aloud. And she was sure that no one else had answered her thought aloud. She tried to open her eyes, but her eyelids felt weighted down.

Sighing, she fell back into a dreamless sleep.

A burning cold touched her side. Ashta gasped, pushing away from whatever was touching her.

Stop moving.

Never, she thought, she needed to get away from the pain. She would not die. She would not let them come for her.

It is for your burn, to help the healing.

She frowned as memories slowly trickled in. The bowl with purple smoke. Enzol pouring it down her side. Screaming in pain.

You are safe, the familiar voice spoke in her head again.

She wasn't sure of that, but she relaxed against the ground, holding herself still as the pain returned to her side. She grit her teeth.

I wish I could take you pain for you. Fingers entwined in her left hand, the thumb gently rubbing along her thumb.

You have already made it better, she thought towards him.

His thumb stilled for a moment. Then continued.

I think she is waking, zHima.

Ashta was surprised when another voice, though distant replied. *I will return when I am done setting the break.*

Whoever was beside her, let her hand go. The cold sting also disappeared.

Curious, Ashta focused on opening her eyes.

Despite the little light in the space, she had to squint to see around her. Above her was a canvas tent and a small hole in the centre of the roof. It was a familiar sight from a year ago. A Yer.

She turned her head and saw a man carefully cleaning a white cloth in a bucket.

It is infused with Ruutka.

Ashta frowned, then tentatively asked in her head, *are you speaking to me with your thoughts?*

The man turned and she was caught in twin amethyst gaze. *Just as you are speaking with your thoughts to me.*

She was frozen, both with the realization that she could mind-speak and that zHar was coming towards her.

He knelt down at her side.

Ashta struggled to sit up, the movement causing her side to flare up with heat. zHar put his arm out and helped her rise completely.

Once she was sitting, she looked around herself. A blazing fire was to her left a pot bubbling over it. The soft white hides of a deer like animal lay beneath her, stuffed into the edges of the Yer to keep the cold out and the heat in. Her eyes tracked the piles of canvas bags that lined all around the Yer, each carefully tied closed. The occasional spear or sword peeked out from the canvas. Above her, the rope lashes kept the canvas tight over the wooden stakes of the walls. She couldn't help but notice the dark stain of years of smoke in the middle. Her eyes tracked the smoke down to the fire that burned beside her.

Finally, she turned to zHar. His hair had lightened since she had last seen him, the ends bleached from the strong desert sun. His sharp jaw was softened by the beginnings of a beard. Ashta's fingers itched to touch it and feel if it was soft or scratchy against her skin.

His mouth twitched. *Go ahead.*

Heat burned across her cheeks as she looked down at herself. She realized she was still naked, furs piled over her legs and a large bandage wrapped around her right hand.

Chuckling, zHar pulled both of her hands into his. Ashta stared at her small white hands, dainty looking in his hold despite the years of calluses built on them.

Why can I hear you? She asked. *I never heard you before in my mind.* Ashta chewed her lip as she finally dared to look up into his purple eyes.

His gaze was soft as his thumbs rubbed along her hands. "It is a long story. Almost as old as time."

Her black gaze sparked with annoyance. zHar smiled. He had missed her fire. He continued in her mind. *A long time ago, our people lost a daughter, and Naankdoen a princess, to Tripsia. And now she has returned to her home.*

Ashta stared at him, not understanding. He tightened his grip leaning in. Her breath left her as he whispered, "*You* are returned home."

Home.

The word did not make sense to her.

Before she could say another word, the tent flap moved and a stooped older woman, no bigger than Trice had been, walked in. Her long white braids almost dragged along the ground.

Ah, you have awakened. Good.

Ashta's eyes widened, and she turned to zHar. Could she hear everyone's thoughts now?

Yes, my child. Just as we can hear and feel everything you push outside of yourself.

Ashta pulled her hands out of zHar's grasp and wrapped them around herself, cold at the idea that her thoughts, her innermost feelings were now open to one and all to hear.

The woman clucked, bringing the bowl of something steaming over to Ashta. She settled down on to her butt, groaning as her legs creaked with age. Ashta winced, watching her move.

"You mustn't worry, my child. For years your true self had been dampened by the *binding*. Now that the marks have been removed, you are as you always have been."

Ashta stayed silent, questions in her eyes.

The woman held out the bowl. "Drink this and I will explain. And you," she said, glaring at zHar, "Will go and find some coverings for the woman."

When he didn't rise right away, a blast of power washed through Ashta that set all of her hairs on end. She watched wide eyed as zHar winced before rising and disappearing out of the Yer.

zHima grumbled before turning to Ashta. *Drink.*

Ashta quickly pulled the bowl to her mouth and took a tentative sip. The milky liquid tasted like black dirt. Ashta wrinkled her nose but took another sip.

The healer smiled. Then she leaned forward and drew in the air a circle in front of Ashta. "Your mind is like this circle, your thoughts and feelings and memories floating in a deep but narrow pool." Then she drew a wider circle around the imagined first circle. "Around the deep pool is a shallower area, and this is outside of your mind. It can be an arm's length around your mind. Some children have a larger pool and some smaller. If a person is standing in this pool, then they can feel and hear your thoughts that swim in *this* depth but not what is in the deep pool." She suddenly gripped Ashta's arms, surprising strength in her hands. "But just as they can hear your thoughts, you are also then standing in their pool and *you* can hear and feel everything of theirs." *Understand?*

Ashta nodded.

Keep drinking.

Ashta grimaced. The bowl was only half empty, and ,impossibly, as the liquid cooled the flavour became stronger.

"Now, if you focus, my child, you can let only the thoughts and feelings you *want* others to think and feel in the shallow waters and keep the rest swimming deep in your mind."

Ashta's shoulders loosened. She sighed. There was a way to close her mind.

But how could she know if she was keeping her thoughts inside herself?

Time, zHima replied.

Ashta frowned.

The woman smiled and patted her arm. "Time and practicing with another until you are sure of your range." zHima turned to the entrance of the Yer.

zHar ducked inside, clothes on his arms.

His gaze went to Ashta, running down her face and arms. Only when he saw she was alright, even relaxed, did he let out a breath and relax. He gave her a small smile.

"Just leave the clothes here. You can wait outside," the majik woman dismissed him.

The smile disappeared. He glared at zHima but did as he was told, placing the clothes beside Ashta before he turned and left as well. Ashta could see his light just outside the entrance.

"Lights?" zHima asked in delight, cackling. She almost fell over from laughter.

Ashta glared at her as well. She finished the last of the disgusting drink. Pulling the furs off her legs, she went to stand but stopped when she looked down. Both feet were wrapped completely in bandages.

The majik woman's laughter slowly dwindled. She wiped her eyes before turning to Ashta's feet as well. "These should be healed now, my child."

As for your lights, she said, her inner voice chuckling, *those are the pools that surround every one of us.*

Ashta watched her as zHima pulled the bandages back. She carefully rose up onto her feet, looking down at the thick scars that wrapped around her feet and up her legs. She craned her neck to see her side. A purple and red mess of blistered skin went from just underneath her breast to around her back and down to her hip.

Her hands were covered in white and red scars, the new ones blending in with the old. Blue ink peeking out from her left hand.

For the first time, Ashta really saw her body. And she was ashamed of what she saw.

Your scars mark you as a survivor. Someone with many tales.

The healer's words soothed her a little. She was glad to pull and twist the rough white cloth around herself, like the other zMun women wore. The bottom covered her legs and some of the scars from her own gaze.

"Now, it is time that you tell me your name, child."

"Name?" Ashta asked as her brows wrinkled.

The woman chuckled, snapping her fingers. "Aye, what you wish to be called."

Ashta opened her mouth to answer but the woman waved her off, "And not who you have been before. Who do *you* want to be?"

zHima walked over to the bucket where several other pouches hung from the canvas wall, leaving Ashta to think.

What was in a name? She had been given Svetlana at birth. And she had earned Ashta in the pits. And her silence had resulted in Darkling amongst the other white lionesses.

Each name had been wrapped around her, woven from the threads of others. And while Ashta had picked one name over the other, one duty over the other, she never had the freedom to choose who she wanted to be.

She was free now.

The reminder of that truth brought a smile to her lips as she stared at the dancing flames in the cooking fire.

As she stared, a memory washed over her, Trice's familiar voice speaking softly for attention…

A father, in despair, made a bargain with the elf king.

He was given a berry that would allow the wife to hold a babe to term. But in exchange for the berry the father had to promise that if the babe was not quite human that he or she be given back to the elves.

Not a year later his wife gave birth. But the babe was strange.

The husband, worried, asked the wiccan what was wrong, and she told him it was Darkling, a babe of the spirits and all things evil.

She had been placed inside the nest, whether it was Tripsia, Bbrski or amongst the other lionesses. Not quite human. The pulse of lights beyond the Yer reminded her of her sudden strength.

If what zHar had said was true, then the legend of Darkling suited who she was more than Trice had known.

The memory of her friend brought a familiar ache in her heart. She had lost everyone she had ever cared for. And now, once again, she was an outsider. Not quite like the zMun.

You are perfect as you are, zHar interrupted her musings.

His thought warmed her chest even as she glared behind her towards the entrance. That feeling grew, the love she felt for her friend pouring through her.

No, she did not know how the legend ended. But she also did not know how her own story ended.

She turned to the healer and said in a clear voice, "I want to be called Darkling."

The majic woman nodded, returning to Darkling's side. "Then Darkling you shall be."

The healer gently grabbed Darkling's hand and tugged her outside. Darkling gasped as rain drizzled down, soaking her hair.

It's still raining.

She looked up at the cloudy sky in awe.

The lights, *the people*, Darkling reminded herself, slowly came closer until their brightness warmed Darkling's face. It was unlike when she walked through the Tripsian people. This brightness did not burn. It lapped around her in a warm gentle wave.

She opened her eyes and looked around her. Every man, woman and child stood around her, each connected from hand to hand. zHar held onto zHima who reached her hand out to Darkling's shoulder.

"Darkling," someone whispered.

Darkling.

"Darkling."

Darkling, Darkling.

Darkling!

"Darkling!"

Her shoulder burned, filling her mind and soul with warmth, cocooning her in love. Darkling turned her face up to the sky and cried.

CHAPTER THIRTY-EIGHT

⌘

Wandering

IN THE MIDDLE OF THE night, the rain stopped for the first time in over a month. The next morning Darkling helped zHima take down the Yer. The other families were also busy, rolling the canvas' up and placing them on the backs of the yak's.

Darkling was a quick study, but her strength had still not returned. Her right hand also was not healed, and the bandage made her clumsy with the ropes. zHima forced the black-eyed woman to sit and rest many times.

By the time midday came around, the sun was high in the sky, baking the desert sand. Mist filled the air, leaving nothing to see but the shift from sky to mist. It was eery and beautiful. Darkling was comforted by the warmth of the mist touching her face.

She noticed that many of the zMun people also paused in their work to feel the mist on their faces. The children laughed and darted through tents and yaks and mist. For the first time, she felt a smile, a *real* smile cross her lips as happiness flickered inside of her, a small candle surrounded by the shadows of her pain and loss.

Maybe she would stay with the zMun.

She had nowhere else to go, she mused. And the zMun were notoriously difficult to find. Darkling herself did not know where they went, for the entries about them in her readings had been few and far between.

After the midday meal, the carts were loaded, and the caravan began. Darkling walked behind the cart that held the majik woman's Yer canvas. zHima had already disappeared amongst the people.

Soon enough a familiar light was beside her. Darkling did not need to look to know zHar walked beside her.

Darkling wanted to ask him a question, but she still was not sure of speaking with her mind. Her speaking voice she knew how to control. And as for her thoughts and feelings, she pulled them close to her chest and hid them, even from herself.

zHar watched the black haired beauty at his side. He was awed by the darkness of her hair. The sunlight did not reflect off her hair, as if it was absorbed inside to light her from within.

His fingers itched to touch a stray lock that had escaped her long braid. Would it be as soft as the curl looked?

He turned away from her and instead looked ahead into the mist. Over the last day, the loudness of his star's feelings had quieted. He was not surprised at her strength. Some of the older zMun were wearier of her.

After a long silence, she asked in a whisper, just between them, "How do they know where to go?" She nodded towards jHora and several young men that walked beside him at the front of their column.

zHar looked over at her and saw only curiosity in her gaze. A wave of distrust hit him from behind. He ignored Ameera, instead taking a step closer so that his shoulder almost brushed against Darkling's. His arms burned from the heat of her skin so close.

Taking a quick breath, he hoped Darkling had not felt Ameera. "jHora is the strongest of our people. He can sense where the Kiang don are."

Darkling's eyes widened but she did not reply.

They continued walking until the sun began to set. The mist lifted and turned into a gentle shower. A few of the canvases were pulled out of the carts and stretched. Darkling found herself sleeping beside zHar, the heat of him at her back unnerving. Her mind was awake as she heard the rustle of the young family sleeping in front of her. And zHima sleeping at Darkling's head.

You are safe, my star, zHar whispered in her mind. When his arm came around to rest on her waist, she did not pull away. She felt safe.

The gentle patter of the rain against the canvas slowly pulled her into soft dreams.

The next day, as they continued walking, several children came to walk beside Darkling and zHar. "Are you going to show us to fight again? Papa said you were faster than zHella himself with a sword!"

Darkling gave a small smile to the boy but said nothing.

zHar bumped her shoulder lightly. "It would be nice to do something during the midday again." And then in a softer voice, "If you want to."

A part of her did want to. She had been trained to fight. She was good at it. And a smaller part worried that one day she would need to fight for her life again. Darkling could still see Ennris's red eyes as she growled at Darkling.

It was only a matter of time.

Darkling turned to the boy instead and asked, "What's your name?"

He smiled a toothy grin, "Naar. And that's my Papa, zHook."

Darkling looked to the side to the older man who walked beside a heavily pregnant woman. The man gave her a nod and a small smile. Darkling waved at him.

The kids introduced themselves to Darkling, excited at the prospect of watching a real warrior fight. They leapt and ran around Darkling and zHar, showing the pair their warrior skills.

Darkling smiled and shared a warm glance with zHar. Her fingers brushed against his hand. But she did not take it.

The weeks passed in an easy rhythm. Darkling spent an hour with the willing men and women to train at the midday. Sometimes the children joined. Sometimes they were too busy playing in the mist to remember to come. Everyone watched when Darkling and zHar sparred afterwards.

Her strength slowly returned, her cheeks filled, and shoulders began to round out. zHar was always near, coaxing a smile or a few words out of the quiet woman.

When they walked, Darkling and zHar would stay near the back of the column. After the first day, Darkling began practising her mind-speak with him, gauging her strength and her distance.

At night, when the rain would return, cooling the desert, zHar would hold her close. Darkling would tell herself it was for warmth as most of the zMun slept in a close pile together. But the tingles that raced across her skin each time were not from simple body heat.

Early in the morning, one day, Darkling noticed the soft desert sand shift to packed dirt. Then small tufts of grass began to spot the ground. Low brush, thick with silvery leaves, grazed their dewy tops against her bare legs.

When they stopped for the midday meal, zHar pulled her away from the encampment. *Come, we shall eat fresh meat today.*

Curious, Darkling let him lead her into the mist. zHar pulled out a small dagger and crouched in the dirt. His hands rubbed the imprint of an animal track. Two claws.

RsAmmm. Still your mind and movements, as they can hear us.

Darkling's pulse began to race with the excitement of the hunt. She followed on silent feet as zHar led her behind a rock. He carefully held his finger to his mouth before pointing at the brush on the other side.

Darkling glanced around the rock. At first, she saw nothing, just silver leaves in the bush.

But then the bush moved.

To her amazement, the bush turned, and feathers shifted that replicated the texture of the bush leaves. It looked like a strange coloured chicken, she thought to herself.

She almost jumped when zHar grabbed her hand. For a long moment, they crouched there in the stillness of the mist, staring deep into each other's eyes. Darkling's gaze lowered to the white scar along his nose. His beard had filled in, making him look rugged and wild, suiting his curling hair. Her gaze caught on his lips, the top one slightly bigger than the bottom.

What would they feel like against hers, she wondered for a moment? Blushing at her thoughts, she looked into his gaze again. Amethyst eyes burned for her. She didn't dare name what she saw in his gaze.

She broke away and looked back at the RsAmmm. She felt the cool steel of a blade against her palm. Looking down, she realized it was zHar's dagger.

Without hesitation, she took it in her good hand.

zHar kept hold of her right hand, gently rubbing the stiff joints that had not healed properly.

With a deep breath to settle herself, she stared at the RsAmmm.

Then she released the dagger.

Squawk!

The bird jumped once before it stopped moving. Darkling jumped up, running to her quarry. She retrieved the blade from its chest, quickly wiping it on her skirt before handing it to zHar who stood beside her.

Her mouth salivated at the memory of cooked chicken. The stews of the last week while hearty were bland at best.

zHar took the bird by its legs, pulling Darkling into his chest with his other arm. Her hands came up against his chest automatically.

Both stilled as they realized how close they were. Only the slightest movement would land zHar's lips on her own. Darkling shivered at the feel of his hot breath tingling across her lips.

She closed her eyes.

Waiting.

The Naankdoena are here, jHora's voice rang through their minds.

Darkling stepped back.

zHar dropped his arm.

In a quiet thought between them, she asked zHar, *Why would the Naankdoena be here?*

Sighing, zHar turned and began the trek back to the encampment. He did not reply. Darkling could sense something brewing beneath, his light suddenly turbulent. Had she done something wrong, she wondered?

Maybe he doesn't want you in that way, a small voice inside of herself said. *You are too old, to scarred, to broken for a man.*

Shaking her head, she focused instead on the crowd that appeared before them. Naankdoena soldiers mixed with zMun. Darkling was surprised to see a male soldier embracing the older woman Ameera.

Her son, zHar answered.

Darkling looked to zHar but stayed silent. She had not thought about the connection between the zMun and Naankdoen. Seeing it was surreal.

But not as surreal when a familiar dark haired man materialised in front of her, his uneven gaze catching her own.

zHavier.

He glanced at zHar with a quirked brow. zHar grunted, turning and leaving Darkling alone with zHav.

She frowned after him. zHar had never been so short with her.

"I had heard the rumours that Ashta the Lion Tamer had joined the zMun."

Darkling turned and glared at him. "Ashta is dead. I go by Darkling."

He held his hands up, a smirk on his face. "I thought only friends were allowed to call you that."

Darkling could feel the anger building up, rolling inside of her. She had not thought she would ever see anyone from her former life again. Least of all the prince of Naankdoen.

She turned away and looked around herself. Several people suddenly turned away from her and the prince, busying themselves.

Suddenly, Darkling wished zHav wasn't there.

zHav ignored her cold shoulder and stepped closer, placing a hand on her arm. She glared at the hand but made no motion to remove it. His heartbeat picked up. Things were different now, he thought to himself.

"Why are you here, zHav," she whispered, her gaze sliding past him and fixed to the mist over his shoulder.

"It was only two days ride to the encampment," he joked.

Darkling ignored his humour, instead focusing on the words. They were close to the Naankdoen border then. The distance between Tripsia and herself eased some of the anxiety that had hounded her for months.

Sighing, zHav looked down at her seriously, seeing the changes of the last year. Her long black hair hung in a single braid over shoulder. White and pink scars lined her arms and legs, disappearing beneath her clothes. His gaze caught on the pale fingers of her right hand and their odd angle.

Without thought, he grabbed her hand to inspect them closer. "What happened?" he growled, angry that she had been disfigured.

Darkling was to surprised at the heat of his touch, the tingles that shivered through her arms. She answered honestly, "They were severed by a sword." His angry gaze clashed with hers. Before he could question, she added, "He's dead."

zHav nodded slowly. He lowered their hands but did not release her.

Darkling shifted on her feet, uncomfortable. She could feel the heat of the zMun watching them.

In a low whisper, zHav began. "It has been months since the last sighting of the Black Death. My people are finally recovering from over a year of siege and starving. The wall has been mended and preparations for a second wave have begun. Ballista have been installed every few yards along the entire length of the wall."

Darkling stared at him, her black gaze closed, giving nothing of herself away. Some things did not change, zHav though as he glanced down at her full lips.

Clearing his throat, he continued, gently rubbing his thumb along her wrist. "There are rumors of a civil war in Bbrski…"

Darkling blinked. This close to zHav she didn't dare think about what his words meant; in case he heard her thoughts. She had not forgotten her time in Naankdoen.

Finally, she pulled her hand out of his. "Why are you *here*, zHav?" she asked again.

He looked down at his hands, suddenly cold and empty.

Taking a deep breath, he grabbed both her hands in his this time. He leaned in close, whispering for her ears only, "Will you marry me?"

Darkling was surprised at the slight burst of heat in her heart from his words. She blushed, but pulled out of his hands again, this time taking several steps back.

zHav was not dissuaded. He followed her, his voice picking up volume. "You don't have an excuse now. You are no longer bound to Tripsia or the Tripsian princess. Your homeland has cut you from the royal line. There is nothing standing between us now."

Darkling took another step back, a flash of a memory overwhelming her, still as strong as the day it happened. Of zHav pulling the arrow back. The finality of Lily's death as the barrel burst in flame.

She took another step back, her head slowly shaking no.

zHav hesitated, finally noticing her wide eyes and the paleness of her face. He stopped from trying to hold her and instead straightened up to his full height. "I know this is fast. The people will be staying here for a few days before moving on. We are here to deal with the healer, jHora, to refill our supply of Ruutka. I will come to you tomorrow before we leave for the city."

He looked deep into those dark eyes that swallowed him whole. "Darkling," he whispered, "Give it a day before you come to me with your answer."

She only stared up at him, her body trembling with fear and something else.

He nodded, more to himself than to her. He turned away, calling over his shoulder, "Until tomorrow. I will be waiting for your answer, Iara."

Darkling shivered as she stared after his familiar black head of hair, as it disappeared into the mist.

CHAPTER THIRTY-NINE

⌘

Broken

FOR ONCE, THE MIST felt like it was pressing down on Darkling. She could not breath. She could not run away.

A small hand curled into hers. Darkling looked down into Naar's big blue eyes. He slowly ripped a bite off of the bun his mother had traded for from the soldiers.

"Will you take a bite?" he asked, holding the bun up to Darkling.

The panic lessened as her heart warmed. She took the bread and took a smile bite before giving it back to the young boy, who was kind and sweet, his milk teeth slowly falling out. He showed Darkling the latest hole with pride as he pulled her to his family's stew pot.

zHook and his wife Amsa, sometimes took Darkling in during the midday meals. She sat with them and Amsa's grandmother as they shared the stew. Their soft voices and kind thoughts gentled her, eased the panic back until Darkling felt surer of her hands.

After the meal, Naar raced ahead as several zMun including zHook collected for the midday sparring. She divided them into pairs. Naar pulled his cousin towards him, an older girl just coming to her first moon bleedings to join the rows of sparring partners. Darkling smiled and gave the children wooden staffs as well.

As she called out the motions and adjusted stances, she kept coming back to Naar, who needed a little more from her. His warmth and acceptance of her filled the space where little Mina had once filled.

Darkling stopped, stalk still as the realization washed over her.

She could have children.

She was no longer bound by the laws of the white lionesses. She could lay with a man if she chose to. She could carry his seed and give birth to a child. She could be a mother, raising and teaching her babe the ways to survive the world.

"Ow!"

Darkling blinked, then quickly went to Naar who rubbed his arms. She pulled his arm closer and noticed the red mark. It would bruise but nothing worse. Naar's eyes watered as he looked up into Darkling's eyes.

"You will heal," she said softly, rubbing his hand.

He sniffed several times, then surprised her by throwing his arms around her neck. Darkling hesitantly wrapped her arms around his tiny body. Just as quick, he pulled away and turned to his cousin Aleeem, his face pulled into a determined scowl.

Darkling set her hand on his shoulder. "Your pain is not her fault," she reminded him, "You control the fight."

Darkling wasn't sure if he heard her, but he took several breaths, just as she had shown the children to help settle themselves. Then he swung at Aleeem.

Releasing her own breath, Darkling continued to walk through the other pairs. The thought of having children excited her. To have a little one who would love her completely, just as Darkling had loved her own mother. It would be everything.

At the end of the sparring, Darkling looked around but zHar did not come for their daily sparring session. Frowning, she decided instead to stretch. Naar and a few of the other children excitedly stood around her, trying to copy her movements.

She smiled at them, as they wobbled, their balance not quite able to handle some of the movements.

Darkling closed her eyes as she breathed through her sun salutations. She tried to imagine her own children. Would they have her family's dark hair?

Unease slid down the back of her neck and settled in her stomach. For some reason, her mind shied away from imagining dark-eyed, dark haired babies. Something deep inside of herself was scared. A vague memory of something bad happening. Darkling couldn't say what, but she opened her eyes and went to help jHora with the trading soldiers.

She only had a day to make her decision about zHav and his proposal. And whether she could marry a prince. A prince who needed an heir.

That night, zHar did not hold her as she slept. He did not even sleep beside her. Darkling tossed and turned, the rain coming down in hard sheets. Eventually she gave up and slipped through the pile of sleeping bodies to the edge of the canvas.

She sat, her long hair a warm curtain around her as she stared out into the darkness. The moon tried in vain to shine through the clouds, hanging low in the horizon.

The rain matched her mood. Darkling could feel the soft cloudiness of the lights behind her as the zMun slept. Ahead, in the darkness she could see the faint light of a torch from the Naankdoena camp.

Could she marry a prince?

She was surprised when zHar walked out of the rain. His hair dripped down his face. Her gaze washed over him, hungry for the sight of him. An ache she had not known was in her chest loosened at having him so near again. The distance of the afternoon was unlike the closeness of the morning. A small part of her wished the prince had never come. But the tension, the feelings that she had always had around zHav had returned quickly, confusing her heart.

zHar stepped towards her. Darkling blinked as she final could see the fur trim along the hood. Bbrski made.

Where did you find a berserker cloak?

The words stopped zHar. Unconsciously, his hand ran down the length. "From you," he whispered.

Darkling shivered at his gravelly voice. At the phantom feel of his arms around her as he carried her through the desert so long ago.

He sat down, settling the cloak around her. Darkling did not move away as he pulled her into his arms. "You should be sleeping," he whispered into her hair, his gaze stuck on the distant torch lighting up the canvas tent where the prince slept soundly.

Darkling shivered. In a small voice, she admitted, "I couldn't fall asleep without you."

zHar turned away from the prince and focused on the woman in his arms, he pulled her into his lap and settled her against his chest. His heart was warm yet ached at the truth in her words.

I need more time, he thought to himself as he placed the barest kiss on her forehead. "Sleep now," he murmured, "I will watch over you, my star."

Darkling relaxed into his strong embrace, the steady beat of his heart lulling her.

The next morning was quiet. The zMun lounged about, some visiting with the soldiers, some disappearing into the mist. There was no purpose to the day, just the knowledge that they would leave soon enough.

Darkling broke her morning fast in silence, not daring to look zHar in the eye.

zHima watched the two with a sharp eye but kept her distance. She snapped at jHora, "Get up and help an old woman with her wears."

jHora smiled softly but did as he was told, not fooled by her words. The healer was stronger than most. She could easily move the Ruutka on her own.

They disappeared into the mist, heading to the soldier encampment to meet, and keep busy, the prince.

Naar ran through and around the many fires of the morning until he stopped, breathless, at Darkling's feet. He looked up at her with wide eyes, "Will you and zHar fight this morning?"

Darkling frowned before looking up at zHar. He shrugged but said nothing.

"After I stretch." The boy jumped up and ran to spread the news to the other children. She shook her head but smiled after him.

zHar reached for her bowl. "You better start stretching then," he mumbled as he stood, quickly walking to the cart.

Darkling stared after him for a moment, admiring his wide shoulders. In a way zHar was similar to zHav. Both were tall, muscled men with a serious air around them. But where zHav's strength came from training with his soldiers, zHar's came from the need to survive in the desert. From helping the struggling families with putting up and taking down their Yer. From hunting for zHima's meal pot, which was shared amongst the hungry and old.

She sighed before quickly going through her motions. By the time she was ready, a small crowd of children and a few adults had gathered around Darkling and zHar.

The first bouts between them were slow. Practiced. As each tested their strength, their flexibility, allowing the other to easily block them.

Then Darkling's eyes sharpened.

zHar smiled softly, his muscles suddenly tense.

She swung at him, then dropped to his side to kick his legs out.

Naar whooped from the side, cheering on Darkling.

Their hands and feet were blurs as they attacked, blocked, parried. Moving around in a circle, a dangerous dance. As the fight wore on and neither gained an edge, the energy shifted.

zHar's hand would linger around the woman's neck before she flipped him over her back.

Darkling's foot would slowly slide against the inside of zHar's leg.

Smirking, he stepped into her, pulling them both down to the packed dirt, still soft from the nights rain. They rolled around in the sand. A flush spread across Darkling's chest as her core tingled. Sweat dripped down zHar's face as he panted, trying to pin her down.

And then suddenly everything was still.

Darkling sat atop zHar her hands wrapped around his neck.

His arms flopped to the side in retreat. His chest heaved as he stared up at her beauty, at the heat in her eyes and the loose curls plastered against her neck. He watched as a single sweat bead dropped down in between her bandages.

Darkling stared at him as he licked his lips. An answering flare of need burning through her own body.

Have you made your mind up? He asked in a deep voice. It wrapped around her even as it cooled her heart.

Had she?

Shivering, Ashta pushed off of him. Before she could stand, he grabbed her arms.

It's none of your business, she snapped at him as she broke his hold.

She stood, not seeing the knowing glances between zHook and his wife's grandmother Ameera. Darkling stalked off towards the outskirts of the encampment.

Energy coursed through her as she paced, out of sight of the Naankdoen soldiers and the prince, and of zHar.

Shivering, she rubbed her arms. She had to make a decision. Today. zHav said he would be waiting for her answer.

And while he was waiting, she had been off sparing with zHar rather than think about zHav's proposal.

Marriage.

She stopped and stared at the shadows in the mist as zMun went about their day.

The hairs stood on the back of her neck. Pieces of visions slowly filtered through her mind. Darkling couldn't help but feel that something bad was coming.

Her whole life, all the people she had cared for had either died or been betrayed by her actions. Kkaar. Ceerie. Carien.

Her mother.

Like the legend, she was a harbinger of death and pain.

Slowly she turned and looked over to the Naankdoena camp. It was almost midday. Darkling could feel the light of the Prince, his energy swirling.

He was waiting.

As she looked out into the mist, Darkling realized there was only one thing she could do.

Slowly letting her arms fall to her side, she stalked to the Naankdoen tents.

A few soldiers milled about, giving her a curious glance as she passed by. zHav stood by the encampment fire, pacing, his hair sticking up in parts as if he had rubbed his hands through it several times.

Darkling hardened her heart at the sight. She needed to be strong.

When he turned, his blue and purple gaze clashed with hers. He stopped, just drinking her in.

Slowly, Darkling walked up to him, keeping an arm's length between their bodies. She looked up into his eyes, letting the warm tingles wash through her. It would be the last time.

"I have made my decision," she whispered inaudibly.

zHav watched her, looking for clues in her face but she gave nothing away. As cold as the ice of her homeland. He rubbed a hand through his hair and asked, "And?"

She looked away briefly and his heart fell.

He was not surprised when she looked back at him and said, "I cannot marry you."

zHav flushed red, his hands tightening into fists as he looked at her. "Can't or won't?" he spat out.

She glared at him. She met his anger with her own, taking a step towards him. Anger radiated off of him.

And something else.

Narrowing her eyes, she pulled inside of herself to listen.

She's mine. I won't let her go. I need her. She knows Bbrski and Tripsia's weaknesses. With her at my side, Naankdoen can fight back against the other kingdoms. Bring the war to their cities. Burn them from the inside out. I will have her-

Darkling snapped back, stumbling a few steps.

zHav reached out to steady her but she twisted away from him, not wanting the monster anywhere near her. Heart racing, she cut him with her words, "I don't owe you a reason, Prince zHavier of Naankdoen."

The anger burned in his glare. Fear shivered through her arms. Darkling pulled out a dagger and stepped close. To the soldiers who had risen to see what bothered their prince, it looked as if they shared a lovers embrace.

Only zHav felt the deadly prick of the blade on his ribs.

Darkling stood on her toes and whispered in his ear. "If you ever try to find me again, I will kill you where you stand. No one will find your body. And you will be forgotten, a name in the wind. Nothing more."

Ice slid through his veins at her threat. His anger cooled as he stared down at cold black eyes. He narrowed his gaze.

"Leave. There is nothing more for you to say," she said, her low voice deceivingly soft.

With no more words to speak, Darkling turned and walked out of the Naankdoen encampment. The mist swallowed her, leaving no trace of the warrior that had threatened a king.

Anger, at himself, had zHav turning to the nearest man and snapping, "Pack up! We leave before sundown."

Just as the zMun's encampment began to materialize through the late evening mist before her, Darkling veered off to the east. Towards the red desert and solitude.

CHAPTER FORTY

⌘

My Star

DARKLING KEPT A QUICK pace, keeping her back to the bright lights of the zMun. She kept her thoughts close, staring aimlessly into the mist. By the time the sun sank beneath the horizon, and the mist dissipated, Darkling could no longer feel any lights at her back. There was only darkness and grey.

Alone.

The first tear dropped soundlessly onto the desert sand. She stumbled her way through the darkness. Loneliness clawed at her as she cried, her vision blurring. She let her emotions free, knowing no one could feel her.

The sharp ache of her solitude after months of the warm embrace of people ripped her in half.

For a short time, she had been safe. Comfortable. Even happy at times. She had begun to believe that she could have a normal life. To give back to the zMun, more than just showing them to fight. To cook, to hunt, to dance. Maybe, to have something more for herself. To find a man who could walk beside her and hold her through the night. Someone who loved her. And who she could freely love back.

Her heart broke as she realized that she would never go back to the zMun. The dream of a life, any life, ripped away by the certainty that she would bring death and destruction down upon those she cared about. How could she bring a child into this world, knowing that her legacy, her *blood*, could be the reason for the death of that same child?

It was impossible.

Unthinkable.

Cruel.

She wrapped her arms around her chest, slow shivers shaking through her as the desert cooled. Darkling looked up to the sky and was surprised to see a million stars, shining brighter than any candles. Not a cloud in the sky.

How strange, she thought morosely, that when her thoughts and feelings were at their dark and murkiest, the great sky above was clear.

Darkling stared at the heavens, wondering if Kkaar was one of those stars. Her friend had helped her through her emotions. Had a clear head and a big heart. Kkaar had showed Darkling what it was to love someone.

Her loss still hurt, but the pain faded with each day, another scar on her heart. She would never forget Kkaar, or any of the lives lost because of Ashta.

But now, at twenty-one, Darkling could not remember what her mother's face looked like. Darkling just remembered the warmth of her mother's dark gaze and drowning in her love. When would the memory of Ceerie's death fade? Kkaar's?

She rubbed her chest as she continued to stare up the sky. She stumbled over the sand, her foot twisting as she sank to her knees. The stinging pain too much for her to stand up. She rolled onto her butt.

A low rumble had Darkling turning around.

Glowing white in the pale moonlight, the male lion padded silently through the sand towards her. When he was near enough to touch, he rubbed along her side, the rumble of his purrs soothing her.

She smiled sadly at him as she wrapped her hands in his mane.

He turned his head, sniffing the scar along her side before licking its entire length. She shivered at the feel of his scratchy tongue.

"It's just you and me now," she told him, turning to look out at the endless sea of sand in every direction. Sighing, she looked straight into his silver gaze, his eyes like two moons reflecting back at Darkling. "Maybe we should sleep here for tonight and continue again in the heat of the day."

He chuffed before rolling onto his side.

Darkling smiled as she crawled to him, then rolled onto her back, her head tucked into his mane, her body along his front. His shoulder moved beneath her as he began cleaning between his claws.

The heat of him gentled her shivers. For the first time that day, Darkling felt at peace. Laying there, in the middle of the desert at night, staring up at the stars. She did not know what would happen tomorrow. What she would eat or drink. If she would live to the end of the day.

Her hand came up to her hair and pulled out zHar's short dagger. As she stared up at the unending sky her fingers toyed with the sharp point. Could she do it, she wondered. Could she take her own life?

It seemed far less pain than slowly starving to death, aimlessly wandering through the desert. She had almost done that once already.

I would mourn your loss to the end of time.

Darkling sat up in shock.

Before her stood zHar. His gaze was shadowed as he looked down at her.

The lion whined as zHar knelt before him, pulling Darkling into his arms. She stood for a moment before her leg collapsed. zHar did not hesitate, swinging her into his arms.

He sat down with ease, settling Darkling in his lap. *Your ankle?* He asked.

She grimaced, *Twisted it in the sand. I don't think I can walk on it.*

zHar was silent. Long enough for Darkling to twist in his arms and look up into his familiar face. His jaw was rigid as he stared out at the sand.

Why are you here? She asked.

He ignored her question. Anger radiated below his skin, making Darkling uncomfortable. She tried to squirm out of his hold but zHar's grip only tightened.

Promise me.

She stilled turning to look up into his familiar warm gaze. There was a vulnerability there that had never been there before. Or she had refused to see it before. She waited.

Promise me you will not take your life.

Her good hand still clutched the dagger. She bit her lip, looking down at the steely length.

Promise you, that I will never take my life? Darkling played with the edge for a moment before reaching up and replacing it into her hair. *Why does it matter?* She snapped at him.

His right hand came up and gently traced her jaw before circling around her lips. Her breath caught in her chest as the tingles of awareness buzzed like a raging fire in her core.

His finger stopped in the middle of her lip, his gaze intent as he pulled it slightly down. Then he looked up into her eyes. Darkling was caught. And she wasn't sure she wanted to escape.

Because I cannot imagine this life without your heart beating against mine, your thoughts brushing mine, your skin touching mine.

He leaned down, as if to kiss her.

Scared, Darkling pushed at his chest.

He stopped, his gaze hardening for a moment before he leaned back again. He sighed then looked out towards the endless sand sea.

"I'm sorry," she whispered, not wanting to hurt zHar.

His smile tipped down into a grimace.

Her heart ached for him, even as fear had a stranglehold on her. She opened her mouth, but the words would not come out, stuck in her throat.

I can't, she said.

He turned to her, his eyes glittering like hard amethyst stone, cold and unyielding.

Flinching, Darkling looked down at her hands, rubbing at the stiff tendons of her right hand. She noticed the pale blue marks on her left hand, the ones that had appeared the first time the zMun had saved her.

His right hand settled on her hands, stopping her movements.

Anxious, she pushed the rest of the words out. *I can't love you the way you deserve to be loved. I can never marry. Or have children.*

She kept the vision of the dying man to herself.

zHar sighed. His hand released hers and reached for her chin. He tipped her face until she was forced to look into his eyes.

At first, waves of warmth lapped around her body. Then the feelings of love. Acceptance. Awe.

And then Darkling was pulled under by his memories.

I've always felt you.

zHar ran to his mother, a giant stick in his hand. He hoped she would be able to bend it into a bow like zHeezek had. As he ran to the Yer, a shock of heat washed through his body. Crying out, he fell to his knees, clutching his arms around his chest.

Pain shifted to gentle warmth. And a steady beat. Like a heart.

Worried, his stick forgotten, he ran to zHima's Yer instead. The old woman stood outside watching him, as if she had expected him. Before he could tell her about the strange feeling, zHima pulled him inside the Yer.

"Now you best keep silent about it," she murmured, letting him go just inside the entrance as she settled on the furs near the fire.

He watched her milky gaze with suspicion before walking towards her. He settled on the fur in front of her. "But what is it?" he asked.

She stirred the cooking pot slowly, her voice distant as she replied. "It's your soul's other half crying out to you."

His eyes widened in shock as his mouth fell open. His soul? He was only five summers old and already he knew that souls shouldn't be separated. "How do I get it back?" His voice rose with fear.

The healer chuckled. "You don't, my child, you wait until she comes to you."

He frowned at her words. But the healer said no more, shooing him back outside.

Years later, on his first hunt alone, zHar was skinning the white hide of an Elkm rA. He had grown use to the quiet hum of warmth of the other half of his soul. At its steady beat. He did not remember what life was like before it.

As his knife sliced through the skin along the chest, the warmth flared hot then cracked. He dropped to the ground clutching his chest worriedly. It felt as if his heart was breaking, and yet he knew it wasn't *his heart*.

He tried to send comfort to his other half. It did nothing for the pain.

When he returned from the hunt to the people, dark circles under his eyes, no one commented. Only zHima came to him and patted his arm.

Memory after memory pushed through Darkling's mind, until finally it came to the first memory that he saw her.

He had been pacing for days. She was close. She was hurt. He needed to find her. But zHima had said that *she* must come to them. So, he waited.

When he felt her heartbeat slipping, he ran to Amkan.

"I need you to run south. You will find a woman in need of jHora. Bring her back."

The boy nodded, eyes wide, as he ran into the desert.

He had felt her heart sputter, her mind slipping into the arms of death. zHar had tried to send his love, his energy, to her through the bond.

When the strange women came, their bound chests and slit skirts marking them as Tripsian, zHar had felt some relief. And a trickle of fear. The woman, her black knotted hair plastered to her face as her chest barely moved, collapsed to the ground.

jHora stepped forward.

The largest woman crawled to the collapsed woman's side.

"Don't," jHora warned. He gently pulled the large woman's shoulder back before kneeling down beside the prone body of zHar's heart.

jHora placed an ear over the woman's mouth and watched her chest. zHar watched, his own chest aching as his fingers itched to hold her, to comfort her.

Then jHora placed a hand on her forehead. With a sigh, *She will live, zHar. But we will need to move fast. There is no time to call on zHima.*

jHora turned to the other women. zHar and his brothers came forward to take the black haired woman back to zHima's Yer.

She was the other half of his soul.

zHar carefully wiped the tears that streamed from her eyes as she looked up at him with awe.

I have waited my whole life for you to return to me.

Her heart ached, with grief, sorrow, love. Her body shook as she cried in loud gasps. Through it all zHar held her close, rubbing her back. Whispering sweet words of love to her.

Weary, she eventually fell asleep in his arms.

Darkling awoke to a soft kiss on her forehead. She shifted her body and realized she was laying half on top of zHar, the cloak beneath them keeping the sand away.

In the east, the horizon slowly lightened. Darkling sat up then crawled on top of him. zHar's hands settled around her waist. His familiar purple gaze was open as he watched her curiously.

Taking a deep breath, she said, "I-I'm not ready."

He nodded slowly, *I know.*

Relief flooded through her as she smiled down at him.

But one day you will be. One day, you will stand at my side, as my wife, our babe in your belly.

She shuddered at the image, her core warming at the thought. It wasn't today she reminded herself. There was time. And zHar made her feel safe like no one else ever had – not even zHavier. Since the first moment she had seen zHar, she had felt it.

One day, she agreed.

Suddenly, he flipped her onto her back and leaned over her. He leaned down until his mouth was just a breath away from hers.

She wiggled underneath him, the tingles spreading up her back and up to her fingers and toes. She wrapped her legs around his waist. Her heart beat to quickly in her throat. With excitement.

And love.

She had been born Svetlana, the last true princess of Bbrski. She had fought and protected as Ashta the Lion Tamer. And today, she would love this man whose soul she shared, as Darkling, a slave no more.

From this day, until her last day, she was Darkling. A daughter, a chosen sister. A friend.

A warrior.

A lover.

She wrapped her hands around the back of his neck and pulled him close, their lips connecting. Sighing, she felt like she had truly come home. She opened her mouth to his, their lips melding as the sun began to rise.

And one day, she would be a mother.

EPILOGUE

⌘

Nineteen Years Later

DARKLING ADJUSTED THE young boy's stance. "You must have your feet apart, to balance. But not too far apart. If they are so close you will sway like the grass and break in the wind."

The boy pouted up at her but shifted his feet until they were shoulder width apart. The five other children, all of varying ages watched Darkling and the boy avidly, adjusting themselves.

The boy glanced behind Darkling, warning her.

zHar wrapped his arms around her middle gently kissing her bare neck. Despite the years with the zMun, Ashta had returned to wearing her hair like the white lionesses. It was comfortable to her. Made her feel strong. And ready.

I don't mind. It makes it easier to kiss your skin.

Ashta sighed, leaning back into his strong arms.

I love you, my star.

Smiling, Darkling closed her eyes. Despite more than a dozen years marriage and two children, the heat between them was as strong as that first night. She did not need to say the words, sending him her feeling instead.

His grip around her middle tightened as one hand shifted down her belly.

A giggle from one of the older girls had Darkling pushing zHar's hand away. He let her go as she turned around and glared at him.

"Not in front of the young ones," she admonished.

zHar's purple gaze sparkled as he smiled down at her, no forthcoming apology on his lips.

She slapped him playfully on his bare chest. "Go," and with a quick kiss on his lips, she turned back to her charges.

Five pairs of eager eyes looked to her, ready to learn.

Off to the side of the small sparring space were the younger children, the ones who had just learnt to walk. Darkling smiled as she watched her son, Lucifer, help one of the girls braid her hair like Darkling's. He had gotten quite good at it, spending hours braiding his twin sister Illya's hair every day.

"Alright, in your ready stance!" she called. All five kids adjusted their hips, wiggling with energy as they brought their staffs up to both hands.

Ashta called out the commands as she walked between them. "Left, high!" They swung high with their left hands. "Left, low!"

The session went quick, the kids energies waning quickly. With the smell of the midday meals coming from several Yer, the children quickly dispersed to their families fires. Lucifer came to stand beside his mother, having surpassed her height last summer.

Darkling could not believe he was already eighteen. She pulled his face to hers, kissing his nose softly. He blushed but did not push her away. "*Mom*, I am too old for that."

Darkling glared at her son. "You are my child. You will always be my child."

He grumbled quietly, but did not say anything, following her to their family Yer.

They slipped inside where zHar ladled the stew in to three bowls. Darkling frowned.

Before she could ask, zHar said, "Illya said she would find her own meal this day. The land is more bountiful than when I was a young boy."

Darkling stayed quiet. Despite the knots in her stomach, she forced herself to eat the stew zHar made for them. She searched inside herself and found her daughters energy, distant but strong.

She's safe, Darkling reminded herself, you taught her to protect herself.

Lucifer shared a glance with his father.

The meal passed in silence. When they were done, zHar grabbed the bowls, leaving mother and son together.

Darkling stared unseeingly into the fire.

Despite their shared blood, Lucifer could feel nothing from his mother, only the brightness of her life. He rubbed between his thumb and forefinger. Taking a deep breath, he decided to speak aloud.

"I was speaking with zHima and she said there is nothing else she can teach me. I've spent the last year with her, as you asked, but I still want to go east. I've heard from the traders that the elves of Kae ol can-"

"No," Darkling barked. She turned the full strength of her glare on Lucifer.

He frowned, "But mom, I'm eighteen, and Amseeka went-"

Again, Darkling cut him off, "I don't care what the others did or are doing. You are not leaving the zMun!"

Anger roiled through the Yer as Lucifer stood up and threw himself outside. The tent flap fluttered closed.

Darkling stood as well and began pacing, her body shaking with anger. And with fear.

A warm hand stopped her pacing. She looked up into zHar's warm purple eyes. He pulled her into his arms, rubbing her back until she melted against his chest. He dropped a gentle kiss on her temple before whispering in her ear, "One day you must let them go, my star. They need to spread their feathers and learn to fly in the hot winds of the desert and the cool breezes of the coast."

Darkling stayed silent but she rested her cheek against his shoulder, just breathing in zHar's scent. Her heart slowed as her anger waned, leaving only a gentle ache in her heart.

She knew she had to let them go. But they were still so young.

Someone has arrived, zHar thought.

Darkling's back went rigid as she also felt the new energy coming towards the outskirts of their encampment.

zHar pulled her outside into the glaring sun of the desert. Other zMun also gathered outside their Yer trying to catch an eye full of the newcomer. It was rare for a person to come close enough to the zMun when they were in the midst of their journey through the desert.

Darkling scanned the crowd but did not see Lucifer's familiar head of black hair amongst them. Frowning she turned towards where the crowd parted to reveal her daughter, Illya. Her black hair was pulled back into a tight conch shell braid. Her sun darkened skin shone against the blinding white bindings she had somehow fashioned in secret without Darkling's knowledge.

Darkling glared at the clothes. The twins only knew that their mother had been a white lioness of Tripsia before joining the zMun. Illya did not understand what that title had cost Darkling. For years.

As her daughter got closer, Darkling could see Illya's black eyes, so similar to Darkling's gaze, sparkling with excitement. Darkling couldn't help but smile.

Her children were full of light and joy, their lives untouched by their mother's legacy.

And it would stay that way, Darkling thought as her gaze slipped past her daughter to the newcomer.

To another woman.

Darkling's heart stopped.

Then picked up double time.

She watched with horror as the two women walked right up to Darkling. Illya stepped up to her father, sharing a quick hug as she turned to her mother. It was then that Illya noticed her mother's frozen stance.

Darkling could only stare at the young woman standing across from her, only an arm's length away. Her hair was white, the blonde leached of all warmth. Her skin was red, peeling across her burnt nose. But what opened a gaping hole of pain in Darkling's chest was the other woman's eyes.

Forest green. Lush like a jungle. Crawling and alive.

It couldn't be.

It was too soon.

Darkling wasn't ready.

But the other woman, now almost twenty summers old stood tall before her, dressed as a common Tripsian. Darkling frowned at the woman's loose clothes before looking beyond her. But there was no one else.

At least the gods and goddesses give small blessings, Darkling thought.

zHar frowned, *what is it my star?*

Darkling ignored him, her gaze focusing back on the woman who also was eyeing up Darkling. Recognizing her conch shell braid before catching on the blistering red mass on her chest and side.

It's her.

Darkling grimaced but waited, aware that her daughter, her husband and the entire zMun people watched the tense exchange.

Finally, those forest green eyes focused back on Darkling's gaze. She straightened her back, her hands curling into tight fists on either side of her.

"I am-" she began, her voice smooth as honey and familiar.

"Mina," Darkling finished.

The girl stopped, her eyes widening in shock.

She knows me.

Darkling sighed. Oh child, she thought to herself. "Come inside," she said as she turned and entered the tent, not bothering to look back. She took a seat.

Mina entered, zHar and Illya behind.

"Sit," Darkling commanded.

zHar came beside his wife, pulling her disfigured hand into his own and gently messaging the rigid tendons.

Illya flounced across from Darkling before sprawling on the ground.

Mina stayed rigid in the entrance. "I don't wa-"

The tent flap was pulled aside and Lucifer walked in. He moved past Mina and took a seat beside Illya. His purple gaze was as bright as his sisters. He stared at his mother expectantly.

Darkling grimaced. "I said sit down," she growled, glaring up at the girl. Before the other woman could argue, Darkling added. "I know why you're here."

Even more shocked, the girl fell down beside Lucifer. Despite her tense muscles, there was a vulnerability in her gaze. Hope. Darkling ached.

"So, you know who my mother is?" she asked excitedly, those forest green eyes flashing.

Darkling glanced at her own children before looking back at Mina.

"Was," Darkling corrected.

The End, For Now…

The Named Again series continues in **Trice the Wolf Hunter.**

Acknowledgements

First off, I would like to thank you the reader. Without you, this whole process would not have been possible. Writing is a lonely job, but knowing that one day it will shape and create worlds for you, the reader, to escape into makes it all worth it. I myself am a reader first and a writer second, and I appreciate the efforts of all the authors whose works of love I have read.

I want to thank the writing community at large. I can't count on my hand how many times I went in search of formatting issues or character development and found a writer who had the answer. We are a small community, but we are mighty! For those of you not published yet, I wish you all the luck on this crazy journey. And know that hard work and dedication pays off. Don't be scared of it.

To my writing group, I want to thank you for the continuous motivation to sit down and write. The pandemic was hard on all of us, and I am glad we reconnected this last summer and started up our group again (And I am excited to one day read and brag about all of your published works!). Those twenty minutes of connection with you, keeping me accountable, mean everything to me. I never would have found the time to start and continue through the boring middle of this book without your jokes and support. I love that I can come to you with my issues of characters doing things I don't want them to, or have magic systems that aren't quite flushed out yet. You answer all my questions with kindness that google can't quite replicate.

That being said, to Google, thank you for indexing all the answers a crazy author could ever need. I can't count on my hand how many times while I was editing, I would open up a Google search on some crazy random topic or a word I couldn't remember.

To Fiverr and your endless resource of great editors, formatters, and illustrators. Thank you! The editing experience was wonderful. Also, the cover art is gorgeous.

Thank you to my family who puts up with my crazy mood swings and doesn't let me get distracted from writing. I know it's not easy dealing with someone with as wide of a creative streak as me. I can't even count how many times you guys took my phone away so I could focus. Jokes aside, knowing you all loved and supported me no matter what I do is a blessing. I appreciate it more than you all can ever know.

About The Author

Morena Stamm grew up in central Alberta as the third of four kids. She has her Bachelor of Communications degree at MacEwan University, in Edmonton, Alberta, in 2017. After graduating, she moved back to her home in rural where she completed her Masters in Intercultural and International Communication at Royal Roads University, in Victoria, B.C. online in 2020.

    She grew up reading every book she could get her hands on, for hours on end. This started her love for authors like Tamora Pierce, Rick Riordan, Scott Westerfield, Gail Carson Levine, and many countless more. These sparked her passion for the fantasy genre and sucked her into the endless world of fantasy and science fiction books, which she has yet to emerge from.

Want to read more from the Named Again Series? Keep up to date on Morena's new releases on her website morenastamm.wordpress.com *or Facebook page @StammMorena and Instagram page @morenastamm.*

CPSIA information can be obtained
at www.ICGtesting.com
Printed in the USA
BVHW070946160521
607400BV00001B/1